FRANK KURNS: TALES OF THE UNKNOWN WORLD

FRANK KURNS: TALES OF THE UNKNOWN WORLD

NATALIE GREY

MICHAEL ANDERLE

DISRUPTIVE IMAGINATION

LMBPN Publishing
PMB 196, 2540 South Maryland Pkwy
Las Vegas, NV 89109

Version 1.03, January 2021
eBook ISBN: 978-1-64202-356-5
Print ISBN: 978-1-64202-663-4

YOU DON'T TOUCH JOHN'S COUSIN

CHAPTER ONE

John Grimes, Queen's Bitch and one of the few massively modified humans in existence, crumpled the newspaper in his hands.

Frank Kurns had called him, giving him the news that a married cousin of his had problems.

Problems he might have taken care of had he been around, not fighting fucking Forsaken for the last two years.

Even if he *could* change being on the team, he wouldn't. Without Bethany Anne's help in the Everglades, he would not be here to do anything about the problem now.

But he was both alive to do something and working on how to do it.

He stood up, six and a half feet of mental muscle and masculinity. No one ever confused John Grimes with a metrosexual. He was clean-shaven and his nails were clipped, but one didn't expect the latest colognes or skin goop to be found on his person.

He hadn't used anything before he received Bethany Anne's blood, and he sure as hell didn't need it now.

He picked up his holsters and slid them on, then grabbed his "MIB" jacket. He pocketed the dark sunglasses he enjoyed wearing so much. He had always made an entrance; his size alone guaranteed that. After he went through the military, he had added danger to his aura. He had been there and done that, and people could sense it.

Then he'd gotten roped into the Forsaken/Nosferatu bullshit. That had opened his eyes in ways he never wanted to share with the world at large.

However, that wasn't the problem at hand. Right now, his cousin Cheryl Lynn had issues of the gang variety.

She was in the middle of divorcing a significantly bad life-choice named Mark, and Mark was now using his not-inconsiderable legal knowledge to put her and their two children through hell for rejecting him. The children, both pre-teen, had chosen their mom, not him.

He blamed them all instead of looking in the mirror.

John grabbed the SUV keys and set out to find his ultimate boss to discuss the situation with her. He might not go since he was focused on keeping Bethany Anne safe, but he knew Bethany Anne wouldn't allow this to stand. He wasn't sure who she would send, but John was certain it would get taken care of.

He was as sure of that as he was that the sun would rise in the east every morning.

What he hadn't figured into the equation was that she would make sure he got a chance to deal with this problem himself.

How? By going along for the ride.

Mark Lindell looked in the mirror and flicked an incredibly small piece of lint off his suit jacket's shoulder.

He turned left and then turned right, eyeing himself in the mirror to confirm what he believed was true.

He looked damn good.

The twenty-one-year-old in his bed, still sleeping off their night together, was another reminder that he hadn't lost his touch in or out of bed.

He had brought her here to one of the more exclusive hotels in Dallas and paid for several days. It was late Friday morning, and he was sated. He didn't need another ego stroke and figured she could find her own damn way home.

He left a note mentioning that the room had another couple hundred on the account for her to order room service and that she should enjoy it for another night, but that he had been called away to deal with work issues. It was so much easier to end it this way.

Besides, he had put a smiley face on the note. That should make it better, right?

He shut the suite door behind him, hoping he didn't wake Sarah. Or was it Jenni?

No, it was Tammy. Jenni had been last weekend.

He waited for the elevator to drop the twenty-one stories from the top of the hotel to the main floor and exited, then headed to the front desk and signed out. He made sure the bill was paid and the suite incidentals credit had a maximum approved amount. By the time he made it to the valet, his Mercedes SLK was waiting for him.

He tipped the valet a twenty and got in. He figured he would at least swing by his office and check a few things. No reason to be a liar. Cheryl Lynn had thrown his lying in his face for the last nine months, ever since she had found out about him being at this very hotel with a pair of twins instead of working late that night with the guys from the advertising agency.

That had offended him. He *had* worked late with the guys from the agency, but they had gone out for dinner. When the sisters looked him over, he knew he had just been put on the "interesting" list. He noticed their glances from time to time during the meal.

He didn't want to be on the interesting list. He wanted to move to the desired list, so when dinner was over, he told the agency guys he was going to rest for a minute before the trip home.

He had been on the hunt, and he had to get his fix in. He needed to feel alive, and there wasn't a better way to make that happen than closing deals. In his world, getting a woman to go to a hotel room with him was closing a deal.

Cheryl Lynn had confronted him when he got in a little past two A.M. He had tried to play it off as a one-time incident, but the little bitch'd had him tailed for the next six months. She got pictures of him with three other conquests—conquests that she just didn't understand met a need in his ego. Sleeping with them was the ultimate proof that he could conquer; the perfect and unarguable truth that he was desired, the incontrovertible proof being when they lost their damn minds and screamed.

The women didn't mean anything to him and he had told her so, but Cheryl Lynn wouldn't listen. Neither of his children would either. The bitch had obviously lied to them about him and acted as if he was somehow not a good man because he still had it and used it occasionally.

He hadn't thought twice when she had confronted him with the pictures and asked, "Am I not enough for you?"

He'd just shrugged. "Been there, done that."

So she'd left and filed for divorce. That had been three months ago.

Dallas Love Field, Personal Jets Area

Chester Dextress was waiting for the private jet to finish their taxi. His responsibility was to make sure they had the hookups to refuel and take care of the wastewater and any other supplies or replenishment they might need.

He was waiting in front of the private hanger for one of the FBOs (fixed based operators) to help the Gulfstream when a black late-model Jeep with heavily-tinted windows drove in, followed by a Mercedes Maybach S600. Chester whistled to himself.

That last was one sweet ride, and downright sexy.

They were heading right for him.

This incoming was apparently a pretty high-level person. He wasn't sure who it was, but with that kind of car, Chester was guessing Fortune 500 CEO. He turned his attention back to the Gulfstream as it slowly made its way to him. He could see the pilot and co-pilot in the cockpit.

His tablet buzzed, so he looked down and reviewed the instructions. The plan was refueling and departure. That worked for him; he liked the in-and-outs. Everyone would be focused, and he wouldn't have to wait around for instructions.

The plane stopped as coolly as could be, and the door was lowering no more than thirty seconds afterward. He watched as a sharp-looking young man stepped down the ladder and walked around, checking the area before calling back into the plane.

King Kong stepped to the door.

Chester wanted to stare, but he was able to get his astonishment under control when Sir Fucking-Large-as-a-Tree came down the steps and scanned the area. This guy had black sunglasses and was wearing a black suit with a white shirt and a blood-red tie. When he finished his review, the first guy went to stand by the steps. The big guy started walking over to the first vehicle, the black Jeep.

A professional-looking black man stepped out of the Jeep and closed his door. He waited for Kong, and they shook hands. As Chester watched, the big man nodded and started walking around the Jeep. He pulled out what looked like a metal pencil that turned into a long rod with a mirror on the bottom when he pulled it out. He walked around the Jeep, using the mirror to look underneath.

Finished, he took a clipboard from the black gentleman and signed it. The driver of the Jeep took the paperwork back, pulled a copy for King Kong, and handed him a yellow copy and a set of keys. Then he walked over to the Mercedes, and it left.

What the hell?

Chester looked around to see the first guy accept a long bag that clinked from someone in the plane and walk it over to the Jeep. Biggie put it in the back.

Chester didn't think that looked like a golf bag, but if it was what he thought it might be, he didn't want anyone to know that.

He turned to see another person leave the plane. This time Chester's mouth *did* open and fail to close.

"Please, oh please." He spoke under his breath, "Please be a damsel in distress!" Chester didn't know how to provide mouth-to-mouth resuscitation, but he was willing to pretend that his experience as an almost-ok-french-kisser was sufficient to make the attempt.

The woman was dressed in a beautiful white short-sleeved top and long flowing black pants and sported some sort of red-soled high heels. It was a cool day, in the low sixties, but she didn't seem fazed. He looked very closely, and her top was tight enough that he would have known if she had been.

Damn!

It wasn't but a minute before she jumped into the passenger seat of the Jeep. Biggie went around to the driver's seat, and they took off.

Chester got his little cart in gear. He would be in a happy daze for a while from the memory of that angel walking across the tarmac.

That was one lucky guy.

CHAPTER 2

Dallas, TX, USA

Cheryl Lynn wanted to give up, sit down and cry. She touched the area by her right eye and flinched. It hurt as bad as it looked, and it looked pretty bad.

She was in the tiny bathroom she shared with Tina and Todd, her two children. Her hopefully soon-to-be-ex-husband had cut off all of her accounts, but fortunately she'd had a rainy day fund where she had put money for Christmas each and every year that Mark hadn't cared about.

She had squirreled over seven thousand dollars into that account, and it had been enough for her to get this mostly horrible little one bedroom apartment and put a few pieces of furniture in it she found on Craigslist. A phone call to get two guys and a truck for fifty bucks, and she and the kids at least could sleep on a bed and a fold-out futon couch.

It was something. She needed a job, but Mark had

placed legal issues on her record, and it was messing up her ability to find a job.

This evening, she had been coming back to the apartment from the small grocery store six blocks away with tonight's dinner and some food for the weekend.

She had been accosted by two guys who had started whistling at her from the doorway of a closed barber shop. One was a white guy who hadn't shaved in a few days. He was wearing jeans and a black t-shirt with a red ball cap. His compatriot was Hispanic. The white guy had been looking at her, elbowing his friend and laughing.

She had ignored them, but when she heard their footsteps behind her, she had tried to walk a little faster, lugging her bags. She had turned around one time and noticed the two guys behind her.

She had four blocks to go. She made the mistake of thinking that cutting through the parking lot of an apartment complex would be both safer and faster. When she had made it halfway through the dark area where the cars were parked, another guy had come out of bushes at the other end and smiled at her. She saw the faint gleam of his teeth in the poor light from the security lamp that had been installed on the side of the apartment building too many years ago.

She looked over her shoulder at the two guys behind her. Nothing to do but go forward, so she'd set her shoulders and picked up the pace. The guy in front was considerably overweight, and his dark t-shirt didn't keep an expanse of his white belly from showing.

It was like a plumbers' crack but on the other side.

When she kept walking toward him, he spoke; his voice

seemed pretty high to be coming out of such a huge guy. "Where you goin', sweetheart?" He talked around a toothpick in his mouth.

Cheryl Lynn glanced at him and made to walk past. "To my kids. They're hungry," she mumbled.

"Not getting by without paying a toll, sweetie."

His little black eyes hinted at a darker meaning than she wanted to think about. "I've got nothing you want." She went to step around him, and he moved to block her.

"Sweetie, you got everything I might want. Food and…" He was surprised when she lashed out to kick him between the legs.

Momma had always told her that talking never solved anything when someone threatened you.

"Goddammit!" The big-bellied guy dropped to his knees, his voice now even higher. Cheryl Lynn heard footsteps running up behind her and started swinging the grocery bags before she even looked.

She hit the Hispanic man upside his head with the canned goods bag and it ripped, cans flying everywhere. The momentum of the other packages carried her too far around, and the white guy grabbed her left arm and clamped his right arm across her face.

She stomped down hard on his instep and bit his arm, causing him to pull it back.

"Fucking bitch!"

That was when she lost her focus and pain flared up in her face. She had been hit with a glancing blow from the guy's other hand, and it caused her to stumble to her right. The first guy was getting slowly to his feet.

She swung her other packages at the guy who had hit her and started running for all she was worth.

Her adrenaline pumping, she took a second to look behind and noticed the white guy helping the last guy, who yelled after her when she went around the corner. His voice carried.

"Mark sends his regards!"

The cold compress she had applied to her face was helping a little. When she got home, she told the children to call for a pizza. She wasn't going back out there tonight. She couldn't make herself do it.

Thirty minutes later, the doorbell rang. She got up to open the door to make sure it was only the pizza guy when Todd ran in from the kitchen yelling, "Pizza!"

"Wait!" she yelled at him, but he was too excited and too trusting.

They were all too trusting. She hadn't ever been in a situation like this in her life. She had grown up in a small town, gone to a small university, and gotten married. Everything had been idyllic—until she had confronted Mark.

Not for the first time, she wondered if she should have stomped on her pride for the kids' sake. She was willing to take the mental abuse and games. She might be willing to fight, but if Mark took his anger out on Tina and Todd, Cheryl Lynn wouldn't be able to forgive herself.

"Hello, young man..." Cheryl Lynn's blood ran cold.

Todd was staring up at someone who had to be tall. The door blocked her view, but his voice was deep.

This wasn't the pizza guy.

Cheryl Lynn's demeanor changed. Those mother-fuckers had come for her children! She raced into her kitchen and yanked open the utensils drawer and halfway screamed, "Get away from the door, Todd!" She grabbed the meanest-looking knife she had, a cheap chef's knife.

Todd was transfixed by the guy as Cheryl Lynn raced to the door. She reached over to pull Todd out of the way so she could try to slam it shut. That was when she got a glance at the guy in the suit and the woman.

She let go of Todd slowly and brought her left hand up to her mouth, covering it. Tears started streaming down her face.

The big man smiled at her. "Hello, cuz. It's been a while."

She opened the door, stifled a sob, and went to hug her cousin, little John.

John deftly took the knife from her as she grabbed him and started sobbing into his chest. John heard a minor commotion behind him and glanced over his shoulder to see Bethany Anne paying a pizza guy down by the street. She also pulled her phone out, and he heard her order more food.

He winked at the young man staring up at him and the girl who had peeked around the corner. John held the knife out. "Todd, isn't it?" The young boy nodded. "Would you take this back to the kitchen?" The young boy took a few steps and reached out to grab the knife. John cautioned, "See how I'm holding this blade, with the cutting edge away from me and the handle to you?" Todd nodded. "You say thank you when you have it in your control. That's when I release it to you."

"Thank you?" His voice was part-curious, part-scared. His mom was still crying into the big guy's chest.

"That's right. Now take it to the kitchen." Todd turned and walked in that direction.

Bethany Anne came up. "C'mon, John, let's get this out of the public view, so we don't become this evening's entertainment."

She was right; no reason to create new stories for people to talk about.

John spoke to the top of the head on his chest. "Cheryl Lynn? We need to go inside."

His cousin nodded and wiped her tears with her hand, then grabbed his sleeve and pulled him into the house. Bethany Anne walked behind him and closed the door, holding the pizza box in the other hand. She said softly, "I got this."

John nodded, "My boss will get the kids fed. Why don't we go talk about this in the bedroom?"

He was able to get Cheryl Lynn to start down the short hallway. He followed his cousin and started to close the bedroom door.

He heard Bethany Anne speaking from the dining room before the door shut. "My name is Bethany Anne. What's yours?"

CHAPTER 3

Cheryl Lynn grabbed the tissues, a little travel package she had been hoarding for the worst cases of sneezing she experienced. Dallas was horrible for her allergies.

John's huge hand held out a handkerchief. She took it and nodded her thanks.

"How did you know?" she asked, trying to dry the tears from her face.

"The group I work with apparently keep tabs on family members. I was told early this morning that things were bad with you and Mark, so I got here as fast as I could."

She nodded, her shoulders slumped. "You always told me he wasn't a good guy."

"No 'I told you so's' from me. We live with our decisions, and you've already paid that price."

A small laugh escaped her lips. "I'm *still* paying that price." She looked up at him. "Did you know that he cheated on me?"

John shook his head.

She looked back down. "He did. Not just once, but a lot.

I found out about at least four times. He claimed he needed to feel like a man. That the women were nothing but conquests. He didn't love them." She sniffed. "At least, that was what he said."

John let her get it off her chest. He had tried to get Cheryl Lynn to see the true Mark back in college. Mark had been into himself then, and he was still into himself. Cheryl Lynn had rebuffed his efforts at first, and that had made him want her all the more.

She told the story again: how they dated off and on through college and she had never given in. She had made him "put a ring on it" before she would go to bed with him. While her personal beliefs had had something to do with her decision, in the beginning, she had been too shy. A late bloomer, she hadn't felt she was attractive, despite Mark's advances and other guys asking her out.

Mark had been the most aggressive guy, and she finally realized he must be telling the truth since he was still going out with her after two and a half years.

Now she realized it had all been about the conquest with Mark. With the ring and the bedroom, she had just been one final notch.

They'd had Tina quickly and Todd soon after. Cheryl Lynn had focused on the kids, and Mark's occasional forays into the bedroom suited her just fine. She hadn't spent much time or effort trying to figure out why Mark was so easy-going with her lack of interest. It had only been in the last couple of years when she wanted adult companionship again as the kids started becoming independent that she had realized she and Mark didn't have a close relationship.

She wasn't stupid. Momma had always said to find out your problems and face them head-on. She tried to be the sexy little vixen she knew Mark liked, but after the first two or three times, he got tired, and it was back to square one.

She had hired the investigator to just cover her bases. She hadn't expected him to come up with so much evidence. The first time she was told about another woman, she had held out hope that it had been a one-time fling.

When she got a call for the fourth time, she realized she wasn't facing her problem head-on. She had been hiding from it and from her disgrace, and from her feeling that she didn't know what to do.

When she was done yelling at Mark, expecting some sort of argument, he merely told her that since the house was in his name, she was welcome to leave that night. The kids could choose who they would stay with.

Mark had expected them to stay with him in the house with their toys and games.

He had finally gotten angry when all three had packed their bags and gone into the garage. He started ranting and yelling about how rejecting their dad wasn't going to help them in life. That leaving him was tantamount to saying they didn't love him.

Both kids had kept their comments to themselves and gotten into Momma's Honda Accord. It had been paid off two years back.

The only thing it shared with her husband's car was the silver color.

The first place she found to stay had been a nice motel.

NATALIE GREY & MICHAEL ANDERLE

It hadn't taken Mark forty-eight hours to cancel all of her credit cards and move the money from shared accounts into others she had no access to.

Then she had to find a place that would accept cash and ask few questions. She had connections with a local church where she had donated money and items. She had never thought *she* would be the one who needed the help.

She asked, "How did you find me?"

John smiled. "The church."

Her brow furrowed. "They promised they wouldn't tell anyone." She didn't like the fact that they were passing on information.

"My boss can be persuasive," was all he told her.

"Your boss?" John pointed his thumb in the direction of her kitchen and dining room. "That lady is your boss?"

He nodded. "Yes, she is. You saw her? I didn't think you were tracking too well."

"I'm not, but I notice everyone who's around my kids."

He asked, "Are the kids skipping school?"

She shook her head. "Spring break. I have to deal with school on Monday."

John heard a knock on the front door and cocked an ear. Cheryl Lynn asked, "What is it?"

He put up a "wait one" finger as heard Bethany Anne answer it and ask what the total was. "My boss ordered more food and is taking care of the delivery driver."

"Oh!" Cheryl Lynn started reaching for her pocketbook.

"Don't. It's already paid for, and she wouldn't accept

your money anyway." John knew how all of his family had been brought up. It was a testament to how upset Cheryl Lynn was that she wasn't out front; normally she would be making them tea or coffee in the kitchen right then.

He looked at her eye. "How did you get the shiner?"

She reached up to her eye. "I was roughed up this evening by some guys Mark sent after me. I think they were supposed to hurt me more, but I was able to get in a few licks and run."

"How do you know Mark was behind this?"

She glared up at him. "Because the prick I kicked in his manhood told me at the very end that "Mark sends his regards.' I ran away before confirming the last name." She practically dared John to criticize her efforts.

"Is that why you came to the door with a knife?"

She nodded.

There was a knock on the bedroom door, and John opened it. A medium pizza box was thrust through. "Eat up; there's more." John grabbed the box, and Bethany Anne closed the door on him.

He turned to the bed and opened the box. She had placed two plates and napkins inside, with a third plate keeping them from getting greasy. He pulled out a pepperoni slice, put it on the plate with a napkin, and handed it to Cheryl Lynn. "Eat this. You need your energy." There was another knock on the door.

He turned back to the door after Cheryl Lynn took the plate and pulled it open. Bethany Anne had two sixteen-ounce Cokes and a small medicine cup. In it, there was red medicine that smelled like cough syrup to John. He took the bottles in his left hand and the medicine in his right. "It will help with the eye," she told him. John nodded, and Bethany Anne closed the door again. He kept his back to his cousin and brought the medicine close enough to sniff it.

There was a hint of copper in the medicine. Blood.

John smiled wistfully. God, he loved his boss.

He turned to his cousin. "Grab a Coke and open it. I want you to down all of the medicine and wait until you can't stand the aftertaste, then drink some Coke. Got it?"

"I have kids, you know. It isn't like I don't have medicine-taking skills. Besides, I don't have any medicine in the house that will help me right now." She took the small cup. "This smells like cough syrup. That isn't going to help."

"Trust me. By the morning your eye will be fine," John said. She raised a dubious eyebrow at him. He shrugged and added, "I'll bet you a 'truth' if I'm wrong."

"*Any* truth?" She and John had played Truth or Dare all the time as kids. John had fallen out of a tree when he was five because she had dared him to climb it. Thankfully, it had only knocked the wind out of him, and he had never told his parents anything other than that he had fallen trying to climb.

When John confirmed with a nod, she downed the medicine with a smile. "I've always wanted to know if Angie Garcia's story about the two of you in the back of the movies was true." She made a face. "Gahh! That shit is awful. I hope she didn't poison me with something out of date. I didn't pay attention to the expiration when I bought that stuff at the dollar store." She lasted twenty seconds before taking a large gulp of the Coke.

"You're going to have to wait for a while to get the

Angie Garcia truth since I'm sure that is going to work just fine."

"Says you!"

John grinned. "Yup, says me. Now, what do you want to do about Mark?"

She frowned. "Why, are you going to go beat him up? This isn't high school, you know."

John replied, "Oh, he will pay for what he has done. I told him before he married you not to hurt you and a promise is a promise. But, if you're asking if I'm going to go beat him up in front of the teachers and everything, then no."

She sighed. "Well, a girl can hope." She smiled when John grinned at her response.

"Trust me, he will wish he had treated you with loving hands. But enough about that dick. How about we find out what you want to do with your life and with the kids? If you could do anything, what would it be?"

"Why, do you know a Prince Charming who is unmarried and wants a woman with children who can make a mean lasagna from scratch?"

John scratched his chin. "Well, they aren't princes, but you will have their interest when you admit you can cook a mean lasagna."

She stood up and reached around her cousin's huge chest. John put his arms around her, and the net of safety she had been sensing finally reached the dark recesses of her brain. There was nothing, she was sure, that Mark could do to her now that little John was here.

"I don't need or want a man right now, but someplace

that Tina and Todd can be safe going to school would be wonderful. You know Mark is going to fight, right?"

John's chest rumbled as he laughed, "Trust me when I say my boss has dealt with bigger and meaner pricks than Mark. Just believe me about the size of the troublemaker. You can see she's still good."

"Is that because she has you protecting her all the time?" Her voice muffled. John's suit coat was getting extremely soggy.

"Maybe, but maybe not." John rubbed Cheryl Lynn's back, trying to give what comfort he could. John grunted as he thought back through all of the times he and Bethany Anne had done operations together.

"Truthfully, usually it's not."

CHAPTER 4

Mark answered the Trac phone. He wouldn't do anything stupid like take calls on his personal phone. "Hello?"

"It's done, but she was a feisty little bitch."

"Hey! Watch how you're talking about my wife. I'm the only one who can talk about the cunt like that."

"Whatever," came the reply over the phone.

"Was she walking when you finished?" Mark asked.

"If by walking you mean running as fast as she could, scared to death with an ugly-ass black eye, then yes."

Mark held in his frustration. "Look, I was explicit that I wanted her to crawl out of a ditch, not run away from three grown men. What, you couldn't hurt one little woman?"

"Which part of 'she put up a fight and caught us by surprise' didn't you understand?" was the gruff reply Mark received.

"The part where I thought you had a clue. When you split only half the money I promised—which I've already paid you—my response might make better sense."

"Don't be a prick, Mark. We are just waiting until after midnight, then we will go back and do a B and E. Eric followed her far enough to see where she went. We've got where she lives."

"Good! Good."

"What do you want done with the kids?"

Mark considered his response and answered, "Frankly, I don't give a damn.

"Why is your hair so black?" Tina asked Bethany Anne while stuffing another slice of cheese pizza into her mouth. Her mom and brother preferred pepperoni, so they always ordered pepperoni and made her take off the meat. Tina thought the grease left too much taste behind and messed up a truly beautiful experience. Cheese pizza done right was an exquisite experience. It was, she considered, the purest form of pizza, and should be held in high esteem.

Bethany Anne cocked an eyebrow at the young girl who had peppered her with questions all through dinner. Bethany Anne had watched the two children eat significantly more than what Bethany Anne thought they normally would.

If they had been fed regularly.

Bethany Anne kept a conversation going with the two kids. Well, Tina mostly. Todd had asked a couple of questions and then timidly asked Bethany Anne if he could play games on her phone. When she agreed, he scarfed down six slices and a third of the chocolate chip cookie dessert she had purchased, then took her phone and went to go play a pigs in space game.

She kept her other ear open to listen to John and Cheryl Lynn. This husband or ex-husband, she wasn't sure if they had been officially divorced yet, was a world-class goat-fucking douchebag. On the trip to Dallas, John had given her the background between him and Cheryl Lynn, which had made Bethany Anne happy she had come along. It allowed her to get a peek into John's early days when his life was climbing trees and skinning his knees and spending long afternoons talking to his friends and family while listening to the cicadas and drinking Kool-Aid or the cheaper Flavor-Aid.

Good times.

Times when he was that guy in high school you didn't mess with, teenage hormones maybe making him a bit quicker to punch someone than he should be. The time before he went into the military that took him down the road that ended in an operation out in the Florida Everglades.

When destiny had sunk a knife deep in his chest.

She came back around to think about Tina's question. "You know, I'm told my mother had the darkest hair; so dark you would think it had blue highlights."

"Really? I don't know the genetics behind that. I wonder if it is a recessive trait since you don't see it too often."

This time it was Bethany Anne who forgot to close her mouth.

"Flies are going to land in there if you don't shut it." Tina smiled and took another bite of her pizza.

Bethany Anne closed her mouth. "What do you know about genetics?" Bethany Anne figured that it was probably safe to eat the three remaining pepperoni slices now, so she grabbed one and reached for the parmesan cheese. Before she had been turned, she would have dropped half a bottle of red pepper flakes on her pizza, and was her happiest when it made her sweat. Now she was very careful. With her modified taste buds, a hot pepper could damn near make her cry.

She wouldn't admit it to anyone, but she had asked TOM to shut down the pain receptors in her mouth the first time she had sprinkled red pepper flakes too heavily on her pizza.

Lesson learned.

Tina swallowed. "I know a little. I liked the class when we talked about it, which was right before spring break. I had started to look for websites to learn more before Daddy got so mad and turned off our web access and phones. Now I'm hoping Momma will let us go to the library so I can look it up."

"You want to go to a library?" Bethany Anne was pretty sure she hadn't wanted to see the inside of a library at her age. At that age, she was still tagging along with her dad to the base and running through all the courses and training classes she could. Sometimes she got on a physical course that was a little too much; she had been lucky to not get hurt.

She had, however, fallen off a log you were supposed to cross that had a four-foot-deep water hole underneath. She had been showing off and slipped, flipped, and landed in the water on her stomach. The pain of the breath getting knocked out, and feeling like she couldn't breathe had brought back the respect she should have had for the course.

Tina answered, "It's the only way I'm going to learn more about genetics."

Not if John and I have anything to say about it, Bethany Anne thought.

CHAPTER 5

Cheryl Lynn left the comfort of her cousin's hug and reached for the little tissue package. It was past time to crack this open.

"Is your boss going to be ok with my kids?"

"As in, will she be safe, or will she want to jump from the window?"

Cheryl Lynn laughed. "We are on the first floor. I don't think she could even sprain an ankle leaping from the window."

"You know, I've no idea. I don't hear any screaming coming from the other room, so I presume she is doing ok." John studied the bedroom.

Cheryl Lynn looked around. "It isn't much. I'm trying to watch my funds to make them last as long as possible. Mark has found me, so I'm going to have to move again."

Her cousin's visage changed, and she got a glimpse of the face that had caused more than a few guys in high school and college to run screaming. Well, maybe that was more figurative than literal.

Now she could see a darker glint in his eyes. "John, I don't want you doing something and getting in trouble. Mark has a lot of powerful friends. He's rich, and he knows a few less savory characters."

John looked at her eye. "Apparently he sicced them on you tonight."

Cheryl Lynn reached up and touched the eye that had turned black and blue. It wasn't as tender as it had been before. That was nice.

John continued, "I asked you before. What do you want to do?"

She exhaled. "I want to leave and go somewhere that prick can't find the kids or me, but I'm not sure what the law will say. Here in Texas, he owes me half, but I doubt I'll see a penny. I don't want it for me, but the kids deserve better than I can give them right now."

John nodded. "I'll want the three of you to pack. We are going to move you to another location. A safe location."

"Are you going to be with us?" She didn't want to beg, but she hadn't felt safe in so long. When she had opened her door to see John, it had felt like hope had entered her life again after a lengthy absence.

"No. I'm planning on seeing if anything happens here, then visiting Mark in the morning."

Cheryl Lynn's voice came out softer and a little strained. "Can't you come with us?"

"That would mess up my plan."

"What plan is that?"

"Find Mark's accomplices and take their signed affidavit to him. He can back off or fight us in court."

"He's got serious legal connections in this town."

John laughed. "Trust me, he doesn't have anything like the ability to pull in resources that we have."

"You know," she said, "you never said who your boss is and why she needs you."

John agreed, "No, I never did. Is it important?"

"Well, maybe I'll want to use my special 'truth' opportunity to see if there is anything going on between you two."

John shook his head. "I'll give you that one for free. I'm part of her team. We have a direction and a goal. I'll take a bullet for her, but it's not my future for anything else." He added, "Besides, she's in a relationship with another guy."

John could hear Bethany Anne's voice. "Am not!"

Damn, that lady was still trying to deny the obvious.

He decided to play with her. He put up one finger to his cousin. "One sec."

John turned to the door and opened it just a smidgen. "You're denying the truth, BA. You've got to start accepting reality or you won't ever be able to understand yourself."

John closed the door and didn't hear a response. He figured she was holding her tongue due to the kids being in there with her.

"What did you just do?" Cheryl Lynn was curious. "Did she say something?"

"Yes. She said she wasn't dating this guy."

"You could hear that?"

He tapped his right ear. "Good hearing. I've had a little surgery since joining the team."

Cheryl Lynn considered trying another tack. "What if the kids and I slept here?"

"You really that freaked out, Cherry Lint?"

She smiled, remembering when John was so young he

NATALIE GREY & MICHAEL ANDERLE

had gotten her name all wrong. She didn't say anything, just nodded.

He looked around. "I can bring the futon in here. The three of you need to sleep on the floor."

"Why the floor?" she asked.

"Lots of people don't shoot lower than waist-high. If they come in with guns blazing, I want to have a chance that you will be safe from a stray shot. Often people will shoot for center mass, which will be pretty high for me." He noticed her eyes widen in alarm. "Don't worry, I'll be fine. They won't have anything I can't survive, plus, we brought along protection."

He noticed her smirk and rolled his eyes. "Chest protection, you deviant!"

At least he made her laugh.

Bethany Anne slipped her ceramic armor on. She had switched bras and undershirt before putting on the armor. John asked, "You clear?"

She grumped, "You need to get laid."

John turned around. "Hey, my cousin laughed at me when I said we brought along protection. Don't *you* start with me!"

She rolled her eyes.

He smirked. "I could start asking questions about Michael…"

She put a hand out. "Let's keep this operational, Mr. Grimes." She smiled. If John wouldn't allow her to use direct methods to get him out and about, she would launch a sneak attack, with Cheryl Lynn helping her. She had to be an outstanding source of intel on her friend.

He snorted. "Man, are you easy now."

She let that comment pass and asked, "You want first or second shift?"

He looked at his watch. "It's half past midnight. I'll take the next couple of hours, and you can take the last few."

"Where are you going to be?"

He zipped up their bag. He had already dressed in black and slipped on his holsters and guns again. He was going to try to keep this quiet if he could, but he wasn't going into a gunfight with only his fists.

"I figure I'll park the Jeep a half a block away, then stay in there and watch. I'll drive away and look around real quick. Hopefully, we aren't already being watched. There isn't anywhere to hide out front. It's the best I can think of at the moment."

"Don't worry, I won't let anyone past me."

John opened the door and smiled at Bethany Anne. "I'm not worried about you. I'm worried that if they get by me, I won't get my chance for a pound of flesh!"

She shrugged. "Why don't I just keep kicking them out to the street until your lazy ass shows up?"

He paused after stepping out of the door. "Ok, that will work." He winked and shut the door.

Bethany Anne bent back until she could hear her vertebrae pop, then put a jacket on so the kids wouldn't see the pistols if they got up and came in here. She left the sword in the corner. Rolling her neck, she took a position in the middle of the floor and slowly closed her eyes.

ADAM, have you tracked down the asshole I asked about?

\>\>Yes.<<

Well, don't make me play Twenty Questions. What do you have on him?"

\>\>His original name was Timothy Spickels.<<

What the hell? Really?

\>\>Yes. Why would I create a false answer?<<

Give it time, she thought to herself. *I'll bring you to the dark side.*

It's called humor, but let's drop that for now. Are you saying that this creep is not the guy Cheryl Lynn thought she married?

\>\>That is correct. He changed his name and his age upon entering the university. I have located the bank accounts for his present and previous identities. He runs multiple businesses through both, and only uses his original a couple of times a month. He goes over to Fort Worth when he does any banking in his original identity.<<

How do you know that?

\>\>Cross-checking credit card receipts for purchases and accessing bank accounts.<<

How much money does he have access to at this time?

\>\>He has less than thirty-seven thousand under his original identity. He has in excess of half a million in cash and over three million in securities under his Mark identity.<<

What a fucking creep, Bethany Anne mused to herself. *That wealthy, and his children live like this.*

ADAM, would you please retain a legal representative to fight for sole custody? Confirm any and all illegal or unethical actions you locate through the records and prepare them for delivery to them. Further, I want to know if Mark has ever communicated with criminals or suspected criminals— anything that would show his character in a bad light that we can use against him should he fight Cheryl Lynn in court.

>>What about a psychological report describing narcissistic issues that result in a lack of psychological awareness, difficulty feeling empathy for others, and hypersensitivity to insults real or imagined?<<

I'm not sure I want to know how you got that information, but that is a hell of a start!

CHAPTER 6

The old white van pulled up two blocks from Cheryl Lynn's apartment complex.

"Ok, this is a B and E. Make sure we break the door's lock in an obvious manner. If you find anything of value, take it. Make sure we tear apart the place, so it's obvious we were trying to find stuff. Everyone got your gloves?"

"What about the kids?" Eric asked. Family was important to him, and while he had taken money to hurt the woman and she had beaten him over the head with those damn cans, he couldn't look his *madre* in the eye if he hurt a child.

"I know you aren't capable of that, so just stay out of it. If they cower, I'll just slap them so I can tell Mark we roughed them up a little. It will be good for them to learn about the street. They can't buy that kind of education without getting a lot worse done to them than we will."

Eric nodded. A street education *would* be good for them, perhaps. It mollified his guilt.

The three men exited the white van and pulled the

doors shut. Ben, his weight belying that he was a pretty fast runner, got out of the driver's side. Eric and Wayne exited the side door. The front passenger door had been stuck shut for over a year. Now it was the depository for trash, often enough.

Wayne grumped, "All I'm saying is to watch out for the teeth. She's like one of those damned honey badgers. First chance I get, I'm giving her a love tap with this bat. I'm probably going to have to get a rabies shot or some shit like that."

Ben came around the front of the van. "Just don't hit her too hard. Mark isn't paying enough for us to off her."

Wayne handed the bat to Eric. "You better take this. I'll just slug her. I might get too rambunctious with that thing."

Eric accepted the bat without saying anything.

The three men crossed the street, the early morning quiet blanketing the area. You could hear a train in the distance, the air horn blaring as it went through inter-sections.

Wayne looked in that direction. "I thought trains didn't run at night?"

Eric answered, "Freights do. They run by my *tia*'s house all the time. Rents are cheap there for a reason."

They turned to go up the sidewalk that would take them to the two doors. The one to the right was their mark's, the one to the left someone else's. There was also a set of stairs that went up a level. The three guys put on their gloves and Ben spoke in low tones. "Remember, make this fast. We want to get in, do our jobs, and get out. The bitch should only be able to crawl if we want the rest of our money."

Ben started to walk toward the door when a deep voice spoke behind them. "Fellas, your lives just became worth shit."

Ben turned to see an ox standing behind Eric. Wayne moved to the side and slipped his hand into his pocket. Ben said, "Listen, stranger, we ain't here for you. The bastard in that apartment roughed up my little girl. We are just here to make sure the cocksucker isn't going to do that to anyone else, *comprende?*"

Wayne thought that was a hell of a lie to come up with so quick.

The ox spoke. "Guys, you have two choices. You can mess with me right here, or you can try to go through that door and your lives will be forfeit. The person who's in there waiting for you won't think twice about killing you."

Ox flexed his shoulders. "What you *aren't* going to do, any of you, is get out of here without the ass-whipping your fathers or mothers should have given you years ago." He paused. "So, what's it going to be? Ass-whipping from me, or are you going to chance door number two?"

Wayne whipped out his pistol. It was a tiny .22, but it would put enough hurt on Ox's ass that they could possibly get their job done and get out of there. He fired three rounds quickly, and it clicked empty.

Wayne didn't spend much money on bullets. He'd never had much use for the gun.

Ox looked down at the three gray splotches that gleamed faintly in the dim light on the street.

"Seriously?" Ox looked at Wayne. "Brother, you need to do something serious. That is only going to piss me off."

There was a tiny "snick" behind Ben. He turned to look

into the darkness where the doors were but couldn't see anything. He turned back when Ox said, "Well, that's done it. You guys are fucked now."

Eric swung the bat in an overhead arc, trying to slam it on the ox's head. Eric was left staring when the bat was stopped by Ox's beefy hand, the bat making an audible *slap*.

Eric's hand's hurt like hell. It was like when you hit a pole or the ground with a bat, the reverberations reaching through it.

Ox took the bat, and quick as a thought, Eric slumped to the ground. He tossed the bat over by Eric, who now had blood running from his scalp.

Ox looked at Wayne and Ben. "One down."

"Fuck this!" Wayne pulled a knife and started weaving it in front of him, angling for a way to cut this fucker. Make 'im bleed, and he'd see a need to let them go, he thought.

Ben started to step backward, keeping Ox in front of him. The ox glanced in his direction and told him, "I wouldn't do that." He returned his attention to Wayne.

Wayne flicked out quick as a viper to slice the guy but grunted in pain when his wrist was caught, then gave a short scream when his wrist was turned ninety degrees and broken. The man popped Wayne in his temple with a closed fist.

Wayne went down.

Ben turned to run into the apartment. If he had a hostage, this freak would have to let him go.

He made it to within ten feet of the apartments when two red eyes started glowing in the inky blackness near the doors. Ben could make out the faint glimmer of fangs.

The darkness was pierced by the blood-curdling

scream of a man who had seen his demons and could do nothing as he fell headlong into their embrace.

Bethany Anne grumped, "All I'm saying is that the Etheric is a pretty clean solution for that trash." She got in the front passenger seat of the Jeep and slammed the door.

John stuffed the bag into the back and got in the front. Ten minutes before, he had made sure Cheryl Lynn, Tina, and Todd had been picked up by a limousine that would drive them to a hotel, where they would clean up and eat. Then the limo would pick them up at nine to take them to the airport.

Cheryl Lynn had come out with her little knife after she heard the scream. She had stood on the porch watching Bethany Anne and her cousin in a whispered but spitting argument about what to do with the three men who had attacked her earlier that night.

Unable to believe her ears, she took a few steps forward to get close enough to hear little John's boss say, "Those fuckers deserve it. No lawyers, no muss, no fuss!"

John replied, "I think you need a little exposure to normality, BA. Everything answer you offer is a Michael one."

Cheryl Lynn almost snickered when the woman stomped her foot in frustration.

The woman put out a finger and pointed it right at her cousin's face. "Fine, but if those fuckers hurt anyone else, I will hunt them down and toss their asses straight in, you

NATALIE GREY & MICHAEL ANDERLE

got me, John? ADAM will be watching, and he doesn't forget either!"

John nodded. "I'll get the ID, but you will need to verify they aren't fake."

Bethany Anne had nodded agreement and turned to take in Cheryl Lynn. She didn't laugh at her little knife or coddle her. Her voice turned matter of fact and she pointed to the group of men. "These them?"

Cheryl Lynn walked over, "Yes." She gestured to the fattest one there. "He's the one I kicked in the 'nads." She pointed to the one who obviously had a broken wrist. "He's the one who gave me this wonderful eye."

Bethany Anne looked like she was considering kicking the guy in the 'nads herself. "Ok. John says we have to come up with some option other than 'kill them all and let God sort them out.'" Cheryl Lynn started to smile but realized this woman wasn't joking.

Bethany Anne had been eyeing the three men with ill-concealed disgust. "How about we find out who they are and if they have records? Then we will notify the authorities, and if not, what?" She looked sweetly at John, who rolled his eyes.

At his emphatic, "No!" Her look became disgusted again. Cheryl Lynn figured out the two were playing.

"Would you really kill them?" Cheryl Lynn realized with a start that she had asked that question out loud.

Bethany Anne looked at her. "If you want to find out how deep the rabbit hole goes, Alice, I'll answer you. But you need to think about it first."

Cheryl Lynn started believing John's comment that she might have saved him more often than he saved her.

Just who the hell was this woman?

What the hell was this woman?

John rolled onto the 35 freeway. "Thank you, boss."

"For what?"

"Letting Cheryl Lynn work at the base."

Bethany Anne shrugged. "Her little girl might be a budding genius, and who knows about her son. He's in the video-game-playing stage. If she isn't careful, that can ruin a guy's desire to move ahead in life."

"I plan on working with him."

Bethany Anne glanced at him. "Another 'Pete' project, John?"

He shrugged. "Maybe if I get involved earlier, it won't take that much effort."

"Maybe," she agreed, "or maybe he just needs the opportunity and he will jump at it. You can't tell until you take away the mental stuff and give him a chance to check it out. Won't matter. He's going to be busy as hell at the base."

"What made you willing to take her on as your aide?"

Bethany Anne asked, "Did you see her when she came out the front door?"

He answered, "No, a few seconds after. Why?"

"She was scared, John, and mortified, but she came out to help. She wasn't going to let us go down without getting involved." She turned to look into the night as they drove toward Mark's house.

"Besides," she continued, "she's family, and we don't let

NATALIE GREY & MICHAEL ANDERLE

family down if they are fighting like hell to do the right thing."

John reached up and surreptitiously wiped his eyes.

He fucking loved his boss. She was the older sister he'd never had but had always needed.

It took them fifteen more minutes to arrive on Mark's street. John put the Jeep in Park. "How do you want to handle this?"

She unclipped her seat belt. "I've got this. This fucker isn't going to bother Cheryl Lynn again." She paused long enough to let John think he would need to ask his question before she continued, "He won't die. I'll even leave him alive in bed."

John could see the red glow kindle in her eyes. "But if you think I'm not going to scare the ever-loving *hell* out of him, you don't know me too well." She stepped out of the Jeep and headed toward the two-story modernist concrete home.

"Actually," John said to the empty Jeep, "I was rather counting on that."

CHAPTER 7

Mark woke up on his stomach. Something wasn't right, but he couldn't tell what it was. He lifted his head off of his pillow and reached over.

No one was there. Yeah, that was right. He had left Toni back at the hotel this morning. No, it was Tammy yesterday morning.

Whatever.

"Hello, Mark."

Mark looked the other way quickly. There was a person in his chair in the dark sitting area. He couldn't make out her face too well, but it was definitely a woman.

He smiled. Just his type.

"God, I hope you're attractive. When a hot female surprises me in my bedroom, I can be pretty receptive."

"Oh, Mark, this isn't going to be one of those meetings. We are going to talk about Cheryl Lynn and that little group of men you sent to rough her up."

Mark turned over fully and got up on his elbows, trying to see her better. "I don't know what you are talking about.

My wife left me. I don't know where the hell she is, she took my kids along with her."

"Save it, Mark. Or should I call you 'Timothy Spickels?'"

"Who? I don't know a Timothy Spickels. What are you, a PI?"

"Timothy, I'm your worst fucking nightmare. I'm going to make you taste death and then beg to die."

He smiled at her overly melodramatic comment. She didn't scare him. No female scared him.

The woman stood up and Mark noticed a body to die for, but the snarky comment died in his throat when she came into the light from the window. Her eyes were red, and fangs protruded from her mouth.

The screaming was brief. It ended a second later when both of them disappeared.

John heard the faint scream and started the timer on his phone. He was surprised when it went past ten minutes. Obviously, Bethany Anne *was* going to keep him alive. John had to admit that he was ambivalent about Mark's survival, but then he had hated the guy for a long time. He might need to be around a grounding influence other than Bethany Anne as well.

Maybe.

Nah, Mark was a dick.

Had he not been staring right at the house, he wouldn't have known that Bethany Anne had appeared on the sidewalk in the darkness provided by the tree in the yard.

John started the Jeep, and Bethany Anne jumped in. He pulled out and drove down the street, backtracking their trip into the neighborhood to get back out to the freeway.

"How did it go?" he asked.

"Our dearly almost-departed Timothy Spickels has assured me that he won't be asking for the children back. Due to his many indiscretions, he understands he wouldn't be a fit father for the kids." She turned to look at John. "You know that prick didn't give a shit about Tina and Todd? I have his money tied up, and once he figured out that he had lost all of his carefully squirreled money he broke down."

"You let him know you had his money and he crumbled?" John asked.

"Well, that was after taking him into the Etheric a few times. Funny how that place drives you insane when you realize there isn't a way to get back if your ass is left there. That man is an anti-parent," Bethany Anne mumbled.

John glance at her. "What was that?"

She explained, "I was thinking that all kids should have both a mother and a father, or two parents anyway, but that guy is so messed up that he is literally the Anti-Parent. I can't think of anything he could contribute to raising those kids."

John wanted to puke, but he admitted, "He did provide shelter, food, and clothes. That's more than some."

"Oh, he didn't get out of that."

"No?"

"Nope. He was happy to provide a million and a half dollars to Cheryl Lynn to divorce him."

John snorted. "Any particular reason he felt so generous?"

"Yeah, I told him all the dirt that Cheryl Lynn had on him, and that if he didn't provide a separation amount, she

NATALIE GREY & MICHAEL ANDERLE

would go to the cops with it. He bitched until we took another trip into the Etheric."

"You dropped him there until he paid?"

"Hell, no. I dropped him there until he quit whining. What a blubbering pussy." She looked out the side window.

"What's going to stop him from being a bad guy in the future?" John worried that Mark, or Tim, or whatever the hell his name was would do this to another person.

"Nothing." She paused, her tone changing to one heavy with anticipation. "God, it would be so nice if he did!"

"You told him you would be watching, didn't you?"

"Of course. He's been warned. Well, to be correct, ADAM is watching, but if he strays outside of what I told him he can do, that information will be dropped at the nearest DA's office."

"What if they don't do anything about it?"

"All of his money disappears, and his credit dries up. If that doesn't cause the women to leave, then that would be the third strike."

"Three times aren't a charm?" John turned on the blinker to exit the freeway.

"Not if the fourth is being dumped somewhere he can't survive, it isn't."

John turned into the private airport entrance as dawn started to break in the east. He pulled around to the hanger.

Their plane, which had gone back to the base, had arrived early that morning. They parked the Jeep, and John grabbed their gear. After storing the weapons and gear on board, they decided a donut and coffee run would be nice. Bethany Anne and John stayed on the plane so Captain

Paul Jameson and his co-pilot for the trip could stretch their legs and use the Jeep to go get something to eat.

The kids had been excited to see the limousine waiting for them as they exited the hotel. Cheryl Lynn was in shock.

She had been fairly well off, so this wasn't completely outside her experience, but the way she had been treated by the hotel's staff and those in the limousines was beyond her expectations.

The gentleman held the door, and Todd jumped in. Tina waited for her mom before she climbed in after she saw Cheryl Lynn's nod.

"Ma'am" The man was big, and he appeared to be Hawaiian or something like that. His nametag said Alika.

Cheryl Lynn stopped before stepping into the limousine and looked at the hotel.

"Something wrong, ma'am?" There was concern in his voice.

She turned back to answer the gentleman. "Alika is it?" He nodded. "I'm just trying to get my bearings. I've had so much happen in the last twenty-four hours. I'm trying to ground myself."

Alika smiled at her. "Feel like you aren't in Kansas anymore?"

She put a hand on his arm and smiled at him. "A big guy like you watches *the Wizard of Oz*?"

When he shrugged, the muscles flexed in his arms. "My grandmother was a fan. We watched it every Christmas."

She nodded and made a quick decision. "Alika, could I

ride up front? I think my life is about to get very strange. I'd like a bit of normal before that happens."

Alika closed the door. "I would be honored, ma'am." He walked to the front passenger door and opened it. "Your carriage awaits, ma'am." He gave her his best smile.

Returning it, she put one foot in the car before telling him, "It's Cheryl Lynn, Alika."

She sat down, and he closed the door and started walking around the front to get into his seat.

"Yes, ma'am, it is."

FINIS

BITCH'S NIGHT OUT

CHAPTER ONE

QBS *Polarus*, Two Hundred Miles off the Argentinian Coast

"What I was told," said Darryl as he slung his overnight bag over his shoulder, "was that Bethany Anne requested that Gabrielle, Cheryl Lynn, Patricia, Ecaterina, and Barb come to her suite here for a conference and no, and I mean 'no' guys are invited." He sat down on the couch in the Bitches' central area that been recently renovated to add a fifth door for Akio since Peter's room was on the *Ad Aeternitatem.*

"Except Ashur," Scott called as he reached across his bed to grab his phone. He spoke a little louder so everyone could hear him. "She even has two hand-picked female Guardians in front of her suite for protection."

"What about Peter?" Eric asked from his room as he packed.

Scott came out, dropped his bag on a chair, and sat down.

"What about me?" Peter asked as he breezed into the

main area carrying his overnight bag. "I was told by Bethany Anne to grab clothes for overnight and to meet you guys here. Where's John?" he asked as he sat across from Darryl on the matching couch and put his feet up on the coffee table.

"Did she call?" Darryl asked.

Peter shook his head. "Nope. Did the mind juju."

"She's getting a lot better at that," Darryl remarked, to Peter's nodded agreement.

Eric came out of his room and shut his door. "That room is not for public consumption!" He gave Peter a fist bump before kicking his legs off the table. "Mind the furniture, shrimp," he grumped. He sat next to Peter, crossing his feet and placing them on top of the table.

"You Bitch!" Peter remarked, putting his feet back on the table. "Where is the esteemed High Bitch?"

"Right here, Sophomore, with our Fish," John said as he walked in with Akio, who was holding a sword. The guys raised their eyes in surprise. John had an overnight bag, and he was fully decked out in "Queen Bitch" dress with patches and everything.

"I think I failed to get the memo." Darryl quipped.

Akio nodded to the men and sat down next to Darryl, still holding his sword.

"No memo was put out," John told him, looking down at his five guys. "What I've been told...no, actually *commanded* by Bethany Anne, was that the Bitches needed a night out. I was told to make sure this group let out some of our energy and 'attitude,' and to come back relaxed. Now, we all know that Bethany Anne just wants us off this ship so we can't figure out what she's doing. That's fine;

Gabrielle is here, and so is Ashur. However, she is right. We need to blow off some steam."

John looked at his guys. "That would normally mean we go to a bar, but I'm not sure how much that would affect us now. While I fully intend to end up in a dive, I think there is only one way to get rid of the pent-up aggression I'm feeling."

"Well, considering how you're decked out," Eric said, "you clearly believe we need to work out our aggression?"

"What I'm thinking," John replied, "is that the best way to get rid of aggression is to fuck up some people who desperately need to be fucked up. So, I've had Frank help me locate a few places that need help. Now, we might not make it to all of them, but by the end of the night, we will have done some major good, and I'll start feeling a little Karmic balance restored. If you guys aren't full up, well, we will just have to schedule another trip."

Peter grinned as he stood up. "Hell, yeah! How are we getting around?"

John pursed his lips. "Well, six of us, and six Black Eagles are available..."

Scott stood up. "God, I've needed to fucking shoot somebody for a while now. You pussies keep getting the action since the Australian incident."

"Oh, is *that* what you call running into an ambush?" Darryl asked as he stood up.

"No, I call that being your shield, and if you would just appreciate it instead of always trying to turn my self-sacrifice around, I'd enjoy it!" Scott grinned and punched Darryl as he walked past him.

Darryl rubbed his arm. "Make sure Scott is up front so

he can shield me all the time." He rubbed his arm a second time. "That way, I can use my size twelves to kick his ass through the door!"

All of the guys chuckled.

Akio stood back for a second and got Eric's attention. "What are we doing?"

"Well," Eric told him, "I imagine John is taking us by the armory to find all sorts of personal mayhem devices. There, we are going to make lewd jokes about how long someone's 'gun' is. Then, six of the most deadly men on this planet have been commanded by their Queen to go 'blow off some steam.' Now, she might have known what John was going to do, or she might not. Either way, John has found a list of the locations of some very bad people who probably need an attitude adjustment. We are going to take six of the most deadly planes in the world to these locations and have a very good time doing very painful things to said very bad people."

Akio asked, "Because this is what our Queen wants?"

Eric closed the door as the two followed the rest down the hall. "She wants us to get rid of our general bad attitudes about Michael, about stupid politicians, horrible people who want shit they had nothing to do with creating, and friends who are no longer with us. John decided the best way to relieve this pent-up anger is to do something righteous with it."

"Something righteous with guns?" Akio asked.

"Of course!" Eric responded as he looked at Akio and grinned. "Righteousness at the end of a .45..." He glanced at the sword Akio was holding. "And a sword, of course."

Eric started humming a recent tune as the guys ahead took a left toward the armory.

"Righteousness at the end of a .45...a .45..." he was singing as he and Akio followed the others around the corner.

"No, give me the long one. This short stick doesn't feel right in my hands," Darryl quipped.

Akio grunted. "Here, let me feel it." Darryl handed it to him, smiling. Akio looked it over. "It's all in the way you handle your gun to get the most bang from it."

John chuckled. "Whatever, you two. Get your damned sticks and whatever personal 'fuck them up' stuff you want."

Dan called from the second room over, "Anyone want some plastique? I'll have to open a new box if you do."

"Seriously?" Darryl turned from joking with Akio. "I'll take me some of that!"

Dan pulled out his key ring. "God, guys. Seriously, don't fuck me over. Bring back video, ok?"

"No worries," John answered. "Our helmets have heads-up upgrades with built-in video. ADAM is doing an immediate download to Frank. He wants to write a story on it immediately to put out as 'fiction.' Hey, here are some knives."

"Someone is bound to see through that shit," Eric commented.

"I'm pretty sure that is the plan," Peter stated as he pulled out a few boxes of shotgun shells.

"Why the hell are you pulling a shotgun when you have those two beasts on your hips?" Scott asked, pointing to the two railgun pistols Peter was packing.

NATALIE GREY & MICHAEL ANDERLE

"These pistols are accurate to as far as I can see, but they won't make near the bloody mess a shotgun will up close," Peter replied, putting the shells into a bag.

Scott shook his head. "Damned good reason."

"Who needs six inches?" John called before finishing, "Shut up, Akio!"

Everyone laughed.

Then laughed louder with Akio's retort. "I start at twenty-seven inches, John."

"I'm out!" Scott called.

"Out," agreed John.

"Ouch…" Eric winced. "I can't play in that park."

Everyone looked at Darryl, who just grinned. "What can I say? Some things are true about black men."

"Fucking liar!" Peter joked.

Dan called, "Anyone want grenades?"

"If you do," Darryl commented, "remember that Mr. Grenade is not your friend, or mine, once you pull the pin."

"I want a few explosive incendiaries," John said. "I want the opportunity to drop them on someone. That shit just seems funny."

"Hey!" called a female voice, and the men turned to see Jean Dukes standing behind them holding a big-ass wooden box. She was straining a little. "I'm not trying to pull the weak woman card here, but someone stop being all woman-are-equal and help a girl out."

Akio and Peter were the closest, and each grabbed a handle. She let go. "Now, put that on the bench. That's from Bethany Anne." She wiped her hands on her pants. "She had me make those last night."

Peter and Akio moved the crate to the bench and Dan

walked over. John looked at Dan, who shrugged. "No, I don't know either."

The men piled around the box to see what Dukes had manufactured. John pulled on the simple master lock, but it held.

Jean said, "Oops" and reached into her pocket to pull out a key ring.

Jean was going through the keys when she heard someone say, "No worries" and metal snapping. She looked up to see John moving a broken lock and set it to the side.

As she stared at the man, she realized no one truly understood the power these guys had. Then, she looked them all over and decided someone, or many someones, was going to have a very bad night indeed.

"Ok, I'm officially claiming Bethany Anne as my Queen….again," Peter said as John started pulling out a rifle. "Scott!"

Scott reached over, and John put a special made tactical railgun rifle in his hands. The grips were stipple-textured on both sides, as well as having deep-cut grooves, both front and back straps, and a beavertail for prolonged firing.

"Oh, my. That is long enough," Akio said, admiring the rifle in Scott's hands.

Peter looked at Jean. "How many shots?"

"Seventy-five," she said. "Bethany Anne wanted to make sure you enjoyed your evening. The rifles have three settings: normal, which will push out the rounds at typical velocities, then twice-normal, and ten-times-normal for when you seriously want to fuck something up. They are coded to your biometrics, so don't leave them around, but no one will be using them against you. Any Queen's Bitch

NATALIE GREY & MICHAEL ANDERLE

can use any gun, but she did have me put your names on each one."

Jean glanced at Darryl, who had received his rifle. "Darryl, she told me to tell you that yours is a quarter-inch longer so your ego wouldn't take a hit." Jean winked, waved, and turned to leave. "Have fun, boys!"

"God, she even makes size jokes! Can there be a more perfect woman?" Darryl asked.

"Who?" Akio wondered. "Bethany Anne or Jean Dukes?"

"Yes," Eric agreed. "Either. Have you seen the way Dukes caresses her railgun barrels? You would require a cold shower afterward, I promise."

John reached in. "Dan?"

"Yes?" He turned from examining Eric's rifle.

John pulled one more rifle from the box. "This one has your name on it, with a note."

Dan grinned as he held his rifle, opened the note, and read it.

"Hey!" Darryl said. "Don't make us ask here."

"She says she knows that I've got too much to do tonight, but that she fully expects me to be free on other occasions should I want to go," Dan finally supplied.

John grinned. "Sign you up?"

"Hell, yeah!" Dan grinned. "I'm up for Bitch's Night Out Part Deux when it happens. Count me in." He handed a box of incendiaries to John. "These are for you."

"Thanks," John took the box. "Looks like we have a shit-load of ammunition in here. I wonder how the hell she was able to carry it all?" John mused and looked back down the hallway where Jean Dukes disappeared.

"Interesting," he thought out loud.

QBS Polarus, Bridge

"Now, what I am about to tell you, Fred, is based on our twenty-year relationship." Captain Thomas spoke patiently, hoping the commander of the aircraft carrier strike force twenty miles away would listen. "I'm about to launch six very small craft, and they are going to go over your position very fast. Don't be alarmed, and for God's sake, don't try to attack them."

Captain Thomas walked over and sat down in his chair on the bridge. "Sure! If you want to try an intercept, I'll even say 'go' for you." Thomas laughed. "No, it won't make a difference, Fred. I'll tell you what: if you guys want a look-see, I'll talk to my boss for a second and confirm she doesn't have a problem. I'll give you five minutes to put your birds in the air and get to thirty thousand feet. Have them hold position like they are planning an air raid on ISIS in Iraq."

Thomas looked at his operator, who held up another line. "Hold one, Fred, other line. It might be who I'm going

NATALIE GREY & MICHAEL ANDERLE

to try to get permission from." He clicked the mute button, held out his hand for the second phone, and put it to his ear. "Boss? Thank you for letting me interrupt. I would like to allow some people I know in the US Navy a chance to witness the Black Eagles flying past a set of F-18s—although, I'd be surprised if they didn't have at least one E2D Hawkeye up there for radar intercept."

Thomas listened for a moment. "Ok. Which do you want to do, show we don't have to be ugly or show them the ridiculousness of competing?" Thomas listened again. "Well, they will want the technology no matter *which* way we do it. I'm sure France has already provided specs on your episode." Thomas laughed. "Well, I found it funny as hell, so personally I'm glad you did it."

"Yes, I *would* like to give them a chance. I'm guessing they already know or surmise most of the capabilities. Mmmm, no, I don't think we've used the flying interfaces yet with the Black Eagles. The Bitches can certainly think fast enough to make it happen." Thomas grunted. "Ok, so I have your permission, and you want me to tell John they should 'have fun?' I can do that. Appreciate it, ma'am. Talk to you later."

Captain Thomas hung up with Bethany Anne and tossed the phone to his comm specialist, then un-muted the other before putting the receiver back to his ear. "Fred? Yeah, sorry about that. Ok, I've got two doors. What's behind the door depends on how well you follow directions, or we might get door number three. That would be really, really bad for both of us."

Thomas listened. "Well, you're the top dog over there, so I'll give you the scoop and you tell me. I've got six of our men heading out, and they have been told to 'have fun.' Now, I can ask them to come up and ride with you guys and maybe do a couple of things, but they are not in good spirits after the bullshit being tossed our way. If you can put levelheaded fighter jocks up top, we have a chance to share some cool shit with permission. If not? Well, they aren't real patient right now, and there isn't anything on an F-18 that can catch them or pull them down. So, level heads and everyone has a little fun together. Assholes and it is just a fly-by, if you are lucky. Sore losers and we have an international incident that won't go over very well."

Thomas listened for a few seconds. "Yes, I know 'level-headed fighter jock' is an oxymoron, but there have to be some Gooses up there. They can't all be Mavericks. Mmmhmmm. Works for me. If it helps, tell the guys going topside to watch the news for strange attacks in Iraq tomorrow morning. If this goes well, I'll share some personal footage we all want to see. All right? That works. Bye, Fred."

Thomas handed the second phone to the comm specialist as he went to find John.

The waves were about four feet as the guys walked out to the deck. John turned around when he heard his name called and scanned the area for a moment before realizing he was hearing footsteps up the port side of the boat. He waited a few seconds for Captain Thomas to appear out of a side hallway and make his way to where his team was loading a boat to transfer to the *Ad Aeternitatem*.

Captain Thomas held out his hand. "Good to see you, John." He nodded to the rest. "Guys!" They all greeted the captain, and he turned back. "I've had a request from a Navy buddy who is heading the group in charge of shadowing us. He would like a nice, polite fly-by to see what we have. Bethany Anne is ok with it, since there isn't a chance they can do shit with it before we are out of here." He stared intently at John. "I want to make sure they understand they want us as friends, not enemies. I've warned Fred not to send up an ass, but you never know what will happen. Bethany Anne says to go manual if you want."

John considered the request. "I won't accept potshots at us, Bartholomew."

Captain Thomas got the message. John didn't use his first name unless it was personal. He would do this for him personally, but there was only so much he was willing to take anymore. "I've told him as much, John." He held out his hand. "Give 'em hell tonight."

John shook the proffered hand. "Who?"

Captain Thomas looked at the six men. "Everyone." He winked and started walking back toward his bridge. "Oh, and Bethany Anne says, 'Have fun!'" He waved before disappearing around the side.

Buenos Aires, Argentina

Tabitha walked into the library and put a hand on the chair Michael used to read in. She ran her fingers across the back, enjoying the texture.

Stepping over to the books, she walked down the shelf,

running her hands across spines before going to the chair across from Michael's and sitting down.

She crossed her legs and took a moment to stare at the emptiness of the chair, which mirrored the feeling in her heart. She had told Bethany Anne she couldn't take being at the funeral; that if she went, she would have to believe he couldn't come back.

Come back from a small nuclear explosion.

"You know that you are my father now." She spoke into the quiet. "The man I finally looked up to, the one who allowed me to be me; the one who respected me for my talent, not my tits."

She sniffled.

"So now I sit in this big house, talking to myself with only mute memories to remind me of your awesomeness." She heard the doorbell and simultaneous knocking on the front door. She stood up. "We aren't finished yet, you and I. I don't believe you're gone. I won't."

Tabitha wiped the tears out of her eyes and straightened as she went down the stairs. She was the owner of the home now, and she would be damned if she would sully the house by acting immature. It was time to be an adult and climb above her fears.

She nodded to the mute memories as she stepped to the door and opened it. Three men stood there, all wearing dark suits. "Yes?" she asked, puzzled.

"I am Francisco," he turned to point to the two men with him, "and these are my compatriots Santino and Mateo." Francisco was a dark Hispanic man with medium-length black hair and brown eyes. "May we come in?"

NATALIE GREY & MICHAEL ANDERLE

"No, I don't believe so, gentleman. It won't go well," Tabitha replied. "I'm in no mood for company."

Francisco turned his head. "Well, our benefactors are expecting to be able to enter the house this evening, so you had better get 'in the mood' very quickly." Francisco's smile turned dark, his eyes losing their charm as he placed his foot to stop her from shutting the door easily.

Tabitha shook her head. "Seriously? You three... You know what?" Her voice hardened and her eyes turned darker, her anger due to her pain rising to the surface. "Why don't you come in?" She opened the door the whole way as she turned to stride determinedly back down the hall, leaving the three men on the porch.

Francisco turned to Santino and Mateo, who shrugged. "Women!"

The three men moved into the house slowly, and Mateo turned to close the door behind them. While there wasn't another house even remotely close by, her screams might carry for quite a distance.

The door clicked and Mateo turned back around, a dark look on his face.

The three men found Tabitha in the middle of a large circular room with two staircases going up the sides. "Just up there," She pointed above them, "is the library I'm about to go back into. Up here behind me," their faces followed her gesture to a railing, "was where Bethany Anne had her last kiss with Michael. And now Forsaken are listening to rumors of Michael being gone, and they want something from his house? *HIS HOUSE!*" she screamed at the three men, momentarily startled by her anger.

Tabitha's voice went deadly quiet. "She might be letting

me weep in peace, but there is something your benefactors should have thought about, which is: my Queen doesn't leave her people undefended. So, let me introduce you to my two mute memories of Michael."

She held out her left hand like she was about to show off a beautiful car. "His name is Hirotoshi." A previously unseen man all in black separated from the wall. "And his name," she moved her right arm as if indicating another beautiful car, "is Ryu." A second man, again all in black with his head covered, separated from the wall to the surprise of the three men. They noticed the gleaming and very deadly-looking katanas by Ryu's and Hirotoshi's sides.

She continued talking. "They have been here suffering with me as I try to pull myself together. You are the third set of *idiots* who have come through the door. Well, I've decided that it is impossible to teach the Forsaken anything with patience. These two are from the Queen's Elite. They are mute not because they can't speak, but because they are honoring me. They also honor me by drinking blood from a mug."

Tabitha's eyes grew dark. "Now they will honor me by drinking from your *necks*!"

Francisco had started out slightly concerned, but he latched on her last comment and smiled as he looked at his two guys. "Necks?" He turned his head back toward her. "Like vampires? Señorita, it is light outside. No vampires are going to..." He pulled his gun, and as he lifted it, the vampire on his right moved so fast Francisco barely registered movement before his wrist screamed in pain. He watched in disbelief as his hand separated and flew to the floor five feet away, blood spurting out from his wrist to the marble floor, gun still in its grip.

"Unfortunately for you..." The first man spoke to Francisco in highly accented English. The three men saw that his eyes had turned red and fangs were growing out of his mouth. "We only need two!"

Francisco felt the sword pierce his neck, then flick to the side.

Francisco's body slumped to the floor, and Santino and Mateo screamed in horror as the vampires came toward them. Tabitha just stood and watched what she had wrought, and she felt peace in her soul.

Unfortunately for the two men, the house was too far away from anyone so no one could hear them scream.

CHAPTER TWO

South Atlantic, Fifty Miles North by North East from QBS *Polarus*

Six F-18s were in position at thirty thousand feet cruising at three hundred knots. That was a good speed for the F-18s, and about forty knots faster than the typical cruising speed for an E2D Hawkeye.

The planes flew in a V formation, with one plane hanging back slightly in the middle. The Hawkeye was stationed five hundred meters to the left of the group.

Their hope was to get the planes, or "Pods," as they called them, to slow down enough so that the advanced radar and other sensing equipment could get a fix on them, allowing the military to get enough data to tweak their systems so they could better tell when the Pods, or whoever used this new coating technology, were in the area. When you are the world's most advanced super-power, it was a kick in the sensitive parts to find out that someone else was significantly more advanced.

America was not fond of playing catch-up.

In the middle radar desk of the three on the Hawkeye, Radar Operator Robert "Styles" Griffin looked at his readings, blinked, and looked again. "Uh, Captain?"

"Go," a voice returned over his headphones.

"Sir, we have approximately thirty aircraft rapidly approaching our vector."

"Say again, was that three-zero?" his captain's voice came back.

"Yes, sir. Wait one. Now I have six zero approaching. They will arrive in… HOLY SHIT!"

"Styles! Can it; keep it professional."

"Uh, sir, you will see them coming up very, very quickly." Styles barely managed to calm his voice.

"What?" There was a break, then, "Never mind. Styles, didn't you say sixty?"

"Yes, sir! Radar is showing sixty, as in six zero contacts."

"Ok, because visual is six," the captain called back. "From a few hundred meters away."

"Im-fucking-possible," Styles murmured to himself. "Sir, can you confirm six again?"

"Yes," came back quickly.

"Sir, they are spoofing their signature, and they are all over the place. Can you tell me where they are?"

"Wait one for Mark-One Eyeball. They are sitting about ten feet above our six birds flying upside down, taking pictures with cell phones. One idiot is using a flash."

"Sir, I have nothing. I repeat, there is nothing showing near our birds," Styles finally managed to get out.

An unrecognized voice interrupted their conversation. "This is Black Eagle One. We will be leaving in a few seconds. I will count down from ten. When I do, we will take off in this same direction, although we will adjust a few hundred feet up so our disturbance doesn't affect your flight. I propose someone takes off when I start counting. The rest is up to you guys. We will not be attaining top speed. Have a nice day."

"Ten," said the deep voice again. Styles saw the first jet fire its afterburners. "Nine..." A second pulled out. The voice got down to one when the last plane fired its afterburners and started rapidly leaving the E2D behind.

Suddenly, six blips appeared where their Pods had been seconds before. They jumped up five hundred feet in altitude before...

They simply disappeared within two seconds from his screen.

"Holy...Fuck..." Styles let out, not realizing he still had an active mic.

His captain came over the radio. "For once, Styles, I concur."

"Well, that was a fun start to our little Bitches' night out. Where is our first stop, John?" Eric called over the comm.

All of the men were playing with the capabilities of their helmets. They gave them complete spatial awareness in a globe around their craft, and also pointed out items in the upper atmosphere or anywhere they chose to look.

"We are going to Iraq. ISIL has been killing all sorts of people, but specifically, Christians. They crucify them and put the videos on the Internet. They have multiple oil refineries pumping for the money."

"Bombing run?" asked Peter.

"Negative. There are a fair number of innocents being used to run the largest plant," John answered.

"We are to save the innocents, and then?" asked Akio.

"Send a Bitches' welcome down."

"Oh, *then* a bombing run," Peter commented.

"Make sure we are clear before we do that, John," Scott mentioned. "I was talking to Marcus, and the shockwaves from the motherpuckers plus the probable concussive force are going to be pretty substantial."

"Come on, don't you want to see what these things can handle, Scott?" John asked.

"Sure. You go first; I'll be the Army Brass sitting in the concrete bunker miles away taking pictures."

Everyone chuckled at Scott's remark.

The team went above the atmosphere and darted over to Iraq before heading down in the twilight. The night had just gotten started when six craft slowed to a stop a mile above the largest oil refinery.

"Are they supposed to have that many fires burning?" Scott asked.

"Yes, they are burning off gasses that form during the processing of the oil. They either don't have enough to capture and use in the process or they are just inefficient." John replied.

"Big fucking place," Scott commented.

"Isolated, too," Darryl added.

There was a small road which led to the huge refinery, but otherwise, there were precious few buildings besides the refinery and the pipes leading to it and away.

"I see two major security bunkers along that road," John answered. "You guys want to play or just nuke them?"

"I'll do the first one," Akio said. "If we drop something, maybe they get the word out, and we lose surprise."

"I'll take the second one," Peter mentioned.

"Pete?" John said.

"Yup?"

"Why don't you let your true self be free tonight? What they don't understand will only make them more scared," John suggested.

"Oh, you wicked, wicked man," Peter replied. "Can I have your babies?" The chuckles went around.

Two of the Black Eagles broke formation and went toward two security emplacements, which were three hundred yards away from the main entrance to the refinery.

John told the rest, "Everyone else, take a side. Drop down and have fun. Don't shoot the good guys."

"How do we know who the good guys are?" Eric asked.

"They won't be shooting at you," John replied.

"I'm telling you, I hear growling!" Hasayne told Aabad.

The two men were in a dugout surrounded by sandbags, and a machine gun poked out of a firing hole. They had some rough-hewn wood and a couple of old doors over their heads to supply protection from above, not that they had any need for it.

"We are two hundred kilometers from any fighting." Aabad grunted. "You hear the machinery behind us." The two jihadis shared a cigarette. "We haven't seen any action since we got here, and if we don't get picked soon, we are going to be here the whole war."

Aabad was taking a drag on the cigarette when the growling got loud enough for him to hear. He turned slowly around to look out the back entrance to their dugout. Two glowing eyes returned his stare.

The cigarette dropped from his fingers.

Three hundred yards from him, two men were playing cards when a figure cloaked in black with red glowing eyes ghosted into their security bunker. Seconds later, he stepped back out after cleaning his sword on the dead bodies.

Akio jogged to the next bunker and took a look inside. His nose had already told him that the men inside were dead.

He looked at the blood and body parts. Apparently, Peter was upset, and had truly 'let his mad out.'

Akio turned and started running toward the large refinery if he didn't hurry he wasn't going to have any additional kills.

John dropped the twenty feet from his Pod to the walkway on the distillation tower with his new rifle. The team had taken a few minutes to zero them back on the *Ad Aeternitatem*. Given the distances here, he wouldn't have to worry about the slug this threw dropping due to gravity. John pulled the gun from his shoulder and rolled his head around, hearing a couple of his vertebrae pop.

He opened his senses as Bethany Anne had taught him and listened to the creaks and moans of the metal around the refinery as the oil went through high-pressure and heated tanks.

He heard the footsteps, the heartbeats, and the grunts as men passed each other.

Fifteen. He had fifteen in his area. John raised the rifle to his shoulder. He had shot once on 10x, and decided unless it called for it, he didn't want the pain that caused again. Even with his advanced healing, it hurt like a bitch.

John looked down and to his left. Two guys were sharing a smoke. He aimed and gently stroked the trigger. The rifle's kick was inconsequential as the metal slug went through the first guy's neck at an angle, exiting between his shoulder blades to enter the chest of the guy behind him. Both bodies slumped to the walkway they were on.

Thirteen.

He turned to watch a guard head down a third walkway and waited for his target to turn to the right. John squeezed his slug through a gap between two eight-inch pipes, and the man's head blew all over the small distillation tank he was strolling past.

Twelve.

The distillation tank now had a small hole in its side and oil started dripping out.

"Somebody should look into that," John murmured.

Thirty seconds and seven shots later, he was down to five.

NATALIE GREY & MICHAEL ANDERLE

Two things happened simultaneously. An alarm went off on the distillation tank he had shot earlier, and one of the dead bodies was discovered.

Two more shots and the latter wasn't an issue any longer. That damned alarm stayed a problem.

John looked over his shoulder and noticed three men jogging toward the tank. One of them had a rifle.

"Way to make yourself a target, asshole." John spoke to the wind. Another twitch and another guy dead. The two running in front of the downed guard heard his fall and turned around. The first in line, who was wearing a tan shirt, drawstring pants, and sandals, pushed the second out of the way as he ran past him to bend down, grab the dead man's gun, and headed back the way the three had come.

John reached up to the small microphone by his mouth. "This is Eagle One. We have a good guy with a rifle about to deliver righteousness to the evildoers, it seems. Try not to kill him."

John clicked off, shouldered his rifle, and started down the stairs to go into the maze.

Scott dropped from his Black Eagle and commanded it to go up. He was wearing a full chest and thigh protection. He kept the helmet on and let it show him everything in the nearby area. It was able to decipher movement and organic sounds with the amplified microphones within the helmet. From this information, it would list likely targets.

Scott smiled under his helmet. "I've always wanted to play Robocop..."

He started walking in a plodding step to the first path. "Please step away from your camels…" he started, then stopped and sighed. "Wow, I can't even make a racist joke about someone I plan on killing without feeling bad. Where is this world going?"

"Who are you?" a voice called from the darkness to his left.

Scott turned to see three armed men in a row. "God, could you guys make this any easier?" Scott pulled his pistol in a blink and shot, and the three men were thrown back with massive holes in their chests, surprise the last expression they would ever have on their faces. "Clean up, aisle one. Aisle two it is." He headed away from the first three dead bodies.

He could see a hundred-yard row of oil containers, dark in the night. "Go infrared." His helmet showed the areas between the tanks, and there were no humans in his view.

Scott looked around. "Bring me the Black Eagle." Scott holstered his pistols and pulled off the helmet. His Black Eagle was in front of him within five seconds, so he palmed the lock. The cockpit slid open, and he placed the helmet in the front seat and reached into the back to grab his rifle.

He hit his microphone. "Take the Black Eagle up to the holding level." His Pod disappeared.

Over the noises of the refinery, a wolf's howl pierced the night.

Scott jerked around. "Motherfucking wolf!" Scott yelled and started running toward the plant. "I'll shoot you myself if you take any of my kills!"

Scott's heart started pumping as he slung the rifle over his shoulder and pulled the pistols. He came around a corner to find himself in a group of four armed men crossing the ground between sections in the plant. Scott jerked his right elbow up, practically exploding one man's skull. He twisted to his left, bringing his pistol around and shot the second in his kneecaps. That man screamed in pain, but Scott was already on the next man to his left.

The third guy in the pack received a bullet between his eyes.

The last man was trying to pull up his rifle and jerked the trigger, sending a burst of bullets into the man in front of him—the same man Scott had kneecapped, blowing the unfortunate guy's chest open from friendly fire.

Scott finished his turn, raised his right hand, and spoke in frustration. "You rotting jizzy-cunt fuck!" Scott shot him in the stomach. "I had fucking plans for him!" Scott shot him in the kneecap. "But now you've gone and killed him!" Scott finished the man with a shot to the head.

He turned in frustration after watching the man's body fall backward. "Fucking shit, how is a guy supposed to—" Scott had to duck to his left when bullets screamed at him from a guy firing off a catwalk fifty yards away.

"Losing situational awareness," John said in his ear, "is a good way to get shot."

Scott bowed his head. John was right. He had been allowing emotion to run his decisions lately. He unslung his rifle, ramped up his speed, darted out from behind his hiding place, and raised his rifle. He could easily see the man at the end of a walkway taking aim at where he had been hiding. Scott continued running toward him as his mark tried to track his target.

When Scott was halfway to the guy, he shot him in the head. Scott was past him before the body fell off of the catwalk to slam to the ground and lie still.

———

Darryl watched Scott step out of his Pod and paid attention as John dropped to the high-level catwalk. "That was smart," he whispered.

"Hey, Eric," Darryl called.

"Yeah?" Eric replied.

Darryl said, "What say we leave those two to ground efforts and play up here?"

Eric smile came through his reply. "What, shoot fish in a barrel?"

"Yes, exactly that," Darryl agreed.

"Works for me. I knew I liked you being around for something besides just getting me a beer."

Darryl snorted. "Prick, I'll bet you a six-pack I get more kills tonight."

"Just say when, old-timer," Eric quipped.

"Now, you cockup." Darryl hit the button for the door and raised his new railgun rifle. Then, it was a silent effort as the two men started aiming and shooting.

———

Scott was running into a more dense section of the refinery when he heard regular rifle shots and then return fire in what sounded like a firefight, but the noises weren't from his group's weapons.

"What the hell is going on?" Scott asked as he stepped onto a catwalk and started jogging toward the gunfire.

John replied, "We have good guys grabbing guns and shooting bad guys."

Scott had just flipped to the main team channel to ask a question when he heard Darryl and Eric. "*Gott Verdammt!* That was *my* kill, you lazy fuck!" Eric told Darryl. "I've got twenty-one, and if you steal my kill again, I'll come over there and slap you so hard your momma will feel it!"

"Oh, try it, you burrito-eating barbarian!" Darryl shot back. "Twenty-three and -four!"

"What?" There was a pause. "Yeah, ok, that was good shooting. But how about this?" Four ear-shattering blasts entered a building to Scott's left, and brick pieces exploded from the wreckage.

"Fuck me! That hurts like a motherfucker!" Eric called. "Why didn't John tell us it hurt so much to shoot these things on ten?"

"Probably so you would do something like that!" Darryl replied. "Yeah, I see four bodies in there. That was slick. I would like to say it was cheating, but only because I didn't think of it first."

"Anyone seen a werewolf?" John's voice interrupted the two.

"Why, did we lose one?" Eric asked.

"Here, Pricolici! Bark, bark, bark!" Darryl called over the net.

"Ahhh, fuck!" John exclaimed. "Akio, see if you can find Peter and get him to change back. I'm getting news that my next hit has moved up their timetable. We have to go. Scott, we are leaving in three."

"Got it!" Scott called. He had arrived at the scene of the firefight. There were ten ISIL members behind a brick wall firing back at four of the previous hostages. "Ah, screw it." He popped the switch to 10x and moved the railgun to his shoulder. "You only live once." Scott held down the trigger.

All hell broke loose.

In a second, seven rods slammed out of his gun at an incredible velocity. The first three shattered the wall into thousands of killing shards, destroying the bodies of five guards immediately. The remaining four went through the two other living ISIL members. The shots blew holes so large in the bodies there was nothing remaining to hold them together and continued into the oil heaters.

That was when the explosions started.

Scott was tossed backward by the continued pummeling from the gun, and tripped over the wire safety railing and flipped off the catwalk. The whole situation became hyper-slow motion to Scott. He tucked his knees to increase the speed of his somersault and paid attention to the ground to stick his landing.

He looked left and then right to see if anyone was going to shoot him.

"I give that a seven for effort but a four for technique." Darryl quipped on the comm.

Fuck, they saw that. He wasn't going to live *that* down.

"Scott, quit fucking around and get your Olympic gymnastics ass in your Pod," John grumped.

Seconds later, Scott's Pod dropped down, and he jumped in to get out of there.

"Where's Peter?" Scott asked.

"Oh, I'm here." Peter's voice came over the net. "I was cleaning my claws when Akio found me."

Akio came on. "Maybe my English is bad, but please explain to me again how swiping your claws through someone's shirt is 'cleaning?'"

John's chuckle came back after Akio's question. "It isn't your English, Akio. It's Peter's definition of cleaning."

CHAPTER THREE

"Are we bombing them?" Peter asked as the six Black Eagles silently ascended a thousand feet.

"Yes," John responded. "Confirm no humans near the storage tanks and use two pucks each to take them out. Eric, I want you to focus on the pipes heading to the southeast. Go out about ten miles and take out a huge section. I'll go to the west and do the same."

Those fighting inside the refinery were startled when ground-shaking explosions went off. They looked to their left to see oil and metal flying high in the air from the sixty-foot-diameter holding tanks. There were no flames, but the destruction was catastrophic, and it was raining petroleum.

The men started running in the opposite direction when two more explosions occurred near them. No one saw the missiles, but everyone suspected they were being used.

From ten miles away and three miles up, Eric released a

four-pound puck at maximum acceleration. Below, a huge explosion of dirt obscured his vision.

"Mission accomplished," Eric reported, then looked over the side again. "I think. I can't see shit down there."

"Mine too," John's voice came back. "It will be good enough. These don't have to be perfect. Close enough works." John switched over to the group comm. "Ok, next stop is Beni."

"Where?" Peter asked.

"Beni," Scott replied. "Shit, sophomore, step up your global mapping knowledge."

"And where the hell," Peter responded, "is Beni?"

"East side of the Republic of Congo," Scott replied.

"You're fucking kidding me, right?" Peter said. "There is no way you knew this already. Did John tell you this?"

John cut in, "No, I didn't, Pete. If you had paid more attention to how your helmet works, you might have this information already."

"Oh," was Peter's sole reply.

"Ok, we are going to visit the ADF, who are resurging. They've killed innocent women and children, often slicing open pregnant women and tying up people before slitting their throats. The politics involve those close to power trying to stop the elections from occurring because they would lose power. Frank heard chatter about a group of about thirty doing a run on a remote village of about eighty."

"Can I come out and play again?" Peter asked.

"No, too much can be a drug, I understand," John answered.

"Yeah, it is a hell of a hit," Peter agreed.

"Ok, guys, we are going to fly in, drop down, and walk down the main street to the path the ADF is using."

"Great! *The Magnificent Seven*," Darryl exclaimed.

"But there are only six of us?" Akio asked.

"I'm counting Peter's ability to change as a split personality, so seven," Darryl qualified. "Or we could say Scott and his arms."

"That are big as tree trunks," Eric agreed.

"Would those be oaks or redwoods?" Peter asked.

"Guns?" Eric asked.

"They should have a few, but they commonly use machetes and other bladed weapons," John answered.

"No, I meant, what guns do *we* use?" Eric clarified.

"Pistols at most, but I'd suggest knives for close work. You are looking a little weak in your hand to hand."

"Whatever, John. Just don't take my kills," Eric said.

"God, still on that? We were even back there," Darryl commented.

The six Black Eagles dropped down over the moonlit jungle to the coordinates Frank had supplied. It wasn't until the team was within a thousand meters that they could see the break in the trees that revealed the small village.

The six Pods quietly landed two at a time. John and Eric got out first, placing their helmets in the Pods, followed by Scott and Darryl, then Akio and Peter. The Pods went back up and disappeared.

John called out loudly in a dialect none of the men understood. When he stopped after repeating his words a third time, they got a lot of movement in houses and people leaving past them, giving the six curious glances as they took in the six men carrying pistols, knives and a sword.

"This way," John supplied, and the six men walked abreast as they started down the dirt main street. Six pairs of boots kicked up dirt as several weather- and time-beaten faces regarded them from cutouts the huts used as windows.

People too old to leave or too old to care anymore.

The six could hear the group coming toward them long before they were visible. They moved to the shadows beside buildings about twenty yards from the jungle, and Akio disappeared up a tree. John just shook his head. He couldn't find the Japanese vampire.

The attacking group congregated just out of sight, and John counted to sixty before the yelling and running started.

The five men on the ground allowed half the group to appear before they stepped from the shadows. Every thug who held a gun was horribly torn apart by the pistols the men fired. Many of the attackers had to pick themselves up off the ground after half-bodies were blown into them as they ran down the path on which only three could run abreast.

The running faltered as the simple village attack turned into an ambush. Many froze when the screaming from those in the back started.

"Akio!" John yelled. "For God's sake man, leave a few!" He pulled his Bowie knife and smiled as he strode toward the closest man, who was holding a machete.

"Let the fun begin!" he growled as he parried the first swing with his knife and kicked the attacker, crushing two of his ribs as he flew into plants next to the path. "NEXT!" he yelled into the chaos of men cursing, slashing, and dying in screams.

The cries of attackers turned to whimpers as each voice was systematically silenced in the night.

The six collected all of the ADF's weapons and placed them in the center of the village. John spied a smaller knife on one of the attackers and a machete two bodies over. He found one body that seemed to be the leader since he was wearing a military-looking coat. Grabbing the knife, he strode over to the body, grabbed the coat's collar, and started dragging it into the jungle. He had gone about a half mile before he placed the body against a tree that allowed him to throw the arms over the lower limbs. He pulled the machete back with both hands and used his massive strength to thrust the machete through its chest and embed it into the tree, then ripped off his Queen's Bitch patch and pinned it to the body with the knife.

It was a warning to the ADF that if they didn't get the message, he would personally come back and deliver it again. Permanently.

You don't fuck with this village. It is under the Queen Bitch's protection.

John walked back through the jungle, complete in its silence until he passed.

Minutes after he was gone, the jungle sounds returned.

New York City, New York

John "the Don" Cherynsky pulled his coat closed as he stepped out of the limo. His two guards had already confirmed that the warehouse, a twenty-foot high affair a hundred feet long and sixty wide, was safe for the meet, so his car drove through the garage door and parked thirty feet from a similar limousine. By the time John came around the front, the SUVs that had followed had unloaded ten men near each limousines.

The agreed-upon number for each side.

John's six-foot-four-inch height and barrel chest usually dwarfed most men, but the Asian man might be his equal. Maybe not in height, but his chest was even larger, and his arms were massive.

They shook, their handshakes firm, with neither playing stupid "who is stronger" games like you would get with immature operators.

"John." The Asian man spoke, a whispered breathing due to an unfortunate "accident" with chemicals in his youth. He had made it out alive. The others had not.

"Jing," John supplied. "I trust the family is well?"

"Yes, thank you, John. You are always a pleasant American to interact with on my trips. Rarely do you speak business first." Jing turned to look around. "It is refreshing."

"Jing, you might find more Americans pleasant if you didn't treat them as uncultured barbarians first, and work up to barely accepting them as civil over a year," John replied, smiling. "Even if, between you and me, it is mostly true."

The powerful Asian man clapped the taller American on the shoulder. "You repeat this wisdom every time we meet, yet I am not wise enough to understand."

"Uh huh." The two turned to walk toward the far wall.

"Why do I feel it has more to do with the television shows we ship all over the world?"

"Because it is true!" Jing laughed. "The reality tv shows you export explain the zombie-like mental state of the unwashed masses!"

"Which, I might remind you, are very 'washed' compared to the rest of the world?" John replied.

"Bah." Jing waved a hand. "Physically clean, yes, mentally full of sugar." Jing put his hands on his ears and pulled them away. "You open it up, and there is nothing but talk about someone's ex-wife or the latest actor scandal."

The two men turned before reaching the wall and started walking back. It was time for the two of them to get down to business.

"So, we have retrieved the four boxes from the cargo containers. Do I have your personal promise these will not be used here in my state?" John asked.

Jing raised an eyebrow. "Did you open them?"

"No, of course not," John replied. "My people are good. You might blame someone's choice of shipping containers. Two of my men are ex-military. They know what an RPG crate looks like."

Jing stopped, turned back slightly toward the wall, and lowered his voice. "John, we have done business for a very long time. I cannot promise where these might be used. I can tell you that they are slated to be used against a CEO who makes her home in Florida or possibly against one of her flying vehicles."

"Yes," John kept his voice low, "I'm aware of the person you are speaking about. There is an open offer of a million dollars for her capture."

"Five," Jing admitted and looked into John's eyes. "But if you bring her to me, I'll double it."

John considered. "Well, that makes the effort worthwhile. I understand, and I respect, your need to keep your options open. If they are to come into my territory, please give me a heads-up. I'd hate to have a team get between your effort to send one of these as a gift and my effort to acquire a guest."

John held out his hand.

Jing nodded and took it. "Agreed."

"Can you believe that shit?" Darryl hissed. He and John were on the roof right next to one of the old windows, listening to the discussions below. Eric and Scott were watching one door, Peter and Akio watching the opposite door of the warehouse. "He wants to off Bethany Anne."

John's face went from dark to impossibly black, if it were possible. "Yes, I can believe it." His voice was quiet, if grim.

"Did you know about it?" Darryl asked.

John shook his head. "No, Frank said that a cache of Chinese weapons was being unloaded at the port, and there was a meeting to pass them over here tonight. So, mafia types and Chinese players. I didn't know they were looking to hit Bethany Anne." John reached around to a pouch on his back and pulled out two grenades, then leaned over to look down into the building again.

John tapped his mic. "Hey , y'all. Watch this shit!"

"Oh, fuck," Darryl whispered and started quickly and

quietly moving to the edge of the roof on the other side of the building as John pulled out one more grenade.

John, face lit by the building's lighting and contorted in anger at anyone who would threaten Bethany Anne, started grinning as he pulled the three pins. "Say hello to my leetle friends!"

On the south side of the building, two sets of boots could be heard running away. On the north side, there was a hushed conversation. "No! John does *not* mean watch this!" Scott tugged on Akio's arm, and the Japanese vampire allowed himself to be pulled away to start running from the building. The two had made it to the street when Darryl came running out of the alley and joined them.

Akio was confused, but started sprinting with purpose now that Darryl was with them. "What is it? Didn't John say to watch this?"

"Hell, yes!" Darryl huffed. "But whenever John Grimes says, 'Hey, y'all, watch this shit,' that is code for 'get the fuck out of there!'" Darryl and Peter grinned when explosions rocked the warehouse behind them.

The three men slowed to a stop and turned around. A massive amount of smoke was billowing out of broken windows, glass still tinkling as it fell to the concrete around the old warehouse.

A few moments, they heard pistol shots from inside the building.

"Does he need us?" Akio asked.

"Oh, I don't think so," Darryl answered. "He's getting his mad out right now."

"What happened?" Peter asked Darryl when Scott and Eric joined the three.

Darryl answered, "The Chinese in there were importing RPGs to use against Bethany Anne, and John heard them talking about it." Two more shots could be detected among the crackle of the flames.

The four men turned from looking at Darryl to staring at the now-burning building. Soon, a figure emerged from the door, walking calmly toward the Bitches as a siren cut the dark in the distance. John had made it about halfway to the group when another round of explosions rocked the warehouse.

"There go the RPGs," Darryl mused.

CHAPTER FOUR

Akio stepped out of the suite's bath. "Next," he called as he shoved his clothes into his overnight bag. He had changed into a nice dark blue pair of pants, a pressed white shirt, and dark blue loafers. A gold watch accented the ensemble.

"All mine!" Peter yelled as he rushed into the shower.

The men had rented a large suite on the other side of New York to clean up. John had had to be brought in through a side entrance because he smelled too badly of smoke to walk through the lobby. The huge fire and dead men inside the warehouse had made the news. The police were keeping quiet so far about how the men had died.

John, Eric, and Darryl were using the connected suite's shower while Scott, Peter, and Akio used this side. Scott had to cut out a small piece of metal from the fight in Iraq and was making sure he didn't have anything else stuck in his body that he hadn't noticed.

John walked through the open door between their suites. "Damn, Akio, you clean up well." He turned to look at Scott. "Are you done, Dr. Demento?" Scott threw up his middle finger. "Told you not to get too close, but you had to go all Rambo and shoot off your Dukes Special on 10!"

"Motherfucking thing should show 11 on the side, not 10." Scott grinned. "God, it packs a punch like a mule." He rubbed his shoulder. "I know the healing is done, but you don't forget that feeling."

"Experience is the mother of all teaching," John said. "We have a limo picking us up in thirty minutes, guys. Carry concealed only; nothing to get us in trouble."

The shower door opened and Peter stepped out in a towel. "Next!"

The six men, all decked out in nice clothes, swept through the hotel lobby, and many ladies followed them as they walked through the front doors to a waiting limousine.

John went up to the driver and held out his hand. "John Grimes."

"Um, Bartholomew," his driver supplied, and shook his hand. The driver stuttered a bit as he watched the men enter his car, his eyes wide in shock.

John leaned forward. "Bartholomew?" The driver nodded his head. "You know I asked for you specially, right? I wanted a Nacht to drive us around."

"No, I didn't realize that," Bartholomew answered as he turned to face John. "I didn't realize that I was on a list for anyone to know…um…what I am."

"Bartholomew, Bethany Anne doesn't care so long as you stay 'good,' ok? Don't go Forsaken, and you will never hear from her. However," John reached into his coat pocket and pulled out a business card, "here's my card. You need help? Call me. We are here to let off steam, and I'm sure you know most of us?"

"Of...of course!" Bartholomew commented. "You're practically rock gods on the UnknownWorld. The only gentleman I don't recognize is the one in the blue slacks."

John looked at the limo. "Akio. He is a Guard, the leader of the Queen's Elite."

"And a..a..." Bartholomew stammered before John could finish it for him.

"Yes, he is a Queen's Bitch as well. We are here to have a good time for the next few hours. Can you help me make that happen for these guys?"

Bartholomew smiled and gave a sharp nod. "Yes, I can, Mr. Grimes."

John put one foot in the car. "Let's go to 245 Eldridge first, Bart." He finished sliding inside.

"Bar Goto it is, Mr. Grimes," Bartholomew said as he closed the door.

"Bar Goto was nice," Akio admitted. "It was a touch of home in this new world. Thank you."

John nodded, and Peter spoke up. "I'm voting Club Purple."

"You're voting for the babes around their pool!" Scott called to general hoots.

"And the bikinis," Darryl added.

"I'm voting for their willingness to drink until they find Peter handsome," added Eric.

The glass separating the driver's area from the back started to open. "We are almost to the last place, Mr. Grimes. Are you sure you want to come here?"

John was sitting on one of the seats that ran the length of the car, so he leaned over to speak to Bartholomew. "I'm positive."

The limousine pulled to the curb in a dilapidated neighborhood, and Bartholomew stepped out and put on his hat. He hadn't expected to take these men from some of the hottest clubs in New York to this neighborhood, which was run by gangs.

Ones that, Bartholomew suspected, had eyes on them right now.

He stepped around the vehicle and opened the door. The first one out was Darryl, then Akio, Peter, John, Eric and finally Scott, who had a look of shock on his face. "Dude!" He turned around. "This is one of my old areas!"

"I know," John said. "You know who happens to be in that two-story a block down with the two guys lounging outside smoking?"

"No, who?" Scott asked, looking down the street.

"A world-class fuck-head pimp who killed a certain prostitute a long time ago. Care to have a word with him?" John asked. "We got your back." He paused. "This can be civil…"

Scott started walking toward the building. "God, I hope not."

Darryl winked at John as he followed Scott. John told Bartholomew, "I expect this car to be right here when we get back."

Bartholomew's eyes flashed red. "Oh, hell, yeah Mr. Grimes. No one is taking my ride tonight."

"Good," John said and followed the rest of his team.

This was going to be a great finish to a lively night.

Buenos Aires, Argentina

"So, I requested that Hirotoshi and Ryu drain them. Well, I asked them to drink from their necks, but I guess I had expected the guys to kill them. So, same thing, Bethany Anne." Tabitha spoke into the phone she had been given to call TQB.

"No, I just got fed up with the bullshit. This was the third time someone tried to send idiots during the day, and this bullshit is pissing me off. I'm tired of using the computer and research as my security blanket."

Tabitha waited for a moment. "Are you shitting me?" she asked. "Yes, I know that." Another pause. "If you trust me, I'll get the fucking job done or die trying. I'm sick of hiding, and none of these fuckers are going to hide from me. They want to raise their heads now that they think Michael is dead?" Tabitha's voice dropped an octave. "Then their heads will be that much easier to take off."

"No, I don't need Gabrielle for this. I'm not suggesting she can't come, just that if she is busy elsewhere, that's fine." Tabitha started laughing. "Yes! I guess Hirotoshi and Ryu make me feel safe."

Tabitha's lips drew tight. "If that is what I need to do, then I'll do it. I hadn't expected to learn how to fight with swords. Yes, I understand. I have to earn the honor, not just point a weapon. I'll make it happen."

The front door opened and Ryu walked in. Tabitha cocked an eyebrow, and he nodded quickly. "Ryu just got back from disposing of the bodies. What do you need me to do?"

She listened briefly. "I'll be ready for the Pod in thirty minutes, then."

A few minutes later she said, "Yes, my Queen, I will. See you shortly."

Tabitha clicked off the phone and turned to face Ryu and Hirotoshi. "I'm going to the *Polarus* to take part in a ceremony to accept Bethany Anne as my Queen. It is a requirement before she can release any additional Elites to help me take out the Forsaken who have been annoying the fuck out of me here. Plus, I am going to need to work out and learn martial arts." Tabitha started taking off her shirt and walking toward her room. "No time like the present. I'm done hiding." She flung her shirt one direction and reached behind her to unsnap her bra as she continued down the hall.

Hirotoshi looked at Ryu, who shrugged almost imperceptibly as the two men watched her ditch her bra before turning into her room.

Two minutes later, she was back out in a pair of leather pants. The men barely raised an eyebrow, but Tabitha caught the slight movements. "Gabrielle's that she left here. Her ass is a little smaller than mine, but I'll be fucked before I wear that other shit anymore." She slid on a black bra and reached behind her to hook it, then put on an Under Armour long sleeve lycra shirt. She finished, her breasts damned near popping out, and noticed that the two men hadn't moved a centimeter while she dressed in front of them.

"Guys?" Tabitha asked. "Woohoo, guys?" She snapped her fingers in front of their eyes. "What's the big deal? You're all gay, aren't you, like Akio?" The men minutely shook their heads.

Tabitha's face turned red as she dropped her face into her hands. "Oh, fuck my life!"

Hirotoshi looked at Ryu and winked.

CHAPTER 6

New York City, NY, USA

The two-story was old-fashioned, with wood planking covering the sides. The hurricane fence had grass growing where the weed-eater couldn't reach too well. The buildings on either side were boarded up.

Scott walked down the street as two more guys stepped out of the house in the early morning chill. They noted the six men heading their direction, but only one seemed intent; the others were hanging back. Probably didn't want anything to do with what the asshole in front wanted.

Scott reached out to grab the gate.

"Yo, homes, that isn't smart," Mars said and pulled his cigarette out of his mouth. "Private property."

"Oh?" Scott stopped at the gate. "So, if I open this gate, like this," he asked as he opened the gate, "and step through like this," he took as long a step as he could and left the gate to swing behind him, "you will call the cops?" He put up both arms like he was questioning the guy.

"No," Mars agreed and reached into his pants. "But we will call the ambulance." He pulled out a pistol and aimed it at Scott, who turned toward John and raised an eyebrow in question. Mars looked at Scott's posse. "Don't think we won't shoot all six of you fuckers." When Mars finished speaking, the other three pulled their pistols and held them down by their sides.

John considered it for a second. "Yeah, I'd call that uncivil."

Mars was trying to understand why they were talking so casually when he realized the first guy was already running toward him. He was hit so hard the one shot he got off was because his hand clenched as he hit the front door on his way through it.

Scott punched the one to his left and kicked the one to his right. The last guy just stared in confusion. "Get the fuck out of here. This isn't about you, dumbshit!" Scott grabbed him by the back of the neck and threw him off of the porch toward the gate.

The rest of the team stepped around him as they walked up to the front door. Scott yelled, "Mario! Get your pimp ass up, you fucking piece of trash!"

"You think we should go in?" Peter asked, and the men flinched when a window shattered above them and a body rolled off the awning to fall into the grass with a thud.

"Is that..." Eric started when they heard Scott yell, "Mario!" again. "Guess not," he finished.

There were two female screams, and the men were almost run over by two twenty-somethings with t-shirts and pants held to their chests wearing g-strings.

Peter watched them run down the walkway and out the

gate, and both hooked a left, heading away from their limo. "Doesn't that floss hurt?" he wondered. "Not that I'm complaining. No lines when the pants are tight, but still…"

The guys turned back around when they heard two pistol shots crack and one shot fired in return, then a cry of pain.

"That would be Mario, I'm guessing," Darryl said.

The men could hear a crying male and the thump-thump-thump of a body being dragged down stairs. Scott was commenting, "No, you don't have any rights, mother-fucker. This is Justice, just a little late. Well, there is my attempted murder first… Oh, and a friend you killed years ago is going to rest easier tonight."

John spoke into his microphone when Scott reached the front door. The men started to leave when a Pod came down from the sky and landed in the middle of the street. John turned to Scott. "Just remember, you have to clean up the blood. See you back at the ship." He smiled.

Scott looked down at the helpless man in his hands and called after John, "*You* would do this, wouldn't you?"

John turned as the four others continued toward the limousine. "Do what?"

"Kill him in cold blood, no trial, no worries?" He looked at his boss.

"Was I worried about the men in the warehouse tonight?" John answered.

Scott paused for a second. "No, but that was about Bethany Anne. I'd have done the same thing." Scott thought about it for a second. "Ok, maybe with fewer grenades."

John nodded in Mario's direction. The pimp was hanging from Scott's fist, trying fruitlessly to get away from him while attempting not to move his shattered kneecap. "He's trash, Scott. If the system does anything, it will spit him back out like it did the first time. Do I care if you kill him?" John asked as Mario redoubled his efforts to get away.

Scott casually took the pistol and popped Mario across the back of the head. He now hung without fighting, but held the back of his head and moaned.

John continued, "No, he shot first. Look around. Is anyone else dead?" Scott turned to catalog everyone. Even the one lying on the lawn was moaning. "No. What use is he to society?" John asked. "But really the question isn't what good he is for society, but rather what vigilantes do for the four hundred million people in this country? It messes up the illusion of a justice system, however good it feels to do it. That's up to the person, and is a personal decision."

"I want Justice done, John," Scott grated out. "I can't just drop him."

John turned toward the limo. "Akio?"

Akio got back out of the limo and quickly jogged over to them. "Yes?"

"Do you think you can command this piece of trash to go to the police and tell them all of his crimes?" John asked.

"Yes, easily," Akio agreed.

Scott turned from Akio to John. "Thank you, John." John nodded and turned to walk back to the limo. "Don't take too long, guys."

The Pod disappeared back into the sky.

Thirty minutes later, near a lonely stretch of beach, six

men got out of a limousine. John stepped over and shook Bartholomew's hand. "Thanks for this."

"It was truly my pleasure," their driver told him. "I've got an hour before sunup if there is somewhere else you need to go?"

"No, but what are you going to do?" John asked him.

Bartholomew turned to look at the city behind them. "Go back to my room in a basement, and wake up tonight and see if someone needs my services." He shrugged before turning back to John. "What I've done for the last eight years."

"You ever wanted to know what is over the horizon?" John asked. Behind him, six Black Eagles descended from the sky, and the other five Bitches grabbed helmets and threw their bags into the back after they landed.

"Why?" Bartholomew asked.

"It's something my Queen does: find people with good hearts and provide them a chance to do something else in life. You've got a good heart, Bartholomew. I can't promise you a long life, but if you want to know what is above the horizon, I'll take you."

Bartholomew looked at the waves and smiled. "Mr. Grimes, you're the first one to offer me anything like this in over six decades. I need to think about it. Right now the Big Apple is all I know, and you guys have shown me there is good to do here. Can I call?"

"You've got the card, so don't be a stranger!" John clapped him on the shoulder and turned to go.

John palmed his cockpit lock open and grabbed his helmet. He slid into his seat and hit the Close button.

John spoke into his helmet. "Good times, everyone,

good times. All right guys, what happens on a Bitches' Night Out…" John started.

Frank interrupted his comment and finished, his voice loud in their helmets, "Gets written about in one of my books!"

FINIS

AUTHOR NOTES - MICHAEL ANDERLE
MARCH 22, 2016

Guess who?

You know, I've actually read something on either an Amazon Forum or on Facebook or someone mentioned seeing that the real author of the Kurtherian Gambit is Frank Kurns, and that "Michael Anderle" is actually a pen name for him.

Damn, now I don't know who the hell I actually am.

Just to screw with people, I should open up another author name account with "Frank Kurns" and then put books out under THAT name.

That will teach us all a lesson. A lesson on how to really screw up your author branding, that's what it will teach us!

So, Margaret, here is the book you asked about. Why am I highlighting Margaret? Because I was on the forum an hour ago and noticed her comment about "When is John's book coming out?." That's when I realized that the beta readers had delivered the document to my Production Editor, who had promised it to me tonight. But then, he pulled a fast one and delivered it early while I was out eating. So, I completely forgot I HAD the document to go through and get it online.

Which, I'm doing right now because Margaret was asking. (See, I get back to the original point eventually).

I hope you enjoyed this small slice of John's life with Bethany Anne as much as I enjoyed writing it. I will do Tabitha next, and if you have a particular person or character/situation you would like to read about, why not drop me a line sometime? Or, better yet, create a Forum post and argue why it should be done, and maybe the Amazon Almighties will wonder just what the H#LL is going on with all of these forum posts/updates on such a tiny Indie-Authors Forum?

Mwuhahahahaha! We are having fun, that's what we are doing :-)

If this is your first book, by now, I think you have figured out that these characters (John Grimes and Bethany Anne) are actually from *The Kurtherian Gambit* Series. So, apologies from me and my readers that you are now part of the family.

I imagine it feels a little like a shotgun wedding.

Love the book? Drop a review! Like the book? Drop a review! Hate the book? Here is another author you might like to read... ;-)

http://www.amazon.com/Veronica-Roth/e/ B004FX672S/ref=kar_mr_-1_99

Just be prepared, if you like my writing: a few people have lost a few days catching up on the series.

Don't say you weren't warned (and I'm not being

egotistical; read the reviews. All of them (good and bad) are real. Except that the first book has been edited since November...like a few times ;-)

Best Regards,

Michael Anderle

BELLATRIX

CHAPTER ONE

Alec Nikolaev lifted the latch and pushed open the door into his parents' kitchen. At almost six feet tall, he had to stoop to get in the older, shorter, doorway. The first few flakes of an early snowstorm clung to his black hair.

"Hello, Mama." He went to where his mother, far shorter than he was and now grey-haired, was kneading bread with the sort of intensity that masked worry. She always baked when she was worried. He kissed her on the cheek. "Why did you need me here in the middle of the day?"

She gave him the answer she often gave: "It's your sister."

Alec walked to the kitchen table and slumped down in a chair with a groan, "Mama, every week you tell me to get Yelena to quit her job and move home." He decided this time, he was going to go to the wall with his mom.

She needed to *finally* accept the truth.

He continued, "Mom, she clearly doesn't want to come back. She's a grown woman, she gets to—"

"She came home." Was his Mom's curt response, hand's strangling the dough.

Alec's mouth dropped open. "What? When?"

"This morning." His mother licked her lips. Her shoulders were hunched. "She took an overnight train."

Alec felt a prickle on the back of his neck. "And? What aren't you telling me?"

His mother finally gave up on her kneading. She sighed and wiped a floury hand across her forehead, and paused to pick her words.

She was a woman who could argue with her children for hours, almost without drawing breath, but now she didn't seem to know what to say. "She'd been crying," she said finally.

She looked older, suddenly. "But she wouldn't talk about it. She said everything was fine. But she was still in her work clothes, and she didn't bring a suitcase. It looked like she just walked out of the house without even a coat, and bought a train ticket."

Alec knew just what his mother was suggesting, but he had one question.

"Mama…." He tried to smile. "You've wanted her to break up with Ciprian for months, and come home. Why don't you look happy?"

His mother went back to kneading, with more force than was necessary once again. She had complained nonstop since Yelena had taken a job a few hours away. His mother hadn't liked the job. She hadn't liked Ciprian, Yelena's boyfriend. She called Alec every few days to plead with him to get Yelena to return home. Now, though, she didn't seem to be celebrating.

She was sad. She looked over at him, finally. "I didn't want her to be unhappy," she said finally. "I never wanted that." Then, she whispered her greatest concern, "And, she's broken, Alec."

Alec sat, frozen. He and Yelena were twins. When they were children, they always knew when the other one was upset. That had faded over the years, especially when they began to live further apart.

Alec had woken up the previous night from a sad dream he couldn't remember, and sat at his own kitchen table late into the night. He was feeling like his heart was broken and not knowing why.

Now he wondered if it had really been him who had been sad ... or Yelena.

What had happened?

He pushed himself up without a word and went down the low-ceilinged hallway to his sister's bedroom, all the way at the back of the house. He half-expected to hear music.

When she was a teenager, Yelena would play music far too loudly and dance all evening until someone pounded on the door and told her to stop. Now, nothing. He raised his hand to knock on the door, and then thought better of it and just pushed the door open. His sister was sitting on her bed, staring at nothing.

She looked terrible. Her black hair was nicely styled, her skirt suit was tailored, but she was too thin and she appeared so exhausted that her eyes looked bruised.

Her makeup had long since worn away, but he could still see the shadow where her mascara had run and she hadn't washed it off properly. Her fingers kept working over one another, twisting.

She looked over at him dully, her eyes lifeless. "Hi."

Alec tried to conceal his shock behind a smile, "Mama said you were home."

She smiled back, the sort of emotionless smile she would give in the law office where she worked. She opened her mouth to say something witty, to tease him—he knew she was planning to come up with some story so she wouldn't have to tell him the truth. Yelena never wanted to tell anyone when she was hurting.

Their parents had always used Alec's sense of her, to figure out when something was wrong, and even then she would lie.

She couldn't pretend this time, though. She crumpled.

Her shoulders hunched and tears began to run down her cheeks. When Alec came to sit by her on the bed, she leaned her head on his shoulder and he wrapped his arm around his beloved sister, and held her close.

"It's going to be okay." He didn't know what else to say.

"No. It's not…." She gave a choking sob. "It's not going to be okay. Work is terrible, and getting worse, and I caught Ciprian with…." She tried to steady herself. "With our downstairs neighbor. Again! I didn't even grab anything, I just left. I wanted to beat him into the floor with my bare hands and I knew I shouldn't do that."

She gave a watery laugh.

At least there was a spark of the feisty sister he remembered. Alec gave a grateful smile and squeezed her shoulder. "I dunno, I probably would have."

Her laugh turned into a sob. "Alec, I didn't know where

else to go. He said he would never see her again, but he…."
Her voice trailed away. "God, how could I have been so
stupid? I was proud of myself for getting him when
everyone else wanted him, and he was just a jerk the whole
time once we were together."

Alec felt a hot wave of anger course through him. His
sister had been a fighter at one time. Once, she would
never have allowed a guy to walk all over her, but she'd
fallen hard for Ciprian. Alec understood why their mother
hated the man—he was arrogant, cold, and he clearly didn't
care about Yelena at all. But, Yelena had refused to hear a
word against him.

He let Yelena cry, her tears soaking his shirt. He didn't
know what else to do. The feeling of helplessness only
made him angrier. After a while, the sobs stopped, and he
tried to think of something to say. Something that *wasn't*
promising to kill Ciprian.

"You could stay here for a while," he suggested.

She picked her head up. "What?"

"I mean; you've got your room here. You could stay for
a couple of weeks, until you find a new job."

I have to go back. He saw the words come to her mind,
but to his shock, she didn't say them. She stared at him for
a moment and she looked terrified. Then she nodded. "I'd
like that," she whispered.

Her eyes filled with tears again. "I don't want to go
back. I hate my job. I've hated it for months but I didn't
want to say because I knew Mom would tell me to come
back." She sighed, "Have I mentioned I hate my job? It was
a mistake moving there, I don't want to go back."

"Then you don't have to." He promised her. He brushed her hair behind her ears. "Hey, you remember Dmitri?"

Yelena sniffed and wiped at her eyes. She nodded. "Yeah, why?" When the two of them were younger, they had spent whole holidays at Dmitri's kennel, learning how to train the dogs, and playing with the puppies. Dmitri had been forty or so then. His public demeanor was gruff, but he'd been kind to the two children.

"Well, Inger—one of the bitches now—just had another litter. I bet he'd let you help out at the kennel if you wanted."

Yelena shook her head, dispirited. "I'd just get in his way. When we were kids, it was fine, but now I would be imposing."

"No, you always had a way with dogs, remember?" Alec nudged her. "You really did. I bet he'd ask you to help, if he knew you were back."

Yelena smiled back, chin trembling. The thought of staying here was crazy. She had a job back home. All of her things were in the apartment she shared with Ciprian. She couldn't really stay here, could she?

Maybe just for a couple of days. She could call in sick to work. She smiled recklessly back at her twin. "Okay. I'll stay. Probably just for the weekend."

Alec knew better than to push her, "Uh-huh. You get some sleep, okay? I'll take you to see the puppies tonight."

Yelena hunched her shoulders against the winter wind outside the kennel. She was wearing some of Alec's old pants and a heavy down vest, warm enough for early winter, but her fingers were going numb holding the phone. "Ciprian—"

"Just come home, Yelena." He sounded desperate. "I messed up, baby. I don't know what I was thinking."

"What you were thinking *again*, you mean?" She retorted. When she walked in on him with their neighbor, she remembered that she had only felt tired and numb. Now, she could feel herself starting to get angry. "You said you'd never even talk to her again. How did this happen?"

"Yelena—"

"You know what?" she snapped. "I don't even want to know. I have to go."

"Yelena." It sounded like he was crying. "Yelena, please."

"I have to go," she repeated, but she was shaken. Ciprian never cried. He would yell and be cold with her, but he never cried.

She could hear him sob, "Yelena, I'd give anything to have you back."

Her voice went cold, "How can I believe that when you couldn't stay away from her? You've been a jerk for months, Ciprian. You don't *deserve* to have me around."

"It's different now!" He sounded panicked, like a prize was getting away. "When I realized you were gone, I went crazy. I've never been that afraid." He paused, just a second. Just enough time to feel...honest. "Tell me I haven't lost you, baby."

You haven't. Of course I'll come back. Yelena bit her lip.

She knew she shouldn't say those words, but she had been weak when it came to him. Ciprian was the one guy wanted by every other woman she knew—and she'd won him.

Unfortunately, the satisfaction of winning him had blinded her to how much of a jerk he really was.

"Please." His voice cracked again. And then, desperately, "At least think about coming home, Yelena, *please*. It's not just us, it's your job. It's everything."

"I hate my job," she spat out.

"You've been having a hard time—that doesn't mean you should walk away from everything! You have friends there. We have a life together. You can't just throw it all away! If you—"

"*Fine.*" Gott Verdammt! She'd give anything to make him stop talking.

He echoed everything she'd been thinking last night. This was crazy, people didn't just quit their job and move back to the town where they grew up. She was being a baby, and she knew it. She looked down at the ground.

She didn't want to go back to it all, but Ciprian had a point … didn't he? She might not stop herself from saying something, but damned if she would totally capitulate to that ass. "Fine, I'll think about it."

She hung the phone up before she could say anything else. Putting the phone back in her pocket she stamped her feet to warm herself up. She should go back in, but needed a moment or two to think.

She looked around at the trees admitting to herself she didn't have the first idea what to do. Alec would be disappointed if he knew she'd even said she'd think about going back to Ciprian. But they had been together for two years, and in the beginning, she had been happy, hadn't she?

How could she just turn around and walk away. God, relationships suck and monumental relationships sucked worse.

Alec poked his head out the back door of the kennel. "You done with your call?"

"Yeah." Yelena nodded and headed in.

"Who were you talking to?" She heard the worry in his voice.

She tried to give herself an easy out, "Work."

He wasn't fooled, "It was Ciprian, wasn't it?"

"Alec, let it be please." She pushed past him, annoyed with herself. "I don't want to talk about it, okay?"

Luckily for her, he didn't get a chance to answer.

"Hey, there!" Dmitri called to them from across the room. The big, barrel-chested, man came to enfold Yelena in a hug. "Yelena! Good to have you back." He wrapped an arm around her shoulders and pulled her across the room. She could hear the yipping of dogs beyond. "So how long are you staying?" His eyes full of joy.

"I don't know," she admitted. She smiled up at him. Once, he had seemed impossibly tall to her. She'd teased him about the salt and pepper in his hair. Now it was all grey, and she was almost as tall as he was, "So, I hear there's a new litter?"

"Right here." He held a door open for her and led her over to a large enclosure. Several black balls of fluff tumbled over one another, yipping, while Inger, a massive German Shepherd, reclined in the corner. She looked immensely pleased with herself.

"Oh, look at them!" Yelena smiled as she reached down to brush her hands over one of the puppies. It tipped over, barked, then righted itself with a shake of its fur.

At this stage, the puppies looked like little bear cubs. She patted one on the head and laughed as another toddled toward her. "This one! She's so tiny!"

"Oh, that's … yeah." Dmitri rubbed his hand through his hair and shrugged. "She's the runt, and no mistake about it. I don't think anyone's going to take her."

"But she's so fierce." Yelena laughed as the puppy struggled for freedom in her arms, giving a growl that was not as intimidating as the puppy hoped. "There, there, little one, you're safe. You're safe." She sat down and let the puppy roam about on her lap. In this moment, she was perfectly content. She watched as the puppy asserted itself, trying to sit proudly and puff out its chest. "Look at her, Dmitri!" Yelena looked up at the older man, then back down at the little puppy, "She's perfect."

Dmitri squatted down next to her. He looked dubious as he scratched his chin. "You have a name for her?"

"Hmm." Yelena picked the puppy up and put it right in front of her face. It opened its jaws to try to bark at her, and got caught in a yawn. She laughed and put it down, and the little black puppy snuggled against her.

Yelena smiled as an image formed in her head. In it, the puppy was the size of a small pony and its fierce growl had the other puppies cringing and rolling onto their backs.

Yelena's smile slowly faded as she noticed more details of the image. Things like it being a little out of focus and the whole scene lacked good three dimensional detail, looking flat.

One last thing started her frowning. She had no control

over the image, she could not change the details to better reflect reality. The image faded, as the little puppy's legs started twitching and she fell asleep.

"Yelena?" Alec shook her shoulder gently.

"Hmm? What?"

Alec pointed at the puppy in her lap, "Dmitri asked if you had a name for this one."

"Oh." Yelena looked away from the puppy, thinking of the little scene she had in her mind. "Hmm, Bellatrix?"

"Bellatrix?" Dmitri raised an eyebrow. "Big name for a little pup."

Yelena looked at the little puppy, all snuggled in her lap. "It means, lady warrior and bringer of light."

"That's an even bigger name," Alec laughed. But he reached out to stroke the puppy's head and Yelena felt contentment radiating from the little ball of fur.

"I like it, though," Yelena told him. She looked over as Dmitri scooped the puppy off her lap annoyed. "Hey, I wasn't done cuddling!"

Dmitri shrugged, "Well, you'll have to come back tomorrow and help me train them, then, won't you?" He grinned. "Your brother told me you might like to. I'd be glad to have you. Never met anyone who can communicate with dogs the way you can."

Yelena wavered, "I really should go back to my job...."

"Just stay a week," Alec suggested. "Say Mama's sick or something, they'll let you take off work."

Yelena wavered, but Bellatrix's pitiful mewl caught her heart strings and jerked them hard. She smiled and reached out to tickle the puppy's stomach. "Okay, one week. Then I go back to the real world," she promised herself.

"Because I like it here!" Yelena's voice rang out. There was a chorus of yips from the other room, and she lowered her voice to a whisper. "I'm happier than I've been since before I met you, Ciprian."

It was true. The last week had been amazing. Every day, the puppies learned something new. Their mother had taken to escaping over a small partition to rest, and only a few of the puppies had figured out how to climb over it and follow her. To Yelena's pride, Bellatrix was one of them.

The little puppy was still smaller than the rest, but she was absolutely determined that nothing would slow her down. She would nap in Yelena's arms for a few minutes after her exertions, and then Yelena would set her down so she could go back to playing, climbing, play-fighting.

She didn't follow her brothers and sisters anymore. She explored on her own, utterly fearless.

"Don't be ridiculous." She could practically see Ciprian rolling his eyes. "What are you going to do, work in a

NATALIE GREY & MICHAEL ANDERLE

kennel for the rest of your life? Wear flannel? Date someone who works in a factory?" he ridiculed her.

"I didn't say I was going to—" Yelena started.

"You don't have a plan." He lectured her like she was a small child. "You're just throwing a tantrum, Yelena. You want me to believe that you would actually stay somewhere there's no hope for a career? That you'd live in a little cabin? Is there *anything* in that town?"

Yelena pressed her lips together angrily. Ciprian couldn't imagine a life here, that much was clear. At one point, she had felt the same way he did. There was no place for a career here, no way for her to earn as much money as she could in the city.

But she didn't miss any of it: not the fancy restaurants, not the suits, nor the elegant apartment. She liked slipping into jeans and a warm shirt at the start of the day, pulling her hair back in a ponytail rather than taking an hour to blow dry it.

She liked not having to wear makeup. And now that she wasn't watching women in thousand-dollar dresses throw themselves at Ciprian, she was beginning to realize he wasn't much of a catch, either.

She was wondering what the hell had made that fish not smell so bad earlier.

Ciprian hadn't realized what she was thinking. "You don't have to say anything." He sounded so smug that she wanted to punch him. "Just don't hurt yourself because we had a little spat. You don't want me to move on and find someone else while you're gone, do you?"

A little spat? Her eyes drew together, her teeth clinched.

"That is not what happened." She was shaking in her anger. "What *happened* is that we broke up, asshole."

"What?" He laughed. He actually laughed at her.

"I said, because apparently we have a bad connection, is we broke up." She paused a moment to think about it, then added, "No, really, *I* broke up with *you*. You cheated on me Ciprian—again if you don't remember—and I left."

Damn, this felt good!

She smiled out at the view of the valley, leaning back in the chair. "So don't call me anymore. I'm staying here. And you know what? Don't find anyone else. It's not about me wanting you—it's for their good. No one should have to put up with your shit. Goodbye."

She hung up. She was shaking, breath coming fast. Had she actually just done that? Had she broken up with him?

Every woman she knew was crazy about Ciprian, and she'd been the one who got him. She'd be crazy to give that up. She visualized what she always did when she made him angry and he left the apartment in a huff. Him, going out to a club and a dozen women, prettier than she was, throwing themselves at him.

But somehow, instead of making her sick with fear, the thought didn't hurt at all right now. For the first time in months, she felt happy. The idea of never talking to him again made her feel like she could fly.

"Hey." Dmitri's voice made her jump. He was at the door to the main room. "You all right? I heard shouting."

She started nodding her head, "I'm all right." Yelena could not stop smiling. "I'm better than all right."

"Good." He smiled as well. "I have an idea. How about you take Bellatrix home tonight?"

Yelena's eyes opened, "What? Really?"

Dmitri shrugged, "Yeah. She's old enough—eight weeks today, actually. I think it would be good for her to explore a new place. You know I'll never be able to sell her as a guard dog. And ... it'd take a heart of stone to split you two up." He grinned wickedly, "Just be careful she doesn't go on your rugs, ok?"

Yelena got up from the chair, feeling too damn good to be sitting still, "I will Dmitri, my Mama would flip out."

She might flip out anyway, but Yelena would be able to say ... well, she'd be able to say that she'd be getting her own place soon.

Because she was staying. She really could not stop smiling.

"All right, then." Dmitri held open the door to let her pass, "Come get a crate and some blankets."

Hundreds of miles away, a door slammed and Ciprian made his way down the stone stairs of his apartment building, fuming.

He was wrapping a Burberry scarf around his neck, pulling on leather gloves that fit him perfectly. Normally, putting on the clothes that showed his wealth made him happy. He knew how good he looked. Men got out of his way on the sidewalk and women looked at him appreciatively—sometimes they did more than just look.

Right now, nothing even dented the fury in his chest. She was leaving him. She was leaving *him*? No one left him, ever!

He paused on the landing two floors down and looked speculatively at their neighbor's door. *She* would ask him inside. She would pour him a brandy and go slip into something lacey, and when Yelena finally came home, she'd find that Ciprian had moved on.

She'd *beg* to get him back.

The thought should have made him smile, but it only infuriated him. He left without knocking on the neighbor's door, walking out into the sun.

He found himself walking without purpose, fairly snarling at people to get out of his way. Dammit, he was going to be one of the city's highest powered attorneys within a year. Certainly worth millions within a few years.

Yelena was throwing a fit, but she shouldn't even dare to think for a second, she shouldn't even dare to pretend that she thought she could do better without him in her life. When she came home she would realize...

He stopped, staring around himself for a moment, taking in the area, the cars, the people and forced himself to stop ignoring the truth.

The truth that was making him so angry, and the realization of the truth didn't make him any happier.

She really wasn't coming back.

When she'd hung up on him this last time, he could feel she'd meant it. She wasn't coming back. She didn't even miss him. She'd just walked out without so much as a by-your-leave and she was happy without him.

He ground his teeth. Then he set off, with a purpose this time.

To the train station.

Like hell she was going to leave him.

CHAPTER THREE

Bellatrix toddled across the unfamiliar rug, a jumble of not-quite-coordinated puppy legs, until she came to an obstacle. She mewled piteously and looked up at Yelena.

"You can do it." Yelena sat cross-legged nearby and smiled down at her. When Bellatrix tried to come snuggle against her, it took resolve not to hug the puppy close. "No, you have to be brave. Come on. Over the books." She trailed her fingers up one side of the stack of books and down the other. "Come on, you can do it. Then you get a bit of bread," she whispered to the little puppy, looking at the door to the room, "if you promise not to tell Mama."

Emboldened by the promise of treats, Bellatrix propped her front legs up on the books and tried to climb up the side.

"No." Yelena started laughing at the spectacle. "You have to jump, Bellatrix. Come on. You can do it!"

A knock sounded at the door and she looked down at the puppy, smiling. "Come on." The knock came again and she remembered that she was the only one in the house right now.

Alec was off skiing, her father had gone to help someone trim a tree that was threatening to fall on a nearby roof, and her mother had gone to the market. "Coming!" She yelled out as she stood up and brushed off her pants.

She pointed at the little black ball of fur, "You need to keep practicing."

She made her way through the house, still smiling as Bellatrix yipped piteously after her. Yelena paused briefly when the image came to her.

The scene the images depicted had been getting clearer as Bellatrix got older. Somehow the little black fuzz-ball was communicating with her. This latest image almost made her laugh. Bellatrix was the size of a mouse and the books in front of her took on the proportions of a mountain range.

She turned to call back down the hallway, "What happened to my fierce Trix? You can do this!" By now, she was almost used to the flashes of what felt like Bellatrix talking to her.

She hadn't mentioned it to anyone else. It should be impossible. She probably just had a sense of the puppy's emotions, she decided.

That would be normal enough, right?

Then she opened the door, and forgot all about the puppy.

Her mouth dropped open, "*Ciprian?*"

He stood outside the door, tight-lipped, in his elegant wool coat and plaid scarf. He still had his work shoes on, black leather, and his suit. He had taken the overnight train, it seemed, and he did *not* look pleased.

The sight of him hit her in the gut, and a wave of anger followed right after it. She wanted to slam the door in his face and lock it.

How dare he come here? Her voice dropped, "What are you doing here?"

"Let me in." He didn't wait for an answer. He shouldered her aside and she fell back, rubbing at her arm where he'd pushed her out of the way.

"What are you doing here?" She didn't like the look in his eyes. "You should go."

"I will." He rounded on her, his hand holding paper. "With you. I got us tickets back to the city." He held them up as if they were a legal document.

She slowly backed up and stopped when she ran into the door. "I'm not going back."

He walked next to her and slammed one hand against the wall. "You are! Stop this nonsense at once, Yelena. You are coming home!" His breathing was heavy, his frustration came broiling to the surface.

"I'm not." She wanted to roll her eyes at his childish banging around. What, did he really think he was going to intimidate her? "And that place isn't home." She turned around and pulled the door open. "This is, now." She pointed outside, "You should go."

He spun her around, his touch sudden and unexpected, and pulled her close for a kiss.

Normally, his kisses melted her. She would forget why she had been mad—it was another woman, it was *always* another woman—and she would forgive him everything.

He would smile and say it was so much better when she was happy, wasn't it? And the fight would be over.

Now she felt a physical revulsion. Her hands were at his chest, pushing him away. She shoved, *hard*, his surprise evident as he watched her wipe her mouth with the back of her hand.

She wanted to spit out the taste of him.

Her eyes furious, she said low and slow, her anger barely held in, "I... said... go!"

He stared at her in shock. "What did you just say?"

"*Go*." She flung her arm out to point at the still open door. "Is that too complicated for you? I told you ... we broke up! Why is that so difficult to understand? Aren't you a full blown lawyer that can figure out the vagaries of documents and rules hundreds of years old? What is so difficult about *we are finished* that you can't understand it?"

"Yelena." His voice was soft now, but something about it scared her. If she were a dog, her hackles would have gone up.

She hadn't ever heard him use that tone before, but she knew it instinctively. He stepped toward her, and it took everything she had to stand her ground. "We're going home."

She said nothing. This was a side of him she'd never seen before. She wasn't entirely sure what to do with it.

"Yelena...." He was losing patience.

And then she was furious. That motherfucker!

"I'm not going." She stood up straight. "I'm. Not. Going. You leave. We're done. Go downstairs from your apartment and beat on 2G or go to a club and have them all rub up against you all night, I really don't give a shit anymore."

He hit her.

He moved so fast she never saw it coming, his boxing training giving weight to that single hit. His hand cracked across her face and she slumped against the wall as she went down. On her hands and knees, fingers tracing over her cheek in shock.

Had that asshole actually hit her?

"Get up." His voice was ugly, his hands clenching and unclenching. "We're going."

She didn't think, she just reacted. Fury hot in her veins.

Like hell he was going to get away with this. She launched herself at his knees and took him down, sprawling in the corridor that was now full of cold winter air. She scrambled up and ran for the door, hearing him yell behind her.

He was raging.

She ran out into the sunshine with him behind her and he grabbed at her, missed—and finally caught her hair. He dragged her back and she swung at him, a punch that went wild and hit his shoulder.

She pulled her arm back and hit him again, in the jaw this time.

He was angry? Well, so was she. She was fucking *furious*. If he wanted a fight, that was what he would get.

But as strong as she was, as angry as she was, he was better. He knew how to fight and she didn't. His punch, his first actual punch, knocked her down onto the gravel. There was a ringing in her head as he came to stand over her.

"Get. Up." He spat the words.

The books were tall, but she was *going* to get over them. Bellatrix scrabbled for purchase on the covers and tried to push herself off the ground with her back feet. Her little bottle brush tail was wagging in anticipation. When Yelena came back, Bellatrix would be on top of the books and Yelena would be so happy.

Bellatrix was absolutely going to make Yelena happy.

She yipped to herself as she tried jumping, and shook herself off when she bounced off the edge of the books and fell on the floor. She rolled on her back for a moment, savoring the feel of the carpet under her back, and then scrambled up.

She was going to do it this time. She wasn't quite sure why Yelena wanted her to stand on the books, but she was going to do it.

Then she heard the scream—and felt the pain. Bellatrix froze, looking over her shoulder. Yelena was hurt.

Yelena was *hurt.* Bellatrix set off, tiny feet marching determinedly over the carpet. There was new, cold air blowing down the corridor and her fur puffed up, but she could hear Yelena—angry, scared.

No one got to hurt Yelena. A growl burst from Bellatrix's throat. She bared her teeth as she scrambled over the floor, little feet scrapping down as she tore down the hallway.

There! Two figures, Yelena and a man. The man swung his arm and Yelena went down. Then she lunged at him and tipped him over, got up and ran.

Bellatrix ran, too. She had to get to her mistress. She had to protect her.

The man never saw Bellatrix coming after him. He picked himself up and ran, too. Bellatrix left the house and jumped off the step to the lawn.

The man and Yelena grappled in the sunlight as Bellatrix tried to make her tiny legs move faster, faster. There was pain again—Yelena was on the ground. The man reached down and grabbed her shoulder—

And howled as Bellatrix's tiny teeth sank into the back of his ankle. He twisted, trying to see what caused the pain, and kicked his foot. Bellatrix hung on grimly, but when his heel hit her in the stomach, she flew away from him and landed on the frozen ground with a yip.

"YOU LEAVE HER ALONE!" The yell burst out of Yelena, and in that moment, nothing mattered but Bellatrix.

Not her jaw, not the ache in her shoulder where she'd slammed into the ground, not how angry Ciprian was. This bastard just hurt Bellatrix, and Yelena was going to kill him.

She was on her feet in a second. As Ciprian made for the prone figure of the puppy, Yelena grabbed his shoulder and yanked it back hard.

This time, her punch was dead on with all of the fury and fear in her heart. Her fist caught him in the nose and he doubled over, blood spurting between his cupped hands.

He gave a sound halfway between a moan and a wail as the blood flowed, getting both hands bloody.

She laughed at his display. He was pitiful.

She'd been scared of this man? God, she should be giving herself twice as much shit for her stupid decisions.

The second she'd really hurt him, he was crumpling like a paper doll. She couldn't believe she'd ever been glad to be with him, an asshole that hurt her dog!

That righteously pissed her off all over again and before she even considered her actions, her arm was already poised...

She hit him again, and once more for fucking good measure, "Asshole!" she spat out, "Kick a dog, will you? Kick *my* dog will you? I'll kick your ass back to your apartment if you ever do that again."

His blood was on the snow and she didn't care. He wanted to hurt someone he thought couldn't fight back?

His ass would be lucky to get out of this alive.

She thought about how he had come into her home and slapped her. She hit him once more and he fell to the ground. She wound up, about to kick him in the side when she thought of whether Bellatrix needed her.

Hurrying, she scooped the puppy up off the ground cuddling her close to her face. "Are you okay? Tell me you're okay." Bellatrix licked her nose and struggled to her feet in Yelena's hands. She was wagging her tail proudly.

"You have ... blood on your teeth," Yelena told her.

Bellatrix only wagged harder, baring her teeth proudly. She stood up on her hind legs, unsteadily, to lick Yelena's face.

"Ew! Blood breath!"

Bellatrix chuffed. It sounded like she was laughing.

"*Yelena!*" There was the pounding of feet and Alec

skidded to a stop by the house, Dmitri at his heels. "What happened?"

Yelena looked over to where Ciprian was still moaning, his leather-gloved hands over his face. "He tried to get me to come back."

"Oh, my God." Alec reached out to her face, his hands shaking. "Did he…."

"Yeah. But we got him." Yelena held Bellatrix close. "Didn't we, Trix?"

The puppy yipped.

"I'd say you did." Dmitri looked Ciprian up and down, clearly unimpressed by everything about him.

He grabbed Ciprian's arm. "Come on, now. The police are going to want a word with you. And in the event that they don't, you can talk to me and Alec." He guffawed. "Or you can have another conversation with Yelena, see how you like *that*."

He made to drag Ciprian away.

"Wait." Ciprian's voice was muffled. He stood up. Blood was streaming over his mouth and chin. He glared at Yelena. "You're ruining your life," he spat. "You're going to wind up with a lumberjack, a miner. You can't do better than me."

The last shreds of fear bled away and Yelena shrugged. She cuddled Bellatrix close, and she smiled. "I think I'm gonna be okay. In fact, I'm gonna be just fine." She turned away without even waiting for a response, and tickled Bellatrix's stomach. "Come on, Trix. We're going to teach you how to jump, and *I'm* going to learn how to box."

CHAPTER 4

<u>**2 Years Later ...**</u>

"I'm fucking cold," Cezar complained.

Emilian lifted one lip in a silent snarl and savored the scent of fear as Cezar's voice trailed away. It was always something with Cezar. If he wasn't cold, he was hungry. If he wasn't hungry, the job was too dirty, or too undignified, or whatever excuse he came up with.

Cezar was always afraid, that was the truth. He never admitted it, he just stank of fear.

All the time.

And he was cruel. Always taking things too far. He never stopped a fight when his opponent was down (he never started a fight, either, just snuck in once someone else was fighting). He liked to kick people, keep hurting them once they were out cold. And the humans who trafficked girls through Europe wouldn't keep working with Emilian's crew if the cargo kept showing up damaged.

Emilian should get rid of Cezar, he knew that.

He'd have to do it permanently, though. Cezar knew

too much of Emilian's operations, and he was just slippery enough to make a deal with the police if Emilian kicked him out and left him alive. Hell, he might even convince one or two of them that Werewolves and vampires were real.

So Emilian wouldn't leave him alive.

Simple.

And with the money from this job, they'd have enough to start making some real strides toward power.

There was a power vacuum in the underworld, left by goody-goodies and cowards who'd decided to clear everything out. They didn't understand the world, but they were about to.

Emilian had known some of the people killed by Stephen. He didn't regret that those people were gone—he wouldn't be anywhere near so close to taking their place at the head of the European underworld if they were alive—but he was looking forward to making a big show of avenging their deaths.

This new matriarch was weak.

At least Michael had had a code and implemented it in a way Emilian understood, strength rules.

It didn't matter. If she was weak, that was just better for him.

It was time for the Wechselbalg to take their rightful place in the world. Emilian's wolf-eyes narrowed in satisfaction. He was getting paid to help humans thin their own numbers. He might not enjoy other people's pain as much as Cezar did, but he liked it enough to take joy in this.

The radio crackled, and a voice spoke softly: "He just started down the hill."

Emilian smiled.

His claws came out.

Theodor Dimitru leapt off the ski lift and landed with a puff of pure white snow under his skis. He surveyed the valley below, savoring the silence. With the Christmas holidays over, he was one of the only people at the resort, and he liked that.

He had even asked his wife not to come with him on this trip. He knew that hurt her, especially as he had been working such long hours while his firm tried to acquire Ionescu Corporation, their main rival.

But, the truth was, he didn't want her to see his weakness. He was badly shaken by the threats made by a man who had once been a friend—and was now a business rival. Theo had been finding messages on his work line, his cell phone, his email.

The messages were graphic.

If Theodor didn't abandon his quest to buy Ionescu Corp, a business Virgil also wanted, Virgil would have him killed. Unpleasantly. "Ripped to shreds" was the term Virgil had used.

It brought to mind claws and teeth, a sort of primal fear —even though Theo knew it couldn't possibly be literal.

He walked awkwardly in his skis to the edge of the mountain and stared down at the pristine white slope. Then he tipped forward and began to pick up speed along the first, straight piece of the path. He told himself he did not believe the threats. That was even true. He could not believe that Virgil would take a hit out on him, not over a business disagreement.

Virgil had been at his wedding! Their grandparents lived in the same neighborhood and still met each week for tea.

The calls rattled him, nonetheless. He had come here to regain the stability and calm he was known for. To regain his resolve. When he was pitting himself against nature, he remembered what it meant to be powerful. On mountains, as in business, there was no room for mistakes. Theo always came back from these trips refreshed and sharp, no matter what was troubling him.

He told himself it would work this time, too.

It was a little ways down the hill, coming around a tight turn, that he first saw the man behind him. The hair on the back of Theo's neck stood up. He only just managed to stay on the course as he returned his eyes to the snow in front of him.

Someone behind him. Had Virgil sent an assassin, after all?

It wasn't possible, he told himself. But the man was coming closer. He was dressed all in old, worn black gear. Most of the people who came here were wealthy, but this man clearly was not.

He had a simple mastery of skiing, moving lightly down the course that tested all of Theo's skill.

Theo gave a despairing look through the trees. They were not far from the resort, the way the crow flies, but this black diamond course had been designed to be both difficult and long. It wound back and forth many times between where Theo was, and the bottom of the slope.

Fear began to hammer in his chest. He wanted to call for help, but he knew the wind would just take the sound. He really was alone on the course, just like he had wanted. He spared a thought for Mariana, his wife, who would be waiting at home for a call. He had been very short with her the last time they talked.

Dammit, he regretted that now.

He tried to focus on the tight turns of the path, but he was getting sloppy. Every time he looked behind him, the man was closer. Every time he looked back, he was a split second from catastrophe. He was still picking up speed. He could not afford to make a single mistake.

He had to be faster than he had ever been. More controlled than he had ever been.

And then he came around a bend, and there was the branch. It was laid out on the crisp snow in front of him, not at all touched by last night's snowfall. Theo swerved to try to avoid it.

Had it been left here as a prank? Or was it this man's colleagues, hoping to lure Theo into a trap so they could kill him on the mountain with no one the wiser?

He tried desperately to correct his course, but his speed was too much. One ankle twisted, he felt the agony as a bone snapped, and then he was tumbling end over end in the snow, branches whipping at his face, sliding downhill with the chill of snow shoved up beneath his coat.

He came to rest deep in the trees. He tried not to sob with pain or fear, but it was difficult to control himself.

He did not hear his pursuer come around the corner, but he did hear a startled shout as the man encountered the branch.

What?

Wasn't it part of his plan?

Theo tried to crane his head to see, and caught sight of a black-clad figure tumbling down the slope. And then….

He must have hit his head. Theo was sure he wasn't *really* seeing a massive wolf pad out of the shadows of the forest nearby, accompanied by humans. They picked up the other skier and his head lolled on his chest.

They slapped him, hard, but he didn't wake up. Was he dead? Theo could not tell. He watched as the humans argued amongst themselves and the wolf snapped at them, and then they set off with the unconscious man dragged between them.

Theo wanted to cry out for help, but he was scared. He was seeing things. Maybe none of them had really been there, but maybe they had—and what if they treated him as roughly as they were treating the other skier? He just had to wait until one of the ski patrols came back later.

They were safe. They were….

It was so cold, and his leg was in so much pain. Theo saw the world fading, and he lost consciousness long before one of the ski patrols came by sometime later. A prone figure in the dense undergrowth, he was invisible to them. The patrolman clicked his tongue at the kids playing pranks, pulled the branch out of the fresh snow, and continued on his way.

He liked getting away from everything. Alec tipped over the edge of the downslope and grinned as the wind began to ruffle his hair. It was perfect out here today, not least of all because there was only one other person on the slope. Alec didn't like coming to places like this when it was busy. People sneered at his well-worn winter clothes. Some of the women liked the thrill of sleeping with a guy they didn't know on vacation—particularly one they knew would never show up in the clubs and spas they frequented back home—but even that didn't make it worth it.

Right now, he wasn't thinking about any of that. He was only thinking about the turns, the way the snow crunched under his skis, the way the winter air felt in his lungs. He was a good accountant—very good—and he took pride in his work. But being out on the slopes was better. This made him feel alive.

He saw the other skier look back at him a few times. Probably worried that someone in shabby winter gear wouldn't know how to pass him safely. Alec shook his head and rolled his eyes. He'd make sure the other guy didn't get so much as a scratch on that expensive parka of his.

Then he came around the corner, and the man was gone. Had he fallen? Alec turned his head sharply and caught sight of a shape in the snow—

He didn't see the branch until it was too late. His skis caught and he went end over end.

He kicked his feet free of his skis, but that wasn't enough: between one somersault and the next, his head struck something hard and the world went black.

He never saw the nightmare that came out of the woods with the men to drag his unconscious body away.

"I'm telling you, I heard it." Cezar struggled along behind Emilian, one of the skier's limp arms wrapped around his shoulders. "Another scream, *before* this one."

Emilian looked back and fixed the man with a yellow stare for a moment. Then he kept walking, disdainfully. He had been daydreaming about ripping Cezar's head from his shoulders, or sinking his teeth into the man's neck.

When he was human, he dreamed about just shooting him, no fuss, but in wolf form, his dreams were bloodier.

"No one else came by," Marcel said. He was breathing hard. The skier was tall and well-built, a heavy burden to drag down the mountain.

Emilian smiled his wolf smile, a curl of the lips, baring his teeth. It was good to be in charge. To make the plans. To watch others carry them out. It was also good to be out in the snow in his true form, his strongest form.

The other Wechselbalg in the underworld had called him weak. They called him a coward. But who was still alive now? They'd drawn attention to themselves and allowed themselves to be killed by a vampire who—if the stories were true—must have one foot in the grave by now. *They* were weak, not Emilian.

"I swear I heard it." Cezar was talking again.

Emilian growled, low in his chest.

Cezar either didn't hear him, or he was too stupid to know to stop. "Shouldn't we go back and check? If anyone saw Emilian like this, it's gonna be all over the news. There are so many superstitious people around here, they're going to believe it. It was a mistake changing, you aren't even doing anything in that form—"

Emilian batted the skier's body out of the way as he

leapt. Long claws raked through the ski gear like it was butter, and he felt them catch skin.

No matter. Their client had told them to make this man suffer before he died.

But he wasn't going to waste time on him yet. Emilian pinned Cezar instead, big paws on the man's shoulders. He lowered his snout to Cezar's face and savored the look of abject terror. He'd hated having the stink of fear around him all the time.

Now he enjoyed it. Cezar *should* be scared. He was about to die.

The bastard started babbling, "Come on, boss, you know it's risky, I'm just trying to tell you the truth. No one else will. Marcel just kisses your ass. But I'll always tell the truth. You shouldn't have—"

The pity was that he had to die quickly. No one could hear screams echoing down the mountain. Cezar's life ended in one snap of Emilian's jaws. His throat was gone, and he bled out under the trees within a few seconds. Emilian stepped off his body and grabbed one of the arms in his jaws. He pulled Cezar's body along without comment as Marcel struggled to keep up, now carrying the skier alone.

Marcel didn't complain, though. Not after that display.

Good.

CHAPTER FOUR

Yelena was training hard enough that her top was soaked in sweat. Her fists hit the bag with dull *whumps* and she savored the feel of exhaustion in her muscles.

Two years ago, she'd learned that her natural strength made her a good fighter, but that a trained boxer could still hurt her more than she wanted to get hurt.

The lesson had come from her ex-boyfriend, Ciprian. A man with startling good looks and charisma, but also a petulant nature that had only revealed itself when she walked away from him.

In the end, she hadn't been as easy to intimidate as he thought. Still, she'd learned something important about the world. She'd learned not to give an inch to people like him. She'd learned that when it counted, you had to be the best in the ring.

Now, she was getting pretty close. She'd started boxing lessons the same week she sent Ciprian packing, and even though the other boxers at the gym had laughed at her when she showed up, she'd earned some grudging respect from them over the past twenty-four months.

She was quick, light on her feet, and she had the stamina to keep going long after most boxers began to get sloppy. Not to mention, she packed *way* more strength into her slender body than anyone ever expected.

She followed her punch with a kick, and was just turning to slam her elbow into the bag when pain hit her. It was distant, but it was as real as if she were there with Alec.

Breathing in cold air, terrified, as the world spun around her and everything went black. And then, even as he slid into unconsciousness, she felt hands pull him up, hit him.

"Yelena?" Boris, the gym boss, was at her side in a second. "What's wrong?"

Horia, one of the other boxers, sneered at her, "You pregnant or something?"

He was one of the guys who still hated her after all this time. He didn't like that she showed him up in the ring sometimes, even though he won frequently. He didn't like how the guys had started to like her and laugh at her jokes.

He also didn't like Bellatrix, and he definitely didn't like that Yelena brought the dog with her to the gym.

She never went *anywhere* without Bellatrix.

The dog was at her side in a moment, a cold wet nose nudging at her worriedly. Bellatrix never worried needlessly, and for a moment, Yelena had the crazy thought that maybe Bellatrix had felt Alec's pain, too.

She shoved that to the back of her brain, where she shoved the thoughts that she could talk to Bellatrix sometimes. During the first year, the images she came to believe were coming from Bellatrix had become clearer, sharper, more detailed. But the last couple of months she was having conversations in her head … actual words. She knew no one would believe her if she said that—hell, even *she* didn't really believe it. Not really. Or so she told herself.

She let Boris help her up and gave him a tight smile. "I think I sprained my wrist." She wasn't even aware of picking the words. She had to get to Alec—*now*. She began to make for the edge of the mat.

"You'll never be a boxer if you quit when you sprain something," Horia muttered.

Yelena pulled a sweatshirt on over her tank top, giving him a glare. "You know what? After two years, if you still don't like me just because I haven't got a dick, you can go fuck yourself."

"Hey," Boris said warningly. He held palms up to both of them. "Not tonight, okay? I have a date, and if I get in the middle of you two, no one's going to want to have a date with me. I'll lose what little good looks I have left."

Yelena gave an unwilling chuckle as she laced on her outside shoes, but only a tiny piece of her was still in the room. She could feel the memory of Alec's pain and it scared her. She gave a smile and clapped Boris on the shoulder, and left without another word, Bellatrix padding at her side.

Out on the street, Bellatrix stayed close to her, either looking for the same comfort Yelena needed right now, or offering it. She looked up once, worry in her unusually intelligent eyes.

Is he all right?

"I don't know." Yelena answered the question she

shouldn't have heard. She shouldn't have answered, but the words were always so clear in her head that it seemed rude not to say something. "I don't know. We have to find him, Trix. I'll call Mama, see where he was going to go skiing this week."

"I thought we fixed this problem." Bethany Anne crossed her arms over her chest and glared out the window into space. "I thought once Stephen took out their leaders, they would understand that things were different now."

John raised an eyebrow at her, "Really?"

"No." She sat down and crossed her legs, kicking out a red-soled Louboutin. "But I live in eternal hope that someday that pile of shit-eating rat-fuckers down there will get their act together and I won't be required to go kill them all."

Just think how bored you would be if that happened.

I think I'd like to be bored, TOM.

Huh, you might be getting old.

Mention a lady's age like that and you'll find yourself strapped to the outside of this ship, TOM.

"Eventually, you have to let some of them live." Gabrielle leaned back in her chair, smiling. She wore a black tank top under a leather jacket, artfully faded jeans, and what appeared to be well-worn boots.

Bethany Anne shook her head. Every once in awhile, Gabrielle liked to play the bohemian.

Maybe it was her years in Paris, but it was weird to see her in faded, ripped clothing, compared to the crisp looks of all the other vampires Bethany Anne had ever met. Now, though, there were more pressing matters. "Ok, explain to me why the fuck should I leave any of them alive?"

"They're like cockroaches." Gabrielle shrugged. "You can never stamp them all out. There's always an underworld. Eventually you need to go after bigger fish."

"That would be a good suggestion … if they weren't forcing my hand." Bethany Anne tapped her fingers on the chair arm. Earth hung below the ship in vibrant blues and greens, streaked with white cloud formations. She narrowed her eyes at Europe. "And if I weren't bored out of my damned mind."

John mouthed silently to Gabrielle, *"That's the real reason."* She nodded back, trying not to smile.

Stephen? She reached out with her mind.

There was a small pause. Then: *Yes?*

"Oh, dear," Bethany Anne said wickedly. Speaking out loud for those near her as well as mentally to him, *"did I interrupt something?"*

John snorted.

How may I help you, my queen?

"So formal. And yet not answering the question, I notice." Bethany Anne snickered. *"I'll let you get back to your girlfriend in a second. I just wanted to let you know there's some trouble in Romania that I'll be handling personally."*

Instantly she felt Stephen's worry, *Is there a reason you do not wish me to handle it, my queen? Have you been displeased with—*

"No. Absolutely not." Bethany Anne spoke hurriedly. Stephen was one of the most loyal, most competent members of TQB Enterprises. She regretted that her words might have worried him. *"Stephen, you know I have no concerns about your abilities. I am going a bit stir-crazy on this ship, and I know you're dealing with other matters, like the reports of laboratories in Bulgaria."* Her lips curved wickedly, a gleam of humor in her eyes. *"And your girlfriend, of course."*

Stephen had been tracking down several groups of enemies, accompanied by Jennifer, a fact that caused no end of jokes on the *Meredith Reynolds*.

Stephen, who had once enjoyed Tinder and could hardly walk into a bar without picking up a stack of phone numbers, had proven to have decidedly old-fashioned and gentlemanly sensibilities when it came to an actual girlfriend, a fact Bethany Anne found endearing ... but still teased him about.

Like, every damned time she had a chance.

She could practically hear the vampire grinding his teeth right now.

It's healthy to sow some wild oats in your old age, Gabrielle chimed in sweetly.

Stephen ignored his daughter. *Will there be anything else, my queen?*

"I'll let you know if there is. Enjoy your romantic getaway." Bethany Anne cut the connection as John snorted with laughter. "All right. So, it's settled. I'll go down tomorrow."

John's smile was replaced with a weary look. "With...?"

"With what?"

"With who?"

"Whom." Pete grinned across the room at him.

John gave him a look, but then returned his gaze to

Bethany Anne. "Do any of us get to go with you?"

"I can handle this on my own."

"I'd be more careful, actually." Gabrielle stretched like a cat and settled back into her chair, raising her eyebrows at the other vampire. "You want to be cautious around the weak ones."

Bethany Anne frowned. "How do you know these ones are weak?"

"Even in the underworld, the pack structure is the same." Gabrielle shrugged. "Stephen took out the alphas. And most of the betas, along with some of the others. So ... who's left? The ones who weren't strong enough to be in charge."

She raised her eyebrows. "And they're the ones who are angry that they are not as strong as the others. They are resentful that the others look down on them. But they can't take any of the others on in a fair fight, so they always watch their opponent, and hit where they are weak."

"So do I." Bethany Anne grinned. She sighed when she saw the same expression on everyone's faces. "Okay, fine,. I'll take some people with me. John, you see who wants to go with me. Cap it at ... six. I'm going to go pack. ADAM tells me Romania is cold as a yeti's balls this time of year."

"ADAM actually said yeti's balls?"

"No," Bethany Anne answered, "That part I modified from the ice age number he quoted me."

"Oh, you mean something less than forty degrees, then?" Peter asked.

Bethany Anne called out over her shoulder as she exited the room, "That's a first class ass-kicking for you, next time we spar fur-boy!"

John smiled at Peter's stricken expression. There was one thing that they all realized after a while with their Queen.

Bethany Anne never forgot who deserved an ass kicking when it came time to spar.

"Mama…." Yelena tipped her head back with a groan of frustration. "Let it be."

"No." Her mother flipped the suitcase closed on Yelena's hand. Her eyes were fierce. "You shouldn't go."

Yelena did not even consider that, "Alec is in trouble."

"So call the authorities! I got you the phone number." Her mother held out a scrap of paper.

"I'm going, myself." Yelena took the piece of paper. "*And* I'll call the authorities. But something is very wrong, and I am not going to just sit here." She looked at Bellatrix. "Even Trix knows something is wrong." She meant it as a joke, but her mother swallowed hard and her face went grave. "Mama … Mama, I was joking."

"You can't go." Her mother's voice was even fiercer now. "Not out there. You stay here, where it's civilized."

"What does that even mean?" Yelena flipped the suitcase back open and shoved a stack of shirts into it. She wasn't paying much attention to what she was packing. Hopefully, she'd have something usable when she reached Vatra Dornei, the ski resort. "When I was in the city, you kept telling me to come back here because the city wasn't good for me." She grabbed a pair of shoes.

"The city *wasn't* good for you. I thought if you came back, you would find a nice man."

"Oh, for the love of—" Yelena pointed a shoe at her mother. "I am not having *that* argument, too. I am perfectly happy right now."

She wasn't, of course, but she was definitely not going to tell her mother that.

Yelena's mother kept telling her to meet 'a nice boy' and settle down. And, while Yelena had no intentions at all of settling down, sometimes she did feel a strange yearning for something ... more. A boyfriend? Maybe. The idea had some appeal. But it was more than that, and she could never put a finger on it. She had her boxing, and a job at the kennel, and Bellatrix. She didn't want to admit that she wasn't happy.

Anyway, right now, it didn't matter. What mattered was her brother.

"Yelena, I am begging you," her mother pleaded.

"What do you *want?*" Yelena rounded on her mother. Her voice yelling in frustration. "This is your *son* out there! Why aren't you begging me to go help him? He's in danger!"

"I don't want to lose you, too!" Her mother yelled back. "It is dangerous, it's more dangerous than you know! There are ... *things* out there that you shouldn't know about! That we moved here long ago so you'd never know about them! To keep ourselves safe!"

Yelena stopped. She wanted to brush off her mother's words and yell at her about Alec being in danger, but the hair on her arms was standing up. Her mother was genuinely terrified. She had always scoffed at superstition now looked like she was really afraid. "Mama … what kind of things?" Yelena asked, her anger chilled.

Her mother looked away. She clearly wanted to lie, she regretted having said anything. Oddly, her eyes came to rest on Bellatrix, and that seemed to help her decide.

"Vatra Dornei is near where our family came from, long ago. I tried to keep Alec from going there, but you know your brother. Tell him not to do something…."

Yelena gave a little laugh, but it was forced. Her mother was trying to make a joke, but fear was coming off of her in waves.

"There were rumors about our family. My family, not your father's." Her mother was twisting her hands. "They said…."

"Mama."

"They said we were changers." Her mother threw the words out, as if even speaking them was an act of courage.

"Changers?"

"Skin changers. Wolves." Her mother's lips shaped a word silently, and then she said it aloud … "Wechselbalg. That's what the Germans call them."

Yelena stared at her mother. The woman was clearly going crazy. "Mama. That's a story for babies."

"It's true!" Her mother looked up. Her eyes were wide. "We had to leave. Something about a pack, and being driven out, and … it isn't safe there. There are people who aren't natural. They aren't human. Bad enough your brother goes, but *you*?" She pointed to Bellatrix. "You have some of it in you."

"*What?*" Yelena shook her head wearily, "You're talking crazy, Mama."

Mama pointed at the big black German Shepherd. "You can hear her talk! I hear you talk to her, answering questions. All the dogs listen to you. They all accept you as their alpha, even the ones who don't like Dmitri. He tells me about it. He doesn't know what it means, but even he can *see* it."

"Mama, I've always been good with dogs, but that doesn't mean—"

Her mother cut her off. Tears were shimmering in her eyes. "If you go," she said, shaking, "I am afraid you will never come back. There are things out there that are dangerous to you because of what you are. I have always tried to keep you from that place." Her shoulders slumped, "Now, you know why."

Yelena could see that she believed. Her mother, who always laughed at folk tales, really believed this one. But it was crazy. The world was connected now and science had shown that none of those sorts of things were real.

Hadn't it?

These myths, they were stories for a time when people didn't know how wind whistled in the trees, and called it werewolves.

She shook her head.

"I have to go find Alec," she said flatly. "He's my brother. I am not going to let him be hurt. I love you, Mama." She kissed her mother on the top of her head, *"I'm going to be fine."*

She picked up the suitcase and left, Bellatrix padding along with her, without a backward glance. There was no time to talk anymore.

Alec was in danger.

CHAPTER FIVE

His ankle throbbed. It was an unceasing pain that he never seemed to get used to. The tiniest shift would make Theo cry out, and he soon learned that there was no way to keep from moving entirely.

At one point, passing in and out of consciousness, he remembered crying. He wasn't proud of it, but this was a bad way to end. Alone, dying slowly, his wife never knowing what had happened to him. He never able to take back the harsh words he'd spoken.

Some part of him wanted the pain to stop, whatever that meant. He knew what it meant, and he told himself he was past caring whether or not he died. He kept eating snow, anyway, and dragging himself slowly over the ground when he had enough strength and will to force himself to movement. He'd cracked some ribs, as well as shattering the ankle. He'd managed to get all of ten feet the first night, and not much further since then.

He told himself it was not far to the resort, but he could not make up his mind whether to go through the woods, the shorter path, or out onto the ski trail, potentially a hazard to other skiers—and visible to whoever had sent the wolf.

He was sure he had seen the wolf.

He was also sure, as consciousness came and went, that Virgil had hired hit men. *Ripped to shreds*, the man had said. And there had been a massive wolf with claws that could do just that.

And they had the wrong man.

That, more than anything, spurred Theo into motion again. He had to find someone and tell them what had happened on the slope. They would think he was crazy, but that was a problem to deal with when it happened. He dragged himself over the ground, gritting his teeth in pain.

It was the faintest noise that caught his attention. In fact, he could not even say what the noise *was*, just that the breeze in the trees seemed different somehow.

He found himself terrified that the wolf had somehow learned to fly, but he knew that was ridiculous. Cursing himself, he craned his neck painfully to look up.

No flying wolves. No, the truth was stranger than that. Black shapes stood out against the night sky, descending toward the resort. As they passed by overhead, Theo thought they almost looked like pods of metal. They weren't falling, though, and there didn't seem to be any sort of propulsion he could see.

The tears surprised him this time. He was actually going crazy. He was going crazy, and he was going to die here. Theo rested his face on his arms, despairing, aware of the pathetically short distance he'd managed to travel, and wept.

"Everyone ready?" Bethany Anne looked around the interior of the Pod. Now dressed in a high necked black shirt beneath a light jacket, having reluctantly traded her new Louboutins for what Ecaterina assured her were stylish winter boots, she was reasonably enough dressed that no one would think oddly of her.

They didn't need to know that she was not troubled by weather anymore.

"Ready." John nodded at her. At his side, Eric gave a thumbs up.

"Ready," came Pete's voice from the other pod.

"Ecaterina?" Bethany Anne tapped the communications unit.

"Ready." Ecaterina's voice was tight with anticipation. "I can't wait to get down there into the snow. I hope we have to go into the mountains to find them."

"What is it with you and cold?" Pete sounded dubious.

"It's not that cold."

"I'm not saying I mind it, I'm just saying I don't think to myself, 'hmmm, what could I do today? Why don't I tramp around in the cold icy snow?'"

Bethany Anne cut off the communications with a shake of her head. Nathan was worried about Ecaterina going on a trip, but even he had to admit that she was both capable of handling herself, and that she was surrounded by a good team—and it would take a heart of stone to ignore the way her face lit up when she found out Bethany Anne was taking an expedition into the mountains of Romania.

167

At least he was smart enough not to say it around his mate.

The Pods deposited them near one of the buildings, conveniently out of the line of sight of any of the ancient security cameras. Once everyone was down, the pods went back up in the air, out of sight.

Bethany Anne crunched through the snow toward the resort.

"Everyone listen for any strange stories," she said over her shoulder. "Remember, the most reliable people can be the ones no one believes. You know, the ones who actually *admit* they've been seeing giant wolves. When in doubt," she pointed behind her, "let Ecaterina do the talking."

Ecaterina grinned. "That's right!" she rubbed her hands in anticipation, "None of you speak like a local who tended bars. Let me find out what's going on!" She continued talking, adding a rough accent to her voice, "Like leading lambs to a Pricolici slaughter…"

Bethany Anne laughed and looked into the trees, where Ashur was slipping through the underbrush like a ghost. "And *you* stay hidden. The last thing we need is for some tourist to freak out and call the cops to shoot a wolf."

Emilian wrenched the curtains back and watched the bound man flinch from the light. He wanted to be in wolf form, but he did not trust anyone else to interrogate this man—or hurt him enough. The client had been very specific. This man was to know just who had hired Emilian and his crew, and was to realize that he had been outplayed. He had been foolish, going to the ski resort alone. He had been predictable. For that, and a multitude of other sins, he would pay with pain. And with his life.

Emilian did not ask what the other sins were. He did not particularly care.

"So." He smiled humorlessly. The man was watching him. Black hair, grey eyes. He smelled interesting, a single note of something Emilian could not quite catch.

Not important.

"You were foolish," he observed. "You were warned what would happen."

The man swallowed. He had been watching Emilian's face, and he looked around himself desperately. He was tied to a chair in the center of the room, stripped of his ski gear.

The marks of Emilian's claws had not been washed; they stood out vividly on his pale skin, though strangely, they already seemed to be healing. His face was bruised from where Cezar had hit him, but that mark, too, was fading. Cezar must have been losing his touch.

It was good that Emilian had killed him.

"Who are you?" the captive asked finally.

"Who I am is not important. I am here because you, unfortunately, made an enemy," Emilian explained.

He picked up a scalpel and savored the fear in the man's eyes. It was amusing, really. The scalpel could not do nearly as much damage as his own claws, but humans were weak and afraid of little things. He walked over to the man and paused, letting the man's fear rise, and then plunged the scalpel into his upper arm. He smiled as the man screamed as Emilian shrugged, "I told you, you were warned," he repeated.

The man's head lolled, and he pulled it up with an effort. He had gone grey with pain.

"Who sent you?" His voice was a rasp.

"Virgil. He told us where you would be skiing. He told *you* that you would be ripped to shreds if you didn't listen to him."

"I don't ... know a Virgil."

"Liar." Emilian hit him in the face, and snarled in disappointment when he saw that the man was unconscious. He pulled the scalpel out of his victim's arm and tossed it onto the tray.

Gott Verdammt, now he would have to wait until the man woke up again.

"Thank you." Yelena smiled at the bus driver as she made her way off. "Oh, don't worry," she said, as the woman began to stand up. "I'll get my bag, myself."

"You're a good kid." The woman smiled at her. "You deserve this vacation. Have fun skiing, dearie."

Yelena hoped her smile hadn't frozen too obviously, "I will." She was hardly going to confide in this woman that her brother had been lost and might be in serious danger. She dragged her suitcase out of the side compartment and went back to give the woman a thumbs up. "Thanks again!"

She hefted the bag as the bus drove away into the night, and then looked to the forest, where a shadow waited patiently among the trees.

I'll be back soon. She had no idea if Bellatrix could hear her. *Don't kill too many rabbits.*

She thought she heard the chuff of the dog's laughter, and smiled. She had not been able to bring Bellatrix on the bus, but she sensed that the dog had enjoyed making her way through the forest from the train station nearby.

At the doors of the hotel, she paused and took a deep breath. Alec might be here, she told herself. He might be inside. Maybe he had taken a fall and sprained his ankle, but they'd brought him right back and he'd be hanging out, flirting with the bartender. Maybe everything was fine, and she was just overreacting. She'd had plenty of time on the train to wonder if he was just going to laugh at her when she showed up.

Somehow, she knew that wasn't the case.

She heard laughter nearby and spotted a group walking through the trees. Tourists, probably, wandering through the forests of Romania at night and telling one another ghost stories about vampires. Yelena rolled her eyes and made her way through the glass doors and up to the elegant desk. A pretty blonde woman smiled at her.

"Hello, I'm Petra." She frowned, as if trying to remember something. "You look familiar."

That made things easier. "Ah, actually, my brother is staying here." Yelena tried not to look sick with fear as she asked the question, "Alec Nikolaev. Is he still here?"

When the woman's face fell, Yelena gripped the desk to keep herself upright. *Oh, no.*

"He, ah…." Petra was twisting her hands now. She looked toward the door that must go to the manager's office. "Let me get—"

"Just tell me." Yelena knew her voice was too high, too scared. "Did something happen to him?"

The woman hesitated, but she couldn't resist the plea in Yelena's eyes. "He went out early this morning," she explained. "Very early. It was just him and one other skier on the slopes. Neither of them … neither of them have been back all day. No one has seen them." She swallowed hard. "We sent out tons of patrols. We *have* tried to find them, I promise, but they're nowhere on the trail."

It was as if a yawning void had opened beneath Yelena's feet. She wanted to sob. Dimly, she heard herself speaking: "It's probably nothing. Maybe he's just at a pub nearby."

Petra nodded eagerly. "Maybe! We haven't asked in the village. We should do that."

"I'll … I'll handle it." Yelena heard the group behind her enter the hotel. They were still laughing and bantering. She thought fast, biting her lip. "Could I, ah … could I get a key to his room? He said he booked a double."

"It was just the one bed." Petra shook her head regretfully.

She had started the lie, and now she had to continue it. Maybe there was a clue in Alec's room, after all. "Well, then I'm going to get some sleep and he can sleep on the couch," Yelena announced. "Isn't that just like a brother, asking me out here and not remembering to book a room for me?"

Petra laughed at that. She pulled something up on the computer and selected a key. "Just like *my* brother, for sure.

Here you go. I'll tell him you're here if he comes back—and to let you sleep."

"Thanks." Yelena tried to smile. She took the key and hefted her bag over her shoulder….

The pain was sudden and blinding, like a knife stuck into her upper arm. She doubled over with a cry. It hurt—it hurt so much. She was sobbing with it, her knees had given out, and a second later, horrified, she realized that she had thrown up. She heard a howl from outside and the stab of Bellatrix's worry.

Don't … don't come in. She could hardly form the thought. She couldn't even see, it hurt so much. Bellatrix tended to unsettle people, with how big she was.

Yelena could not bear it if something happened to the dog because of her.

"Hey. Hey, now." A man's voice, speaking English. Gentle hands helped her to a chair.

When her vision cleared, Yelena's jaw dropped open.

The man in front of her was one of the most gorgeous guys she had seen. He was crouching, but when he stood up, he would be far taller than even she or Alec, and he was *ripped*. The guys at the boxing gym were nothing compared to him.

A moment later, a woman's face swam into view.

"Hello." She smiled, and switched to Romanian. "Are you a local?"

"Yeah." Yelena nodded at her gratefully, and gave a pained look at where Petra was cleaning up the vomit from the floor. Her face flamed. She'd just thrown up in front of the most gorgeous man she'd ever seen. "I, uh…."

"Are you alright? I mean, really all right?"

No. My brother is out there alone, and someone is hurting him. But what could this woman do about that? Yelena tried to smile, for all that she felt tears in her eyes.

"I'm just … I'm really tired. I'm so sorry. Thank you for helping me. Can you thank him, too?" She nodded her head at the gorgeous man. She couldn't bring herself to meet his eyes. "I'll get out of your way." She sniffed, trying to hold back a sob that was bubbling up.

The man squeezed her fingers. He looked genuinely worried.

She was going to burst into tears if she stayed here. "I have to go." Yelena pushed her way up and fairly ran for the elevator.

"Wait!" the woman called after her. She ran, too, and laid a hand on Yelena's shoulder as the elevator doors opened. "My name's Ecaterina. You can ask at the front desk if you need help with anything, okay?"

"Thanks." Yelena hunched her shoulders. She smiled as the doors closed, but just so that the woman would feel better. No one could help her with this.

She slumped back against the wall of the elevator. Bellatrix's worry radiated in her mind.

We need to find Alec soon, Yelena thought.

Bellatrix's instant agreement didn't make her feel any better.

"I'm worried about her." John dumped the bags on the floor by one of the beds. The team had gotten four rooms, but everyone had crowded into this one for now. "Something about her ... well, she didn't just seem sick or anything. I'm worried it's more."

"Maybe she has migraines," Ecaterina suggested.

"Maybe, but she looked very upset." John frowned. He couldn't get the black-haired woman out of his head. It wasn't that he was thinking of cheating on Jean. Even if he hadn't been sure she'd kill him painfully if he did so, he had no desire to do so. The black-haired woman had just seemed like she was in over her head. It got to him that he hadn't been able to help her. "I feel like something more was wrong."

"I think you're right." Pete exchanged a look with Bethany Anne.

"How so?" John looked at them both, "Should we go make sure she's alright, is she in danger here?"

It was Bethany Anne who answered, "I don't think she's in danger right now, but she might be soon. She's a Wechselbalg."

"What?" Ecaterina shook her head. "If she were a Wechselbalg, she would have smelled you guys, me, Pete. She would have known there was something different about everyone. She would have had some pack mannerisms."

"She's not *full* Wechselbalg." Pete nodded his head. "Distant ancestor, I'd guess. But she's got some of the nanocytes. At a guess?" He shrugged. "She heals fast. That's usually the only part that sticks when the bloodline gets diluted. That, and being crazy. But she doesn't seem crazy, though."

"So what was wrong with her?" John asked. He sat down in one of the chairs, frowning. "She looked really upset."

"I still think you're all overreacting. You've clearly never had a migraine," Ecaterina interjected. "They're terrible. She might just have been tired and—"

"You're thinking like a tour guide," Bethany Anne told her gently. "This woman's not a normal tourist. I didn't want to look into her head without a reason, but it's clear she's not just here for a visit. And she was afraid, I could smell that. Also … there's more to this. Pete and I talked to the receptionist. Two people went missing here today, and one of them was that girl's brother."

Ecaterina looked around herself. "You think she came here to find him? How would she know he was in danger?"

"It is possible that that he might also have the nanocytes? If he's got them, too, she might know if he's in trouble." Pete frowned. "I hate to say this, because she seems nice, but he might also be one of the guys we're looking for. We know they're operating around here, and we know they're weak Wechselbalg. He might just be stronger than she is, and she doesn't know what he's a part of. Some of the old packs in the underworld, they have old rules. He might be marrying her off to someone to get them to be loyal—and even if the bloodline is thin, there's a possibility it might breed a strong child."

"Well, then it's our job to save her," John argued. "The underworld should have had the decency to die out. We are not just going to let them *sell* people."

Bethany Anne spoke up, "If her brother was selling her off, that still doesn't explain why he is missing." She walked over to the window, frowning.

She stared out at the trees and the snow, crisp under a clear sky. There were too many parts of this that didn't quite fit together, and she didn't like it. Gabrielle had mentioned to be wary of the people here. Was it possible that the girl was one of the people they were looking for, meant to gain their sympathy?

Bethany Anne didn't think so.

The fear and pain she'd felt rolling off the girl had seemed sudden, beyond the girl's control. There had been no awareness when Bethany Anne and her team walked in, as they could expect if the girl was meant to be a distraction or plant.

Something told her this girl was for real. And—

Her eyes caught on something in the woods, and she swore under her breath.

"Son of a horse-humping...." She murmured

"What is it?" The rest came to look out the window as well, and there was a collective gasp.

In the moonlight, Ashur's fur shone, and he was nose to nose with a massive black German Shepherd. The dog looked small next to Ashur, but Bethany Anne and the rest knew just how big Ashur was. This dog, for a normal, mortal being ... was big.

Bethany Anne pressed her hand against the glass, narrowing her eyes as she reached out with her mind. Her eyes still closed, she told them about the dog, "It's hers. The girl. And it's not a normal dog. It used to be, but she's changed it. It's starting to absorb ... what she is."

"On purpose?" Pete frowned.

"No." Bethany Anne shook her head. "I don't think she understands what she is. The dog knows, I think." She frowned in concentration as she searched through the dog's thoughts. "The dog trusts her. She's not mean to it."

She smiled as he saw the black-haired woman through the dog's eyes. The woman had named it, trained it. She could see food held in a palm, and a ready smile and a treat when the puppy sat or lay down or came to heel. "She's a good person, this one. If her brother is part of all of this, then he's nothing like her."

"And if she is looking for him," Ecaterina bit her lip. "She's in danger, isn't she?"

"Yep." Bethany Anne tapped her fingers on the windowsill. "And we're not going to let anything happen to her." She turned away from the window, "Pete, you keep watch. She might try to leave tonight. John, please speak with the receptionist and see if she knows where the sketchy people around here hang out." She walked to her suitcase, "I think I'm going to go pay them a visit as soon as we find out. Hopefully, we can deal with them before this girl goes out looking for her brother."

CHAPTER SIX

After an hour of searching, Yelena slumped onto the bed and put her head in her hands. If it were not for the quiet contentment she could feel coming from Bellatrix, out in nature and amongst rabbits and squirrels and snow, she would have gone mad already, and she thought she might go mad now.

There were no clues here!

Alec always traveled light: a change of clothes or two, his ski gear, maybe a book. Yelena was not even sure what she had been hoping for. Maybe a journal. Maybe if she were going to wish for things, it would be a day planner with an address list … that he had not brought with him to meet whoever had hurt him.

She pushed herself up and began to pace. It had been a long day, but she was not at all tired. She was beginning to feel the same, simmering anger that had led her to beat the shit out of Ciprian two years ago. The anger told her that this was not fair, that no one should have any reason to hurt Alec. That no one should be allowed to take her twin from her. It was wrong.

She wasn't going to just sit here and let it happen.

That thought made everything crystal clear. Yelena grabbed a hair tie and began to tie her hair back, narrating to herself as she went.

"They said he went out to ski and never came back."

She wrapped a wide scarf around her neck, with the cloth over her mouth.

"So the first place to look is on the slopes."

She pulled on her boots and laced them up.

"They said they sent someone, but clearly they missed an important piece of information."

A stab of pain caught her as she grabbed her coat, and she steadied herself against the wall. A moment later, she realized what the pain meant.

She whispered, "If Alec is still in pain, *he's still alive*."

Yelena grabbed a map in one gloved hand and set off for the back stairway out of the resort.

The thought that he was in pain brought tears to her eyes, but she wiped them away angrily. Now was no time to be weak. Alec would hang on as long as he could. He was a fighter.

And so was she. She was going to go find her brother.

"This is perfect." Ecaterina tipped her head back and stared up at the sky happily. "Don't get me wrong, I like seeing stars from space, but there's nothing like a winter sky in Romania."

Pete grinned and leaned back against the wall of the hotel, crossing his arms. The winter air didn't bother him. Minor discomfort did not bother most of those who were enhanced by nanocytes, and he would not have allowed any level of discomfort to keep him from obeying Bethany Anne's orders—and protecting an innocent woman.

He also had other obligations. Even if there had been no orders, he would have been out here with Ecaterina. Nathaniel had been very, very clear.

If anything happened to her, Pete was going to be turned completely inside out.

Pete cared too much about Ecaterina to let her go into danger—human or not, she was his pack mate.

But he also had no desire to find out whether being turned inside out was a thing Nathaniel could actually manage.

"So you used to hike up into the mountains on your own?"

"All the time." Ecaterina shrugged her shoulders. "You must understand, right?

"The world has all of these rules and trivial concerns, and after a while, you just want to be yourself, alone. Matched against nature." She hunched her shoulders, looking sad. "It feels ridiculous to talk about that sometimes. Almost everyone I talk to is more than human now and even I have lost some of the feeling after I changed."

"You know none of that matters," Pete told her. He came to stand beside her.

He could feel Ashur nearby—and the other dog. She was interested in them, but had not yet come out of the trees. Caution would serve her well, and he did not want to interfere by calling to her. He focused on Ecaterina instead. He could see the self-doubt in her face and it tore at his heart. "You are smart and strong and kind. You earned your place with Bethany Anne."

"I guess so." Ecaterina crossed her arms and looked away.

"You really did," Pete assured her. He nudged her with one elbow. "Plus, you keep Nathaniel in a good mood," he joked. "I'm sure a few of us would be dead if he didn't have you to make him nicer."

Ecaterina laughed at that. She opened her mouth to speak, but the sound of the door opening made them both turn.

It was the young woman from before, her grey eyes wide as she saw them there.

Clearly, she thought no one would be here. Her eyes got even wider as Ashur padded out of the forest with her dog at his side.

Yelena was surprised to see some of the others there. She remembered Ecaterina, and something about the man at her side made Yelena feel comfortable. She had the strange thought that they smelled familiar, and realized she was being ridiculous. Feeling Alec's pain was enough weird, supernatural crap for one day. She was not going to start believing that she could smell whether or not someone was trustworthy.

But her jaw dropped when she saw Bellatrix with the other dog. Her dog was unusually large, large enough to make people uncomfortable even in her little town, where everyone knew her *and* knew that Dmitri bred giant German Shepherds. But Bellatrix looked small next to the pure white dog, and both dogs looked perfectly happy.

The white dog chuffed at her.

He's saying hello.

"Hello," Yelena said to the white dog, before she remembered that there were people watching her. She felt her face flush and looked over at them. "Ah, I mean...."

"Can you understand him?" the woman asked curiously.

"Of course not, I was just saying hello." She said the words more emphatically than she needed to. "I, uh ... I have to go. Sorry. Come on, Trix."

The man and the woman exchanged a quick look. "We can't actually ... ah, you stay inside tonight." Ecaterina looked worried. "It's really dangerous out here."

Something inside Yelena snapped. "Yeah. I know. My brother's out there somewhere, hurt. I've got to find him."

"Maybe we can help." Ecaterina bit her lip.

"How can you help?"

"We can find people. And if he's in trouble, we can make sure...." Her voice trailed off. "Well, if he got mixed up in something—actually, would you know if he was mixed up in anything bad?"

Yelena laughed shortly. "Alec? No. He only cares about skiing. I mean, he's an accountant, too. But that's just to pay bills."

"He doesn't have any friends who might be mixed up in bad things?"

"No," Yelena said impatiently. "He came out here alone.

Look, you've been really nice, but I have to go find him. Come on, Trix."

Bellatrix did not move.

"Wechselbag." He raised an eyebrow when Yelena's head jerked around. "The word means something to you?"

Yelena tried to remember her English, and couldn't. She wasn't entirely sure she'd understood the second sentence, but she knew the word Wechselbalg. She looked over at Ecaterina.

"You know the word," Ecaterina suggested.

"It's just old stories," Yelena said. "It doesn't *mean* anything." She muttered, "Even if Mama thinks it does."

"Your mother told you about Wechselbalg?"

Yelena shook her head. "I need to find Alec. I don't have time for this."

"What did your mother say?" Ecaterina pressed.

Yelena spit out, "That our family has changer blood, all right? But I know it isn't true. I'm not a crazy person, all right? Whatever Alec got mixed up in…."

Pete stood up, "Give me … aww screw it."

"What?" Yelena asked. But, all he threw off was his coat, then the man changed.

"You pups always make messes," Ecaterina said and grabbed the shirt around his neck and tossed it off as the wolf stepped out of the destroyed clothes.

He stood bigger even than the white dog, unmistakably a wolf. He padded over to her and nudged her hand with his nose.

"Oh," Yelena said faintly. She swayed slightly as she looked down at the eyes staring back at her.

"They're real," the woman said. "And your mother is

right. You do have their blood. So does your brother. We think maybe he got taken by the people we're hunting."

The wolf growled softly.

"We don't know that for sure," Ecaterina said.

"Don't know what for sure?"

"He wonders if your brother might be using his Wechselbalg blood to become part of the underworld around here," Ecaterina explained.

"He would never," Yelena said hotly. She felt lost, her voice trembled just a bit, "You really think they have him?"

Yelena looked around, it was just too much.

There was a giant, shape shifting wolf, and the idea that maybe she could do that, too, and the thought that she could never rescue Alec if she were up against something with claws like knives.

Ecaterina spoke gently. "You might not be able to take on a Wechselbalg or three by yourself," she said. "But we can. You should come upstairs, meet Bethany Anne."

It was Bellatrix who decided her. *You can trust these people.*

With one more glance at the wolf—definitely still there, definitely still a wolf—

Yelena followed Ecaterina back into the hotel to meet the woman called Bethany Anne.

***

"Emilian." Marcel waited awkwardly in the doorway. "Our client is on the phone for you."

"Thank you." Emilian stood and walked to the other room, not looking at the man. Marcel was clearly still bothered by Cezar's death. That he should let his discomfort be seen was not acceptable.

Emilian would have to talk to him about that. He could hardly take over the underworld if his employees could not deal with a little blood. As he picked up the phone, he thought that he would have to come up with a way to make Marcel understand.

"Hello?"

"What is your status?" The man's voice was sharp. He was an impatient man, Emilian had learned. "The wife is worried. I don't want there to be any chance of him being rescued."

Emilian felt an instinctive flare of rage. How dared this man question his methods? He clenched his fingers as he answered, telling himself that he was using the humans for their money, and reminding himself that it amused him to play them off one another. "You wanted him to suffer," he said shortly. "He is suffering."

"He has suffered enough." The man gave the order carelessly, "End it. Use the beast you told me about."

The beast is me. Emilian smiled. "I will."

"Tell me when it is done, and I will tell you what to do with the body." The man hung up without waiting for a response.

Emilian drummed his fingers on the desk for another moment, and came to a decision. They could take some time, he decided—especially if the man's pain could serve two purposes.

"Marcel." He waited for the man to appear. "You will torture the man. These are things you will need to know if you are to be of use to me." The look in his eyes showed Marcel that if a man was not of use … he would be dead.

As Marcel disappeared, looking sick, Emilian flipped through what they had taken from the man. The ski gear was ruined by his claws, and the man's documents were in a plastic pouch. Emilian took the papers out, and froze.

Worry made him sick. ALEC NIKOLAEV, the papers read. Their target might have made false papers, hoping to keep Virgil from knowing where he was going.

Or he might have been telling the truth. He might not know Virgil at all.

They might have the wrong man. Emilian ran for the torture room, shouting for Marcel. They had to find Theo —and this man had to die. He could not be allowed to tell the world what he had seen.

CHAPTER SEVEN

"The receptionist says there is an old house at the edge of town that's being rented." John closed the door behind him. He poked a finger into his ear and popped out an implant Jean and Bobcat had made for the Bitches, with TOM's help. A language device that translated what he heard, and allowed him to speak translated words.

It took a while to get used to opening his mouth and having words come out that he didn't understand, but the device was useful. Bethany Anne had realized that while many world leaders spoke English, often it was random people on the street who noticed strange things and were willing to admit to them—and those people rarely spoke more than one language, and it wasn't always English.

It helped to speak the local language.

John rubbed at his ear and grimaced. He still preferred speaking his own language. "The people in the house now are younger guys. They don't seem to work anywhere. It was being rented for years, but no one was ever there, as far as anyone knew. But now people have moved in."

"A bolt hole, maybe?" Eric suggested.

"A retreat." Bethany Anne agreed. "So, what do we know? We know that Stephen dealt with the leaders. We know that the leaders were reckless and preyed on humans. We also know that the ones left behind are weak. So they are weak, and they are using systems set up by people who were reckless."

She smiled. "I'd say we have a good shot to take them out easily. In time for breakfast, even."

Bethany Anne was reaching for her coat when voices sounded in the hallway. A moment later, Ecaterina came in with the black-haired woman they had seen in the lobby. The woman looked shocked. She blushed again when she saw John, and shifted her gaze to Bethany Anne.

"She was going to find her brother," Ecaterina explained.

"Where's Pete?"

"He changed, so…." Ecaterina grinned. "Someone needs to bring him some clothes."

"Or," Eric suggested, "we *don't* bring him clothes and make him get up here naked without being seen."

Bethany Anne tapped her chin with a finger before pointing at Eric, "You guys kill me. And Pete's going to kill *you* if he ends up out there naked."

"I'll go bring him some stuff." Eric grabbed workout shorts and a t-shirt out of one of the bags and left the room with an appreciative glance at the black-haired woman.

Bethany Anne frowned. "I would have heard a fight. Why did Pete change?"

"To show her that her mother's stories were real." Ecaterina jerked her head at the woman. "This is Yelena, by the way. Yelena, this is Bethany Anne." She had shifted back into Romanian.

John sighed and put his translation unit back in.

"It is very nice to meet you," Yelena said politely. She swallowed, clearly torn. "We do not have much time. I do not want to be impolite, but whatever is going on here, my brother is in serious danger. I can feel it." She said the last words almost defiantly, as if she expected Bethany Anne to think she was crazy for saying them. Her hands clenched. "If he has really been taken by changers, then I need your help."

Bethany Anne cocked her head to one side, "You do not like admitting that you need help?" she asked her.

"Of course I don't!" Yelena crossed her arms. "Trouble comes for you when you're all alone, but it isn't smart to rely on other people."

Bethany Anne nodded, "I understand that way of thinking. And for a long time, I did not like to rely on anyone, either. But my team is made up of people like you. People, who push themselves very hard because they do not want to be weak or vulnerable. Like you, they want to help other people. I have learned to recognize people like you, and to trust them. Everyone in this room—and Pete, who showed you that the Wechselbalg are real—is someone you can trust."

Yelena looked like she wasn't quite sure if she believed that, and Bethany Anne realized it might be the sort of thing that could only be learned by experience.

"We are going to confront the people who have taken your brother," she told Yelena. "These are dangerous people, so you should stay here for now. If your brother is there, we will rescue him and bring him back."

"Nuh-uh." Yelena shook her head. "Absolutely not. I am not staying behind."

Ecaterina put a hand on her arm, "It is impossible for you to take on creatures like these on your own."

"I don't care," Yelena said instantly.

"Don't be foolish," Bethany Anne told her. The truth was, she did not want this woman to come with her, only to find out that her brother was a member of the underworld.

She was still worried that Alec Nikolaev might not be as good hearted as his sister was. But was worried about suggesting that to the young woman, "What good will you be to your brother if you should get hurt?"

Yelena countered, "Why should you get hurt on my behalf? That doesn't make any sense, either."

"We have our own score to settle with them," Bethany Anne explained. She knew her voice was growing deeper, taking on a tinge of her "Queen Bitch Mode," as the Bitches called it. "And they will not be able to hurt us."

Yelena had backed up into the wall when she heard Bethany Anne's voice. She swallowed hard. She was clearly out of her depth, between Bethany Anne and Pete, but she refused to back down just because she was afraid.

"I'm coming with you," she said simply. "He is my brother. Maybe you don't think I can help. Maybe you're right. But I love him. I will protect him as long as I am able to do so. And I am not staying here if I know he is in danger, wolf or no wolf."

Bethany Anne nodded. She understood the call of

honor. She knew that for Yelena, the chance of death meant nothing in the equation, and she would *respect* that. "Remember that we are hunting these people because of the things they do," she explained. "We want to take them down because they prey on people. We will help you rescue your brother."

"Alec," Yelena nodded. "His name is Alec." She said it like a prayer.

"Alec." Bethany Anne nodded. "We'll save him, Yelena. Everyone, get your gear. We are going to check out the house right now."

None of them were willing to consider the idea that it might already be too late for Alec.

Yelena noticed the sword Bethany Anne pulled out of a pack and the pistols they all slotted into holsters before their coats covered them up.

Just who were these people?

Emilian raced through the hallways, shouting for Marcel. The man they had, needed to give them information now. Before, Emilian had just tortured him for fun … and because their client wanted the man to suffer.

Now he had to know if they had the right man at all.

He found Marcel in the room, nervously holding his hand in a fist, hesitating as the man in the chair strained at his bonds to get away. Emilian took a moment to curl his lip in contempt at both men. The man in the chair should know he could not get away—and Marcel should not be hesitating.

NATALIE GREY & MICHAEL ANDERLE

Emilian ordered Marcel curtly, "Hit him."

Marcel did, though the hit was not as strong as Emilian knew he could summon.

"Again."

Marcel hesitated.

"I said, *hit him again.*"

Marcel closed his eyes for a moment, but his sense of self-preservation was strong. His fist shot out and the man in the chair grunted in pain. The cuts on his chest were almost healed, and they had not festered as claw slashes usually did on humans, but Emilian was too distracted to think about that right now.

"Tell me your name, " Emilian demanded.

"Alec Nikolaev." The words came instantly through cracked lips. The man looked up at him. "Who are you?"

"The scalpel, Marcel." Emilian watched the man pick it up. "Cut him on his chest."

Marcel's face was screwed up with distaste, but he did as he was asked.

Over the sound of the man's cry, Emilian explained: "You do not ask question. I ask questions. What is your name?"

"I told you?" He tried to explain through the pain.

"Keep cutting," Emilian told Marcel. "I will ask again. What is your name?"

"Alec Nikolaev! Please! I am telling you the truth!"

Cold certainty settled in Emilian's stomach. The man was telling the truth. But it could not be true, he could not *allow* it to be true.

He grabbed the scalpel out of Marcel's hand and jabbed

it down into the captive's thigh yelling at him, "TELL ME YOUR NAME!"

"I'm ALEC, my name is Alec!" The man was screaming the words hoarsely. "You don't want me, I haven't done anything! You want…."

His head lolled. He was losing consciousness, damn him.

Emilian slapped him across the face. "Wake up! Who do I want? Tell me or I'll cut you again."

The man's eyes couldn't focus. Blood was spreading over his thigh. "The other skier," he slurred. "The man ahead of me."

Emilian stared at him silently before mouthing the words slowly, "What. Other. Skier?"

"Fell on the branch. Dunno where he went." The man's eyes went wide. "No—no! Don't hurt him. You can't hurt him!"

Emilian smiled at him coldly. "I *can't*? You are in no position to dictate terms. Marcel, go back to the slopes. Find the other skier, and finish the job. At once. Call me when it's done. And you, Alec Nikolaev…." He smiled as he picked up another instrument from his set. He turned it in the light, looking at the blade.

"You are going to suffer. Because I have had a bad day. And you are part of that. And because you tried to give me an order. You are going to suffer, as all humans will suffer when I come to power … if they defy me." Emilian smiled down at the tied up man, "No one will say I can't be benevolent when I want to be." He shrugged as he slashed out to Alex's cry, "I just rarely want to be."

Out in the hallway, Marcel did not stop running until he could no longer hear the man's screams.

He did not want to do this. He did not want any of this. But what could he do?

He knew he could not fight Emilian. A human could not do anything against a shape shifter.

He did not want to die. Slowly, trembling, he started into the woods. Either way, someone was dying tonight: him, or the other skier. That was just the way the world worked sometimes.

CHAPTER EIGHT

Jamie Constantin paced outside the old house.

His breath was making clouds in the air and his feet were going numb, but there was no way he was going back in there, even for a few minutes. The screams had barely let up for the past hour.

He had taken this job despite every instinct. He told them he could patrol around the house, yes. No, he didn't care if he wasn't allowed to go in except to one room on the first floor. Whatever. Rich people were weird, and the pay was all right.

Now he thought his instincts had been correct, though. What was this place?

First there was the guy who looked at people as though they were beneath him, and sometimes he actually goddamned *growled*. Who did that?

Then there were the screams.

He slumped against the wall. His mother was going to yell at him. She was going to remind him that this was the third job in three months. She was going to tell him that

Cristina would never stay with a guy who couldn't provide for her and the baby.

The scream decided him, though. He had to get out of here. He'd given them a fake name, on a hunch he wouldn't even put words to. Hopefully they couldn't find him. He took off down the road without a backward glance.

Better unemployed than dead. Only one of those two situations could be fixed.

He skidded around the corner and stopped when he saw the group in front of them. Huge guys that looked like bodybuilders, and a few women, all of them pretty. None of them seemed scared to be out at night.

"What are you running from?" A woman, in all black, strolled forward. She had a look in her eyes that said he didn't want to mess with her.

He wasn't going to. He wasn't a total idiot. Jamie looked over his shoulder and gulped. "My boss is torturing someone."

One of the women gave a little cry.

"So you just ran away rather than helping?" she demanded, her eyes narrowing in anger.

"Please." Jamie held out his hands. "Please, you don't get it, this guy is terrifying. He growls when he's mad, three of the guys have gone missing in the past week and there's blood on the stairs. I got a baby to take care of. I can't get killed."

The woman reached out. She didn't look like a body-builder, but she dragged him close without any effort at all. Her eyes stared into his very mind without emotion, and Jamie felt more terror than he had ever known. When the woman released him, he thudded to his knees on the frozen ground.

"You are *fortunate*." The woman's voice didn't seem human now.

When Jamie looked up, he screamed. Her eyes were red, and glowing red lines threaded along her skin. The air around her seemed to crackle with power. He scrambled to kneel and pressed his forehead onto the ground.

She was not of this world. He could only pray for mercy.

"I am letting you live because you did not participate in the torture," she told him. "And because it would not be fair to your child if I were to kill you. But let this be a warning, Jamie Constantin."

"How do you know my—"

"Stop … talking," she told him before commanding, "Look at me."

Trembling, he did so.

"You will never do something like this again," she told him. "You will never again stand by while someone is hurt. If you do, the next time we meet, I will not be merciful. Do you understand?" he nodded.

She stepped around him without another word, and the rest of the team followed her.

Screams drifted faintly on the breeze and Jamie huddled on the ground, sobbing with fear. Eventually, he picked himself up and began to stumble back to town.

Never again, he promised himself. He would not ever think he was too good for work. He'd go back to working at the butcher shop in the morning. Good, honest work where he didn't have to stand by and listen to people get tortured.

They'd never be rich, but he'd provide for the baby and Cristina.

He stopped at the bottom of the hill. The house behind him lost in the trees, but he looked back anyway. Then, he was smiling.

That bastard was about to get what he deserved.

In spades.

"I think you're getting soft in your old age." John flashed a smile at Bethany Anne as the group ran up the hill. He wouldn't have dared say anything like that normally—at least, not without expecting a hundred push-ups while Bethany Anne stood on his back in *very* pointy heels—but Yelena looked like she was going to throw up.

"I got her!" Ecaterina slipped an arm around Yelena to help her and the others went ahead of them for the last little bit.

They could hear the screams now, and with every one, Yelena gave a whimper. She stumbled, and John remembered Ecaterina saying that Yelena felt her brother's pain. He couldn't imagine what this was like—but he knew this woman wasn't going to let anything keep her from getting revenge.

"Let's deal with this dickless regurgitated piece of mouse shit, and then you and I can see if I'm getting soft, Mr. Grimes," Bethany Anne chuckled.

As they came up to the door, she brought up one foot

and kicked it forward. The heavy old door, a thick slab of wood banded with iron, practically disintegrated with the force of her kick. She strode into the house, the energy radiating from her and Yelena noticed two pieces of iron glowed hot when she passed. "He's upstairs, I saw in that guy's mind that he was never allowed onto the second floor."

"It smells like weak werewolf in here!" Pete called. He changed a moment later, following Bethany Anne up the stairs with a snarl and a clatter of claws.

Yelena could feel her brother's pain radiating through her. She steadied herself on Ecaterina's arm, and felt Bellatrix at her side.

"We have to help him, Trix." She used the words to steady herself. "We have to."

Upstairs, she could hear yelling and snarling. She forced her shaking muscles into a run. Her brother's screams were echoing in her ears, unstoppable.

Alec, I won't let him kill you.

She came around the corner to find Bethany Anne suspending a man by his neck. His feet kicked and he yelled contemptuously at her.

"Who the hell do you think you are?" he half screamed, half gurgled.

"I'm the fucking Queen Bitch, you cunt-rotting testicle wanking fuckwitted bastard!" Her eyes were glowing.

In the corner, Alec was slumped in a chair. Yelena ran to him, her heart in her throat. She could sense the pulse of life in him, but his skin was covered in bruises and cuts.

She worked at the bindings on his hands, "Alec, please. Please wake up, Alec. Alec, it's me. It's Yelena. Are you still with me?" Her voice pleaded, "Please wake up, *please, please, please....*"

She was the Queen Bitch? Fuck that. The vampires were gone, dead from fighting amongst themselves. Everyone knew that. The rumors about space, about TQB—they were just rumors. The vampires weren't seeking out new challenges, they were running away because they knew they were weak.

Of course, he didn't have a particularly good explanation for why the woman's eyes were glowing, but he sure as hell wasn't going to let her steal his place. He had waited too long for this.

"Listen, bitch—"

Her fist sent him sprawling to the floor the very next moment. He could taste is blood as he choked on his teeth and bit his tongue.

"That's Queen Bitch to you, you ass-faced monkey-fucking wank addict!" The woman stared him down. At her side, a huge wolf bared its teeth.

He was hallucinating. That was the only possible reason for this. Vampires weren't as strong as this one was. She'd brought humans with her—humans they actually seemed to fight with. The humans needed to be shown that Emilian wouldn't just roll over and play dead for them, that he wasn't as sentimental and weak as she was and they would follow a real leader.

And he knew just the way to do that.

Yelena was crying. Bellatrix sniffed worriedly at Alec. She could feel his pain. She could feel whatever Yelena felt.

When her mistress was happy, Bellatrix was happy. When her mistress was sad, nothing was right with the world.

Right now, her mistress was terribly afraid. She was whispering to her twin, to the man who smelled so much like her and yet so different. He was nice, Bellatrix thought, even if he didn't couldn't understand Bellatrix the way her mistress did.

He was trying to talk now.

"What did you say?" Yelena leaned close as he fell, and she caught him. "You're safe now. You're safe."

"Another … skier." Alec's lips were bleeding. He clutched at Yelena's shirt, leaving a bloody smear. "I was … wrong guy. They're going to kill him. On the slope. Have to save him…"

All of a sudden, Bellatrix's hackles went up. The Enemy, the man with the weak scent like a wolf, was looking at Yelena. And Bellatrix did not like the way he was looking. He snatched at something on the ground.

The man screamed, "There is only power!" his hand raising up.

Get out of the way!

But Yelena didn't hear, all of her attention was focused on her brother.

There was no thought, no hesitation. Bellatrix leapt in front of her mistress as the gun went off with a roar.

"NO!" The scream was raw, ripped from her throat.

Yelena heard a sizzle of energy and a blaze of heat nearby, and the man with the gun screamed in a way she was sure she would never forget, but she couldn't pay attention to any of it. She was at Bellatrix's side, pressing her hands desperately over the flow of blood. "No, no, take me—take me, instead. Trix. *Trix!*"

Tears were running down her cheeks. She had come here to save Alec, and while she had Alec, she had gotten Bellatrix killed.

Yelena was sobbing, rocking back and forth as Bellatrix wheezed with pain. There had been no doubt in the dog, nothing but the absolute, pure love of one pack mate to another.

She didn't deserve that kind of love. "You saved me," Yelena whispered. Tears were running down her cheeks. "You saved me, and I can't save you. I'm so sorry."

You saved me, too. The thought held no pain and no fear, only love. *I would never let you be hurt.*

"Gott Verdammt! ERIC!" Bethany Anne shouted and then Eric was there. The man levered his arms beneath Bellatrix's body.

"Come with me," he told Yelena.

"No—no, just let me be with her." It was a childish plea, but she couldn't bear to let Bellatrix be in more pain.

"We will save her." He picked Bellatrix up and ran for the door.

"It's not possible," Yelena whispered.

But Ecaterina hauled her up. "Come on. Leave your

brother with John, he'll be okay. We have to get to the Pod!"

"Go," Alec called weakly. He had blood smeared around his mouth for some reason, but he already looked stronger. "I'll be fine, *go*."

Yelena didn't know what a Pod was, and she didn't care. She took off after Eric. If there was a chance of saving Bellatrix, she would do anything.'

Bethany Anne watched the black Pods take off, heading into the sky. She'd given Eric very exact instructions but she had another task and called Pete to join her.

The trip through the forest was quick, and they found the underworld lackey without much trouble. He was flailing around in the dark. Perhaps he thought he was quiet, but both she and Pete could easily hear him. When they stepped out from the trees in front of him, the man froze.

"Hello," Bethany Anne said pleasantly. Her eyes went red, her fangs slid out. "Going somewhere?"

The wolf next to her chuffed in anticipation.

The man stumbled back. "Emilian?"

"Not so sadly, not with us any longer." Bethany Anne stalked forward. "He's paid for his sins. Are you ready to pay for yours?"

"Please—please, I was only trying to stay alive!" But he felt her hands on his head, dragging him down as she looked into all of his thoughts.

"Earlier this evening, I found another one of you assholes. Do you know what I told him?"

"No." He was sobbing with fear.

"I told him that I would let him go because he had a child to protect ... and because he hadn't actually taken part in Emilian's crimes."

Oh, no.

"Marcel, you are judged and I have found you *guilty.*" The last thing Marcel ever saw was red eyes blazing down at him. He only lived another moment, but it was a moment filled with every agony he had inflicted on the man back at the house.

Multiplied.

Bethany Anne let the now inert body drop into the snow. "What you sow, so shall you reap. Your deeds will come back to you tenfold. Enjoy hell."

She looked around herself. It only took a few moments before she sensed a faint pulse of life nearby. As she pushed her way through the underbrush, she let herself fade back to looking human.

The skier lay on the ground, half delirious. His eyes focused on Bethany Anne. "Are you ... real?"

"I'm real." She crouched down next to him in the snow. "We have to get you to safety."

"Dangerous." He barely made out the word. "And I'm going crazy. Saw a big wolf. A big wolf. So big."

Bethany Anne motioned to Pete to stay back. "Now, now, I'm sure you didn't see that."

"I know." The skier's head lolled and he winced as she picked him up. "It's ... crazy, right?"

"I hear people hallucinate all sorts of things," Bethany

Anne told him, her voice soothing. "But there's no reason to be afraid. No wolves around."

"Uh-huh."

Theo passed out before he thought to ask just how a slender woman was carrying him so easily.

On the G'laxix Sphaea, Hidden in a Romania Forest

Three days later, Yelena opened her eyes, and stared up into a friendly face.

"Hi!" Ecaterina offered her a hand to get up. "So. How are you feeling?"

"Good. Better than good." Yelena stretched. "I feel like I slept for a week."

"Almost." Ecaterina handed her a shirt and pants. "You're all healed now."

"I wasn't hurt." She felt a bit guilty about that. "How is Bellatrix?"

"Out and frolicking in the snow. Absolutely fine." Ecaterina gestured to a heavy winter coat. "You two just took a while to wake up so you got moved in here. And you might not have been injured, but you could say the poddoc cures ... everything. So old injuries, muscle knots, all of that. You've been upgraded. So has Alec."

Somewhere across the room, Alec gave a sleepy mumble.

"Alec!" Yelena went over to look down at him, and winced when she saw he was naked. "Get this man some pants."

Ecaterina threw them across the room, laughing.

"How do you feel?" Yelena asked him. Her brother's

skin was completely clean. No trace of the torture remained there, and she could not even see the scar he'd gotten when he was twelve, on a sharp rock in the river.

"Good." Alec sat up. "I had some weird dreams, though. And where are we? Some kind of hospital?"

Yelena and Ecaterina exchanged a look.

"Sort of," Yelena explained. "We'd better take you to see Bethany Anne and then get you setup in a hotel."

CHAPTER NINE

Virgil Baciu settled back into his chair. His smile was confident. He had heard nothing from his contacts in the countryside, but Theo was still missing.

Whatever had happened, it was clear that his rival was not coming back. He thought of Theo's wife, Mariana, and a cold smile touched his lips.

It had never been about business for Virgil. The truth was that he could never forgive Theo for winning Mariana's heart. And now that Theo was gone, Virgil was sure it was only a matter of time before he could make Mariana fall in love with him.

But first, he would take everything else Theo had valued—starting with his business. He looked down at the contract on the table in front of him. The people selling him the business were late for this meeting, which irked him, but there were no other buyers now that Theo was out of the picture. They would have to sell to Virgil to avoid bankruptcy, and Virgil had also readied himself to buy Theo's company for a pittance when word finally broke that the man was dead.

Maybe he should take up skiing as well. He laughed softly to himself.

The door opened behind him, and Virgil allowed contempt to touch his voice.

"You're finally here. Good."

"How interesting." The voice was amused. "I didn't think you'd be pleased to see me."

Virgil spun in his chair, his jaw gaping open. "But you...."

"Should be dead?" Theodor Dimitru smiled coldly.

He certainly wasn't dead, and to add insult to injury, he looked ... well, taller than Virgil remembered. More muscular. The very picture of health.

"I'm so glad to see you alive." The words tasted bitter as Virgil forced them out.

"I don't think you are," Theo said quietly. He reached out to open the door, and two policemen came into the room. "And they don't, either. They know everything, Virgil. They know you hired people to kill me."

"Wait—how did you—" But Virgil was hauled out of the room before he could say anything else.

Theo smiled after him and then took a moment to look over Virgil's contract as the business owners filed into the room. He smiled up at them.

"Well, now, gentleman. Should we talk about transfer of ownership? I think I can offer you *much* better terms than my competitor."

"Thank you so much." Yelena hugged Ecaterina tightly. "Thank you all," she added, grinning at all of them. She couldn't stop smiling these days. Sometimes, she was so happy she thought she might cry—though she thought of what her no-nonsense grandmother would say to that and kept her tears inside. She couldn't stop the smiles, though.

"How is your brother?" Bethany Anne pointed to the door of the hotel room.

The door opened a second later. "I thought I heard voices," Alec said, peeking out into the hallway.

"You should be resting!" Yelena shooed him back toward the door.

"I *should* be dead," Alec said simply. He smiled at his twin, and then at the group assembled there. "Instead I just feel a bit tired from the healing." He flexed an arm, "I think my muscles may be getting bigger."

"Yeah, that sounds about right." John nodded. He put his hand to his ear for a moment and leaned in to talk to Bethany Anne. "The Pods will be here to pick us up in a moment."

Bethany Anne nodded, but she was still looking at Yelena. "So ... do you want to come see the rest of the crew?"

"Where are they?" Yelena didn't understand for a moment, and then her eyes got huge. "Wait. In *space*?"

"Why not?" Bethany Anne grinned. "You're both doing well."

"I can't leave Bellatrix."

"You don't have to. Ashur lives on the ship with me," Bethany Anne explained. "And, by the way, about Bellatrix—"

"She's bigger," Yelena interrupted. "And that's saying something. And last night…."

"Yes?" Bethany Anne smiled. She had a feeling that Yelena's nanocytes were doing new things now that she'd been exposed to the pod-doc.

"I had the weirdest dream," Yelena muttered. "It was like I was…"

"A wolf?" Pete suggested.

"No, not quite." Yelena shook her head as she tried to remember. "I had paws, though. I wasn't human. I was…." She broke off, and her eyes got wide. "I was Bellatrix!" She shrugged, "Weird."

"I don't think that was a dream," Bethany Anne suggested. "I would think, based on my time with Ashur, that what you are experiencing is real."

Yelena's lips pressed together before she replied, "I really was seeing something from inside of her head, you mean?"

"Yes. And it's something we could test for you up on the ship. I'm sure the whole team would be interested." Bethany Anne thought about something for a moment before continuing. "And I think Ashur and Bellatrix are sweet on each other, too, so there's that."

"They are, aren't they?" Yelena grinned. "Well, I suppose I could at least go *see* it. What d'you think, Alec?"

He smiled but shook his head, "I think I'll go home and be the responsible twin for once," he chuckled. "You go, I'll get home on my own."

"Can you?" Yelena asked.

"Maybe I'll need to be tended to by the cute receptionist for a few days." He winked. "Seriously, I'll be fine. You go."

"And you promise—"

"No, I won't tell Mom where you went."

"Thanks," Yelena said, in relief and turned to Bethany Anne. "Okay, let's go."

Eric led the way down the corridors and out into the sunshine. There was a scuffling noise in the forest and all of a sudden, Pete started laughing.

"What? What is it?"

Ashur emerged from the underbrush, snow coating his fur. Bellatrix followed him, also disheveled.

"Uh, I don't think they're just sweet on each other," Pete explained. "I think you might have some puppies on the way."

Yelena sank her face into her hands as everyone started laughing.

CHAPTER TEN

"Bobby B!" William called out as he strode across the floor of the hangar bay. "That lager came in, if you want to come test it." He looked at Bobcat's latest effort to play with a helicopter. "Ah, what's that you're working on?"

"Better stabilization for Shelly 3.0." Bobcat held up a tiny piece of equipment with a triumphant grin. About the size of a marble, it emitted a tiny ticking sound as he plugged it into a drone. "This little beauty means that even our Queen isn't going to be able to make my girl flip."

"Was that a problem?" William frowned as he stared at the drone. He stepped back as the blades whirred into motion and the drone rose into the air.

"Hell yeah. Do you have any idea how much force she can summon when she jumps somewhere?" Bobcat mumbled, playing with the controls.

William watched the little bladed devil. His friend was hell on wheels in a real helicopter, but there had been Band-Aid accidents in here before, "I thought she could just … you know, disappear." He asked, keeping his eyes focused on the little killer.

"She can." Bobcat maneuvered the drone into the center of the open area. "But let's just say, sometimes she likes to make an entrance. And *I* like my girl not to flip over when she does. Watch." The drone had been loaded with projectiles. As Bobcat pulled a tiny trigger on the controls, the projectiles shot out one by one. The recoil should have sent the drone tumbling, but it barely rocked as it hung in place.

William nodded and grinned, and then ducked and turned as one of the rotors came flying off, "Hey!"

Bobcat's eyes lifted, "Of course, there are other problems," he shrugged as he landed the drone. He retrieved the rotor and looked at it, "That should teach you always to have on your eye protection. Now we need to make new blades. But I've got Jean helping me with that. Some of the stuff she makes the armor out of, and…." His voice trailed away on a strangled note, his eyes not looking at the blade in his hand.

"What?" William looked behind him to see what had caught Bobcat's eye.

"Uh … hi." The woman lingering in the doorway waving her hand back and forth was tall and slender. Black hair flowed down over her shoulders, and her grey eyes were large. Her face was fine-boned, her mouth small—but smiling tentatively as her eyes took things in around the work area. "Am I interrupting anything? I'm just exploring."

"Uh, you should, um…." Bobcat swallowed.

William's smirk was tiny, so far. "Hi, I'm William. And you are?"

"Yelena." She stuck out a hand as he walked over to her.

Bobcat had the sudden, strong urge to beat his friend with a broken drone. Well, it would be broken as soon as he hit William over the head with it.

Repeatedly.

"You really should stick to the civilian portions of the ship," William was explaining. "If you came in with the last batch of civilians—"

"Oh, I thought … uh, I came up with Bethany Anne and Ecaterina and everyone." She shrugged her shoulders. "I'm sorry, we met in Romania, and she invited me up. If you've seen a big black German Shepherd, that's my dog, Bellatrix."

He nodded, "I did hear something about that." William rubbed his chin. "So you're allowed to be around here?"

Yelena's voice was polite, but pretty positive, "Oh, yeah. John said I could look around."

Bobcat groaned. If he was competing with John, he didn't have a hope in the world. Except that Jean had John and Bobcat could get John re-focused by accidentally on purpose saying something to Jean.

Hopefully, it wouldn't get John killed before the truth came out.

The woman stared at him curiously. "I'm sorry, who are you?"

"Well," he ran his hand through his hair, smiling. "Bobcat."

"Bob … cat?" She pronounced the name carefully. "Is that an American name?"

"Nah, it was my call sign and it just stuck." Bobcat wiped his sweaty palms on his shirt before shaking her hand. It was funny, he'd had all sorts of things he was planning to do today—something really important, as far as he could remember—but he couldn't think of a single one right now. "So you're, uh … you're staying on the ship?"

"Just for now. To look around. And they want to do some tests on me and Bellatrix." She hunched her shoulders. She was smiling at him.

Smiling. *At him.*

Dimly, he thought he heard William say something. He looked over at his friend, who for some reason was smirking, "Huh?"

"Lager," he pointed back behind him, "I said, are you gonna come test that lager?"

"Yeah, be right there." Bobcat could almost taste the cold beer sliding across his tongue.

Yelena's face fell. "I'll get going, then. It was nice to meet you—William, Bobcat." She gave Bobcat a smile as she said his nickname.

He stood rooted in place. He'd never been so torn. He looked at William in mute appeal, and had the distinct impression that the other man was trying not to laugh.

Beer.

She looked so sad.

But *beer*.

He heard himself say, "I mean, I could put off tasting the beer, though. Someone should give you a proper tour of the ship, after all."

There was a clatter as William dropped the drone rotor. His jaw hung open. He closed his mouth and opened it again several times, but no sound came out.

William looked around and muttered, "Where the hell is Marcus when I need a third party bet review?"

"That would be great!" Yelena was smiling again. She bit her lip. "I mean, I wouldn't want to mess up your day or anything."

"No, not at all." Bobcat held out his arm and felt a shiver as she took it smiling to her, "First, let's go see Jean...."

As they left, William walked quickly to one of the communications panels. He jabbed at the call button furiously. "Meredith! Please, get me Bethany Anne. Now. *NOW*."

It was a second before her voice came on the line. "William, what's wrong?"

William's voice came out in a rush, "Bobcat just fell for a girl."

Bethany Anne hummed for a moment before replying, "Okay...."

William searched the best way to prove what he was saying. "No, I mean, he's showing her around *instead of trying new beer.*"

Bethany Anne was silent for a long moment.

"You know what this means, right?" William was practically dancing in front of the communication panel.

"Ok, yeah, I believe you William," Bethany Anne agreed. "I owe three ounces of gold," another pause, "Dammit! That man should have tried the beer, first."

But she was laughing when she hung up the call.

"This place is wonderful." Yelena looked out the huge window of the bar, her accent making Bobcat feel tingles up and down his spine. "The best wonderful. Most wonderful? Did I say that right?" she asked as she looked back at him.

"You can say it however you want, if you keep talking in that accent." Bobcat grinned at her.

Yelena blushed. Something about this mechanic made her want to smile so hard her face ached. Her eyes had locked on him the first moment she stepped into the hangar bay.

She watched him pilot the drone, explain it to his friend. She'd noticed his hands—callused, streaked with grease. Honest hands, as her grandmother would say. And he had a way about him, like he took real pride in his work.

If it weren't for the fact that he was in space, he was just the sort of guy her parents would be crazy about for her. She could just see him fixing cars with her father, debating skis with Alec, laughing in a pub at night. This wasn't a guy who needed suits or fine wines to enjoy his life. He just wanted to do his work and laugh with his friends over a beer.

"What is it?" he asked her.

Yelena flushed bright red. She'd been staring at him, she realized. And he'd caught her. She wanted to melt through the floor. She cleared her throat and busied herself with a pretend coughing fit. "Nothing. I am sorry."

"I'll get you some water." Bobcat knew the coughing was fake, but he wanted to be able to grin to himself in private. She'd been smiling when she looked at him, like she

220

approved of him. Him! With the dirty mechanic's hands and the casual clothes. How long had it been since he'd even tried dating? All the women he'd seen years back had rolled their eyes at how he doted on his helicopters. This girl, though, she seemed to like hearing him talk about Shelly.

She listened. She asked questions.

On a sudden hunch, he pulled her a pint and turned around. She had followed him down from the viewing area. "I thought you might want a beer instead."

Her eyes lit up. "You have *beer* in here?"

He was in love. He was absolutely, positively in love. If he'd had a ring, he would have proposed on the spot. As it was, he had only the beer, and so he handed it to her reverently. "Try it."

She took a big gulp, wiping the foam from the corners of her mouth with a self-conscious laugh. Then she took another drink. And another. "This is amazing. Where did you get it?"

"Actually...." Bobcat took a seat. "I brewed it myself."

"Really?" She took another drink. "This is so good. Could you teach me?"

"To brew beer?" He grinned pretty damned wide. "Hell yeah! Want to go learn about it in the back now?"

"But we have the whole rest of the ship to see..." her voice trailed off as she looked down at the beer, and then over to the door. Down at the beer again and slowly to the door once more.

Her eyes rested back on the mug, "Ok, Let's brew some beer."

Bobcat nodded, "Good choice. Come on, I keep the

supplies through here...." Bobcat led her away, pausing only to fill two more mugs for them.

As soon as they were gone, Bethany Anne, William, and Nathan came out from the other side of the restaurant / bar.

They'd been in the bar and hid when Merideth told them the two were heading in this direction. They stared after Yelena and Bobcat incredulously.

"He found a woman who likes beer as much as he does," William admitted.

"He found a woman he likes more than beer," Bethany Anne agreed.

"If they ever have babies, they are going to be born holding steins," Nathan concluded.

Beside them, Bellatrix chuffed with laughter.

FINIS

AUTHOR NOTES - NATALIE GREY
DECEMBER 21ST, 2016

This is Michael and I'm going to write Natalie's first Author Notes. Why? Well, two reasons.

First, she is leaving for vacation with her family early in the morning and is out of touch and I didn't make sure to get one from her :-(

The second, and possibly just as telling, is that she really isn't that fond of attention. She is, in my experience so far, the first author that says that she doesn't want too much attention...and like, means that.

So, as you might guess, I'm trying to get her to open up a little. I've asked for an Author Notes from her (about five minutes ago). and we shall see if I get something. If I do, I'll add it below this so you get both of these ;-)

I met Natalie AKA (Facebook name withheld on purpose) on 20BooksTo50k. She is helping me with this book (ALL OF YOU DOG LOVER'S REJOICE - That means you too, Stephen Russell). Further, she is going to do a series of the happenings in the three years between The Kurtherian Gambit 13 (My Ride is a Bitch) and The

Kurtherian Gambit 14 (Don't Cross This Line) called The Dark Years Illuminated. These stories are going to be anchored by Stephen and Jennifer.

I'll give more information about Natalie when I'm given permission, and we shall see if I can get her to enjoy opening up about this author thing that she does so well.

Please give a warm welcome to the VERY FIRST lady Kurtherian Gambit Author!

(I received a quick Author Note from Natalie before she left last night...Here we go ;-)

AUTHOR NOTES - MICHAEL ANDERLE
DECEMBER 21ST, 2016

As always, can I say with a HUGE amount of appreciation how much it means to me that you not only read this book, but you are reading these notes as well?

This book about Bellatrix was not only a fan desired book (ok, some fans demanded the book) but also my editor Stephen Russell was bugging the shit out of me to get it done.

Like…weeks ago (as soon as he saw Bellatrix in book 14).

Now, you may not know it, but Stephen Russell previously bred dogs, and he has been a big supporter of Ashur through all of these stories. As one of my editors since book 5, he has had a lot of time to bug me. Now, he had ANOTHER dog to champion, and he was using the fans clamoring for a story to bludgeon me because of HIS desire for a story.

So, I told him to write some ideas down, and then he and I worked with Natalie to flesh out the story, and the two of them gave it life. I edited and provided commentary

225

in the beginning, and then I polished the final draft changing some things that wouldn't work in the universe.

So, due to their hard work, we have BELLATRIX, and I have to say, there were two scenes that brought tears to my eyes.

Dammit!

Merry Christmas Natalie, and to all of you as well!

Michael Anderle

CHALLENGES

PAYBACK

BY NATALIE GREY & MICHAEL ANDERLE

CHAPTER ONE

Buenos Aires, Argentina

Gabrielle took a sip of her wine and settled back in her chair with a purr of contentment, "I swear, this is the best steak I've had in years."

"It *is* what we're known for." Tabitha forced a smile and sniffed the wine tentatively.

"Drink it. You'll like it." Gabrielle lifted a glass to toast. "It's a *bonarda*—a type of wine I haven't had since Italy, *way* back in the day."

"How 'way back?'" Tabitha clinked glasses and smiled. She took a cautious gulp. "Oh, that's good."

Gabrielle watched, amused. After centuries spending time with both the richest of the rich and the starving artists of the world, she had learned an appreciation for the finer things in life—both food, and art.

And occasionally other types of hedonism.

She cleared her throat hastily.

"Way, *way* back."

Gabrielle lapsed into silence as she cut another bite of

steak. She was worried about this excursion. In many ways, Tabitha reminded her of some of the artists Gabrielle had known over the years: insanely talented with souls like bright fires. But they hadn't often been happy, those people. Sometimes a soul burned so brightly it ate a person up.

And Tabitha didn't have the hard edge Gabrielle associated with the bohemians she had known. Despite everything, Tabitha seemed to lack the air of cynicism that so often came with counterculture.

That wasn't to say she didn't *try*. From the tattoos to the piercings to the dyed hair, Tabitha went out of her way to look like someone with sharp edges. Someone you didn't want to get close to.

The thing was, when you were a few centuries old you started to get a feel for when that was an act. Tabitha was a talented person, someone whose talents had put her in the middle of a game she was really too young and naïve to play.

A game she was walking back into tonight.

And that was why Gabrielle was worried. "I've been thinking about what you told me," she said. She paused as the waiter came by and gave Tabitha's clothes and hair a nasty look. The man took one look at Gabrielle's cold eyes, however, and was gone like a shot. Gabrielle watched him go and turned back to Tabitha. "You said you wanted to make sure people were safe."

"A lot of people sheltered me over the years," Tabitha explained. "And I want to make sure that none of Anton's old friends are hurting them."

"Anton's crew is done," Gabrielle assured her.

"Anton wasn't picky about who he used," Tabitha said bluntly. She put her knife and fork down as if she were oblivious to the expensive food in front of her. "Anton and his higher-ups aren't around anymore, but he worked with a lot of people once or twice, humans who were on the wrong side of the law. The sort of people no one was going to miss. They didn't know what Anton was—most of them didn't, anyway—but they do know how to be very, very mean. All they care about is themselves."

"Wait, back up. Some of them knew what Anton was?"

"It's not... Um..." Tabitha searched for the words. "It's not always the same in the human underworld as it is in the normal world. People there are likely to believe all sorts of things. They believe in angels and demons and curses and that kinda stuff, so when they found out about Anton it wasn't like this was some big revelation. It was something they'd always believed in anyway."

Gabrielle sat back and considered this.

This was dangerous. She knew it was up to her to make sure all who were aware of the vampires were either convinced that they were wrong or otherwise taken care of.

But frankly, if they were the type of people she suspected they were, she wasn't going to spend much time trying to persuade them. She was going to bring them to justice instead.

"So you want me to hurt these people," Gabrielle said finally.

"*No!* No." Tabitha shook her head. She took a bite of steak and chewed, mouth partly open as she thought.

Gabrielle bit back a smile. Michael and Stephen would

NATALIE GREY & MICHAEL ANDERLE

be having an aneurysm right about now if they were here to witness this. Tabitha ate and drank with the focused air of someone who'd gone hungry before and viewed food mostly as fuel.

Tabitha said finally, "I want to make sure people are okay, that's all."

"Oh?" Gabrielle had long ago learned not to direct the flow of conversations by guessing at what she thought the other person might say. The longer she spent as a vampire, the less she seemed to understand how human minds worked.

"Look, I...put people in danger." Tabitha looked miserable. "I got in over my head, and other people could have suffered for it. A lot of them. My whole family, and all the people who sheltered me. I didn't want to take help, but I needed somewhere to stay. They could have been hurt because of me."

Gabrielle smiled. "When I was very young—okay, younger than I am now—I got mixed up with some revolutionaries who thought they were going to assassinate a whole bunch of government officials. I was...stupid." She shook her head. "I was very idealistic in those days, and I was trying to be very moral, very...chaste." To be honest she'd been prudish, but she didn't feel like sharing that. "Well, I fell in love with this young man who wanted to go around butchering officials and their families, and he talked about all the injustice in the world and how he would save things. I foolishly believed him."

Tabitha took a bite of her food as she listened. Gabrielle was easily one of the most beautiful, elegant people Tabitha had ever met. She was so otherworldly that she didn't even make Tabitha feel self-conscious. Trying to compete with her would be like competing with a statue or a sunset. Gabrielle was on another level.

Tabitha would never have thought that Gabrielle would do stupid things.

"Well, someone in the revolutionary group started to have second thoughts. They argued that it wasn't right to go around killing people's families, and Henri—that was his name—killed the dissenters in front of all of us.

"I should have known right then that he wasn't about to listen to reason. Luc had made very good points. He was being very respectful, but Henri always had an impulsive streak. In that moment the scales fell from my eyes and I realized I had aligned myself with a common criminal. Henri wasn't really a revolutionary. He was just a violent man who wanted to be important."

"So what did you do?" Tabitha's eyes were very round.

"I stayed," Gabrielle said bluntly. "I kept working with them for weeks after that because I wanted to keep loving Henri and I wanted to keep feeling like I was part of a group that was fighting for justice, even though I *knew* that wasn't what they were doing anymore."

"So why did you stay?" Tabitha asked.

"You tell me." Gabrielle studied her, and then looked down at her plate. "These steaks are so good I could almost have another one."

"This is nothing," Tabitha said absently. "The best food in Argentina is *choripan*."

"What's *choripan*?" Gabrielle plucked a menu from a passing waiter and scanned it. "It's not here."

"Of course it's not there. A place like *this* would never

serve it." Tabitha gestured at the four-star establishment with a wry grin. From the white-and-black clad waiters to the subtle clinking of crystal and china, the whole place was worlds away from where she'd grown up. "*Choripan* is street food. It's a sort of sandwich with sausage in it."

"And it's better than this?" Gabrielle gestured at the steak and the wine.

"Oh, yes." Tabitha sighed happily at the memory. "Sometimes when I had enough money for more than rice and beans—which wasn't very often—I'd go get a *choripan*. I never had enough money for anything really, so I felt so guilty buying it. I would wolf it down in an alley, but I remember it was just the best food ever. A *choripan* and a Coke." She grinned and shrugged.

Gabrielle smiled. "Best food ever? I'm going to need to have one of those."

"We'll get one in my old neighborhood, I promise." Tabitha wolfed down the rest of her food.

"So," Gabrielle began, "have you thought about what I asked you?"

"Wha'd'you mean?" Tabitha swallowed a large bite of steak. "What?" she asked again.

"The reasons I stayed in the revolutionary group?" Gabrielle asked her.

"I don't know." Tabitha shrugged.

"Because it's easy to keep making the same mistakes," Gabrielle told her. "It is very, very easy to see the world one way, and then even when it leads you down a bad path you don't change your behavior because you can't see the choices you actually have. I was so desperate to keep being a person who was fighting for justice, who loved this wonderful man, that I got tangled up in something that wasn't justice with a terrible man. I kept making that mistake until I could believe in myself."

"You were a vampire then, weren't you?"

"Yes, but—"

"So why didn't you realize you could leave?"

"Because I would have had to reevaluate who I was and how I believed the world worked. Believe it or not, sometimes it's easier to stay around a homicidal maniac than it is to challenge your beliefs about the world."

Gabrielle sighed. She knew what she needed to say here, but she also knew that Tabitha might not believe her.

That was always the problem with speaking the truth. People tended to be highly resistant to it.

"I am going to tell you something that may sound absurd," Gabrielle said finally. "As absurd as me telling you that this steak is better than *choripan*, for instance."

Tabitha laughed, and it was such a young sound that Gabrielle paused for a moment to drink it in.

She had to say this. Tabitha had her whole life ahead of her, so it would be better if she could live it in a good way rather than being trapped by her past.

"When you were young, you made mistakes," Gabrielle told her. "You know that. It's not new information."

Tabitha sobered at once. She nodded. "I know," she admitted bravely.

"To be fair to you, Anton was much stronger than you were, both physically and in terms of power. You were right about that. But as you said, you also made mistakes. You let them blackmail you and draw you deeper into their world."

Tabitha looked down at her lap.

"So why did you come back?"

"To protect people!" Tabitha looked up at her with tears in her eyes. "I swear it's true!"

"I know it's true," Gabrielle said with a small smile. "I don't think you're lying to me. But ask yourself why you're doing this now and you didn't do it before."

"Oh." Tabitha looked away.

She didn't know what to think of that question. When she'd been a nobody, hiding in the shadows and trying to run away from the people who practically ran her life, she'd been scared all the time. The world had felt too big for her. Now...

"They don't have control over me anymore," she said finally.

"Exactly," Gabrielle told her. "They don't. You know that in your head. But in your heart, I think maybe you still believe you're the same person—the one who made mistakes and is still vulnerable and weak. If you're going to change how you behave here, you're going to have to *believe* you're a different person now."

"But I'm *not* a different person," Tabitha said at once.

Gabrielle bit back a smile. She reminded herself that she'd expected this response. "So what's different?"

"The world. Anton is gone, because of you guys. I...just got lucky."

It was clear Tabitha could not yet understand that she was becoming a stronger person, herself. Less of a victim.

And Gabrielle couldn't convince her of that. Tabitha had to realize that for herself.

"I see. So you wanted my help." Gabrielle poured herself

another glass of wine, eyes fixed on Tabitha. "For what exactly, since you don't want me to hurt them." She paused. "Unless that meant you wanted me to kill them painlessly."

"God, no!" Tabitha looked around herself guiltily, as if someone might have overheard them. "That wasn't what I meant at all!"

"Mm-hmm." Gabrielle took a sip of her wine.

"I don't want you to solve my problems for me," Tabitha said defiantly.

"So why am I here?"

Tabitha swallowed hard. "Because…I'm afraid I can't do it on my own."

There was a silence. Tabitha looked away, so Gabrielle had the opportunity to study her. There was more sympathy in her gaze than Tabitha likely would have guessed. Gabrielle understood what it was to feel young and outmatched by the world.

Contrary to popular belief, being a vampire didn't make you feel invincible. Sometimes it made you realize just how big the world was, how easy it was for even someone so strong to be overwhelmed. Michael and his children had picked sides in World War II because they couldn't change something that big or avert it entirely.

Gabrielle hesitated, and then reached out to take Tabitha's hand. "You can't do it on your own," she said bluntly.

Tabitha's eyes widened. "If that's what you think of me—"

"That's not an insult," Gabrielle said. "People don't go it alone in this world. There's always luck and other people helping to get you where you are. If people didn't need help sometimes there would never have been a Stephen or any of the others—Michael would have done it on his own. Bethany Anne wouldn't have built TQB. The people who fight at our side for love and loyalty are a part of us. Being able to have those friendships shows who you are as a person."

Tabitha hesitated. "I just want to be able to solve my own problems."

"Sometimes you can." Gabrielle lifted a shoulder. "For this, I am guessing that you will need a bit of both. You will need some help, and you will also need to believe that you are a new person now."

Tabitha's face was pale. "I'm not sure I can do that. I want to be better and braver. I'm not sure I am, though."

"Try." Gabrielle smiled. "I'm here to help you face your past, not deal with it for you so you can run from it. Now finish your wine. I'll cry if you let that go to waste."

CHAPTER TWO

"All right, come on." Tabitha, now out of the four-star restaurant and back on the crowded streets, seemed to have returned to her normal self. She directed an impish grin at Gabrielle. "I'll show you the best spots in the city." She whistled. "Can't believe I'm back here with a—um, with you," she corrected herself hastily before she said "vampire" loudly in the middle of a crowded street.

"I think that was some personal growth," Gabrielle said with a grin. She shook her braid back over her shoulder and took in a deep breath. She loved the cities of South America. They truly *lived*, the way cities like Paris and Venice had at one time. They were a jumble of people and smells, everything wildly alight with color.

The thought of modern-day Paris, now a city of fairly clean streets and landmarks restructured for tourists, just bummed her out.

As they wound their way south Tabitha explained, "I don't want to freak you out, but we're going to Barracas."

"Different city?" Gabrielle raised an eyebrow.

"No, just a neighborhood. Um, it doesn't *look* like a great neighborhood maybe, but it's actually safe. Safer than the rich areas."

Gabrielle bit back a guffaw. She was here as the muscle, after having spent years in some of the worst neighborhoods the world had ever seen, and here was a little girl telling her not to be scared about... Hmm, she was going to guess it was nothing more than some rundown buildings and a neighborhood drunk or two.

But it was sweet that Tabitha didn't want her to be scared.

Gabrielle kept a close eye out as the buildings grew a bit dustier, their paint chipping and peeling, and the signs over the shop doors got less slick. Fruit and vegetable stands were being packed up while the sellers called out ever-lower prices. Mothers walked with children in tow, and there was the sweet smell of the evening bake coming from the *panaderias*.

In the more upscale streets Gabrielle and Tabitha had been assessed as tourists. Between Tabitha's piercings and tattoos, not very common here, and Gabrielle's expensive clothes, they must have looked like rich foreigners.

But as they walked confidently toward Barracas, Tabitha chattering in locally-accented Spanish, there was a different sort of assessment going on. Men in doorways watched the two women with a frown.

Gabrielle returned those frowns with a picture-perfect smile that would turn any man's blood to ice, and her smile grew smug when the men looked away hastily. They didn't know *what* she was, but they knew enough to be scared.

They knew they didn't want her to notice them.

Tabitha stopped dead at one of the intersections, sniffing. "*Choripan*! I smell it!" She looked down the streets, which radiated in all directions, and frowned. "Oh, that's maddening. I *swear* I could smell it a second ago." She gave Gabrielle a sad look. "Now my mouth is watering."

"You just had some of the best steak in the world and you're upset that you can't chase it with a sandwich?" Gabrielle put her hand over her heart in mock agony.

"Right, thank you for dinner!" Tabitha waved her hands as she started south again.

"Say thank you to the cow. It died for you!" Gabrielle drew upon centuries of theatrical training as she followed her. "Ungrateful child."

"You were probably an ungrateful child once."

"I was *never* an—"

"Are you sure, because I heard Stephen say—"

"This discussion is over," Gabrielle said, with great dignity.

"Uh-huh." Tabitha wore the expression of someone who knew she had won the argument, but she started looking around with a frown. "Now where would he be?"

"Who?" Gabrielle put her hands in her pockets as she strolled at Tabitha's side. She'd chosen black high-heeled boots, faded and artfully ripped jeans, and a deep red tank top for the night's activities.

She could have dressed in slightly more robust clothing and perhaps hidden some guns and knives on her, but she had no worries about her ability to defend Tabitha. And, besides, it was better if the muscle didn't look like the muscle.

Not to mention, she loved these boots.

"Howie," Tabitha explained. "He always knew everything about everyone, and he used to sit around here. I hope nothing's happened to him. He was so— Hey, Joaquin!"

She took off, and Gabrielle followed at a speed most people wouldn't be able to manage in high heels. She'd had a *lot* of practice, after all.

She found Tabitha chattering excitedly to a cagey-looking man with brown hair and black eyes. He looked up as Gabrielle approached and his face flickered through a quick assessment: the expensive clothes, the lack of weapons. A faint frown of confusion creased his face.

Gabrielle smiled at his expression. He was smart enough to realize that Gabrielle was a strange friend for an Argentine street kid, but he couldn't figure out where the danger lay.

"Gabrielle," Tabitha gestured to the man, "this is Joaquin. He let me stay on his couch a lot after I left home."

"Nice to meet you, Joaquin." Gabrielle kept her expression completely blank.

"Uh-huh." Joaquin was busy looking over his shoulder. "Look, Tabby, why are you here?"

Tabitha frowned. "I came to see people. I wanted to make sure you were all doing okay. Why, what's wrong? Is there trouble?"

"I mean…" Joaquin shrugged his shoulders. "No. No, of course not."

Tabitha frowned. Joaquin had always feared the work she did on the dark net. He told her that she was getting in over her head and she might not be prepared for the consequences.

At the time, as much as she'd thought he was being ridiculous, she had also appreciated his concern. She'd tried to stay with a lot of other friends, only to find out that they wanted things from her she wasn't prepared to give. Some friends *those* were. Joaquin had seemed like an older brother—uncool, always worrying about stuff he shouldn't, but someone who wasn't going to take advantage.

And of course, he'd been right about her getting in over her head.

That was probably what he was worried about now. He saw Gabrielle, who looked well-off, and thought that Tabitha had gotten involved in another gang like Anton's.

She hastened to reassure him, "I'm doing fine, Joaquin. You were right about some of the jobs I pulled, but I'm doing much better now. I just wanted to…see everyone, you know? Make sure they were doing all right."

Joaquin stared at her for a long moment, then swallowed and looked away. It seemed he'd come to a decision.

"Well, thanks. I'm still in touch with most people. I can tell you how they're doing. Cup of coffee?" He jerked his head at a nearby café.

"Sure!"

Gabrielle frowned as the two of them walked off together. Tabitha was practically glowing with happiness to see her old friend, but something was definitely off about the way Joaquin was behaving.

She smiled grimly a moment later. Joaquin had better

hope he was on the level. If he was planning something with Tabitha, he was going to be very sorry.

When she got to their table, she pulled up a chair and turned it around to sit on it backward, resting her arms on the back and directing a brilliant smile at Joaquin.

"So you two go way back, huh?"

"Yeah!" Tabitha smiled so happily that Gabrielle's heart ached.

She'd been that young and naïve once too. Come to think of it, she had hidden it behind fake worldliness the same way Tabitha did.

"Tabitha was a good roommate," Joaquin said, and produced a forced-looking smile. "She tried to give everyone everything she had—except those notebooks, of course. She was always scribbling in those."

"I know." Tabitha gave a secretive little smile. Her research into Anton's family had been in those notebooks, cleverly disguised with abbreviations and tons of little hearts. She knew that everyone from Joaquin to her employers had thought she was a stupid little girl.

She'd used their belief to shield herself from them.

"What ever happened to all of those?" Joaquin asked. "I thought of you the other day and went looking for them, but they were gone."

"I took them with me."

"Important stuff in there, huh?"

His tone was just a bit too casual, and his smile was strained. This man could not be throwing up more red flags if he tried, but Gabrielle knew that Tabitha hadn't seen them yet.

The poor girl was going to have a very unpleasant realization fairly soon.

"Just private." Tabitha's habitual ingenuousness about her notebooks was there in full force. She knew how much some people would have paid to know what she knew, and she didn't want Joaquin to have the first idea of what was in there. It would only be dangerous for him. "It was really just silly stuff. You didn't tell anyone about the notebooks, did you?"

She thought she saw a flicker of something in his eyes, but he laughed. "No, of course not. I mean, I *might* have told a mutual friend that you were a bit boy-crazy back in the day, always doodling lists of boyfriend names and coming up with their whole life stories..."

"Who did you tell?" Tabitha's voice was suddenly tight.

"Tabby..." Joaquin reached out to cover her hand with his. "It's all right."

"Yeah, but who did you tell?"

"Emmi came around asking about you a bit ago, and we started reminiscing. She misses you."

The words were all wrong. Tabitha frowned. Joaquin had been weird since she'd gotten here, and now he was making a big deal about the notebooks.

It could mean nothing, but if someone had figured out how much she had known...

And she'd never liked Emmi anyway. The woman liked to play at being scared so she could weasel her way out of getting really involved in Anton's gang. Tabitha could sympathize—she'd never wanted much to do with it, either —but she'd noticed that Emmi seemed to like the attention she got from Anton's underlings.

Emmi was stunning—tall, with curves in all the right places and reddish-brown hair—but that didn't mean she tolerated any competition. Even tiny little Tabitha with her piercings and her chopped-off blonde hair, trying as hard as possible not to be attractive to anyone, was too much competition for Emmi.

Emmi had made her life miserable. Why the hell did she care where Tabitha was now?

"Tabby?" Joaquin was looking at her worriedly. "What's wrong?"

"I don't know." Tabitha looked at Gabrielle for reassurance, and then back at Joaquin. "What *is* wrong? What aren't you telling me?"

Joaquin looked between her and Gabrielle and laughed awkwardly. "Everything's fine. I don't know what you mean."

"Oh, really?" Gabrielle leaned in. "So it's not, for instance, that you sold Tabby out and now you're feeling guilty?"

"*What?*" Tabitha glanced between the two of them. "He didn't..." Her voice trailed off and she looked down at her lap before looking up at Joaquin with eyes full of betrayal. "Did you?" Her voice was very small.

Gabrielle's heart ached. She hadn't meant to interfere, but it had been hard to watch Joaquin toying with Tabitha, and she knew that the younger woman had been struggling to believe the evidence that was right in front of her eyes.

Joaquin tried to laugh it off again, but finally he looked away with a sigh. His hand clenched.

"Look, did you bring the notebooks?" He looked hopefully at Tabitha's messenger bag. "If you have them here, you could just leave them and go."

Tabitha's jaw set. "What. Did. You. Do?" She ground the words out.

Gabrielle smiled proudly. Tabitha wasn't going to be frightened into selling herself out.

"I didn't mean to!" Joaquin could not seem to stop shaking his head.

"*What did you do?*" Tabitha pressed.

He had to keep her here for just a few more seconds. Joaquin swallowed and tried to come up with something to say that would keep her in that chair. They'd be here soon, and his debt would be clear.

Hell, he knew some people would pay handsomely for the tourist Tabitha had brought with her. She made the hair on the back of his neck stand on end, but she'd be their problem once they had her.

And then the tourist said sweetly, "Tell her what you did."

He hadn't meant to, but he found himself telling the truth. How had she been able to make him do that?

"I... They knew where my family was." He bent his head, clenching his fingers around the cup of coffee. "I didn't want to turn you in, Tabby, but when you were spotted earlier they sent me out to find you. They said to get those notebooks and, ah..."

"And?" Gabrielle prompted. She was trailing her nails up and down his arm, lazy as a jungle cat ready to pounce.

"And they said I had to keep you two here until they could—"

The men appeared from the shadows around them with the distinctive dull clank of body armor and weapons.

The street was suddenly empty, and no one stirred inside the café.

"Until they could surround us," Gabrielle said.

Tabitha looked at Joaquin mutely, his betrayal bringing tears to her eyes.

Gabrielle looked around at the circle of gang members, "Well, seems like things are finally going to get interesting."

CHAPTER THREE

"How could you do this?" Tabitha shook her head at Joaquin. "You could have told me to go. You could have just let me walk out of here, but—"

"*I didn't have a choice!*" Joaquin looked around himself wildly. "They know who I am. They know about my family. They said they'd do horrible things to them. I can't take the chance. And this is all because you stayed with me!" He threw the accusation at her.

"What? How did they even *find* you? Emmi didn't know who you were. No one did. I made sure no one ever followed me home at night. If they found out I stayed with you, that's on you." Tabitha took refuge in the facts.

There was a long silence, during which none of the men surrounding them spoke at all. They didn't seem to care what happened, as long as Tabitha didn't get away.

"I needed more money, so I tried to get a job," Joaquin said finally. "You'd told me some things about where you worked, so I went and found them."

Tabitha declared, "And then you had the *cojones* to turn

around and try to blame this on *me*? You knew how dangerous they were! I warned you about them!"

"I needed the money!"

"So drive a fucking cab in your spare time!" Tabitha shot back.

Gabrielle was trying to hold in her laughter. She wasn't the least bit worried about the men surrounding them. They all seemed at ease with their weapons, but she knew that most of their experience with keeping the peace had actually just been posturing, showing up to make a visible statement of their employer's strength.

And they were human—she had checked every one of them. Not one of these people was going to have the time to react once she unleashed her fury.

Since she didn't have to worry about the impending fight, she was free to find humor in Tabitha utterly rejecting Joaquin's bullshit. The man had tried to guilt her and frighten her and had told her that his predicament was her fault, and maybe Tabitha might have fallen for that if she were younger.

But she'd grown up a lot since joining the Queen Bitch's crew, even from the sidelines.

"I came to stay with you," Tabitha said quietly, "because they would have found my family otherwise and I couldn't afford for that to happen. I took measures to keep you safe. I told them my landlord was a bastard who liked to hit me when he was drunk so they'd think I hated you. I never told them where I lived."

"Tabby—"

"Don't *call* me that! I did everything in my power to make sure that no one close to me got hurt just because I'd screwed up. But you? You weren't just careless. You walked me into a trap." She could feel the tears building in her eyes again. "That was low. I can't believe you'd fucking do that."

Joaquin stared at her wretchedly. "It's your fault," he said again, sullenly. "If you hadn't gotten mixed up in this in the first place I wouldn't have either."

"Yeah, keep telling yourself that."

"All right." The leader of the group surrounding them had apparently heard enough. "Let's get moving. On your feet."

Gabrielle leaned forward slightly, raising her eyebrows at Tabitha.

"I could get us out of this." Her voice was smooth and low. It wasn't the sort of sentiment to make the guards reach for their guns, but the offer was there. She was only too eager to start kicking some ass.

Tabitha looked down at her hands.

She could take Gabrielle's offer. She could tell herself that it was useless to try going it alone, but...

She didn't want anyone to save her. She wanted to look whoever was doing this in the eye and figure out what they were up to. She didn't want to be the scared little girl anymore, the one who kept getting in over her head and telling herself there was no way out.

"No, let's go." She shook her head and stood up, avoiding Gabrielle's eyes.

"Good choice," the leader said sarcastically. "Come on, Red, you'd better follow your friend's example."

He'd been eyeing the way that red tank top clung to Gabrielle's form, and he had some hopes of getting to see what was under it later. Thiago, their employer, was a generous man with people who did good work for him.

But as the woman stood, she gave him a look so cold he felt his cock shrivel.

Maybe he didn't want to get tangled up with this one.

They moved through the streets in silence. People closed their doors or turned their faces away. Everyone made very sure not to see the men with the guns. The implication was clear. When the police showed up, everyone would say they'd seen nothing.

The gang's rise to power must have been recent, Gabrielle thought. In neighborhoods riddled by violence the people in the streets had a wary look. Most of the men carried weapons, and there were always signs of strife: missing doors, broken windows, chips of paint where bullets had hit houses.

This place, however, looked like it was simply a slightly poorer-than-average neighborhood. The streets were clean, there were curtains in the windows, and the children didn't look scared. Even when the gang had shown up, their parents had had to haul them inside.

If the gang hadn't gotten a toehold yet, it was going to be easier to boot them out.

Gabrielle shook her head at her own foolishness. She didn't know any of these people, and there were bigger fish to fry than one minor gang in one neighborhood in one city. She knew from experience that you couldn't fight every battle.

But when she saw places like this, places that reminded her of the kindly old bakers' wives slipping her pastries and the down-on-their-luck artists she had known over the years, she wanted to save them.

And although she knew she couldn't save Tabitha from her own choices, she wanted to save her, too.

Tabitha kept her mind resolutely blank as they walked.

The truth was, she wanted to cry her eyes out at Joaquin's choice. When she had left home, it had been a long string of one bastard after another trying to back her into corners, telling her how grateful she should be for a roof over her head.

Joaquin had sheltered her, worried when she didn't come home for a few days, always tried to make sure she ate enough.

Why did it have to be *him* who had sold her out? Emmi she could have dealt with just fine—she'd never liked that bitch. But Joaquin?

Tabitha's mother had always told her that God made sure the wicked received their punishment. Tabitha had been of the opinion that the punishments never seemed to come quickly enough.

And it didn't help to think that Joaquin might pay for what he'd done someday. It didn't take away the fact that he'd done it, and it would never take away Tabitha's pain.

Maybe that was why she hadn't wanted Gabrielle to let loose on these guys.

What would have been the point? No matter what Gabrielle had done, Tabitha was still going to be the girl who trusted the wrong people. Who had to be bailed out. That wasn't ever going to stop.

They stopped in the shadow of an apartment building and one of the men rapped on the door. It opened from the

NATALIE GREY & MICHAEL ANDERLE

inside, and he motioned to the two women to enter. "We're here. Don't get any funny ideas. We were told to bring you in alive...if we could."

It was an obvious bluff, but Gabrielle wasn't planning to call him on it just yet. She swept ahead of him into the darkness and had to fight every instinct not to lash out as hands grabbed her and ran over her body searching for weapons. She was shoved down a dark hallway, a tactic more effective for disorienting humans than vampires, and watched as the same search was performed on Tabitha. Tabitha's messenger bag was ripped off her shoulder and given a cursory search, and Gabrielle caught sight of notebooks.

Oh, shit. *Had* Tabitha brought the notebooks? The information in those was far too important to be floating around.

"Tabitha." The voice that spoke out of the darkness was genial.

A light clicked on, briefly blinding her, and Tabitha squinted at the man who had greeted her. She knew that voice...

"Santino."

Shit. She wasn't sure who she'd expected, but it hadn't been him.

Santino was the very definition of a jumped-up thief. The man had grown up in one of the worst neighborhoods and had stolen for the gangs since he was a small child. He was the sort of person who'd never have amounted to anything if his sister hadn't been sleeping with the gang leader.

But because she had, Santino had been *family*. And that

meant he got put in charge of things. He got to oversee jobs and take a higher cut. He got to wear suits like the one he was wearing now, with expensive cufflinks. He got booze and women whenever he wanted.

You're just a guy who stole cigarettes, Tabitha thought as she stared him down.

But she was screwed, and she knew it.

Because she didn't know Santino from her time in Anton's group. No, she knew Santino from her home neighborhood, Abasto. Santino's gang was pulling jobs in the worse neighborhoods by then—and sometimes the rich ones—but a lot of them were from Abasto so Tabitha had known their families.

And they knew hers.

"It's been such a long time," Santino said, embracing her. "Little Tabitha. No one thought you'd grow up to be a *hacker,* and you were one of the best, weren't you?"

"Not really." She didn't want him to keep talking about this. It was, in fact, the last thing she wanted. *I'm nobody. Nobody important, and I can't do anything for you.*

"Oh, don't be so modest." Santino looped his arm around Tabitha's shoulders and drew her away, after one last lascivious glance at Gabrielle. "You were a *star* in our world, you know."

Tabitha said nothing. The hallway sloped down toward the basement, and she found that she was fighting the urge to scream.

They wanted her to, though.

So she wouldn't. She told herself that if they wanted her to be scared, she would refuse to be. If they wanted her to feel trapped, she would remember that she was—

God, she was the same person she'd always been. Despite her resolve, she wanted to cry. She wanted to scream at them with every expletive she'd ever learned—her months with Bethany Anne's team had been *very* enlightening on that front—and tell them to go to hell and leave her alone. But she knew what she was. She was one of the people who didn't call the shots.

She had promised Gabrielle that she would try to change, but she didn't see how that would help.

The hallway led to a double door that opened into a massive room. Water pipes ran along the ceiling and the grimy floor the group walked over held puddles.

There were people everywhere. Women in tiny dresses turned to watch, their eyes skipping over Tabitha and going straight to Gabrielle. The men, some in jeans and some in suits, mostly did the same, although a few had the good sense to wonder why their boss seemed so invested in a tiny chick with piercings and dyed hair.

Tabitha, trying to ignore the stares, looked toward the end of the room, where Santino was leading her.

When she stopped in her tracks she heard Santino's low laugh.

"You remember Thiago, my dear."

Thiago. The man sat behind a large desk as if he were Anton himself and not just another jumped-up criminal. His blond hair was parted neatly, and his suit had been expertly tailored. He rested his elbows on the arms of his chair and stared at Tabitha over his steepled fingers.

"I don't remember Thiago," Gabrielle said innocently. "Who's he?"

Tabitha gave her a panicked look, but Santino only smiled.

"I have no doubt that you'll become very well acquainted with Thiago," he told Gabrielle. "He held this little group together after Anton disappeared."

Gabrielle looked at Thiago with renewed interest. She would not have picked him out as Anton's ally—for one thing, he was human—but Tabitha's fear made it plain that he had in fact been involved in the organization somehow.

"Tabitha," Thiago called to her with a smile. "How lovely to see you. You look just like I remember. And what have you brought me?" He looked over as an underling handed him Tabitha's bag, and slid the notebooks out of it with a reverent look. "Your research?"

At his shoulder, Emmi gave a smug smile. "I told you she wouldn't have destroyed them. Little Tabitha was always so proud of everything she knew."

Tabitha swallowed.

"I see you're thinking of leaving." Thiago's voice sounded regretful. "And I really can't allow that." He raised his voice. "Matteo, Santino. See to...securing Tabitha's family. The rest of you are dismissed. And you, Tabitha... You can come here. You really must introduce me to your charming friend."

CHAPTER FOUR

"So," Thiago said, as Tabitha and Gabrielle were brought forward by the guards. "Who is this charming woman?"

Tabitha looked away. She had learned how to be quiet while the people around her played this game—everyone pretending that they weren't posturing and threatening— but she had never learned to play it herself. She hated saying words that were the opposite of what she meant.

"Oh, come now. I am an eminently reasonable man." Thiago smiled.

The smile made the hair on the back of Tabitha's neck stand up, and from the look on Gabrielle's face she wasn't impressed, either.

"I just want you to do one little thing for me," Thiago explained. "*Very* easy, really—for you, anyway. I need you to hack into the Central Bank and get me a little something."

Gabrielle watched him, trying to make sure her face showed no expression.

Tabitha had to decide what happened next. She had

NATALIE GREY & MICHAEL ANDERLE

spent years being exploited under Anton's thumb. True, she had been young and naïve, and she was vulnerable to people of Anton's persuasion. The question was whether now, when she had a crew to back her up and the ability to free herself, would she be the same.

She knew the importance of freeing oneself from one's problems. The story she had told Tabitha had been as much a reminder to herself as it was to the younger woman.

—

It had been Stephen who had found Gabrielle in the burnt-out wreck of the rebellion's safe house all those years ago. She'd been sitting in the corner, arms wrapped around her knees, staring at Henri's charred body.

I sent you a message weeks ago, Gabrielle told him.

I know. Stephen stared down at the body. How did he die?

I killed him, if you must know.

Oh? Why? Stephen's handsome face had held a small smile. He knew, but he wanted her to say it.

She could have said anything. She could have mentioned the look on his face when he killed, or the way he pressed the younger women to find their way into government officials' beds to get information, even when the young women didn't want to. She could have said that Henri had gone crazy, and he didn't care about anyone else as long as he got to feel important.

All she said was, He had to die, and I had to be the one who killed him.

Stephen had stared at her for a long moment. And that's why I didn't come when you sent the first message, he said finally. You had to free yourself. You're more now than you were before, Gabrielle. It's easy to get caught up with the wrong people when you're trying to do the right thing—we all know that. Michael has seen atrocities committed in the name of causes he fought for, and so have I. So have all of us, but we're not helpless. We take care of those people. Now that you're one of us, you have to do the same.

There had been more—quiet murmurs shared over a pitcher of wine in some terrible bar until Stephen's latest mistress had shown up and tried to stab him over his alleged misdeeds with the latest ingénue at the opera—but it was that moment Gabrielle remembered: staring at Henri's body and hearing Stephen tell her that she had to be the master of her own fate.

—

Thiago had tipped Tabitha's face up, two fingers below her chin.

"Come on, now, sweetheart," he cajoled. "It would be so *easy* for you. No one is as good as you are."

Emmi, who was standing behind his chair, crossed her arms, annoyed by the attention being paid to another woman—even threats.

Tabitha made her eyes as wide as she could. "I'm just scared. They're getting better and better at finding people, and what if they find out it was me? They might hurt my family."

Gabrielle tried to refrain from sighing. Tabitha was playing up her innocence and youth. Hopefully it was the start of some con, but at this point Gabrielle didn't have much faith in that.

"I'll keep your family safe," Thiago assured her. "I promise. My men are looking after them right now, aren't they?"

Tabitha looked down at the floor. If she did this job for him maybe she could find a way to set him up, and given that time she could figure out a way to rescue her family and—

And that was exactly how she'd gotten into this mess in the first place.

She looked at Gabrielle. "Okay, do it."

Gabrielle's face split into a huge grin. "*Really?*"

"Yeah." Tabitha could feel fury beating in her suddenly. "You know what? Fuck this. Fuck all of this."

"I agree," Gabrielle said delightedly. She smiled at Thiago. "You really are a total idiot, you know. A little two-bit criminal. You think you're Anton's successor? I can pretty much guarantee you he would have used you as cannon fodder without hesitation if he needed some. Anyone who meant anything to him got taken out with him by my people."

Thiago opened his mouth to tell the guards to shoot, but...

He never got the chance.

Gabrielle turned smoothly to slam her fist into the head of the nearest guard. He was wearing a helmet, but that did next to nothing to protect him at the speed she was moving. His head snapped sideways and he went down. He never saw the red eyes, the claws, or the teeth for one simple reason: he was dead before he hit the ground.

Thiago yanked Tabitha toward him and pulled an old ornamental pistol out from under his coat.

"You brought a narc?" His face was white with fury. "You thought you'd bring a narc in here? You're going to pay for that, little bitch."

But Thiago had always been better at posturing than acting. Tabitha's fist connected squarely with his nose and his shot went wild, taking one of the guards in the shoulder.

The man's scream and the roar of the pistol distracted the other guards, which only made Gabrielle's job easier. She laughed, taking advantage of the changed timbre of her voice. A vampire's voice in hunting form tended to terrify unwary humans.

"You lot are no fun."

She knocked two of the guards' heads together and dropped the bodies to the floor after quickly slashing their throats with her claws.

Tabitha looked down at Thiago, who was now lying on the floor with his hands over his face. His nose was fountaining blood all over his expensive suit, but all she could do was laugh. She had always known on some level that Thiago pretended to be more dangerous and important than he was, but it had never been quite so obvious to her before.

He was pathetic.

"You think you're going to stand there and laugh at me, bitch?" He pushed himself up off the floor, and there was murder in his eyes. "I'll end you right here, right now."

He rushed her, and Tabitha did something she'd watched the Bitches do in training once or twice: she popped her leg up, planted her foot right in the center of his chest, and *pushed*.

She wasn't quite expecting the impact so she gave a little cry, but it turned out there was a good reason for using that technique—it worked wonders. Thiago went flying back against the desk with a shout.

"*FINISH IT!*" Gabrielle yelled. "Don't pause, just finish it!"

"I don't know how!" Tabitha yelled back.

"Find a way!"

Tabitha muttered, "Oh, right, that helps."

But as Thiago gathered his strength to rush her again, she felt herself react. She couldn't turn and run, and she couldn't duck and wait for him to focus on someone else. She had to act, here and now. She had to do something for herself.

She punched him again and this time she punched slightly lower, putting every ounce of her fury into her tiny fist.

Thiago's scream was cut off abruptly and he sank to his knees with a wheeze, clutching his crushed throat. His face was incredulous as the light died in his eyes.

Tabitha stared at his body for a moment, then turned around and threw up on the floor.

Gabrielle decided there would be time to comfort the woman later. Right now there was the small issue of four more armed guards. One of them took aim at something near the wall and shot, and there was another scream as Emmi—running for her life to escape the carnage—slid to the floor, leaving a smear of blood on the wall.

"All right." Gabrielle wrenched the gun out of his hand and dragged him close to her by the throat. "I'm not going to say I liked her very much, but that was pretty fucking low of you. And since you like this gun so much, why don't you keep it?"

She embedded it in the front of his skull and let his body drop to the floor.

"So which one of you stupid bastards wants to be next?"

None of the men answered. Instead, all three turned and ran.

She *loved* it when they ran. Gabrielle took two steps and launched herself into the air, coming down on the middle one's back while his comrades left him to die.

"How does that feel?" she asked him when he realized they weren't coming to his aid. "Are you thinking maybe you should have made better friends? Because you should have."

"Please don't hurt me. I'm just—"

"Someone who hurts whoever he's told to?" She snapped his neck without waiting for an answer. "God, I hate cowards. If you don't have the strength to own your actions you shouldn't carry weapons. *You two, stop right there.*"

The two last guards heard her, but neither one of them stopped.

They both died by their comrade's gun, and Gabrielle grimaced as she dropped it to the floor. She was used to a higher quality of weapon these days.

The door burst open and Santino stood in the entry, gun drawn and face pale as he saw what remained of the room. He tried to leave again, but Gabrielle grabbed him and dragged him back into the room.

"Tell me all about the guys watching Tabitha's family and I'll let you go."

"I'll tell you everything!" He held his hands up pleadingly. "Everything!"

"Okay. You can start anytime."

Tabitha snorted.

"There are five guys on the block and two guys on the opposite side of the street on the roof." Santino was shaking. "I'll call them off if you want! I'll do anything! Just let me live!"

"He's not a very brave man, is he?" Gabrielle tilted her head to the side.

"No," Tabitha agreed, "but he didn't have to do anything to get where he is. He just piggybacked on other people's hard work."

"A lot of crime bosses do," Gabrielle informed her. She glared at Santino. "Anything else?"

"That's all, I promise." He held out his hands. "I could work for you."

"No," Gabrielle said simply. "You see, I don't think I can trust you alive."

"*What*? You said that you would let me live if I told you!"

"And you all told Tabitha that her family would be let go as soon as she was done with this job." Gabrielle's face was like stone. "A lie for a lie, Santino."

There was a gunshot and Santino lay still.

Tabitha stared down at the body while trying to remember how to breathe.

"Are you okay?" Gabrielle asked her. "That was the first person you ever killed, wasn't it?"

"Yeah." Tabitha hunched her shoulders. "And...I'm not sure if I'm okay. Can I just not be sure for a while?"

"Yeah." Gabrielle looped an arm around her shoulders and pulled her close. "Yeah, that's okay. Should we go get those fuckers outside your family's house."

"*Yes*," Tabitha said emphatically.

"Wait, don't you need the notebooks?" Gabrielle looked over her shoulder.

"Nope." Tabitha started laughing. "Those are fake. They *look* a lot like the ones I used to have, but they're not. And anyone who tries to use them to track Michael down is going to find themselves following a *lot* of dead ends, and possibly ending up with a few felony convictions in Kansas."

"Kansas?" Gabrielle gave her a look. "Okay, first things first… Let's go kick some ass. But I'm going to need to hear more about these fake notebooks."

"Sure!" Tabitha grinned. "I'll tell you over a *choripan*."

CHAPTER FIVE

Ciprian Alvarez was not having a good night.

First off, he'd pulled the late shift. He *hated* the late shift. In most jobs the late shift was dead and you could play cards, but not when you worked for Thiago. Night was when Thiago did *everything*, because he liked to be like Anton.

Ciprian had only met Anton once—which was to say, he'd been in the same room once—and he didn't see what all the fuss was about. Anton was dead now anyway, so how scary could he have been?

That still left him with the late shift. Not only that, his girlfriend Serafina was off at a club with another man. Videl *claimed* not to be interested, but Ciprian was sure that the man was just waiting for him to turn his back before he made a move on Serafina.

And so far it had been a slow night. That hadn't improved his mood at all.

They didn't even need him here.

Sure, there had been some excitement when Orlan's

group had brought in some tiny tattooed chick and a tourist, but the police weren't going to trace the tourist here until later this week—if they did at all.

So they were back to square one, bored and resentful.

Renaldo, his shift-mate, spoke from the darkness. "Ciprian?"

"Huh?" He didn't feel like saying anything more.

"Did you hear that?"

"What?"

"Two gunshots, almost at the same time. I thought I heard one or two earlier, but I wasn't sure. I'm sure about these two."

Ciprian looked at his colleague with a withering expression. There were *always* gunshots nearby. There was always some gang trying to prove itself by encroaching on Anton's turf. Most people in the city didn't know Anton was gone yet. Most of them, in fact, hadn't known who Anton *was*, just not to mess with his deputies, but recent rumors were leading other gangs to think theirs was weak.

Thiago wasn't helping. The man *was* weak.

And then Ciprian heard another gunshot, and he understood why Renaldo was worried.

The gunshots were coming from inside the building.

The two men looked at one another anxiously. There were two options. One was that someone had attacked Thiago and the other was that Thiago was in a bad enough mood that he'd just shot three, or possibly *five*, of his people.

If it was the second one, it might make sense to just leave. When Thiago got in one of these moods no one was safe.

And then they heard the yelling and the shooting in the hallway just inside.

The two men barely even had time to exchange a look before the door flew off its hinges and clattered into the street a few yards away.

A woman in a red tank top, faded jeans, and black boots emerged. Her hair was the same dark red as the tourist who had gone in, but her face...

"*Madre de dios,*" Renaldo moaned.

He died with claws through his neck, and the woman let him slide off those claws onto the ground.

"Not. Even. Close," she informed him.

She looked at Ciprian and he fell to his knees. To his horror, when he opened his mouth to plead for forgiveness his mind flashed faces before his eyes. Some had died on Anton's orders, some had died on Thiago's—and some, Ciprian had just watched die, never intervening.

"You know you don't deserve mercy," the woman told him. "Just as there is no second chance for the lives you took, so there will be no second chance for you."

Ciprian's life ended before he'd even had time to accept that he would die.

"May I ask... What will you do if you see Joaquin again?" Gabrielle and Tabitha were making their way through the streets toward Tabitha's house.

Tabitha looked at her in surprise, "I hadn't thought of that. He didn't come with us to Thiago's hideout, did he?"

There was a long silence.

NATALIE GREY & MICHAEL ANDERLE

"If I let him go, would you be disappointed in me?" Tabitha asked finally. Her voice was very small.

"It's your choice," Gabrielle told her.

"That doesn't answer the question."

Gabrielle paused in the shadow of a building. Children were playing nearby, although they were keeping a wary eye on the two unfamiliar women.

"In a way that *is* your answer," Gabrielle said finally. "Whether Joaquin lives or dies is your choice." Of course if he actually tried to kill Tabitha, Gabrielle wasn't going to pull her punches, but she wasn't going to tell Tabitha that.

"What do you think Michael would say?" Tabitha asked. Her tone was wistful.

"That your sense of honor has to be yours and yours alone," Gabrielle said firmly. "Do you want to be merciful to Joaquin?"

"No!" Tabitha said instantly. Her eyes widened at her own admission. "Wow, I'm a vengeful bitch, aren't I?"

Gabrielle laughed. She started walking again and grinned down at Tabitha. "It's one of the things I like about you."

Tabitha relaxed slightly.

She remembered when she'd first awakened in captivity after the bank job. Her colorful language, tattoos, and piercings had seemed to make people think that her outward appearance was a direct indication of how courageous she was.

And when she was out of Anton's sight, it almost *had* been. Tabitha liked joking with people, putting them off-balance and sharing a laugh with them. Without the constant fear of someone finding her attractive or wanting

274

her to get ever-deeper into risky and immoral schemes, she had found herself enjoying the person she had pretended to be for so long. She loved the tattoos she'd gotten and she *liked* spiking her hair up sometimes—and frankly, Michael's expression when she did that was really the icing on the cake.

Coming back here had brought her fear roaring back, though.

But she was changing. Standing up to Thiago had taught her that.

And she wasn't about to let anyone hurt her family.

The snipers, secure in the incorrect assumption that they would hear anyone coming onto the roof, died within seconds of one another. Gabrielle rolled their bodies away as Tabitha peered through the rifle scope at the street below.

"I only see four of the guys," she told Gabrielle.

"The fifth is in the shadows just around the corner on the left." Gabrielle pointed at him.

"It must be nice to be able to see that well," Tabitha said disgustedly.

"It is," Gabrielle agreed sweetly. She gestured at the street. "What do you want me to do?"

Tabitha had already thought about this, "I want to make sure no one in the house hears. Can you do that?"

"Sure, but why?" Gabrielle sat back, crossing one ankle over the other as she frowned at Tabitha.

Tabitha twisted her hands. "I'm...not sure I want my

family to know I'm here, and I'm *definitely* sure I don't want them to know they had assassins waiting for them outside," she added hastily.

"Wait, back up… I thought you came here to check on people?" Gabrielle's frown deepened.

"Yeah, and the first person I saw sold me out!"

"Your parents aren't going to do that, right?"

"No, they aren't. They wouldn't!" Tabitha shook her head. "But Joaquin was a wakeup call. I thought I'd come back and tell people I was all right and they'd be glad, you know? I thought it would ease their minds to know I wasn't dead, but they have whole lives here, and maybe they're angry at me, and maybe they don't really want to see me."

"But you wanted to know if they were all right," Gabrielle protested.

"I can do that without seeing them," Tabitha told her. "Santino and Thiago are dead. The human side of Anton's gang is just going to fade away now; they only had it because he built it anyway. My family will be safe." She looked down at her hands. "I think I'll just leave them a message that I'm alive. That way they don't have to see me if they don't want to. After all, I *did* just disappear on them. I bet they're angry, and they have every right to be."

Gabrielle's heart ached for the younger woman, and she tried desperately to act as carefree and nonchalant as she did most of the time.

"Okay," she said. She stood up and helped Tabitha to her feet. "Your wish is my command. Five very quiet ass-kickings coming up."

"Thanks."

Tabitha followed her down the fire escape and dropped from the last level to the ground. She looked up to see Gabrielle's expression of surprise.

"I lived on people's couches," she explained. "And sometimes... Let's just say they didn't know I was there. I'd sneak in during the day when people were at work. I got good at climbing up and down fire escapes."

"While eating... What are those sandwiches?"

"*Choripan*. And that would have been difficult." Tabitha grinned as Gabrielle dropped lightly down beside her. "Okay, let's do this."

The guard around the corner from the others was the first to meet his maker. He was just lighting a cigarette when Gabrielle sauntered up to him out of the dark.

"So." She plucked the cigarette out of his fingers and took a drag. "Working tonight?"

"Yeah." The man stared, transfixed, at the red lips around the cigarette.

Gabrielle took one last puff and dropped the cigarette on the ground, grinding it out with her boot. "I swear, no one makes good cigarettes these days."

"Huh?" The guy just looked at her.

"So what are you doing for work tonight, hmm?" She trailed her fingers down the side of his face. "Keeping a family hostage?"

"How did you—" He stammered the words out, suddenly worried. A woman this pretty—and unarmed— should be afraid of him if she knew what he was doing.

"I know a lot of things," Gabrielle told him. "I know you work for two lowlifes named Thiago and Santino. And I know they're dead now."

NATALIE GREY & MICHAEL ANDERLE

"What? W-why?"

Gabrielle snapped his neck. "Because they do things like this," she told his body. She stepped over him and peered around the corner.

Two of the guards had gone on their patrol around the block, which left only two across the street from Tabitha's house. She'd take those two first so they didn't notice that the patrol didn't come back, and then take out the patrol when they came around the corner.

The next two to die lurked in the shadows, watching the door. They looked left to one corner, then right to the other, panning their eyes along the building's front.

They were trying to be diligent, but really, they were so predictable that their diligence was next to useless.

Gabrielle slipped across the street while they were looking to the right, and was between them before they had much of a chance to react.

"Hello, boys." Her voice was a low purr, a reminder of the days when she had indulged in every kind of pleasure she could find. "Who's up for some fun?"

The men looked at one another and then stared at her. She could see the mental calculations going on. Did they want to risk Santino's ire by leaving? Maybe, if their night was going to be good enough.

"Uh, what kind of fun were you thinking of?" one of them finally asked. He was trying to sound nonchalant, but she could see the pulse jumping in his throat.

"Well..." Gabrielle drew the word out, rolling it in her mouth. "I was thinking you two could start running in opposite directions, and I'll see if I can kill you both before you make it to the ends of the block."

Both men froze.

"And lest you think I can't do it," Gabrielle said sweetly, letting her eyes go red and her teeth grow, "you should know that Thiago, Santino, your two snipers, and the guy who snuck off for a cigarette are already dead."

One of them drew in a breath to scream.

"Ah, ah, ah." Gabrielle punched through his bulletproof vest and pulled his heart out. "No screaming. That's against the rules." She smiled at the other man. "I guess it's just you and me then."

His gun clattered to the ground and he took off for the end of the block like a man possessed.

He made it barely three yards, and Gabrielle disappeared into the night to find the two members of the patrol.

Tabitha emerged from the shadows to stare at the two bodies. These men would have killed her family without hesitation, she knew. It was strange, just how much she hated them for that. If Santino had ordered it, they would have gone into the house and killed everyone there for no reason at all.

She didn't like it, but she was glad he was dead.

And then before she had the chance to move, the door opened and light flooded into the street.

"*Tabitha?*" her mother whispered.

CHAPTER SIX

Tabitha froze. She turned her head away, trying to think—but her mind was a muddle. Did she want to go? To stay?

And then her mother was there, tears in her eyes, and wrapped Tabitha in a hug. "You're alive," she whispered.

"How did you even recognize me?" Tabitha whispered. "With the hair and the—"

"You're my daughter," her mother said firmly. "I can recognize my daughter even when she has bits of metal through her face. Why you had to do a nose ring I'm not quite certain, but it does suit you in a way. I'm sure you'll find a man who..." She practically dragged Tabitha through the open door, chattering all the while.

"*Tabitha?*" Her younger sister Selise jumped out of her chair at the kitchen table and ran to hug her. "Dad, it's Tabitha!"

Tabitha swayed. Everything hit her at once: the smell of her mother's cooking, the orange-scented soap she always used on the dishes, the way the wooden tables and chairs gave off their familiar oak-y smell. There was a new dog at the edge of the kitchen, wagging a fluffy tail cautiously as its humans laughed and cried over this strange newcomer.

From the street, Gabrielle watched as Tabitha's father came to enfold her in a hug as well. She smiled. She had hoped Tabitha would speak to her parents, and she was glad that there was none of the anger or resentment that Tabitha had been afraid of.

Tabitha, meanwhile, caught a glimpse of Gabrielle in the shadows as her mother shut the door. There was time to see Gabrielle nod. She was standing guard, and would wait.

How many hours passed in that kitchen Tabitha was not sure. She was careful to give an edited version of recent events, but knew that her parents would be able to connect the dots on some things. After all, they had lived in Buenos Aires for years. They knew what could happen when someone got caught up in the gangs.

She expected them to be angry at her for being so stupid as to get caught, but her parents, it seemed, were proud of her in their own way.

"I have missed you, my dearest love," her mother said with tears streaming down her face. "We would have kept you safe. We would have helped you—but how could I be mad that my daughter would do such a selfless thing to help her family?"

Tabitha, who knew that her mother could not have called in anyone strong enough to have taken Anton on, just smiled and clasped her mother's hands.

"Can you stay now?" her father asked quietly. He was not a man who cried, but once or twice in this conversation she had seen a suspicious sheen in his eyes.

"I can't," Tabitha explained. "I mean, I *could*. I'm not being hunted anymore, but the organization I'm with now —they are trying to keep those types of people from hurting anyone else. They work to keep people safe, and I want to keep working with them. I'll be around more, so I can come visit. And I can email and call! I just won't always be here."

"That will set your mother's heart at ease," her father said, "although you could also set it at ease by not doing ridiculous things with your hair."

"*Dad!*"

Her mother smiled to hear the two of them bickering, and got up to go to the door.

"Where are you going, Mom?" Tabitha asked her.

"Well, there were two men sleeping in the street near you, and I think I should try to hurry them along in case the police come through."

"Oh! Uh, you probably don't need to do that." Tabitha winced, hoping against hope that her mother wouldn't realize what she'd seen was two dead assassins. "You know, Mom, you really don't need to—"

But the street was empty when her mother opened the door. Apparently Gabrielle had been busy getting things taken care of.

Tabitha sagged against the door frame in relief. "Phew."

"Hmm?" Her mother looked at her.

"Nothing. I, uh, have to go. Selise needs to finish her homework, and I'll be home again soon, I promise." Tabitha wrote down a new email address. "I don't have a phone right now, but I'll get one so I can call you."

"Please do." Her mother kissed her on the cheek and

enfolded her in another hug. "I never lost hope, but part of me always feared the worst. To know you are alive and safe—it's a miracle. I can hardly believe it. Those who helped you escape, they are heaven-sent. I will pray for them."

Tabitha thought about Michael's sensibilities and smiled. "I think they'd like that."

She left her family waving at her from the open doorway and headed into the streets with her hands in her pockets. Her heart was full.

A shadow appeared at her side with the distinctive click of heels on pavement, but Gabrielle didn't speak. She let Tabitha walk in silence. It was clear to her that Tabitha was happier now, and that she had done what she needed to do. She'd not only made sure her family was safe, but was the one who had taken action to ensure it.

"Thanks," Tabitha said finally. "I know this wasn't exactly a fun girls' night out with bad jokes and drinks and all that."

"Believe it or not, I quite enjoyed myself," Gabrielle said cheerfully. "I'm glad you were willing to accept help. Choices you have to make on your own, but as for what you do, you can always call on your allies."

"D'you think..." Tabitha swallowed, and considered. "Do you think that someday maybe I could help someone else like you helped me?"

Gabrielle answered without hesitation, "I do. I really do."

"I'd like that," Tabitha confided.

But she stopped dead the next second, the smile fading from her face.

Joaquin stood in the road in front of them. He was unarmed, and his expression was miserable.

"I heard," he said finally.

Tabitha crossed her arms and said nothing.

"That Santino and Thiago are dead," Joaquin clarified. "It can only have been you two, so I thought I'd make it easy for you to find me."

Tabitha still said nothing.

"You can kill me," Joaquin told her. "I won't make a fuss. Just... If I can bargain for anything with you, please don't hurt my family. Let my death be the end of it."

Something in Tabitha snapped.

"You think I want to harm your family?" she demanded. "You think I'd take my anger at you out on defenseless and innocent people?"

"I hurt you. I sold you out." Joaquin shook his head. "Your family could have gotten hurt—I saw the guards there."

"So maybe that means I know how awful that is, not that I would ever do it!" Tabitha shot back. "You know what sucks about all this? About seeing you again? You're a coward now, and you're stupid—even stupider than I was. I was, what...thirteen? Fourteen? Well, what's *your* excuse? Even *I* didn't let my family get caught up in my shit."

"I don't have any excuse." He met her eyes. "Even though I knew it was stupid, I told myself I had no choice. I told myself the city was big enough that I could disappear and not have them know where I'd gone once I'd made enough money, but I was wrong."

Tabitha stared him down.

Still at her side, Gabrielle watched patiently. Killing

285

Joaquin would hardly be difficult. She could be at his throat before he even had a chance to scream, but she found that she had no idea what Tabitha would do now.

Tabitha had admitted to wanting Joaquin dead, but it was one thing to want that when you were powerless, and another to have that power in your hands.

Joaquin sighed, and his shoulders slumped. "I did the wrong thing. I know that."

"Oh, for the love of… I'm not going to kill you, okay?" Tabitha shook her head angrily. "I don't just go around killing people because they made a couple bad choices. Those guards are dead because they stood by and watched innocent people get killed—or killed those people themselves. Santino and Thiago are dead because they didn't care who they used or how they used them as long as they got whatever they wanted. You… You're just stupid."

"You're not going to kill me?"

"No. For one thing, I like that you had the balls to argue for your family." Tabitha gave a surly shrug and blew out her breath. "For another, someone gave me a second chance not too long ago."

"I-I can't… Thank you."

"Don't thank me just yet." Tabitha gave him a look. "Here's the deal, okay? I'm going to let you walk away tonight, and you're going to go home and say something nice to your family. And if you ever, *ever* try to screw someone over again 'because you needed the money,' I will make sure that what happens to your dick is a warning to every other man on the planet. No, you know what? Let's throw everything in there. I want it to be a warning to *everyone.*"

Gabrielle stifled her laughter with her hand.

"And I *will* know," Tabitha said, pointing a finger at him. "You might think I won't, but I will. Remember that. Oh, and one other thing."

"Yes?" Joaquin's face was grayish now.

"Get the hell out of here, I don't want to see you ever again."

Gabrielle pretended to shade her eyes as she watched him practically run down the street. "Wow, look at him go."

"Uh-huh." Tabitha tilted her head to the side. "Got some good speed there."

Gabrielle nodded. "I think you did the right thing, for what it's worth. He screwed you over, but you were right. He *did* argue for his family, and he didn't try to escape the consequences of what he did. If you killed everyone over the first infraction, you'd—"

She looked around in confusion. Tabitha had disappeared into thin air. It took a moment of looking and a few exploratory sniffs to identify the direction the woman had vanished in.

"Tabitha?"

"Over here! This way!" Tabitha shouted. "It's urgent! Come *on*!"

EPILOGUE

"I have to say," Gabrielle said a few minute later, "I don't think this qualifies as *urgent*."

"Good *choripan* is always urgent," Tabitha explained.

The little hole-in-the-wall restaurant was furnished with rickety chairs and metal tables covered with red and white tablecloths. Smoke hung heavy in the air, as did the smells of oil, onions, meat, and fried bread.

A man came out of the back and set down two bottles of Coca Cola, and Gabrielle stared at the soda, then back at Tabitha.

"Coke? Really?"

"That's what you drink with *choripan*," Tabitha explained. She picked up her sandwich and took a nibble. "Mmmm..."

Gabrielle took a bite and chewed. "You know, this is pretty good."

"It's hard not to just wolf it down," Tabitha explained. She shook her head. "But I want to savor it, you know?"

"Well, you're going to be nearby most of the time,

right?" Gabrielle asked. "So you can get these when you come to see your parents or whatever."

"I suppose I could," Tabitha agreed. "You know, it doesn't taste quite like I remember, though."

Gabrielle smiled. "You mean, it doesn't taste the same way it did when you were half-starving and living on rice and it was your one indulgence?"

"I suppose," Tabitha said, around a large mouthful, apparently having given up on her plan to savor the sandwich.

"I've been there," Gabrielle confided. "Food tastes better when you've been sleeping on rocky ground and living on limited rations. You're tired, you're hungry—well, humans get hungry, anyway—and a bite of something even a little luxurious tastes like heaven. Hell, if you get hungry enough even rice tastes good."

Tabitha smiled wanly. "I guess that's true. I just wish it tasted like… Well, like it used to." She shrugged and brightened, and picked up her bottle of Coke to clink it against Gabrielle's. "Now it'll taste like freedom, I've decided."

Gabrielle laughed and toasted her. "A good meal for freedom. No lines, no need to dress up. Just you in your old neighborhood, enjoying your favorite food."

"Exactly." Tabitha scooped up a stray onion. "You know, this night has been really weird. When I was here before, everyone else controlled everything. Now *I'm* in control. It's unsettling."

"That's growing up, *cherie*." Gabrielle smiled at her. "That's growing up. And yeah it feels weird, but it's *good* weird, isn't it?"

"Very good," Tabitha admitted. She considered. "So

what do we do now? We told Michael we might be gone for a couple of days."

"Oh, sweetie." Gabrielle grinned. "I'll tell you what we're going to do. We're going to shop our asses off. We're going to get a super-swanky hotel room with the biggest beds you ever saw. We're going to get massages. We're going to have amazing drinks. And we're going to get a few more *choripanes* while we're at it."

"Hell. Yes." Tabitha held up her hand for a high-five. "Let's get on that."

FINIS

SEED VAULT
BY NATALIE GREY & MICHAEL ANDERLE

CHAPTER 1

Romania

Alexi loped through the forest, big paws striking the ground and propelling him forward, rich dirt and loam redolent in the air.

He knew what humans thought of bears: that they were big, lumbering, terrifying. But to him, this form was freedom.

He felt graceful as a bear. He was muscle and purpose, a creature that did exactly what it was made to do.

Things were simpler when he shifted.

Simpler, but not entirely without sadness.

He was missing Ecaterina today. His niece had left years ago now to aid TQB, and though Alexi knew she was happier there than she had ever been here, he missed her smile, her humor, and her company.

Ecaterina loved the outdoors. Like Ivan, she could handle herself in a forest or in the mountains. She understood the dangers and respected them without letting fear trap her.

NATALIE GREY & MICHAEL ANDERLE

More and more, children like Ecaterina and Ivan were leaving to go to the cities. They were growing up with different concerns than a love of the forest.

It made Alexi sad to think about it.

He was hopeful that he might see her soon, however. Ecaterina had had a daughter not too long ago, and had promised to bring the baby home to meet everyone.

And Alexi approved of the man she had found. Nathan was a strong Wechselbag, a man with innate command but no love of power. He would make a good match for Ecaterina. He was the sort of man you trusted implicitly.

The spring breeze was carrying the scent of snowmelt and new greenery to Alexi's nose when he heard the unmistakable clang of a trap and the anguished scream of an animal in pain. He skidded to a halt, head whipping around toward the source of the noise.

He ran as quickly as he could while still being careful. If there was one trap, there was always another. That was a rule in the forest.

Anger was starting to beat low in his chest. He could hear a growl bursting out of him.

The scent of blood caught him not too far away and he slowed, padding carefully and avoiding the piles of recently disturbed leaves. There would be traps there, as well.

A young buck was thrashing wildly in the jaws of the trap. His foreleg was shattered, and he had snapped another in his panic. There was foam at his jaws, and his eyes rolled sideways in terror when he saw the bear appear.

There was no saving him. Too much blood was on the

leaves, and too many bones had been broken. Alexi snarled his frustration, and immediately regretted it when the buck gave a scream of terror.

And without words, there was no way to tell the buck what must happen. Alexi hung his head for a moment. Then, as the buck quieted, he padded closer.

All that was left was the quickest, most merciful death.

But this death should never have happened at all.

He tried to keep his anger from being visible as he looked up to meet the buck's eyes. The buck knew his death was coming. He knew, too, that he could thrash his head and hurt Alexi, but he did not try as Alexi came closer.

He stayed still as Alexi took his life in one quick slash of his claws, and the light faded from his eyes.

All that was left then was to deprive the trappers of their prize. Alexi snapped his jaws at the trapped leg, and dragged the body into the underbrush, to a place he knew was safe.

There, he shredded the body patiently. He took bone and meat, raked his claws over the hide, and left a body that would feed the wolves of the forest well enough ... but be useless to a human hunter or fur trapper.

Alexi had no qualms with the hunters who stalked their prey patiently through the forest. Wolves and bears hunted with claws and teeth, humans hunted with bows and guns. It was the way of things.

Everyone had to eat.

But when a hunter decided to stay in the comfort of his own home, and use metal traps to kill a beast he never saw alive, never took the time to hunt himself—then Alexi had a problem.

And he was going to make sure they paid for what they had done.

Then he left for his home, and for the bar where he found both friendship and information.

He wanted to find out who had left these traps out ... so he could make them tell him exactly where each one was.

QBBS *Meredith Reynolds*

Bethany Anne unrolled the blueprints with a flourish and smiled up at the assembled crowd.

There was a long pause.

"Well?" She grinned at all of them. "Come on, what d'you think?"

Gabrielle looked fixedly at the ceiling. Ecaterina was chewing on her lip. Bobcat had the vague look in his eyes that meant he was thinking of Yelena, and Yelena had the faint blush of someone who knew she was being thought about.

Ashur and Bellatrix offered no opinions.

"Uh...." Nathan finally cleared his throat. He didn't want to be the one to ask, but clearly, no one else was going to. "What *is* it?"

"You're kidding, right?" Bethany Anne tapped at a picture embedded in one of the blueprints. "It's the seed vault at Svalbard."

"Yeah...." Nathan looked around himself for someone who might take up the questioning.

Everyone studiously avoided his gaze. Ecaterina had

discovered a deep and abiding interest in her fingernails, Gabrielle was adjusting her shoes, and Bobcat and Yelena still seemed unaware that anyone else was in the room with them.

Nathan sighed. He wasn't going to get any backup on this. "And what's a seed vault?"

"Really, none of you know about this?" Bethany Anne looked around at all of them. "It's super cool, it's been on the news...."

"Since when are you interested in gardening?" Gabrielle asked delicately. She rubbed a thumb over deep purple nail polish and crossed her legs, sitting back in her chair with a faint frown.

"It's not *gardening*," Bethany Anne said, disgruntled. She couldn't believe that not a single person in this room had heard about this. She and TOM had stayed up the night before, reading all about the facility at Svalbard—but she had known about it for years before that. "And I'm allowed to have non-military interests, you know."

"We kind of thought you'd covered that with the shoes," Nathan offered.

He then took one look at Bethany Anne's face and resolved never to speak again as long as he lived.

ADAM projected his voice over the speaker systems in the meeting room. "The seed vault at Svalbard is a repository that can hold up to 4.5 million different types of seeds, serving as insurance against the loss of biodiversity."

"I see. Thank you, ADAM." Nathan looked around, glaring at the others to start talking. "Anyone else have any questions?"

It turned out he didn't need to be quite so emphatic.

Ecaterina was now genuinely interested. She guessed, "You want to build one for us."

She had always loved the abundance of flowers, berries, and trees in the mountains around her home, and had wondered often about how the relatively simple gardens on the *Meredith Reynolds* would affect the community they were building.

She had kept such thoughts to herself until now, not thinking that anyone else would be interested.

But it seemed like Bethany Anne *was* interested.

"Yes." Bethany Anne smiled at Ecaterina's obvious enthusiasm. "I know it's not a top priority, because we'll have enough food and air treatment, and military projects really need to be where we spend most of our energy.

"But I think it is good to have projects that aren't so...stressful."

Nathan nodded. It had been well-known in his pack that the Wechselbalg who tried to devote themselves entirely to duty without any time to decompress or have a good time, burned out quickly.

Hell, Gerry had even liked to bake. A surprisingly large number of conversations about the pack had taken place over fresh scones and elaborate braided loaves of bread.

If Nathan ever told anyone about that, though, he was sure he would be dead by the next morning.

He cleared his throat hastily, "Yeah, sounds like some downtime would do us good."

Bobcat was also nodding. His pet projects, including his own vehicles and his beer, were what had kept him sane over the years of intensive work. Something like this, with completely different specifications from anything else they were working on, would be a good side project.

Ecaterina could think of only one thing, however: "Where will we get the seeds?"

Bethany Anne smiled. The start of the meeting hadn't necessarily been promising, but this new wave of enthusiasm was making her very happy.

"I'm sure ADAM can find the list of seeds stored at Svalbard," she explained. "Not to mention, a way to get them all in the most efficient way…. But, as we just discussed, this is a project to let us blow off some steam. I don't think we really need to be 'efficient.'"

"Efficiency can be fun," ADAM said mournfully.

"Right." Gabrielle shot a wry look at the speakers. "Because you *never* take time running analyses in unusual ways … or spend time researching strange topics … or make ridiculously complicated algorithms to approximate humor."

"Those processes take mere minutes of your human time! I am not diverting necessary resources away from TQB."

"I don't think that was Gabrielle's point," Bethany Anne explained patiently. "I think her *point* was that you also like to do fun things."

There was a pause.

"I see. So…finding these seeds inefficiently would be fun for you?"

"Yes," Ecaterina said. "Instead of ordering the seeds online, for instance—"

"I don't think Amazon Prime delivers here," Bobcat said, grinning.

Ecaterina gave him a look. "As I was *saying*, we could order the seeds online, but it might be more fun to travel and find them by talking to farmers and scientists and so on."

"That makes a certain amount of sense."

"Oh, really?" Bethany Anne asked wickedly. "What amount? Do you have a percentage?"

"I am never able to determine that," ADAM said with great dignity.

Bethany Anne guffawed. "Right. Okay, everyone start thinking about places you want to go and plants you want to make sure are included. ADAM, you get that list. And Ashur and Bellatrix...you just keep making sure there aren't any rats on my nice shiny space station."

Ashur and Bellatrix gave her an alarmed look, and took off at high speed.

Bethany Anne chewed her lip. "I really need to work on sarcasm with them."

Yelena shrugged. "Eh, it should keep them occupied for a few hours."

Bobcat settled down on the office chair in his private sanctum and spun slowly.

Bethany Anne wanted plants? Well, he was going to make sure he got some hops. Marcus and William would kill him if he didn't.

He gave a sigh as he stared at his beer. He'd been so sure those rare hops he'd gotten in Spain were going to give him an edge in the competition, but now the other guys had them too.

He was back to Square One.

He let his head thunk back on the headrest and considered his options. He could just hope his brew was better. He could start over with totally new ingredients. He could....

Black hair and an angelic face derailed his thoughts. He had been taking Yelena for tours of the *Meredith Reynolds.* He was taking far more time with them than he needed to, and he was beginning to suspect it was obvious.

She didn't seem to mind, though.

She was one of the best people he had ever met. She was quick to laugh, and quicker to smile. Her joy in Bellatrix' presence had no jealousy to it—she seemed delighted that Bellatrix had found Ashur as a companion. More than once she had sat with Bobcat in the bar while the dogs tumbled about, wrestling and giving playful yips.

Everything about her was perfect, and—

He was supposed to be thinking about beer. And plants.

Bobcat let his head drop onto the desk and groaned. When he picked himself up, he could only shrug wearily and type a query into the search bar: *How to make the best beer*

He scanned down the list of results, shaking his head. There were tutorials for how to make beer, basic questions about what equipment he needed, and...

Well, that was interesting. "PUREST MYRCENE OIL ON THE MARKET," a website proclaimed.

Myrcene Oil? Bobcat clicked the link.

Myrcene is an essential oil found in the hop plant, the page read. *As the secret ingredient in many well-known beers, it is known to smooth and deepen the flavors, creating a rich finish that cannot be matched otherwise.*

Our employees come from many of the largest beer brands across the globe, and set out to recreate Myrcene Oil in order to bring this advantage to smaller brewers.

We've done it! Our Myrcene Oil is produced using rigorous standards, and we believe it is even better than the oil we used in our former jobs.

Pick the type of beer you are brewing below, and we will give you our recommendations of which oil to use.

"Myrcene Oil." Bobcat's eyes were huge. "God, is this real?"

"Bobcat?" Yelena's delicately-accented voice called.

"Hi." He spun in his chair, face lighting up involuntarily.

"You look happy," Yelena said. She was smiling. "You have been so sad about your beer the past few days. I am very glad to see you happy like this. What is it that is making you smile?"

You, Bobcat wanted to say.

"It's, uh... Well, it's the beer, actually." It was half-true. This lead was promising.

"Oh? Did you find something to help?" She clapped her hands. "It would be wonderful if you won!"

Visions flashed through his head... Bobcat holding a trophy aloft as Yelena smiled and cheered, staring up adoringly at him. Without another thought, Bobcat pressed the BUY NOW button flashing helpfully at the bottom of the screen.

Nathan whistled as he walked along the hallway, bouncing Christina in his arms. She laughed and waved her arms, singing along with the tune he was whistling. Even at five years old, she liked to be carried occasionally.

He paused to kiss her cheek and accept a somewhat sticky kiss back. Having a family, however painful his memories of old times, fulfilled something primal in him. This wasn't a replacement. He knew that. He never forgot it, in fact.

It was its own thing, and it made him happier than he had been in years.

A big part of him had feared he would never have this again. He simply hadn't had a lot of luck meeting a woman he wanted to settle down with, until Ecaterina. Hell, he hadn't really *wanted* to, until Ecaterina. He'd been too afraid to face the past until she came along.

Now they had a life together, a life full of purpose as well as love, and they had Christina, who was just about the happiest child he'd ever seen.

Lord knew, she was spoiled rotten between Bethany Anne, Gabrielle, Jennifer, and a veritable horde of honorary uncles including the Queen's Bitches. Of course, she was probably going to be less happy about that horde of tall and intimidating uncles when it came time for her to start dating.

Nathan shuddered and decided not to think about that. "You should talk to Barnabas about becoming a monk," he suggested to Christina. "I heard it's very rewarding on a personal level."

Christina might not understand the joke, but she knew

her father was making one. She laughed. "Okay, Dada" she said, with the tiniest lilt of her mother's accent in her voice.

"I'm taking that as a binding verbal contract, you know." He shouldered open the door to the apartment he shared with Ecaterina.

His wife was on the phone—or a contraption rigged up to seem like one, at any rate. It was one of the *Meredith Reynolds's* latest successes. "Of course," she was saying. "Well, I'm not sure if we can bring her for most of it, but maybe for a little bit. All right. Yes. All right. And you're *sure* you're okay?" She was frowning. She listened as the person on the other end spoke rapidly. "Okay. I'll see you soon."

She hung up and crossed her arms, staring at the phone.

"Who was that?" Nathan settled Christina in a chair and went to get some food, sighing slightly as she immediately slid down and went off in search of toys. Life had been easier before she got mobile.

"My uncle." Ecaterina returned to packing, stuffing high-end hiking gear and designer clothes into the suitcase absentmindedly.

"Don't let Bethany Anne see you treating couture like that," Nathan advised. "Is something wrong with Alexi?"

He was worried. Alexi was a good man, protective of his family and a strong Wechselbag. Under his guidance, Ecaterina had become the self-sufficient, headstrong woman Nathan loved with all his heart.

"He *says* he's fine," Ecaterina said. She stopped packing for a moment and looked at Nathan. "He's lying, though."

"He'll probably tell you when you're there, right?"

Nathan offered a bowl of soup to Christina and held it while she ran back to the table.

"He'd better," Ecaterina said darkly. "No more of this 'I don't want to worry you over nothing' *crap*. If it was nothing, *he* wouldn't be worried." She zipped the suitcase shut and sighed. "So will you be okay while I'm there?"

"Actually, I thought I'd come with you." Nathan smiled.

"Really?"

He went over to pull her into his arms, dancing his way across the floor while she giggled. "A nice, romantic getaway to where we first met...and you first scammed the hell out of me...."

Ecaterina threw her head back and laughed. "I did not—"

"Uh-huh." Nathan twirled her and kissed her. "I figured we could go out with Bethany Anne, have Alexi meet Christina, and then Bethany Anne could take Christina back and we could have a little time to wander the hills, maybe stay a few extra days in a nice secluded hotel somewhere...."

"Oh, that does sound nice." Ecaterina smiled as Nathan twirled her again. "And the whole point of this project was to have fun, right?"

"Right," Nathan said seriously. "The way I see it, Bethany Anne has pretty much *ordered* us to relax. It would be very disrespectful not to do so."

"Dada," Christina chimed in, "what's a scam?"

Nathan settled into his own chair and gave a mock glare at Ecaterina. "Oh, I have no doubt your mother will teach you when you're older."

CHAPTER 2

QBBS *Meredith Reynolds*

"Oooooh…" Gabrielle held up a pair of deep blue heels. "I love these!"

"Eh." Bethany Anne looked up from her research and frowned. "I don't think they go with most things I own. The black version, I can't wait to wear. But those…"

"Tell you what." Gabrielle grinned. "I'll break them in for you."

"Feel free." Bethany Anne looked back at the seed list, then up again. "What are you going to wear them with?"

"I was thinking that ripped pair of jeans and a tank top." Gabrielle tilted her head as she considered. "I'll need some jewelry to bring out the blue…"

"Ripped jeans?" Bethany Anne looked pained. "Can't you just…wear clothes in good condition?"

"It's a *look*," Gabrielle told her. "Why do you have to be so stuffy about your clothes?"

"It's called *classic*."

"Classic? Sweetie, I was born a few hundred years before you. I know from classic."

Bethany Anne considered this. "Yeah," she said finally, "but you're French."

She ducked as Gabrielle whipped one of the shoes at her head, laughing madly.

"We *invented* fashion!" Gabrielle yelled. She threw the other shoe.

"Well, if you don't want the shoes, I'll find some way to wear them. Maybe a nice un-ripped gown—" Bethany Anne threw one of her own shoes back at Gabrielle.

"Oh, please." Gabrielle picked up a shoebox and threw it. "When you go to dinner parties, they turn into shoot-outs!"

"That was *one time!*"

"What the hell is going on?" Eric asked from the doorway. He ducked as two boxes of shoes headed toward him at high velocity. "Seriously, what the ever-loving fuck did I do?"

"Sorry," Gabrielle said sheepishly.

"Instinct." Bethany Anne was totally unrepentant.

Eric gathered up the shoeboxes in the hallway, "Were you just fighting over who gets to wear the shoes?"

"*No.*" Bethany Anne shook her head, "we were fighting about what to wear *with* the shoes."

"Totally different thing," Gabrielle agreed, nodding sagely.

"Uh...huh." Eric set the boxes down. "Well, I'll go tell the crew that's what the yelling was about, then."

He left after one last suspicious glare at the two of them.

"Men," Gabrielle said, sighing elaborately. "They just don't understand."

"Not at all." Bethany Anne retrieved her right shoe and slipped it back on. "And fine, you wear the outfit and I'll at least give it a chance."

"If you like how it looks, maybe I'll get *you* a pair of those jeans."

Bethany Anne shuddered. "Let's not get carried away." She checked the clock. "Now, give me a second. I need to figure out which of these we can have couriered to Romania while Ecaterina and Nathan are there, and then I'm going to take that whole crew out."

Marcus stared out the window of his private office, narrowing his eyes at the black outside. Usually he found this view comforting, but in this instance he wanted to beat his head on the window.

"You look troubled," Barnabas said suddenly.

Marcus jumped and swore. Between his Kurtherian upgrades and his years as a monk, Barnabas had developed the ability to move absolutely silently. It was something Marcus was having trouble getting used to.

"Uh…" He tried to remember what he'd been thinking about. "It's just, I'm a little worried about the competition."

"Why?" Barnabas looked at him. "You have made a superior beer. Unless something such as sabotage should occur, I can think of no reasons that you should not feel confident in your product."

"Yours and mine," Marcus pointed out. "You chose the final hop combinations."

"I merely offered advice." Barnabas seemed untroubled. "I am given to understand that advice is allowed in this competition."

"It is, but I'm the newest brewer here." Marcus sighed and rolled his neck. "What if Bobcat finds something else like those hops?"

Barnabas looked serene, as always. "I do not think it is necessary to worry."

"But what if he had some secret ingredient?" Marcus protested. "Shouldn't we go check and just see? Look through his notes or something?"

"That would be against the rules," Barnabas said. There was a tinge of disapproval in his voice. "It would not be sporting, surely."

"He risked our lives to get those last hops!"

"For which he gave recompense in the form of the hops themselves, yes?"

Marcus shrugged and muttered, "I suppose."

"You have made an excellent beer," Barnabas told him. "To you I advise the same thing I would advise anyone: focus on the fundamentals. Tricks and shortcuts do more harm than good. It is mastery of the basic concepts that produces results."

"Right." Marcus sighed. "Thank you."

"And now if you will excuse me, I must speak with Tabitha." Barnabas inclined his head and disappeared as quietly as he had come.

Marcus sighed again and leaned on the window. *Focus on the fundamentals.* He had spent hours measuring and re-measuring his hops and getting the temperature exactly right. Barnabas' approval had been very heartening then.

But was perfection enough to outdo William and Bobcat and any tricks they might have up their sleeves?

He sat behind his desk and tried to focus. He really shouldn't snoop. Barnabas was right, that would be dishonorable.

And he really didn't want to piss off Barnabas. In his experience, the quieter a vampire, the worse it was if you annoyed them.

He'd just have to hope his beer was good enough without any tricks.

William chuckled to himself as he loaded the program and, with a flourish, hit one last key.

His screen flickered and was replaced a moment later with a different desktop.

Bobcat's.

Still grinning, William took another look at the video surveillance. Bobcat had left his computer a few minutes ago, heading out with Yelena so quickly that he forgot to shut the computer off.

Rookie mistake.

After all, as far as William was concerned, all was fair in love and brewing competitions.

He brought up the web browser and looked through the recently viewed sites, and one stood out immediately: MYRCENE OIL.

"Myrcene, like hops?" William brought up the website and looked through it.

His first thought was that it was a scam. Surely if Myrcene Oil were real he'd have heard of it before, right?

But Bobcat had bought some, and Bobcat knew a lot more about beer than the rest of them did.

William frowned at the page for a very long time.

Then he brought it up on his own computer and placed an order.

Like hell he was going to let Bobcat get the advantage.

Romania

"*Unchi!*" Ecaterina held her arms out to Alexi with a smile.

"*Puiule.*" Alexi enfolded her in a huge hug and smiled over her head at everyone.

It was a gorgeous day. Summer had come in earnest and the scent of greenery was heavy in the air. Picturesque white clouds drifted lazily across a blue sky, and crickets were singing in the fields beyond the town. The mountains stood out against the sky, and Alexi saw with satisfaction that every member of Ecaterina's party was looking around in awe.

"Beautiful here, no?" He smiled.

"Beautiful," Nathan agreed. He hefted Christina in his arms, and pointed to Alexi. "That's your mama's Uncle Alexi. Do you want to say hello?"

"Hello, Uncle Alexi." Christina held out her arms immediately, and Ecaterina felt her face split in a smile as Alexi took the child. It was clear that the two had an instant understanding despite the gap in their ages.

"So..." Ecaterina looked around. "Where's Ivan?"

"Bucharest for a few days." Alexi's voice was quiet. He looked suddenly grave. "He said he wasn't sure your friends would be pleased to see him. He said it would be better for everyone if he weren't here when you arrived, and that you'd call him if you wanted to see him."

"Ah." Ecaterina rubbed her head. She hadn't even thought of bringing Gabrielle with her, for that exact reason.

She supposed it was nice of Ivan to anticipate that, though it was also a bit dramatic in her opinion.

Well, that was Ivan. She rolled her eyes with a sibling's good-natured humor. She'd call him—and make sure to give him crap for being a coward.

She drew Alexi away from the others a little bit. Here at her uncle's house, with its gently sloping roof and rough-hewn walls, there was a sense of contentment radiating from every tree and flower. Ashur and Bellatrix were already leaping through the gardens, sneezing and yipping happily, and Yelena was following them with a distracted smile that said she was thinking of Bobcat.

Nathan, meanwhile, had Christina's hand in his own and was walking with her through the meadow grass.

Something in Ecaterina's throat constricted for a moment. She had expected, for many years that she would raise a family here. In this town. Near these mountains. Under this sky. It was only later, when she saw how the men of this town behaved when confronted with a woman

NATALIE GREY & MICHAEL ANDERLE

as strong-minded as she was, that she realized her dreams would not come true.

She'd found Nathan, and for that she was happy beyond belief.

But seeing Christina here in Alexi's garden made her wish, just for a moment, that she could live out her days here.

She would have to spend as much time here as she could before they went through the gate. Christina should know her family.

She looked back to see Alexi smiling at her. "It's good to be back, but a bit sad, I think," he guessed.

"Yes," she admitted. "I've been so busy that I lost track of time. I wish I'd come back more often."

"Bah," he said with good humor. "I've never seen you so happy. Sure, that spaceship—"

"Space *station*."

"Doesn't have mountains like this, but you are doing good work, yes? And you have a good man and a good child and good friends. That one, with the dogs—she is trustworthy." He nodded decisively in Yelena's direction. "Dogs always know," he added, as if he hadn't imparted this very piece of information to Ecaterina dozens of times before.

She smiled at him. "Yes, Yelena is a good person. And she's turning into a hell of a boxer, too."

"She is…"

"She has Wechselbalg blood, yes." Ecaterina nodded. "She can't shift, but she can understand Bellatrix."

Alexi nodded.

He lapsed into silence, staring at the mountains with his arms crossed across his broad chest.

His research into the traps had gone nowhere, and as much as he wanted to talk to Ecaterina about it, he didn't want to worry her. It was obvious to him that she worried about having left, and he did not want her to feel as if she owed it to him to stay.

He had meant what he said about her being happier now than at any other point in her life. Ecaterina had always been headstrong, able to survive on her own in the mountains, and fiercely intelligent—but a piece of her had been missing before now.

Alexi had never said as much to her. For one thing, he valued his life. But now that she had a life that made her happy, he didn't want her to give it up for anything.

He had failed to remember, however, that Ecaterina knew all his moods.

"What is it you're worried about?" she asked him bluntly.

He looked over at her guiltily. "What?"

"Oh, come on." She stepped out of the way as Bellatrix shot by at high speed with Ashur in hot pursuit, and Christina running after both of them, shrieking happily. "I could tell something was wrong even on the phone."

Alexi sighed. "First tell me why you are here."

Ecaterina hesitated, but a moment later she was recounting the story of Bethany Anne's seed vault animatedly. Her hands waved as she described the concrete-and-glass building at Svalbard, and she began to discuss how the seeds would be stored on the *Meredith Reynolds*.

She knew that Alexi would appreciate her thoughts on

the base ship's gardens, and so she launched into a discussion of the types of plants she wanted to bring from the mountains surrounding their town.

"I thought we could take Christina out," she suggested. "I want to show her the forests."

"Not yet," Alexi said instantly.

"What? Why?" When he said nothing, her eyes narrowed. "*Unchi*, tell me."

He sighed. "I have been finding traps in the forest."

Ecaterina was instantly alert. Most people in their town knew the old ways well enough to respect what they hunted and hunt their own game in the old ways. But every few years, someone came along who thought they were above taking lives themselves, who preferred to let their prey die in agony simply for the hunter's convenience.

She hated such people with a passion. She had grown up seeing her uncle pay visits to such people. He would hand them their traps back and say a few words—she didn't know what words, since she wasn't allowed to listen —and usually the man would go pale and stammer an apology.

And the traps would stop for a while.

But this time he had not been able to find the owner of the traps.

"We will find out who it is," she promised. "And they will take all their traps up."

He shook his head, "Child, I do not think it is a local person."

"What?"

"When it is a deer or anything someone might eat, the

body is not taken. It is...left by other traps. I think they are trying to get wolves for the pelts."

Ecaterina swallowed and shifted uncomfortably. Fur trapping was one of the least honorable ways to hunt, in her opinion. Not only was it trapping, it was wasteful, sacrificing all the wrong animals instead of taking what the forest offered.

Because that was the thing about traps: they did not differentiate between a fawn and a buck or a wolf and a rabbit. They took life without compunction.

And that, Ecaterina could not stand.

"We are going to find these people," she said fiercely.

"*Puiule*, I was afraid you would say that. You do not need to be responsible for—"

"This was my home," she told him. "I will not leave while something like this is happening." She smiled and looked at Nathan. "If they want wolves, then maybe they had better be careful what they wish for."

CHAPTER 3

Hainaut, Belgium

Secret ingredients were good, but that only gave William an insight into Bobcat's strategy. And Marcus' was going to be more difficult to reproduce.

Marcus, after all, had Barnabas.

William knew better than to even try to bribe Barnabas to give up Marcus' secrets. He suspected that might be fatal. On the other hand, Barnabas was not the only person in the world who knew the secrets of Trappist beermaking.

Which was how William found himself in Scourmont Abbey, generous donation in hand and with the ostensible mission from Bethany Anne of looking through the monks' library for a full accounting of local plants.

One of the monks, a man who called himself Brother Michel, led William through the herb gardens and pointed out various varieties of herbs.

"Like many monasteries, we have maintained our own gardens for centuries," Brother Michel told William. "Over that time, we have developed our own strains of herbs for potency and medicinal properties."

William dutifully took notes. He knelt by a flower with five sky-blue petals and bent to sniff it, then jerked his head back.

Brother Michel laughed. "That is borage. It smells foul, yes, but it is believed that borage has natural antidepressant properties, and an oil made from the seeds can be used for skin ailments."

William asked him, "Would you include it in the seed catalog?"

Brother Michel considered. "Likely not. Its uses are not well known, and each use can be better approximated with other plants, if you can recreate the correct growing conditions. We maintain it as a part of our tradition. Each of these plants has been maintained for many generations."

Despite his focus on the beer, William found himself drawn in. "You seem..."

Brother Michel tilted his head in question.

William shrugged. "I don't know how to describe it. You seem to find meaning in cultivation of these plants."

"There *is* meaning in it," Brother Michel said quietly. "I think your employer knows this. We were born here on this Earth, surrounded by these plants. Watching them grow, learning to be attentive to their needs, making them into medicines...it is a part of who we are." He lifted one shoulder contemplatively. "In truth, anything can be made into a prayer if you want it to be one. Here we seek to find meaning in every task."

William thought that perhaps Bethany Anne should have come. Though she did not speak of it often, he knew that her faith was deeply important to her. For her, it was not simply the rote recitation of prayers or the habitual attendance of services—sometimes she did not do those things at all.

Bethany Anne's faith was a piece of who she was. It affected everything she did, and every choice she made.

He wondered if Brother Michel was correct—if Bethany Anne did not want to make a seed vault because of logic and caution, but instead because she knew that cultivation of plants from Earth was important to humans.

Perhaps it was part of what made them human.

He was going to be thinking about this visit for a while.

"In the libraries, you will find early manuscripts detailing the proper way to maintain a basic herb garden as well as an extensive one," Brother Michel told him. "That information is freely available. I wanted to show you the garden first, so that you would appreciate the words on the page."

"Thank you," William said honestly.

Between the man's calm words and the buzz of the bees that flitted from plant to plant, he felt a strange clarity washing over him.

He liked this place.

"I had one other question, actually."

"Oh?" Brother Michel smiled and spread his hands. "My time is yours."

"I don't want you to feel obligated because of the donation," William said.

"I do not," the monk assured him. "Truthfully I am very interested in this project of yours, and I think you will do good things with the information."

William nodded.

"Now, what else did you wish to know?"

"Well..." After the seriousness of the last subject, William felt a bit embarrassed. "You see, I'm in a contest with two friends. We are each brewing a beer, and another friend will judge them."

"Ah." Brother Michel's eyes lit up. "Then you must come to our brewery. It is famous, you know." He laughed. "I shouldn't be proud of it since I do not even brew the beer myself, but I am. I would be happy to help you find inspiration."

"Yes! Inspiration." William nodded eagerly. "You see, one friend has been brewing beer for years, and the other... Well, he's working with a man who, ah...was trained in beermaking by Trappist monks." That seemed like the easiest way to explain Barnabas.

"Trained?" Brother Michel looked truly intrigued. "That is...unusual."

"Yeah, he's a pretty unusual guy."

He'd never uttered such a massive understatement in his life.

"I see. And you say he trained for...how long?"

"Uh, maybe thirty years?"

"I see," Brother Michel said again. He laid a hand on William's shoulder and looked at him gravely. "You should drink a few beers with us."

"So I can learn about them?" William asked hopefully.

"No," the monk said. He looked a bit awkward. "Let us say, to ease your disappointment."

"What?"

"I fear very much there is no way for you to win this

contest." Brother Michel hid his arms in his sleeves and regarded William. "However, you must look on the bright side."

"Which is?" William asked, prickly.

"Your friend will make you very good beer. Such things are worthy of celebration in and of themselves." Brother Michel gestured to a building nearby. "Now, come... Let us look at the libraries and then drink many beers."

Romania

Ecaterina laced up her old boots and smiled.

She really should be wearing something newer. The boots were old and not in the best repair. but going to the closet in Alexi's house and pulling out her own clothing and footwear had been too much to resist.

They had both woken up as the very first light of dawn was making the horizon grow pale. Ecaterina had come downstairs to find Alexi making a pot of strong coffee in the kitchen, and the two of them had chatted over coffee and eggs.

As Alexi spoke of where he had found traps so far, Ecaterina built a map in her head.

She suspected that these trappers were motivated by profit, not by hunger. Anyone who lived in this area knew where the deer roamed and knew what types of traps to set for smaller game as well. A hungry man did not disdain rabbit or squirrel for a meal, and he was careful to set his traps where there would be the most chance of getting food.

These traps, however, were scattered almost randomly.

Or so Ecaterina thought at first. However, the closer she looked, the more a pattern began to emerge. At last she fell silent, cradling her now-empty coffee mug in both hands.

"You see it too," Alexi guessed. "They are trying to trap the wolves."

She could only nod.

Once she would have thought that this was simply a coward's way of trying to control the forest. People feared what they could not understand, be that bears or wolves… or even thunderstorms at one time.

Now, knowing what she knew about Wechselbags and having seen the world through different eyes herself, these traps sickened Ecaterina.

Still, she tried to give them the benefit of the doubt, "Has it been a bad year for wolves?"

Sometimes in lean years, the wolves turned to poaching livestock when there was no game to be found in the forests. And while a well-fed wolf would always avoid habitations, there had been times when starving wolves would prey on humans. Those stories endured.

But Alexi shook his head. "No. There are many deer. If the wolves have snatched even a chicken, I have not heard about it."

"So *why*?" Ecaterina demanded. "Why set traps up in the high snow? Why set them in the runs between the deer dens? What could they gain?"

"Pelts," Alexi said simply.

"They want the *fur*?" Ecaterina was furious. She had done her best to believe that this was not the case, but it was true.

"It is the only answer. I have checked the traps and sometimes they are gone. The bodies are not left. I also see fewer signs of wolves. They know, I think."

Ecaterina's hand fisted, and she tried to flatten it on the table without any success. With her emotions high, a shift was threatening.

Alexi, a Wechselbag since birth, understood this well.

"Patience," he advised.

Her head whipped around and she glared at him, only to have him laugh.

"Do you truly think that with this much anger and all the cunning you have had since you were a child you will not stop this? *That* is what I mean by patience, Ecaterina. Have faith in yourself."

Her shoulders slumped and she laughed. "That is a good way to say things. Thank you, *Unchi*."

A few minutes later, Ecaterina slipped upstairs to kiss Christina and Nathan goodbye. Christina had slipped out of her own bed before Ecaterina left for the morning, to nestle between her parents. Now, she was curled up on Ecaterina's side of the bed, her fine hair spread across the pillow, her face peaceful in sleep.

Nathan propped himself up on one elbow sleepily. "Where're you going?"

"Out into the forest with Alexi." Ecaterina smiled at him.

"I know that smile." Nathan sat up with a groan and rubbed his face. "You're going to go rain hellfire down on those trappers, aren't you?" He threw the covers aside. "I'll come with you."

Ecaterina was laughing, "Go back to sleep. No hellfire this time, I promise."

Nathan looked at her suspiciously.

Ecaterina held up a hand solemnly. "I promise. We're just going to look at the traps and see if we can find anything out about who set them. We don't plan to be seen at all."

"If there's one thing I've learned in Bethany Anne's service—"

"Oh, come on—"

"It's that things never go according to plan and we bring the wrath of God down on people regularly."

"Mmmhmm." Ecaterina leaned over the bed to kiss him. "And I promise I'll bring you along on any mission to scare the crap out of these people." Christina had started to wake up, and Ecaterina ruffled her hair. "There's coffee and eggs and pastries downstairs. Have a great breakfast!"

"But—"

Ecaterina was already gone.

Grumbling, Nathan kissed his daughter good morning and headed for the stairs. "Come downstairs when you want breakfast, munchkin."

Pastries *did* sound good.

To his surprise, he found Yelena already up and about. She smiled at him and poured him a cup of coffee before pushing the plate of pastries his way for him to select one.

"Why are you already up?" Nathan asked. "Are you one of those disgustingly cheerful morning people? We may have a problem, if so."

Yelena laughed—not a good sign, in Nathan's opinion—

but shook her head. "I'm not. Well, I didn't used to be before Bellatrix, but now I guess I do wake up early."

"Oh?" Nathan settled down at the table and picked a square pastry that smelled of cheese.

"I think…" Yelena's voice trailed off and she hunched her shoulders awkwardly.

Nathan frowned.

To his surprise, Yelena laughed again. "I'm so used to feeling embarrassed about this because people would think I was crazy, but you'll believe me! I wake up when Bellatrix does. There's a link there."

Nathan nodded. Those who were descended from Wechselbags, like Yelena, often had experiences in their early lives they could not explain to others. Some, with family guidance, could channel their talents into useful pursuits, even if they were not Wechselbag, themselves. Yelena, however, had not been so lucky in her family.

Nathan shook his head regretfully, "It must have been hard for you, not knowing what was going on."

Yelena considered this, taking a bite of her own cheese pastry. "In some ways, yes," she agreed finally. "Ciprian would never have understood, I know. He was my ex-boyfriend. I didn't tell a lot of people about Bellatrix for that reason. But I had her, you see, and that made it easier."

Nathan nodded, his eyes distant.

"What are you thinking about?" Yelena asked him.

"There were legends across the world of druids and shamans who could speak to animals," Nathan explained. "And some about warriors who had animals as their familiars and fighting partners. I wonder if they were from the Wechselbalg lines like you."

"I hadn't ever thought of that." Yelena gazed out the door to where Bellatrix and Ashur were dashing around the garden at high speed. "That would make sense. Perhaps they could not even explain it. Sometimes I questioned my abilities with Bellatrix because I didn't know *how* I knew things."

Nathan smiled and nodded.

"So where did Ecaterina go?" Yelena questioned Nathan. "She looked very happy."

"She is going out to track down the trappers," Nathan replied. "She says that she and Alexi will only be observing the traps today, not hunting the ones who set them…but I have my doubts."

"You are not worried?" Yelena was surprised by this.

She was further surprised when Nathan chuckled. "Ecaterina can take care of herself. And Alexi is also a Wechselbag—he takes a bear form."

"*Bear*?" Yelena asked incredulously.

"Oh, yes." Nathan smiled. "And both can fight quite well, so I suppose we shall see what happens."

Yelena considered. She had been excited to accompany Ashur and Bellatrix on the trip to Romania. Though Yelena was not someone who particularly enjoyed hiking or other outdoor pursuits, she knew that Bellatrix would be over-joyed to be able to race around in the wilderness.

She had also been looking forward to getting to know the others on this trip. She had learned a little about the members of Bethany Anne's team, but she wanted to know more. Each of them had a story to tell.

Each of them had a strong sense of honor, too—something she was not used to in an organization so big.

Now she was getting a chance to learn about each of them. She smiled and sipped her coffee, utterly content.

She did not know it, but Nathan was watching her. Even though Nathan was no longer a second-in-command, he still retained the desire to vet each new member of the organization.

He approved of Yelena. He had been impressed by the way she cared for Bellatrix, even when she did not understand the bond she shared with the dog. He had heard the stories about her, and had even shared in some of the speculation about her and Bobcat.

In his opinion, she would make a good addition to the group, as long as she could come to terms with the self-sufficient independent streak each member had.

He was not particularly worried about that, though. Yelena seemed to direct her worry toward other people, not herself. He'd heard that even outmatched, she'd done some real damage to her jerk of an ex-boyfriend.

In time, she would learn that other people could take care of themselves too.

He stood up. "Should we go see the town? I'll get Christina if so."

"I'd like that." Yelena nodded and sipped at her coffee as Nathan took the stairs two at a time, and came back in time with Christina all dressed. They picked a pastry for the little girl, and all headed outside.

It was a beautiful day. Yelena tipped her head back into the sunshine for a moment, and then waved at the fence, where a group of passing men had stopped to look at the dogs. "Hello!"

They waved back and disappeared hurriedly.

Yelena shook her head, suddenly worried. "Maybe we should leave the dogs here."

"Why?" Nathan frowned back at her.

"People are always afraid of Bellatrix," Yelena explained. "In my home village people knew me, and they knew I worked at the kennels and my dogs were always well trained, so they trusted Bellatrix. Here they do not know me. I don't want to make anyone upset."

"Good point." Nathan smiled at the dogs. "And they seem quite happy here. Listen up, you two," he called to the dogs. "We're heading into town. Try not to eat too many bees."

Ashur chuffed indignantly, and Nathan laughed as he and Yelena made their way through the gate and into town.

CHAPTER 4

QBBS *Meredith Reynolds*

Stephen emerged from a shower, his dark brown hair still drying, to find Jennifer curled up in one of the armchairs with his copy of *Master and Commander*. She was frowning in concentration.

"What's a 'minim?'" she asked him.

"A single drop," Stephen explained. "It's a unit of measure."

"Did people really used to say that instead?"

"Language used to be less…regimented." Stephen shrugged. "People spelled things all different ways and used different words for things all over the place."

"Really? I thought…" She chewed her lip. "I guess I thought language used to be more formal."

Stephen laughed, "Not really. Remember, people didn't travel as much. It wasn't uncommon for people to be stuck in the same place with the same people all their lives. Even in a city, they often kept to their same class or ghetto or wherever, so they developed their own ways of speaking."

"I hadn't thought of that." Jennifer watched as he put on a suit. "Where are you headed to, all dressed up?"

"Nowhere special. I'm listening in on a conference call for this seed vault Bethany Anne started."

Jennifer grinned and shook her head. "So why are you wearing a suit?"

She already knew his answer, but she wanted to hear him say it.

He gave her a dignified look. "After so many weeks covered in dust and blood, I wanted to look nice for a change."

"You look very nice covered in dust and blood," Jennifer told him with a grin. "All sweaty, in a shirt I can see your muscles in..."

Stephen adjusted his tie without comment, but he smiled into the mirror as he did so.

"Although you do look quite nice in a suit as well," Jennifer told him. She grinned. "It's just that I feel like a slob, still being in my pajamas."

"I think you've earned a good few days in pajamas," Stephen told her as he stooped to kiss her. "And a good few bubble baths. And champagne. And maybe a nice dinner tonight, hmm?"

Jennifer grinned up at him. "I like that idea. And I think I might just go take a bubble bath, then. Unless you think I should be on the conference call?"

Stephen shook his head. "This was specifically mentioned as a project for relaxation. I'm only going because I'm curious." He headed for the door with a rueful smile. "It's certainly a nice break after our last few projects."

"Yes, I don't think many seeds are homicidal maniacs determined to create a new world order by subjugating Wechselbalg," Jennifer quipped.

Stephen was laughing as he slipped out the door. "Exactly."

He made his way through the hallways quickly. Every time he came back here it seemed there was more progress on the base ship. It was becoming a fine place to live, almost a self-sufficient city.

The seed vault intrigued him for this reason, as well as what it represented: a slice of home they would take with them when they left.

He knew now that he was part-Kurtherian, a product of the universe beyond Earth, but Earth was all he had ever known and at heart he was human. He had wondered sometimes if he would miss Earth when they left to go through the gate.

Maybe Bethany Anne was wondering the same thing.

Marcus laughed as he settled back in his chair, "That cannot possibly be true."

"It is!" Tabitha exclaimed, clearly insulted to be doubted. "She's very sneaky!"

"You're telling me that Gabrielle killed several commandos in Buenos Aires while wearing Louboutins?" Marcus shook his head and took another sip of his beer. "No way."

"Vampires are less constrained by the limitations of the physical form," Barnabas said gravely. "Gabrielle is able to move more quickly than a human, even when she is wearing high heels." He frowned as he took a sip of his own beer. "Of course, such affectations are not helpful to her any more than they are to a human."

Tabitha rolled her eyes, "You don't think so? Every man there who saw her immediately decided she wasn't a threat. That gave her an opening."

"When one can move as quickly as Gabrielle can, an opening is not as necessary." Barnabas looked grave.

"Maybe she just likes being sneaky, then," Tabitha said. She gave an impish grin, "You know, like you do."

Marcus gave a low whistle. "Oh, really?"

"I beg your pardon," Barnabas said, with great dignity. "I am not *sneaky*."

"You are too sneaky," Tabitha said. She gave Marcus a knowing look. "He *loves* tricking people."

"Tabitha—"

"He likes tricking them by behaving in ways that help them make unwise assumptions," Tabitha continued in a stage whisper. "And then he says that if they weren't so hasty, if they just took more time to examine the issue, they wouldn't have been tricked."

"*Tabitha!*"

"Hmm?" Tabitha looked innocently at Barnabas. "Am I wrong?"

Barnabas gave her a look. "I do not employ cheap trickery."

Tabitha considered this. "I wouldn't call it *cheap*," she said finally.

"*Tabitha!*"

Marcus wished he hadn't taken a sip of beer. He was

trying desperately to keep it from going up his nose as he laughed, and it was only with great effort that he managed not to spit it down his front.

His laughter only got worse when Barnabas gave him an aggrieved look.

"You should teach me how to do that," he suggested. "It sounds useful. Make people rely on incorrect assumptions so they hamstring themselves instead of me having to do it for them. It sounds like a neat trick."

"It is not a trick," Barnabas insisted with great dignity.

"It's definitely a trick," Tabitha whispered loudly.

"It is not a competitor's duty to explain to his competition that incorrect assumptions have been made, after all."

"Even when you encouraged them to make those assumptions," Tabitha continued, still in her loud whisper.

"I will box your ears," Barnabas told her.

"I don't even know what that means."

"*You're* about to." Barnabas gave her an eerily calm smile.

Tabitha shut up.

"Now, as I was saying," Barnabas looked at Marcus, "a competitor can always benefit from another's incorrect assumptions. Perhaps *you* might, in this case. However, the true measure of a competitor is in his own actions, not in others' failures. Simply execute each stage of your brewing correctly, and you will be most of the way to winning."

"Right," Marcus agreed mournfully.

It seemed like Barnabas was absolutely determined to make Marcus win this without any tricks at all.

But he doubted that he could succeed against the other two without them.

Maybe Tabitha would teach him how to use Barnabas' tricks…

Bethany Anne looked up with a smile as Stephen came into the room, "How are you doing?"

"Very well, thank you." Stephen nodded and took a chair, unbuttoning his suit jacket as he sat. "It is good to be back."

Bethany Anne nodded, "Especially after a mission like that, I would think."

"Exactly." Stephen shook his head slightly. "Every time I think I understand people…"

Bethany Anne opened her mouth to speak, then thought better of it. It sounded as if Stephen's experiences in Europe had brought him some new conclusions, and perhaps he needed to speak them rather than have a conversation.

Though none of her team were naïve—by a long shot—everyone had been shocked and horrified by what Stephen and Jennifer had uncovered in Europe. A man named Hugo Marcari had, in a maniacal quest for power, abducted whole clans of Wechselbalg and attempted to break them to his will so he could build his own personal army.

It wasn't the lust for power or even the cruelty that bothered Bethany Anne. Oh, she would fight and die to save the world from those things, but she was not surprised by them. Neither, she suspected, was Stephen. It was something about the meticulous planning and the sheer breadth of the cruelty that had shocked her.

She did not say any of this.

She wanted to hear Stephen speak of it first. She liked to hear his thoughts on the world. He always had insights that surprised her—or reminded her of her values.

Stephen seemed almost unaware that she was still there. He was gazing at the far wall with a frown on his face.

"I keep thinking that I understand greed," he said finally. "I saw it enough with the others." He looked at her then, his eyes jarringly old in his young face. "I saw what they did to Michael."

Bethany Anne swallowed and looked away.

"I should not have—"

"Not speaking of it won't change anything," she said simply. She took a moment to steady herself, and looked back at him. "What were you going to say?"

"Just that... I think I understand greed, and that I will be able to recognize it and anticipate it. But greed wears so many faces." Stephen's mouth twisted. "I never recognize it when I see it, and I am always surprised. I am like a child... I am shocked when I should simply expect such things now."

Bethany Anne could feel TOM's interest, and she had the sense that ADAM was waiting silently for more information. It was clear to all of them that Stephen's experiences with the torture facilities in Europe were haunting him in more ways than one.

"Hugo made himself believe that what he did was right," Stephen said quietly. "I am sure that with enough...pain and time, one could have stripped away the lies and he would admit that he simply wanted power, and he couldn't bear to have people defy him. But on every real level during every interaction, in every *thought*, Hugo believed that what he was doing was right and necessary."

Bethany Anne nodded quietly. She was beginning to see what was troubling Stephen.

"If he could convince himself that such horrific things were right," Stephen asked quietly, "what could I convince *myself* of? What *have* I convinced myself of?"

"You know you are nothing like Hugo," Bethany Anne said quietly.

"I don't know that," Stephen said bluntly.

"In the pursuit of all moral causes, there are those who become extremists," ADAM said.

Both Bethany Anne and Stephen looked up in surprise. Neither would have expected ADAM to weigh in on such a matter.

"It is said by some that the pursuit of specific social change is an inherently selfish endeavor," ADAM continued. "The cause resonates strongly with those who follow it, so they seek satisfaction within themselves by pursuing change."

Stephen considered this. "Do you believe this?"

He was interested to hear the AI's conclusions on the matter.

"I believe it is a correct interpretation of the data, but not necessarily an important one," ADAM said after a moment. "If an injustice has occurred and it is righted, is the happiness of the one who righted it the important thing, or is the most important thing the fact that justice has been served?"

Stephen smiled. "An interesting conclusion. So how would you answer my question, then?"

"I think you are aware that an organic mind can create delusions, and I think you have surrounded yourself with those who would tell you if you engaged in harmful delusions like Hugo did. Consider the fact that Hugo punished those who contradicted him. You do not do this. Therefore, I think you have arranged your life—whether on purpose or not—so that you pursue good social endeavors, and you will not be allowed to slide into extremism." ADAM sounded proud of himself.

There was a pause.

"It takes a great deal of processing power to examine organic minds," the AI admitted a moment later. "And I never know if I am correct."

"Sounds exactly correct to me," Bethany Anne said. She nodded at Stephen. "What do you think?"

Stephen was smiling slightly. "I think that was a very good analysis, ADAM. I would like to talk more about this at some point, if it would not be too tiring for you."

"I would also like that very much."

Bethany Anne smiled at the conversation as she spread blueprints out on the table. "Count me in. I'd like to hear everyone's thoughts. Now, I've had a few ideas on building materials. Is the call connected? Good. Bobcat, tell me what you think of this..."

Romania

Over lunch in town, Alexi and Ecaterina shared their findings with the others.

At Alexi's insistence the dogs had been brought along. Alexi enjoyed much the same reputation in his town that

Yelena had in hers. He was known to have a somewhat innate understanding of animals, although there were a lot of jokes about how livestock seemed to hate him.

People were only too eager to tell Yelena how so-and-so's horse had taken an immediate dislike to Alexi, or how so-and-so's chickens fled the yard, squawking whenever he arrived. It was clear that everyone in the town considered this hilarious.

Yelena, who knew there was more to the story, only smiled.

Ashur and Bellatrix, brought along under stern instructions from Yelena that they were to be on their *best* behavior, were making a big show of being dainty. Ashur fairly pranced, and Bellatrix preened whenever someone complimented her coat.

Alexi had insisted on sitting next to Christina, and she was presently clambering onto his shoulders and his head with an expression of dogged persistence, heedless of the fact that they were in a restaurant.

No one seemed to care. This was hardly a formal place, and children were woven into the life of the town here.

Nathan smiled at her before looking at Ecaterina, "So, what did you find out?"

"They're rich," Ecaterina said at once.

"How do you know?" Nathan asked her in confusion.

"The traps are very good quality." Ecaterina nodded to her pack. "I'll show you when we're back home, but they're coated so that they won't rust, they're very sharp, and they're complex, not just a simple trip."

"They're powerful." Alexi looked grim, or as grim as it

was possible to look with a small child climbing on his head. "They can shatter bones."

"And there are a lot of them," Ecaterina added. "We picked up as many as we could, and disabled others."

"Is it worth letting them know that you are on to them?" Yelena asked worriedly. "If they see that someone has been taking or disabling traps, maybe your hand will be tipped."

Ecaterina smiled. It was not a *nice* smile, and Yelena had the sudden motivation never to do anything that would annoy her.

"I don't think we need to worry about that," Ecaterina explained. Her smile turned almost conspiratorial. "We *want* them to notice. Whoever they are, we've just undone a lot of their work. There's going to be a flurry of activity, and as soon as we have one of them, I'm fairly sure we can *persuade* him to tell us who they work for."

Alexi laughed, shaking his head at his niece. "Wasn't so long ago that you were making mud pies and skinning your knees, and now here you are, making plans like that. Why, if I didn't know better, I'd say that husband of yours was a bad influence."

Nathan laughed. There was too much fondness in Alexi's tone for it to be anything but a joke...and he knew enough to know that Alexi valued Ecaterina's rather unconventional style of solving problems.

Their laughter was interrupted by a sudden spate of barking.

"Bellatrix!" Yelena was up and to the dog in a moment. "Don't bark like that. You—"

She stopped suddenly. Having worked in a kennel, she

343

had been taught to value good manners in a dog, but she had also been taught to trust a dog's instincts.

And right now Bellatrix was on high alert.

Bellatrix, who up until now had hated no one in the world except Ciprian, Yelena's ex-boyfriend.

Yelena followed the dog's gaze. A man across the street was watching her. His eyes met hers briefly, but it was Bellatrix he was watching.

And Bellatrix was watching him, a low growl building in her throat.

He disappeared around a corner a moment later, but not before Nathan got a glimpse. Yelena had crouched next to Bellatrix and was apologizing for doubting her reaction, whispering over and over that she would never let that man hurt her.

She looked up at Nathan. "Was that…"

"One of the men who was staring this morning?" Nathan finished. "Yes." He looked over his shoulder at Ecaterina. "You said you were looking for people who might be trading wolf furs, right? Well, we might just have brought the perfect bait to lure them into the open."

CHAPTER 5

Bobcat turned the truck up an unpaved road and savored the heavy chug of the engine. Dust was rising behind him in the heavy midafternoon air. Though it was turning to autumn and the chill was evident in the mornings and the evenings, the days still had that hot, dreamy quality to them.

Bobcat hadn't spent much time in the Midwest in his life, but he was finding that it suited him.

Outside the major cities the land turned quickly to a dotted landscape of fields and tiny stands of trees, houses set far apart, and barns with silos. Cows grazed peaceably, horses swatted flies with their tails, and the lines of crops about to be harvested curved hypnotically over the swells of the hills.

This, Bobcat thought, *was the sort of place a man could lose himself peacefully for a few decades.*

He wondered if Yelena would like it here.

Maybe, he decided. He could easily picture her striding through dew-soaked tall grass in a heavy sweater and knee-high rain boots, surrounded by an adoring pack of German Shepherds.

The thought was so distracting that he missed his next turn and had to back the truck up. His face heated. It wasn't shame, exactly, he just found that he felt more alive when he was with Yelena or even when he thought about her. His heart was going faster than normal.

He guided the truck up a low hill surrounded by trees and emerged into a broad clearing. A couple of battered trucks sat outside a garage with peeling paint. One of the truck beds held a wealth of vegetables, perhaps to be taken to a farmers' market, and the other was filled with a huge crush of tools.

The farmhouse itself was old and stately, and the trees had been cleared on one side of the hill to allow a clear view of the fields below. Sheep and horses grazed on the land between, and Bobcat took a minute to soak in the view.

He'd forgotten how big a sky could be.

The sound of the door opening recalled him, and he turned to see an older man heading down the walk from the house. The man wore weathered jeans, stained from heavy use but recently washed, a flannel shirt tucked in, and work boots that looked well broken-in.

He stopped and gave Bobcat a onceover, but it wasn't clear from the look on his face if he liked what he saw or not.

He turned his gaze to the truck, but spoke to Bobcat. "You're the one my son talked to, huh?"

"Your son is Jim McHugh?" Bobcat asked. The man on

the phone had sounded old and gruff. How old was *this* man?

"Yep, that's him." The man nodded decisively. "I'm Dick. Wasn't plannin' to give you the time of day, but Jim liked the sound of you."

Abruptly Bobcat felt guilty.

When he had called around to the farms in the area he'd told them that he'd never been to the Midwest, but had come into a little bit of money and was hoping to buy some land, maybe start a small farm.

Jim had been suspicious—and rightly so—but Bobcat had pressed onwards. He wanted to know how the crops worked together, he said. It wouldn't be a large-scale farming operation since he didn't have that much money, but he wanted to know all about the pests and what depleted the land and what fed it. He asked about livestock. He mentioned being interested in reviving some of the old varieties of crops, and asked about curing meats.

It seemed that he'd managed to convince the man, and now he felt guilty for lying.

But what could he say? *I'm a representative of TQB—yeah, that TQB—and the Queen Bitch wants a lot of seeds just in case?*

"Let's walk down to the fields," Dick suggested. He started walking without waiting to see if Bobcat would follow. Like many patriarchs before him he just assumed others would obey, and he had the gruff, commanding air that ensured they would.

Bobcat fell in beside him and climbed up over a stile into the field.

"Watch the muck," Dick suggested pragmatically.

Then he fixed Bobcat with a stare.

NATALIE GREY & MICHAEL ANDERLE

"So what's your story?"

"I told Jim—"

"Yeah, I know what you told Jim. You want t'learn about seeds. Why?"

In his pocket, Bobcat's phone buzzed and he struggled not to pull it out. It might be a shipping confirmation on the myrcene oil. Once again, he saw happy visions of Yelena laughing and cheering as he won the beer competition...

He cleared his throat hastily.

And whether it was something in the view or the air or Dick McHugh's weathered face, he found himself speaking as honestly as he could. He talked about living life with a purpose, and how he felt when he'd watched the sun rise over the fields this morning as he drove. He talked about wanting to give Yelena a farmhouse in the country and a place for her dogs to run. He mentioned the feel of dirt under his fingernails, and how he'd always worked best in the mornings when everyone else was asleep—and how, when he got an idea in his head, he was stubborn as all get-out.

He could tell Dick was intrigued. Somehow—Bobcat would never later be sure *exactly* how—the farmer got the story out of him about piloting helicopters, working on his own machines, and even a bit about the mysterious employer who had given Bobcat the money to buy seeds with.

"She a farmer?" he asked in surprise, and Bobcat laughed.

He pictured Bethany Anne's couture and her sudden ferocious violence. She was as far from being a

Midwestern farmer as he could imagine, and yet he thought Bethany Anne and Dick would get on very well.

"No," he said. "Just practical."

Dick McHugh nodded. They had reached the dirt road that ran alongside the fields and were staring contemplatively at the corn. It was nearly ripe for harvest, and Bobcat, to his surprise, could smell it. His mouth watered.

"Yeah," Dick said finally. He nodded and looped his thumbs through his belt buckles. "Don't know if you'd make a good farmer, t'be honest, but I like the look of you so I'll help you figure out which seeds you need. I can make sure you get 'em, too."

Bobcat grinned and held out his hand to shake. "Thank you. You have no idea how much this means to me."

To his surprise, he wasn't telling even a bit of a lie.

The more he saw places like this and was surrounded by things growing and the smell of rich tilled earth, the more he thought there was really something to this seed-vault plan.

Romania

Ecaterina's phone rang that evening, and she strained to reach it without dislodging Christina. Her daughter had fallen asleep nestled against her, seemingly totally untroubled by the noises around her, but Ecaterina knew that as soon as she moved, the girl would wake up and be grumpy.

To her great surprise, she found she didn't mind very much.

"Hi," she answered.

349

Bethany Anne's voice was cautious, "Is everything okay? You're talking very softly."

"Christina is asleep," Ecaterina explained. "I really don't need to be quiet, but it's just an instinct around sleeping kids, you know?"

"I do the same thing," Bethany Anne laughed, "but that kid could sleep through a *hurricane.*"

"Yeah." Ecaterina kissed the top of her daughter's head. "Yeah, she could. Funny how she can't put up with broccoli, though."

"Still having the broccoli fight? Better you than me." Bethany Anne, a woman of iron will, nonetheless knew when she had met her match—and Christina, faced with a request to eat broccoli, was a match for anyone. "So how are things going down there?"

"Well, actually, it's good for Alexi to see Christina, and I can't wait to start looking for seeds. In fact, I have Nathan and Yelena off cataloguing plants." Ecaterina chewed her lip. "There's just, uh…something I have to do before that."

Back on the *Meredith Reynolds*, Bethany Anne propped her feet up on a footrest and grinned. The deep, deep blue of the shoes winked back at her, visible only briefly as the shoes caught the light. She took a moment to admire her new footwear and then returned to the matter at hand.

"I know that tone of voice. Someone did something bad."

Ecaterina was trying not to laugh too loudly. "Since when do I have a tone of voice for that?"

"You learned it from your husband," Bethany Anne explained. "It was always a lurking tendency, and he definitely brought it out in you."

"A lurking tendency... Good Lord, woman." Ecaterina snorted.

"You're very justice-minded. Everyone who works for me is." Bethany Anne settled into her chair with a pleased grin. "So what's going on?"

"Someone's trapping wolves for fur," Ecaterina told her. "I don't know if I can explain to someone who didn't grow up hunting for food, but—"

"That is the most cowardly, dishonorable, *useless* thing!" Bethany Anne exploded. "Those raccoon-humping shit-guzzlers had better hope their dicks rot off before I find them or I'm going to make them *eat* them."

Ecaterina stared down the phone and wondered vaguely if she should have covered her child's ears.

"So what I'm hearing is, you don't mind me taking some time to mess them up before I head back?" She kept her voice calm, but there was a laugh threatening.

"No, I fucking do not." Bethany Anne was still heated. "What's your plan?"

"Well," Ecaterina grinned, "Alexi and I came up with one this morning, and Nathan put the finishing touches on it. Did you know my husband is an evil genius, by the way?"

"I did. It's one of his best qualities."

"Indeed. So..." Ecaterina detailed the plan, grinning as she did.

By the end, Bethany Anne was back to her good humor. "That's amazing," she told Ecaterina. "They aren't going to know what hit them. Let me know how it goes, and say hi to everyone for me."

Marcus and Barnabas strolled along a country lane. The smell of lavender hung in the air, and Marcus gave a disbelieving laugh.

"What is it?" Barnabas asked curiously.

"I didn't, uh... I didn't think it would actually be this picturesque." Marcus shook his head. "But it really is as gorgeous as it's supposed to be. I wish I had someone to bring here," he added mournfully."

"Self-pity is not becoming," Barnabas said severely.

"It's just annoying," Marcus muttered. "John has Jean, Bobcat has Yelena…"

"John does not *have* Jean." Barnabas' tone had grown sharper, and he fixed Marcus with a glare. "Nor does Bobcat *have* Yelena. Both have cultivated meaningful relationships with the ladies in question. As could you."

"But on a space station—"

"I refuse to waste any further time speaking of this."

"*Fine.*" Marcus was just opening his mouth to ask about the seeds they were hoping to get when Tabitha raced past them at high speed.

"Woohooooooo!"

She had seen a rental shop for bikes in the nearby town and had absolutely insisted that she be allowed to rent one. While Barnabas argued that it was a tourist trap and vastly overpriced, Marcus had quietly shelled out the money to the shop's proprietor.

When Barnabas fixed him with a glare, Marcus shrugged. "We have more money than God."

That only made the glare worse. Barnabas had a rather old-fashioned concept of heresy.

However, he was not immune to the sight of Tabitha racing around on the bike, and he smiled fondly after her.

"See, you're glad she has it!" Marcus said now.

"I am," Barnabas admitted. "I forget sometimes that Tabitha's youth was rather interrupted. It is good to see her enjoying something so simple. I worry about her at times."

"Oh?" Marcus glanced at the farmhouse they were approaching. It was still a ways down the road, but he was beginning to pick out details like the tiles on the roof, the smooth sides of the building, and the garden in front.

"She is young," Barnabas said simply. "She is very clever, of course, but that only makes her lack of experience more dangerous. She believes she can always work her way out of problems. And..." He cleared his throat almost awkwardly.

Marcus looked over in silent amazement. From brewing beer to combat, he had never once seen Barnabas be the least bit awkward.

"I do not want her to be hurt," Barnabas admitted. "I care for her."

There was a crash and a shriek from up ahead, and some cartwheeling limbs announced that Tabitha had been thrown from her bike into a ditch.

"Rather like an idiot niece," Barnabas said contemplatively.

Marcus' shoulders shook. He wasn't sure if he was supposed to be laughing at this.

A shout from up ahead alerted them to the farmer's

presence. Perhaps lured out of his house by Tabitha's bike crash, he was now hurrying along the road.

"Let us go obtain some lavender," Barnabas said serenely and quickened his pace without seeming to move more urgently at all.

"Vampires," Marcus muttered as he hurried after him.

Romania

Ecaterina hopped off a ledge into the underbrush, "All I'm saying is, someone would know if it was a person in town. You would have heard about it."

"Are you *sure*?" Alexi asked doubtfully. "If they were using the money for these traps…"

"If someone came into that much money there'd be talk. You know they wouldn't be able to hide it or resist buying some rounds at the inn, and word would creep out, especially from anyone doing this sort of trapping. They aren't going to do it alone. They're cowards, remember?"

"I suppose. Found another one." Alexi knelt to examine the trap carefully, then retreated to a safe distance to trip it with a long stick.

He winced as the trap clanged shut. It wasn't particularly good for the traps to slam shut when there was nothing inside, but then again, he wasn't worried about damaging the equipment.

What he *was* worried about was the force of the traps. The way they came together was strong enough to shatter bone, but not sever a limb. The injured animal would not have the chance to die with dignity, it would be forced to lie in the trap and bleed out slowly.

The thought made him feel almost physically ill.

A shout from up the hill made him turn to look.

"Ecaterina." He didn't look back, just kept his eyes locked on the man heading toward them. "We have company."

"Interesting." She came to stand beside him and he saw her assessing the man's gait. "I feel like I've met him before, but I can't place him."

"It's old Mihai's grandson," Alexi answered. "His mother and father raised him in Brasov, but when his mother died his father shipped him back here. I think his name was Alexandru."

"Andrei—I remember him now." Ecaterina tilted her head. "He must not remember you though, if he's the one setting these traps."

"Or you," Alexi said with a chuckle. "You may not always have been able to shift, but even *I* didn't want to get on your bad side when you were a child."

Ecaterina muttered, "So that's where Christina got it." She raised her voice. "Andrei. Good day to you."

"What are you doing with these traps?" Andrei demanded.

Ecaterina and Alexi exchanged a look. Perhaps Andrei wasn't behind this at all. Perhaps he was just as offended as they were by the presence of the traps there.

"We're disabling them," Ecaterina said. Even if Andrei was behind all this, she wasn't particularly worried. People in this town could be easily kept in line by the reminder that the whole town would shame them for bad behavior. "Do you know who set them up?"

"Yeah," Andrei said combatively. "I did."

So much for hoping. Alexi shook his head wearily.

"Child, do you have any idea what you are playing with?"

To his surprise, a gun appeared in Andrei's hand. "Do *you*?" Andrei demanded.

CHAPTER 6

Ecaterina felt a sudden surge of anger and tried to keep her emotions in check. The last thing she needed was to shift forms without warning. For one thing, the existence of Wechselbalg wasn't something that should be widely known yet.

For another, she really liked these jeans.

Plus, Alexi had always solved these things with talk before.

"Andrei." She tried to keep her tone soothing. "Why are you pointing a gun at us?"

Andrei blinked. Clearly he had not anticipated this particular question.

His face hardened again a moment later. "Shut up."

She could practically smell the fear rolling off him.

Alexi could smell it too, and he was intrigued. In his confrontations with trappers he had seen greed, laziness, and yes, sometimes anger. In his experience, when people did something they knew was wrong, they only got angrier when someone called them on it. Once or twice he'd seen exhaustion and hunger, and he'd made sure that those families got what they needed.

This was different. Andrei's fear was part desperation, part panic, and the nice clothes and shiny gun, as well as the very well-made traps, showed that money wasn't the issue.

Or was it?

"Andrei, do you know who I am?"

"You're old man Alexi." Andrei had the sense not to be outright rude, but he clearly wasn't happy with this conversation. "But it doesn't matter who you are, you can't just interfere with this."

Alexi was determined to deescalate this.

"How is Mihai?" he asked the boy.

"Fine," Andrei said sullenly. He shrugged.

For any other boy, Alexi would have had a stern reminder about manners. Most boys, though, didn't point guns at him and his niece in the forest.

He wondered if it might not still be advisable.

"Why are you setting traps out?" he asked.

"For—" Andrei bit his words off and looked between them warily. "It's none of your business."

"These are our forests," Ecaterina pointed out. Her voice was soft and kind. "Children play here, Andrei."

Andrei looked uncertain. "Well, they shouldn't be out alone."

"And the balance of the forests—"

"Oh, please." Andrei rolled his eyes. "Don't give me that 'living forest' crap. If we went back to the old ways we'd all be living in caves. We wouldn't have doctors. Or toilets. Is that really what you want?"

Ecaterina's eyes narrowed.

Even she, with her almost constant escapes into the wilderness, had not truly understood the force and necessity of nature until she had largely given it up. The *Meredith Reynolds* was a true technological marvel, and Bethany Anne's dedication to making it self-sufficient *and* pleasant was impressive.

But building the seed vault only drove home the truly staggering complexity of ecosystems. It was almost incomprehensible to the human mind, the sheer number of plants and animals that interacted to create these forests.

And she refused to believe that Andrei had no concept of this.

She told him, "There is a difference between understanding the forest and wanting to live in caves."

"Sure." He sneered at her and jabbed the gun. "You think animals are more important than humans."

"Not *more* important—"

"People need to live and eat, you know!" He waved the gun.

Alexi's eyes widened. Never had he seen someone be so careless, and he was worrying that this situation would escalate too quickly to control.

Whatever happened, he would *not* allow Ecaterina to be hurt.

Andrei continued, "When people need to make a living, it's not fair to expect them to preserve some pristine forest just so other people can tramp through it."

Ecaterina tilted her head. It was just an inkling, but she was pretty sure that these weren't really Andrei's words. It sounded like he was repeating a justification someone else had told him.

"Who said that to you?" she asked curiously.

It was both the right and the wrong question to ask. Andrei's face got white and scared, and he pointed the gun with sudden determination.

"You do not know who you're playing with." He spoke the words carefully, very slowly, as if he wanted to impress upon them the importance of what he was saying.

"The person who hired you," Ecaterina pressed.

"Ecaterina..." Alexi began.

"He's not playing around," Andrei said quietly. He looked truly afraid. "And he's not going to tolerate you messing up his plans. If you know what's good for you, you'll back off. I could..." He looked around suddenly, as if terrified that someone might be listening in. "No, best you just go and hope he never finds you."

"Tell us who he is," Ecaterina pleaded. "We can help you."

Alexi bit his lip rather than interfere. Saying anything might break the spell Ecaterina was weaving, and he could sense that Andrei was wavering. The man knew that what he was doing was wrong, and he wanted to believe he could get out of this mess.

Then the fear came crashing back, followed by terrible resolve. It was an expression Alexi had seen only a handful of times, and he hated it. It said, "I have to save myself first."

And his finger tightened around the trigger.

Ecaterina might have been trying to resolve this matter peacefully, but she was ready for it to turn violent. With the reflexes bestowed by both her recent changes and her inborn instincts, she was already diving out of the way as Andrei fired.

By the time she rolled and stood up, she was in Pricolici form.

Andrei fired again. Once he had started shooting, in his panic he just kept doing so. But the wolf was far faster than he was. It evaded each shot, slinking and weaving until his magazine was out, and then it leapt straight for him.

Bowled over onto his back on the forest floor, looking up into the face of the massive wolf, Andrei gave a low moan of fear.

The wolf dipped its snout close to Andrei's face. "You-uuuu willllll tellll meeee evvvverythiiiiing nowwwww…"

There was a long pause, and then the wolf nudged Andrei's limp form. The man had passed out in terror.

"Orrrrrr innnn a minuuuuute…" the wolf muttered.

Alexi laughed until he was doubled over, hand over his belly. Then he settled down with his back against a tree to wait.

"It isn't that simple," Ecaterina said later. She was pacing back and forth in the small kitchen waving her arms.

"How is it not that simple?" Bethany Anne's voice filtered out of the speaker. "He's doing all of this—he admitted it. He knows it's wrong."

"People mess up," Nathan pointed out.

"Not checking the takeout order before you leave is messing up," Bethany Anne said, annoyed. "Listening to someone who sweet talks you into killing innocent animals is on a totally different level."

Ecaterina wavered. Her shoulders were hunched as she leaned against the wall.

"I just don't think he really wants to do it," she said quietly.

"No, he wants the money, and he's willing to kill innocent animals to get it."

There was no answer to that.

Nathan sank into silence. He was seeing this from both sides, as he knew Ecaterina was as well. Her impassioned speech when she got back from the forest had persuaded him to check his natural impulse to punish the wrongdoers.

She had explained to him that in towns like this, small towns in the aftermath of the Soviet Union, subsistence living was often the norm. One learned to expect lean times and to jump at work when it was offered, and so people were especially vulnerable to those who, pretending to be reasonable, preyed upon the natural instinct to provide for one's family.

And those people, she had told him, were brutal. They controlled through unpredictable violence and fear, and left one choice: obey and be richly rewarded, or disobey and be killed painfully. No matter how much they might, on some level, realize that they could be in the line of fire at any time, people kept their heads down out of instinct.

They told themselves that everyone did whatever they needed to do to survive.

They told themselves that they and their families had to be their first priority.

Even Alexi of all people had agreed. He mentioned the times he went to talk to villagers about their traps. He had kept his concerns from the police, from being enforced by outsiders—and he always made sure that the families in question had enough to sustain themselves.

To Nathan, much of this was unfathomable. Right was right, and wrong was wrong. It shocked him that two people he thought so highly of, who were as passionate about justice as he was, could defend Andrei's actions.

But he had learned that when people did things outside the norm he expected, he needed to ask why. He needed to dig deeper in order to understand.

He looked over to where Ecaterina was chewing on her lip unhappily, and listened to Bethany Anne's silence.

His Queen was not waiting for mindless obedience, Nathan knew. She was waiting for an explanation. She wanted a *reason*, not simply a wish.

She knew how easily a well-meaning desire for mercy could turn into something poisonous down the line.

"I want to learn more about Andrei," Ecaterina said finally. "Maybe he hasn't been a willing participant in this —if he was scared for his grandfather or something. I want to find the others and ask them the same thing. Any of them who refuse to admit what they did was wrong— who are too far gone—I will deal with, but they should have the chance to make amends. People who have slipped once can become the strongest defenders of justice sometimes."

Bethany Anne didn't miss a beat, "Very well, I leave it up to your discretion. Does anyone else have concerns or matters I should know about?"

NATALIE GREY & MICHAEL ANDERLE

"How's Bobcat?" Yelena asked. The moment she realized what she had said she flushed scarlet.

"Locked up in his lab doing something with the beer competition." Bethany Anne's voice had a wicked tone, but she didn't make a big deal of Yelena's slip. "He's like a man possessed. All he does is drink beer, plan beer—and work on ships."

"You know, that sounds pretty normal for Bobcat," Nathan pointed out.

"Yes, but we finally had him doing things other than that." Bethany Anne sounded long-suffering. "Yelena, we need you back. You persuade him to come out of his office sometimes. No one else can do that. Anyway, if there's nothing else, I'm off to train. You kids have fun ridding the countryside of degenerates."

The line clicked off, and everyone hid their grins at Yelena's shy little smile.

QBBS *Meredith Reynolds*

Bobcat hurried into his study. The door to the main room was locked behind him, as well as the study door—both locks. He looked around suspiciously to check for cameras.

He only half-thought he was being ridiculous. He was the best brewer, and the other two knew it. Therefore, it stood to reason that they might be trying to put him under surveillance.

He covered the camera on his computer and looked around once more.

Good, he was alone.

Almost reverently, he opened the nondescript box and pulled out the two bottles of myrcene oil. Both bottles had been packaged securely, and appeared to be undamaged. When he sniffed, not even a hint of the oil's scent could be sensed.

That was good. If a package had shown up smelling like hops, he was sure either Marcus or William would have heard about it.

He set one bottle on the table and unscrewed the cap of the other, inhaling with a lazy smile.

Then he inhaled again.

The oil, as far as he could tell, really didn't smell like much of anything at all.

He sniffed again, then put the cap back on the bottle and crossed to his store of hops. He inhaled, and was greeted with the usual sharp scents.

He looked at the myrcene oil, then he went back to his computer and searched for it. His shoulders settled back happily as he saw hundreds of results come back. Blogs came up, some with references as far back as ten years prior. Commenters on message boards asked in vain where they could get myrcene oil, and more recent posts showed a flurry of activity—a supplier had been found!

Panic gripped Bobcat. If this technique was suddenly becoming popular, then it was possible Marcus and William might find out about it.

The idea came to him in a flash: block the mention. He knew enough to get into the routers, and carefully began building a program that would block all pages with any mention of the oil. But, he reflected, that wasn't quite enough…

"May I ask what you are doing?" a computerized voice asked.

Bobcat jumped. ADAM...he'd forgotten ADAM.

"Uh..." He looked around worriedly.

"There is no need to look for me. I am everywhere."

"That's not reassuring," Bobcat muttered.

"Oh, dear. You appear perturbed. Is this my fault?"

Bobcat considered. He had at first assumed that ADAM would fault him for his actions, but it appeared that the AI did not intend to chastise him.

"I'm trying to make sure Marcus and William don't steal my newest trick for the beer competition," he explained.

"You are worried that they will find the same trick on their own, or that they will learn it by watching you?"

"By watching me." Bobcat looked at the program. "Or that they will find it on their own," he admitted.

"Isn't that unethical? You are denying them a valid technique."

"Well, yes..." Bobcat hunched his shoulders.

"I think you should leave the webpages unblocked," ADAM said after a moment.

"Why?" He tried not to sink his face into his hands. He didn't really want to hear a treatise on morality from an AI.

"Because if you win the competition by denying others the same technology you have access to your victory will be meaningless, and you will come to have negative associations with the memory. Victory should be happy, not painful."

Bobcat looked around again.

"I do not have a physical location," ADAM reminded him.

"Right, right." Bobcat stared at the screen. "Thank you for your input. That was helpful." He only narrowly managed to avoid using the phrase, "Surprisingly helpful."

With a sigh, he undid the blocks. Now anyone could find and use myrcene oil.

"You had better hope Yelena is still impressed," he muttered.

CHAPTER 7

<u>**Romania**</u>

Andrei woke up in the forest alone.

The fall evening was getting cold, and he was chilled. Shivering, he pushed himself to his feet and groaned in pain.

He remembered—or more accurately was desperately trying to forget—screaming in terror, babbling answers to the wolf that had spoken to him, and seeing spots as he passed out time and again from fear.

The wolf hadn't been impressed with the lies he told.

So he had told the truth. He had sold his employer out. Panic made his knees weak again.

You did *not* sell out Ioan. Ioan killed people for disobedience and betrayal. Even talking back—hell, even a noncommittal look—was enough to earn a severe punishment.

Sometimes, it was whispered, Ioan killed people who had done nothing at all. Andrei hadn't seen it, himself, but he believed it.

It was enough to make him think he should never have gotten mixed up in any of this.

In fact, he was beginning to think he should get out.

It was going to be difficult. He would need to get his grandfather to come with him, and Mihai was a man with a stubborn attachment to the town he'd grown up in. He would protest, but he had to come with Andrei. Ioan certainly knew where Andrei lived. He would kill Mihai in a heartbeat to make a point.

As he stumbled back up the slope toward town, Andrei rubbed his arms to warm them, and tried to come up with a plan. His breath clouded in the cold air, and his brain was filling his thoughts with warm blankets and cups of tea.

But he needed to focus.

You didn't run from Ioan without a plan.

He would go in tomorrow, he decided. He would tell that weaselly Grigore that he'd managed to find out who was disabling the traps, and he'd killed him and hidden the body. Let Ioan hear that Andrei was a loyal servant. That way, when he disappeared they wouldn't come looking for him immediately.

Meanwhile he'd pay someone to help him and Mihai disappear. It wasn't impossible, and Ioan would only spend so much time and effort to make a point.

It was a good plan.

At least, it had been a good plan until he came around the edge of the path into town and saw a black car idling by his house.

The air seized in his lungs and Andrei heard himself whimper. Ioan was here, and he was waiting in Andrei's house. That could not possibly mean anything good.

Between that moment and his death, Andrei would deeply regret his next actions: he turned, and ran. His master-plan of a clever bluff was thrown aside, and he ran like a coward. He ran like an animal. He ran like prey.

So they hunted him like prey. He heard the yell behind him as he plunged into the woods, heedless of the branches whipping past his face. He had no plan, he had only panic.

Of course they caught him. They were used to people running and they let him struggle too, so that when he was at last dragged back to Ioan's car he was exhausted and almost crying with fear. He had the chance to see Ioan's merciless black eyes.

Then they put a bag over Andrei's head and the car lurched into motion.

QBBS *Meredith Reynolds*

Marcus made his way down the hallway of the *Meredith Reynolds* distractedly. He was mentally rechecking final proportions of hops as well as an exhaustive step-by-step list, and looked up periodically to make sure he didn't trip over anything.

It didn't work perfectly as a system, but he only ran into two doorways.

He thought he heard giggling as he crossed the open bay to his office, but thought nothing of it. The area was hardly deserted. It was only when he crossed the threshold that he realized the delighted giggles were coming from his office. Tabitha was bouncing excitedly on his office chair and grinning at him like a tiny lunatic.

Marcus stopped dead. This seemed like an ominous development.

In his experience, things that made Tabitha laugh were likely to end in catastrophe.

"Can I help you?" he managed.

"I got you a leg up in the beer competition," she informed him smugly.

"You did?" He grabbed the other chair and scooted it closer. "Tell."

She hiked her legs up to sit cross-legged and leaned back in the chair with a grin. "I hacked Bobcat's emails."

Marcus froze. "You what?"

"Yeah, apparently he got something called—"

"That's not ethical."

She frowned in confusion, "You were trying to do it. I saw the traces in the system. You tried to look, so I thought I'd help."

"No, I was *going* to look and I stopped." Marcus looked around uncertainly, half sure he would see Barnabas hanging upside down like a bat in one of the corners. "I… want to do the right thing, although I was tempted to do the wrong thing." He looked around again; Barnabas might still be listening. "But I *didn't*," he added, just in case.

"Who are you talking to?"

"No one. Nothing." Marcus settled back in the chair as smoothly as he could manage. "You were saying?"

Tabitha was watching him like he was going crazy, and perhaps he was.

Then she gave a very soft, "Aha." "You're worried about Barnabas."

"Shhhh!"

She started laughing again, one hand over her mouth as she hiccupped with laughter.

"You don't need to be scared of him, I *told* you, he's really sneaky."

"He keeps insisting that the only good way to do things is to focus on the fundamentals of brewing beer and hope that wins the competition!"

Tabitha rolled her eyes. "Look, Bobcat nearly got all of you killed to get some special hops. William has hacked Bobcat. *They're* both stacking the deck, so why shouldn't you?"

"William hacked Bobcat? Aw, man." Marcus slumped. "I'm never gonna win."

"Exactly!" Tabitha leaned over and patted his knee.

"Comforting."

"Oh, for— No, that's why I helped you with the hacking." She gave him a sweet smile. "And Barnabas doesn't have to know, does he? *I* won't tell him."

"But..." Marcus rubbed his temples. "Oh, I don't know what to do."

"It's easy." Tabitha gestured. "Look at the screen. Read the emails. Win the competition."

"I can't just—"

"Oh, but you can."

He wavered. He sneaked a peek out of the corner of his eye.

He stood up so quickly his chair fell over backwards. If he stayed, he was going to look.

"Where are you going?" Tabitha called as he walked quickly back across the bay

"To have a beer!" he yelled back. "It'll provide clarity."

"That is *not* how beer works!" She hightailed it after him, slamming the door behind her, and poked his arm for emphasis as they walked. "Look, if you'll just listen—"

"I'm not listening! Nope! Lalalalalalala…"

"Oh, for God's sake. They got something called 'myrcene oil.'"

"Not liiiisteniiiiiing! Wait, what?"

Tabitha gave him a smug look. "See, was that so hard? Myrcene oil. Ever heard of it?"

"No." *Shit.*

"Well, all the emails are up on your desktop if you want them." She gave him a sweet smile and glided off, leaving Marcus staring after her, wide-eyed with indecision.

He looked at the office door. He looked after Tabby. He looked back at the office door. Then back after Tabby. Then he sank his head into his hands with a muffled groan of distress.

He'd never even *heard* of this stuff. What was he supposed to do now?

Romania

Andrei barely managed to hold himself together as the car slid smoothly through the streets.

Once, only once, he gave a little whimper and received a blow to the side that made him cry out. A second blow fell, and then another and another. The pain multiplied, each hit landing on tender skin until there was so much pain that it was beyond him to respond at all.

He sagged onto the floor. There was only this moment, then the next one, and then the one after that. Each moment was filled with pain and since he could not see, pain was the only thing in his world. Each moment was indistinguishable from the next.

He had the sense that time had disappeared entirely.

He must have stopped crying out at some point, because a rough voice said, "That's better. You make no sound unless you are asked a question, and then you will only answer the question."

Ioan's voice, smooth and filled with contempt, added, "Are you capable of understanding that?"

"Y-yes." Opening his mouth meant that he wanted to let another whimper escape, but he pressed his lips together until he felt skin break and tasted blood.

He couldn't make a single noise or they would beat him again, and even this moment—filled with bruises, feeling every little jolt in the road—was better than being beaten.

Ioan waited for a few moments as if hoping that Andrei would break again.

But when he spoke, his voice was satisfied. "Good."

Andrei squeezed his eyes shut under the hood to keep back tears. He was afraid to do anything that would set Ioan off again, but he knew that this was just borrowing time. All he would buy himself was torture while they questioned him.

And then they were going to kill him.

He wished, not for the first time, that he wasn't such a coward.

"I still don't know what to do." Ecaterina sipped at an earthenware mug of tea and stared blankly at the wall of the kitchen. "I don't know what to *do*."

Nathan looked out the window as Christina ran shrieking through the garden. When he looked back, Ecaterina was glaring at him.

"What? What did I... What?"

"What do I *do*?" Ecaterina asked him.

"Oh." Nathan considered his answer carefully. It was different to give this sort of advice to one's spouse. "You should do what you think is right."

"What does Bethany Anne want me to do?"

Again Nathan hesitated. Ecaterina had seen Bethany Anne in action all these years, but she did not run her own operations very often and was therefore unaccustomed to Bethany Anne's style of management. If it *could* be called management, that was.

Management sounded like something you did involving cubicles and toner cartridges, not shapeWechselbags.

"She wants you to make a choice you think is right," he said finally.

"But what if I make the wrong one?" Ecaterina asked. Her voice was tinged with panic.

Calm down? No, that wouldn't go over well.

"Uh..." Nathan took a large gulp of tea, burned his throat, and choked.

Alexi pounded him on the back as he came by to take a seat.

"Thanks," Nathan managed. He looked at Ecaterina. "Look, here's the deal. Bethany Anne knows that no one is infallible. If it were her operation she would kill Andrei and everyone else involved, but she trusts your character, and that you're not stupid. She trusts that if you disagree with her there's a good reason."

"But what if there's not?"

Nathan stood up and dropped a kiss on his wife's lips. "There is," he assured her. "I don't know what you'll decide to do, but I trust you and so does Bethany Anne. This is your home. I trust that you will make a sound decision, and I will follow your lead."

He nodded to Alexi as he left the kitchen. He hoped that Alexi understood that Nathan was not denying this was Alexi's home, too, but trying to keep Ecaterina from simply doing what Alexi suggested.

She would make a good decision on her own, he was sure of it.

Alexi nodded back. He did understand. Ecaterina was part of a world that Nathan and Bethany Anne had not seen as much, and both were stepping back to let her lead the way—a good thing for a member of Bethany Anne's team to be able to do.

He tried to hide his smile, therefore, as his niece slumped back in her chair and grimaced.

"What the hell do I do now?"

Alexi sipped his tea and said nothing.

"You too?" she accused. "Why is everyone so sure that I should make this decision?"

"There's no way to get through life without making decisions," Alexi pointed out.

Ecaterina shook her head in frustration, "Yes, but when I joined Bethany Anne's team—"

"As I understand it, you promised to be a part of an

NATALIE GREY & MICHAEL ANDERLE

organization that does the right thing—however difficult that is."

"But *every* choice in this situation is the difficult one!" Ecaterina dropped her head into her hands. "How am I supposed to know which one is right by how difficult it is when they're *all* difficult?"

"That's the most ridiculous thing I've ever heard."

"What?"

"There's no math you can perform to figure out which decision is the right one," Alexi explained. "You have to trust yourself."

She said nothing, crossing her arms and sinking her chin onto them contemplatively.

"I'm afraid that if I let Andrei go the way I wanted to, he won't do the right thing from now on," she admitted.

Alexi nodded silently.

"But I'm afraid if I kill him, he *might* have done the right thing in the future and now I've come in and condemned him for trying to keep his family alive. We all make mistakes..." Her voice trailed off as she remembered Bethany Anne's definition of a mistake. "I'm trying to balance mercy with justice," she said finally, "and I don't know any of the probabilities that either is the right move. I *know* it's not math," she added hastily, "but I just... I wish I knew more."

Alexi nodded again. "If it helps, I asked myself the same question many times when I would go to speak with people about their traps."

Ecaterina looked over at him with interest, and jumped when Ashur thunked his head on her thigh. She had been so involved in the conversation that she hadn't noticed the gigantic dog padding into the kitchen. She scratched behind his ears absentmindedly and gave him a smile.

"I don't suppose you have suggestions," she said to him.

I suggest you keep scratching my ears.

She laughed and obeyed. "I should have known that would be your answer."

There was a silence as they all pondered.

"And here's what I don't get," Ecaterina added. "The man who's running all of this—Ioan, was it? Andrei is terrified of him. I always knew about men like that, but now I'm finding myself wondering why he does it. I understand what he does, I get how he controls them. But why bother about something so small as furs?"

Alexi gave a rueful smile.

"Some people seek control of others more than they seek money, child. This man has become deranged. He warps people like Andrei, he sweet-talks them about how it's necessary to do the wrong thing sometimes, and then he binds them to him with absolute fear until they forget that this is furs and not a matter of life and death. To this man, his control of Andrei and the others is worth more than anything. Being questioned sends him into a rage." He shrugged. "The furs are just today's reason for him, and I hope you have the good sense to know you'll never change *that* one. He'll throw everything he's got at you until you fall in line too, or you're dead."

Ecaterina considered this for a long moment and then gave a decisive nod. "Okay, I've made my decision."

"Good." Alexi smiled, "What is it?"

"I'm going to hit Ioan where it hurts. I'll see what Andrei does. If he's willing to keep killing people and

NATALIE GREY & MICHAEL ANDERLE

animals for Ioan, then we'll have our answer about him, but we gave him a chance to run away and pick a different path. Maybe he'll take that chance now that he's been reminded it's there."

"Maybe he will. We can always hope." Alexi looked around as Nathan came in the door. He grew wary at the look on the man's face. "What is it?"

"One of your neighbors came to ask for your help," Nathan said grimly. "He says a man named Mihai was taken from his home by men in suits, and that Mihai's grandson, Andrei, was seen running away from those same men, only to be dragged back and put in a car and both of them taken away. They want to know what to do."

Alexi looked at Ecaterina.

"We're going to go and get them back," Ecaterina said decisively. "We'll give Andrei the chance to show his true colors, and judge him on that."

CHAPTER 8

They hauled Andrei down into the basement of a house, his feet scrabbling and bouncing off the wooden stairs, and tied him to a chair. When they wrenched the hood off, he squinted in the light of a single bare bulb. All of them were blurry shapes, hidden in the shadows.

This was the sort of thing you laughed at in TV shows, Andrei thought despairingly. It was just psychological; they were trying to scare you.

The thing was, it *was* scary. It was terrifying because he was already hurt and he couldn't see them, and they were going to hurt him more. They would hurt him until he told them what they wanted to know out of sheer terror, trying to get them not to kill him.

And then they would kill him anyway.

He knew that.

He wished he had the courage to defy them so they would kill him now, but he wasn't that kind of person. He wasn't like those people in the forest, who had truly believed they could fight Ioan.

"Why don't you tell us what's been going on?" Ioan suggested. His voice sounded eminently reasonable now. He settled down on a couch on the other side of the room, and Andrei saw the glint of his eyes and the bright flash of flame as he lit a cigarette.

Deep breaths. Calm. Andrei grasped at what little sanity remained and swallowed.

"Two days ago I scanned the hill, and there were no new pelts. It seemed odd so I went to go check the traps, but many of them were missing."

"Did you notify Grigore?"

"No. I wanted to solve the problem on my own."

"I see." There was a touch of dangerous amusement. "And how did that go for you?"

"Right before you...found me at my house, I went into the forest to confront the people taking them. I had figured out who they were. It was a woman who had just come back to town to visit her uncle. She used to live here, but she left to marry an American. She brought two pelts with her—magnificent. I was going to take them after dealing with her."

It was a lie, Andrei realized. When it came down to it, he hadn't *wanted* to shoot her in the forest. He could have killed them both easily; he was a good shot, and they hadn't immediately thought he was an enemy.

He was fairly sure he could have killed them anyway, but if what happened next wasn't just some nightmare...

"Was that the end of the story, Andrei?" Ioan's voice was sharp now, and at his nod, one of the guards stepped forward to give Andrei a hard blow on the jaw.

Andrei forced himself not to cry out. "No."

"Then continue, and do not waste my time."

"I swear to you I am telling the truth," Andrei whispered. He had a sudden fear that if he explained what happened with the wolf they would beat him until he passed out. "The woman—she turned into a wolf. A massive wolf, bigger than anything I had seen. She pinned me to the ground and asked me questions about you."

There was a silence.

"I didn't answer her," Andrei lied desperately. "And she was too weak to kill me for it. I was coming back to tell you, but I thought you wouldn't believe me and I was afraid. That's why I ran."

"That is..." Ioan's voice trailed off, then came back strongly "The stupidest set of lies I have ever heard. You know I can't just let that go."

"No, please! I'm telling the truth. *I'm telling the truth!*"

But the blows fell, and they were so hard that the chair tipped over and Andrei tasted dirt until he was flipped onto his back. He thought he felt wooden rods raining down on him, and fists, and the jolt of the chair as it was kicked, and he began screaming again.

This was how it ended, but he wasn't ready to die. And it had been the truth!

When at last he fell silent one of the guards looked up at Ioan. "Do you want me to kill him?"

Ioan threw his cigarette onto the floor and strolled over to study Andrei's prone form. He considered.

"No. When his friends arrive, have them bring him and his grandfather back home. They'll serve us better as living reminders not to cross me."

. . .

QBBS *Meredith Reynolds*

Bobcat leveled off the top of the grain scoop and eyeballed it. "Eh, close enough."

Brewing was as much an art as a science, after all. Plus, he had a secret weapon. He gave a look over at the myrcene oil and grinned as he dumped the wheat into the boiling water. He inhaled, waving the steam toward his nose. It was already smelling sweet.

The hops lay nearby and he dumped scoops of those into the wort as well.

"One, two, three... Eh, add a bit more." His list lay nearby with the measurements, and he took a moment to scrawl *and a bit* next to one of the types of hops.

Art.

Excellent. He sat back on a couch and took a pull of one of his latest beers. It had been a rousing success, yet another reason to suspect that he was going to win this competition by a mile.

He indulged in the happy daydream of Yelena throwing her arms around him in front of everyone. Good beer to drink, Yelena's adoration, and bragging rights—it really didn't get much better than that. Throw in some tinkering on his newest vehicle and he'd call that a perfect day, in fact.

He was especially going to enjoy leaving Barnabas in the dust. What did Barnabas know, anyway? He was relying on outdated techniques. The world of brewing had moved on, and Barnabas would be telling Marcus just to use the old Trappist methods and nothing else.

It was definitely William who was the wildcard. Bobcat narrowed his eyes and considered. Yes, William and Pete.

"ADAM?"

"Yes?"

"Do you know if anyone looked up the myrcene oil? You know, since I didn't block it?" He had minor regrets on that front.

"There have been no searches for myrcene oil or returning results including myrcene oil since then."

ADAM waited for Bobcat to ask the relevant follow-up question: "And were there any before then?"

But Bobcat did not ask, and ADAM, in the spirit of competition, did not feel it sporting to offer the information that William had already procured some of the oil.

Romania

"Okay." Ecaterina stabbed her finger down on a crudely-drawn map. "This is where Ioan is hiding out, according to Andrei. It's this big old house that hasn't belonged to anybody in years. I thought it was just filled with squatters, but apparently not."

"Big old house, huh?" Nathan narrowed his eyes. "I don't like the sound of that. He could be hiding anyone in there, or any*thing*."

"We don't think there are many people there now," Ecaterina explained. "As far as we can tell, Ioan left the day-to-day running of the operation to three men in town: Andrei, Grigore, and Mathieu. Andrei says Grigore was supposed to be in charge of them. Apparently he's a nasty piece of work."

"So we should only have...what, six people?" Nathan shrugged. "Or five. Ioan's here now, or at least I'm going to assume that was who was in the car. Andrei, Grigore, Mathieu, and probably a bodyguard or two."

"Exactly, and we want to hit now before Ioan calls in anyone else. He might not, but why take the chance?" Ecaterina shrugged.

"You have three Wechselbags," Yelena pointed out. "You can take on way more than six guys."

"No sense taking *any* chances," Ecaterina said unequivocally. "I'd rather it be stupidly easy."

Nathan leaned back against the wall and grinned. He was proud of her. Too often people running their first missions would try to do things the hard way, thinking that it was more heroic to fight more people. They risked a lot of lives that way, and he was pleased that Ecaterina wasn't falling into the same trap.

"Nonetheless," Ecaterina said warningly, "I am guessing Ioan can call on backup pretty much immediately. I'll bet furs aren't the only thing he sells, and I'll bet that *also* means he is prepared for things to go wrong at a moment's notice."

"So what do you propose?" Alexi frowned.

"Andrei will almost certainly have told Ioan about us," Ecaterina explained. "He will probably even have told Ioan that I can shift into a wolf, but there's no way to know if Ioan will believe him. Either way Ioan now has a target, and it includes two noncombatants." She nodded at Yelena and Christina.

"I can fight," Yelena said, irritated. "I'm getting really good with a gun, and I'm a pretty good boxer."

"Yes, but you haven't gotten any upgrades for healing yet," Ecaterina said. "And we need someone to watch

Christina. Will you do that for us while we take on Ioan's crew?"

Yelena knew there was no reason to argue with this. Her pride was stung, but Ecaterina was right. Three of the four adults in this room were much better suited to combat than she was.

"You're really not missing much," Ecaterina said softly, "if that helps. People talk a lot about the fights Bethany Anne's team gets in, but fights are just messy and bloody. You are also integral to the plan."

Yelena nodded silently.

Nathan nodded as well. Ecaterina didn't have the silver tongue of an experienced leader yet—she would have headed Yelena's concerns off at the pass if she had—but she had the good sense to recognize those concerns when they surfaced and address them directly.

"So what am I doing?" Yelena asked.

"We're all going to go into the forest," Ecaterina explained. "We'll make sure they see us. As soon as we're there, you'll take Christina and go to a hunting stand Alexi built. No one else knows about it, and that way you'll be out of sight. Stay there until we come *into* the hunting stand to get you. Don't move until then."

Yelena nodded.

"Meanwhile, the rest of us will go through the forest and pretend that Bellatrix or Ashur has gotten snagged in a trap. While we seem to be distracted by that, we think they will attack us." Ecaterina looked around. "And I personally think Ioan will confront us to show his superiority before he has us killed. That's when we strike." She stood up and looked between Alexi and Nathan. "I think it's important that we deal with them as fast as possible on the off-chance that he does have more people waiting in the wings. No words, no explanations, no speeches—we just deal with them."

Nathan nodded. He could feel his smile widening. "It's a good plan," he told her honestly. "Let's go rid this town of Ioan."

QBBS *Meredith Reynolds*

"Let me just check again," William said worriedly.

Pete groaned. "You've been over this ten times. *I've* been over this ten times. The proportions carry over. You've worked out all the timings. The equipment is ready." He took William by the shoulders. "Enough worrying about beer. *Have* a beer."

"I just—"

"Nope." Pete turned him around and marched him over to the bar. "Sit. As your mentor in this process—"

"Assistant."

"*Mentor.*" Pete glared. "As your mentor, you should listen to me when I tell you to stop worrying. We can brew anytime." He set a mug of beer down on the counter. "Drink."

"Right." William drank. "God, this is good. See, this is why I'm worried. This was Bobcat's last one. Sure, we have the oil, but he's a good brewer."

"So he's a good brewer." Pete shrugged. "Wouldn't be much point in a contest if he sucked at it, would there?"

"I...guess not?"

"Right. Meanwhile, you've worked out all the hop

concentrations and we're good to go. I'm telling you, you've made a winner. Whatever this myrcene oil crap is, we'd have a good beer anyway without it. Stop making yourself crazy."

"Right." William nodded. He drained his beer and set it down. "Then let's get to brewing."

"Excellent." Pete clinked his mug against William's empty one. "Be with you in one sec... Right, okay." He wiped at his mouth. "Let's get to brewing, indeed."

CHAPTER 9

Romania

The group dawdled on their way to the forest. It was a nice afternoon so there was no reason to hurry, and Ecaterina and Nathan made a big show of introducing Christina to the forest, as well as the dogs pretending to be total pushovers for anyone who would rub their bellies.

"It's not *entirely* an act, you know," Nathan told Ashur.

Ashur chuffed at him contemptuously.

"You are!" Nathan asserted. "A total pushover for tummy rubs."

Ashur asserted that he would push Nathan over, and then Nathan would give him tummy rubs and *Nathan* would be the pushover.

"That's...not how that works. Oh, you know what, I give up."

Ashur gave a self-satisfied grin.

About halfway to the forest, Ecaterina and Nathan exchanged a pleased look.

Alexi made sure not to look around himself, "What is it?"

"We're being followed. I'm guessing it's Grigore; he has a very smug look about him." Ecaterina stole a glance behind her in a shop window and tried not to laugh as Grigore darted artfully into a doorway. "Yeah, he's real spy material. *Super* sneaky."

Even Yelena had noticed him by this point, and was trying not to laugh.

As they approached the forest, they were still calling loud hellos to their neighbors and waving delightedly, never once looking toward their incredibly obvious follower. They walked slowly, and it was only when the trees closed around them that Ecaterina handed Christina to Yelena and they all started to run.

"Come on, come on." Alexi bundled Yelena and Christina toward the hunting stand. "This way. And…there we go, nice and comfy."

"Are you ready to hide?" Yelena asked Christina. "I don't think your mom's going to find us, do you?"

Christina giggled.

"Yeah, and there are a bunch of other people playing too, so we'll have to be quiet when all of them go past, okay?"

Christina nodded solemnly.

"Awesome." Yelena held the little girl close as Alexi hurried away again to rejoin the rest and continue their very loud, very easily-followed trail through the forest.

Not long after, she watched Grigore bumble by. He was snapping branches, almost as loudly on his own as the rest had as a group, and he swore every time something snagged his expensive pants.

He clearly had the idea that someday he would run an organization like Ioan's, and Yelena rolled her eyes at him. She'd seen a lot of men like Grigore in her day. They always ended up petty and mean, taking out their frustrations on their families and pets because they didn't have the wealth and power they thought was theirs by right.

It was a good thing Ecaterina was taking this group out. Yelena held her finger to her lips and nodded to Christina to stay quiet even though Grigore was gone. Ecaterina was right, she *was* doing something very important. She was keeping Christina safe.

Her arms tightened around the little girl and she kissed the top of Christina's head. At her side, in its holster, the gun was waiting.

Just let anyone try to hurt Christina. She'd make sure they didn't live to see another day.

Ioan adjusted his cuffs as he strode down the hallway to his study. He stopped when one of his bodyguards came out into the hall to incline his head respectfully,

"Sir, Constantinou's team from the castle will be ready as soon as they are alerted."

"Excellent." Ioan looked at Mathieu.

Since he had brought Andrei's limp body upstairs, the man had been pale and prone to jumping at small noises. He bowed his head instantly when Ioan looked at him.

Good.

"Mathieu."

"Yes, sir?"

"I will require you to stay here and alert Constantinou's team, as well as make an emergency call to report the vicious attack these people are about to make on us." Ioan looked smug. "As soon as I give the signal, tell Constantinou and his men to surround the group."

"Yes, sir." Mathieu bobbed his head nervously.

The problem with his excessive deference was, of course, that Ioan could not see the expression in his eyes.

"Mathieu, I understand that you are shaken by what happened to Andrei, but you must understand that Andrei has put all of us in danger. He gave these people our address and they will call in the police, who do not care whether or not you need your family, and who will perhaps arrest you. I will try to keep us safe, but you must remember it was Andrei who put us in this precarious situation."

"Yes, sir." Mathieu met his eyes briefly and swallowed hard. He nodded.

"Good. I will send you a signal in a few minutes." Ioan nodded to his guards and they headed into the forest.

It wasn't long until they found a trap.

No one had to look behind them to know that Grigore was still following. Anyone with ears could hear the sound plainly as the man struggled and swore his way through the bushes.

His path had not wavered at all since they had started

into the forest, and Ecaterina knew he was too stupid even to have counted the figures below to notice that there were fewer people now than he'd followed to start with.

If Ioan was trusting his organization to people like this, he deserved to lose everything from stupidity alone.

She rolled her eyes.

When Bellatrix pawed at the ground and whined, the whole group gathered around.

"This is it," Alexi said grimly. "Are we ready?"

"Ready," Ecaterina said. She turned to look at Ashur. "You ready too?"

Ashur chuffed.

"Good." Ecaterina took a long stick and reached out to tap the trap.

The sound of it clanging shut made everyone jump, but Bellatrix and Ashur didn't miss a trick. Ashur yelped as if he were in terrible pain, and Bellatrix started keening.

"Okay, quick... Ashur, you come lie down here." Ecaterina patted the ground next to the trap and smiled when Ashur flopped down in the leaves. "Good, now I'm going to put some of this on you..." She splashed the fake blood on him and it was vivid against Ashur's white fur. "They won't even think to question that you're wounded. No, don't *lick* it yet."

Ashur informed her that he *would* be licking it.

"I know, but hold off. They have to see it. We want them to think we're all distraught and you're out of the fight."

Ashur agreed that it was probably best they thought he was out of it, or they'd never try to take the group on. He was too formidable an opponent.

NATALIE GREY & MICHAEL ANDERLE

"Yes," Ecaterina agreed with a straight face. "Exactly. You'll have to act *very* well to fool them or they won't even come close."

Ashur flopped his head back dramatically on the forest floor. It was the same pose he always used when his food bowl was empty.

Nathan hid a snort of laughter behind his hand.

"All right, now everyone start wailing," Ecaterina instructed. "Make a big fuss, as if we have no idea what to do."

She could already spy three more figures making their way through the forest nearby.

Ioan had come out to play.

He heard the yelp and the howl. Ioan's eyebrows shot up and he looked at the guards in amusement.

Was it possible? Had they actually been so foolish as to let one of their own team be taken down by traps? His lips curved in an involuntary smile. And one of those magnificent pelts Andrei had mentioned...

Yes, this was a delicious irony.

Ioan enjoyed trading in furs. While drugs were always good money, and guns as well, those markets were crowded and vicious and there was always the risk of losing one's goods to the border patrol.

Furs, on the other hand...

Furs were used only by the rich. Ioan's trade, illegal as it might be, was protected from all but the most zealous customs agents, and even they were easily made powerless by the immense weight of the bureaucracy above them.

He'd had numerous arrest warrants thrown out and citations wiped off the slate. He had cultivated relationships with the customs agents, the sort of relationships that would last for years if only he continued to slip them some good brandy here, some caviar there.

If he ever got stopped the rich would demand to know why their furs weren't available any longer, so he was never stopped.

Now he was rolling in cash, and absolutely untouchable in a market few others had even tried to claim.

It was a good place to be.

And he liked the furs. It was foolish, but they were gorgeous and he enjoyed the sheer luxury of it all. He'd even kept one or two.

His breath quickened as he saw the wolf lying on the ground, bright red blood against its white fur. It was magnificent, and he was torn—the thought of what he could get for that pelt, not only in cash but in gratitude, was exhilarating.

On the other hand, he might like to keep this one for himself.

He pressed the hidden button at his wrist to signal Mathieu. Now he just had to keep the idiots talking.

"So." He stepped out of the trees nearby and was delighted to see their shocked expressions. Some attackers they made! They'd been so caught up in their own worry about the dog that they weren't paying attention to their surroundings.

397

The other dog, jet black to the first's pure white, growled low in its throat.

"I trust you will control the animal."

Ioan had no fear of this situation. Those with numbers and even weapons were still easily cowed by confidence, and he had confidence in abundance. He would simply promise them that all the legal trouble he could get them in would go away if they just left now.

He was lying, of course, but it would be easy.

He scanned the trees. Constantinou's team wasn't visible yet, but they would be soon. He could see Grigore hiding, waiting for his moment.

"What do you want?" a woman demanded of him. Her eyes were wide.

"Ah." Ioan smiled. "I'm so glad you asked."

Mathieu stared at the phone. His hands were shaking.

He needed to call the number. Ioan had signaled him, and he needed to call Constantinou. The man would bring his guards around and all of this would be over.

He wasn't quite sure why he couldn't seem to make himself pick up the phone and dial, but something in him was telling him not to do it.

What was it?

He had been terrified since they had brought Andrei back with his grandfather. Andrei they had kicked around until his screams echoed through the house. The grandfather they had only slapped around a bit—but the bruises were vivid enough.

Whatever Andrei had done, the grandfather surely hadn't done anything.

Mathieu swallowed hard. He didn't like helping Ioan in little schemes like this. He *knew* that Ioan was going to play with these people and then kill them painfully just for fun. Ioan was like that, and Mathieu hated it. If he hadn't had debt he needed to pay off, he'd never have gotten tangled up in this mess.

Truth to tell, he admired the people who were attacking them. Every time Ioan mentioned a customs agent or a police officer who didn't want to take bribes, Mathieu secretly hoped they'd shut Ioan's operation down.

He had been disappointed when none of them had.

And he didn't want to help Ioan now. On the other hand...

His eyes went to where Andrei was lying, breath wheezing. To his surprise, Andrei was watching him and he whispered something.

"What?" Mathieu crossed the room. "I couldn't hear you."

"I said..." Andrei winced. "Don't do it. Don't help him. You were right, we never should have gotten involved." He pressed a hand over his ribs.

"I have to help him," Mathieu said despairingly. "He knows where my family is and he spared your grandfather once, but he won't again."

He jumped when Andrei's bloody hand clamped down over his. The man's eyes were bright, almost manic.

"Not if these attackers kill him," Andrei whispered. "We could let it happen."

"They'd only kill us too."

"Maybe, but won't Ioan too someday? You know he will." Andrei closed his eyes and grimaced. "And there are the...others. In the basement. They should know about them."

Mathieu wavered.

"Don't help him," Andrei repeated. "Let's make sure the others go free. Whatever happens, isn't being free of Ioan worth it?"

"Listen." Ioan spread his hands. "I know that you two, at least—" he looked at Ecaterina and Alexi, "are locals. You understand the way things must be. You know that the laws and the police only aid the rich. You know that in order to survive, common people like you and me must break those laws."

He looked around. Constantinou really was taking a very long time.

From a few paces away, Nathan looked at Ecaterina. He said in rapid-fire English, "I thought you said you wanted to kill him immediately, not take any chances."

She gave him a delighted smile. "I did, but you see, I think he's waiting for someone and I don't think they're showing up. And now that we're here, I want to watch him figure that out."

Ioan was definitely worried now. He took the time to adjust his face into a pleasant smile.

"You know that whatever the laws are, they can be bent for the very rich, and it is the very rich who enjoy these furs. Now, it is clear to me that you came here to halt my operation, and for that you would find yourself in jail for a very long time. As I said, the laws can be bent and the rich will not be pleased to be deprived of their goods. But if you leave me this pelt, I will forget you were ever here. I will let you go back to your village, and nothing more will ever be said. In fact…"

His voice trailed away and he stared at them.

"Why are you smiling?" he asked finally.

Ecaterina took a moment to enjoy his discomfort. It was risky, she knew—the backup could arrive at any moment—but in the meantime Ioan showed the annoyance of a man accustomed to obedience warring with the self-preservation instincts of a man who knew his minions weren't obeying him anymore.

She spoke in Romanian now, strolling forward. "I think you know why I'm smiling. As you say, I came here to halt your operation. You thought you held all the cards, but you don't, do you? I don't know who you're waiting for, Ioan, but they're not coming."

Ioan's face twisted.

"Shoot her," he instructed curtly.

The guards frankly never had a chance. From where they stood they had the very brief impression that two wolves came out of nowhere.

Very brief, because within seconds they were dead.

They were quick. Both had gotten their hands to their holsters, ready to draw their guns, but they didn't get the chance to fire.

Ecaterina raised her head from one guard's throat and

looked Ioan in the eyes. In this form she could smell the fear rolling off him.

"It was true." He crossed himself. "*It was true!* My God, he was telling the truth. You're a... You're a monster."

"Iiiii ammmm noooo mooonnnnster." The wolf's voice seemed to have the echo of howls and cold nights even as it reverberated inside Ioan's bones. It seemed to him to be something entirely beyond the Earth he knew.

He didn't realize how right he was about that.

"Youuuuuu hurrrrrt people. Iiiiii willll ssstoppp youuuuu."

Nathan prowled behind Ioan, teeth bared. He had been ready to shift since they had entered the forest, but instinct and rage had made him quicker than he would otherwise have been when Ioan ordered Ecaterina's death.

The guards had signed their own death warrants when they hadn't even wavered. They had been willing to kill a woman simply because their boss requested it.

They had known, as Nathan had, that Ioan's offers of mercy were lies, but unlike Nathan they had no moral distaste for what Ioan asked them to do.

They were the sort to say a job was a job and morals were for others.

He wondered where Andrei was.

Ioan, however, had now realized just how alone he was.

"Spare me." He thudded to his knees in the leaves. His expensive suit was out of place in the forest. It was his armor when he was dealing with other smugglers and his rich clients, but here and now it was only a hindrance.

"Spaaaaaaare youuuuuuu?" Ecaterina gave a laugh that made Ioan scream. "Whyyyyy?"

NATALIE GREY & MICHAEL ANDERLE

"Because I was doing what I needed to do to survive! I brought money to your little town, I helped your people! They could never have done this on their own, could they? Have you no mercy in your heart for them?"

"Forrrrr themmmm, yesssss." The Pricolici paused. "*Sommmmmme* mercyyyyyy," it amended, "noooooot unlii-imiteeeeed."

Nathan huffed a laugh and Alexi grinned where he leaned up against a tree.

"I'm a businessman, nothing more! You would hold me to standards that mean nothing? You would make a world out of a fantasy!" Ioan's voice was desperate.

"Hmmmmmmm." The giant wolf came to stare into his eyes. "Iiiii thiiiiiiink … Iiiii willlll giiiiive youuuuuu to Ashuu-uuuur and Bellllllllatrix."

Ioan had no idea what that meant, but he knew enough to see the end result plainly.

"Grigore!" His voice was raw. "*GRIGORE! HELP!*"

Alexi's head whipped around. The man who had been following them was crashing back up the hill. He didn't even pause when Ioan screamed, but Alexi didn't find that funny at all.

Grigore was bumbling right toward Yelena and Christina.

Mihai was testy about being locked in one of the storage rooms.

"In all my years—" he started.

Andrei cut him off. "Please, Grandfather. Let me make

things right without having you suffer for my mistakes."

Mihai's old face softened. "Ah, you were always a good child."

Andrei smiled ruefully, and winced when his lip cracked. "You said I was always a selfish, cowardly child."

"That too." Mihai lifted his shoulders. "I feared you would be just as selfish and cowardly as you grew older instead of following your better nature."

"I was," Andrei admitted.

"Well, the day's not over yet." Mihai stepped back into the storeroom and gestured to the door. "Do what you need to do, then."

"Thank you, Grandfather." Andrei closed the door and began limping along the hall. "Give me the phone," he told Mathieu.

"Why?" Mathieu asked nervously.

"Just give it to me."

Mathieu hesitated, then handed it over. In truth, he was a little bit scared of this new Andrei. The friend he remembered from childhood was, exactly as Mihai had said, a good boy, and one who was selfish and cowardly.

In grade school, Andrei was always the one to give you his snack if you said you were hungry. He waded into a spring river once, overflowing its banks, to save a cat that had gotten stranded. When their friend's parents had grounded him over a schoolyard incident, Andrei was the one to go over and argue that the grounding wasn't fair, that the friend had been standing up for a younger child.

But he was also the one who might lure you into ditching school and then leave you to get caught if he had a way out. He was the one who would snatch candy from the store sometimes, and even if he shared it with you, you were just as likely to get caught as well.

Always, Andrei had been...*more* than other people. He laughed more, he shouted more. He seemed to contain more energy in his body.

When he had talked Mathieu into joining Ioan's group he'd done so with the same silver tongue he'd used to persuade people all his life, and Mathieu had agreed with the familiar despairing thought that this was just as likely to go well as poorly.

Andrei had changed today.

It was as if the beating had freed a man Mathieu had never seen before. Andrei was calm and determined. He did not deny the risks anymore.

The only thing that remained was his insistence that Mathieu should do something risky and defy Ioan.

As Mathieu watched, Andrei talked to Constantinou.

"Ioan just called. They're heading back from the forest, so they won't need you." He listened to the words. "You'll still get paid. Of course you will."

He lied as easily as he had when they were children, Mathieu thought with a grimace.

He hadn't changed *that* much.

"No, they were scared by the mention of the customs agents." Andrei faked a laugh, and though he winced in pain he kept his voice level. "And the police are on their way to their house. They'll regret meddling." He listened to the voice on the other end. "People here are tightly knit. It is too risky to kill them if he doesn't have to. He already made two examples today. That's enough."

Another pause while Constantinou argued.

"No, no, you can go back to the city. The money should show up in your accounts in a few minutes. Just remember this, eh? Remember you got good pay for doing nothing, and maybe when you have to choose jobs you choose us?" He smiled. "Good, good."

He hung up and smiled at Mathieu. "There. Now they'll leave Ioan to rot, and no one's the wiser."

Mathieu groaned and dropped his forehead into his hands. "But if Ioan survives…"

"Mathieu." Andrei put his hand on his friend's shoulder. "You and I both know Ioan deserves to die. If he comes here, I know what I will do. You should think about what *you* will do?"

"Why?" Mathieu asked nervously.

Please, please let Andrei not be turning into another Ioan.

"Because a lifetime is very long, and you will think of yourself with pride for all those years if you do the right thing, but you will carry shame in your heart if you do the wrong thing," Andrei said seriously. "I already have more shame than I want to carry. I want no more." He nodded his head to the basement stairs. "I am going to free the others. Will you come with me?"

Will you come with me? It was a risky plan and a silver-tongued speech, but it was different than it had been before. Andrei was taking all the risk for himself, and merely offering for Mathieu to follow him.

And if Andrei could change, Mathieu thought, *so could he.*

"I will come with you," he said, and was rewarded by Andrei's smile.

Ioan demanded complete loyalty, and it made sense to give it when he had all the power and wealth in his hands.

But when he was clearly going to die, it was every man for himself.

That was Grigore's opinion, anyway. He'd been raised in these forests, so he knew that wolves did not hunt humans unless they were starving or sick—or unless there was something very wrong with them.

He also knew what he'd seen: wolves larger than any should be which had appeared from nowhere. A white one rising from the trap apparently unharmed and a black wolf just as big who had participated in tearing Ioan to shreds.

He'd thought they were dogs, those two wolves. He must have been wrong, though.

Dogs didn't get that big, did they?

And he knew the humans who controlled those wolves were coming back this way. He couldn't outrun wolves, so he had one choice: find a hunter's stand and hide there.

It was a risk, but it was the best option.

He saw the faint outline of one ahead, the littlest distortion in the way the branches lay, and he kept running. He'd always hated hunting. He wasn't quiet, it was always either too hot or too cold, it was boring, and he wasn't a good shot.

But his father had dragged him out here enough that he at least recognized a hunting stand when he saw one.

He heard someone running behind him and yelling, and he dived for cover.

He made it. That was his last thought before the shot went off and Yelena pushed his dead body back out of the hunting stand onto the ground.

She looked behind her to make sure that Christina was still looking away with her hands over her ears, and nodded to Alexi as he plunged into the clearing.

"You told me to look after Christina," she said defiantly. "I wasn't going to give him even the chance to think of her as a hostage."

Alexi sagged with relief. He'd had the same thought: Grigore realizing that the child was the same one he'd seen before, would know that he could bargain for his freedom. In situations like that adrenaline got the better of people sometimes, and hostages got killed.

He pressed a hand over his pounding heart and nodded.

"You did well," he said. "Thank you. From the bottom of my heart, thank you."

Next to him, two Pricolici transformed back into humans. They kept running even through their transformations, and Ecaterina and Nathan enfolded Christina in their arms.

Ecaterina turned after a moment to embrace Yelena as well.

"I told you that you were an important part of the plan," she said.

Yelena smiled. "I won't doubt that ever again."

A shout caught their attention, and they turned to see Andrei.

Alexi drew in his breath sharply. The man had more bruised skin than unbruised, and he walked with a cautious limp as if both his legs and his ribs were injured.

"There are more who need your help," he said. "You can kill me afterward if you want, but at least let me show you to them."

CHAPTER 11

Ecaterina was the first to follow Andrei down the steps into the mansion's basement.

Nathan, watching her as he followed her, was proud of her. She walked with purpose, her eyes alert. She knew this might be a trap and she was determined that no one else would take the risk of it.

She had made a good plan. They had killed those in the woods quickly, and she had left Yelena—known to be a good shot, known not to hold back in a fight—to guard Christina.

His heart was still pounding at the thought of Grigore trying to use his daughter as a hostage, but Nathan knew that was only adrenaline.

No one had ever had a chance to hurt any of them.

When he saw what was in the basement, though, he stopped dead. They all did.

The walls were lined with cages, and in those cages were dozens of wolves. Many were too weak to stand now, their fur matted and dull, but others paced and whined when they caught the scent of the Wechselbalg.

In the center of the room stood a man none of them had ever seen. Mathieu, Nathan guessed.

Ecaterina looked over at Andrei. "Talk, and don't even think of glossing over your part in this."

"I knew he kept them," Andrei said. His voice quavered, but his chin was high. "It was his pet project. No one else was allowed down here, and often one of the guards stood at the door. I didn't know how many there were, but I knew they were here."

"*Why?*" Ecaterina's voice was full of frustration and raw horror.

"Trapping for pelts is random," Andrei explained. "If you were able to breed wolves, though, you would always have some to use. It was…insurance for him."

He had tried to explain it dispassionately and realized his mistake a moment later.

"Insurance?" Ecaterina asked dangerously.

"You asked me to explain. I am doing so." He shook his head. "I didn't think it was right."

"But you didn't think it was wrong enough to stop it," she said. Her voice was still deathly soft.

"No." He swallowed, but he met her eyes. "It wasn't enough to push me over the edge, no matter how wrong I knew it was. Even when you confronted me in the forest my plan was to go back, take my grandfather, and run away. I wasn't planning to save these wolves."

"What changed your mind then?" She crossed her arms and stared at him.

Behind her, Nathan fought the urge to growl low in his

throat. He was glad Ecaterina did not just accept this man's good intentions now.

"To be honest with you, it was the danger to myself." Andrei looked down at last. "Even the good things I have done today are because I knew the only hope for saving my own skin was to let Ioan die in the forest. I was the one who made sure his backup never arrived."

Ecaterina didn't say anything, but one eyebrow lifted in amusement. "I wondered. Go on."

"What more do you want me to say about my own culpability?" Andrei clasped his hands together behind his back to stop them from trembling. "You know everything I have done. I ignored others' pain in hopes that Ioan would not hurt me. I turned a blind eye to what he was doing to these animals. I went into the forest this morning with the intention of shooting you if you would not comply.

"I only did what I did today because I saw clearly that there was no way to stay on Ioan's good side, that I would only become more and more compromised, and sooner or later this game would kill me."

"That's not entirely true." Mathieu spoke for the first time. "You argued for me to stand up to him, too. You said that we knew what he was doing was wrong. You wanted to save your grandfather. We could probably just have run away, except you insisted on going and finding these people for them to set the wolves free. They wouldn't ever have known if you hadn't told them."

Ecaterina took a deep breath as she considered this.

"My grandfather raised me to be a better man than I am now," Andrei said. "Whatever you think of me, my actions are not his fault. He told me every day that I would regret what I was doing, and that I knew it was wrong. I never told him what I was doing, but he knew I felt guilty about it."

He paused in shame.

"I don't think he ever dreamed I would do something this bad," he said. His voice was quiet. "I ask you not to hurt him."

"I won't hurt *him*," Ecaterina said, annoyed. "I am not Ioan."

And me? Andrei said nothing. Even his hope made him feel ashamed.

He knew he did not deserve to feel hope. He knew she should open these cages and let the wolves tear him to shreds.

Finally she sighed.

"I said earlier today that I would attack Ioan and stop him, and that we would see your character from what you did," she told him. "And you didn't help him, you helped us. You did the right thing, so I'm going to let you go."

Andrei said nothing. He could hear the *but* in her voice.

"But I don't like it," she told him bluntly. "I think you have a lot to make up for. I think you let yourself ignore far too much cruelty. I think that if someone asked me to justify why I was letting you go, I would have to acknowledge that beyond my word that I said I would there're a lot of good reasons to punish you instead. And I want you to know that. I want you to know this isn't something I'm sure of."

Andrei had expected to feel relief, but instead he felt only a sinking sense of shame.

He had meant what he said to Mathieu earlier: he had more than enough shame to last a lifetime. Two lifetimes.

"I'm also not sure I *can* make it up," he nodded to her, "but I'll try." He looked at Alexi. "I hear stories about you. I know that when people do things that are wrong, you talk to them and set them straight. I will try to do the same. I will try always to do the right thing, no matter what it costs me. I hope I will balance out the bad things I have done."

"Go," Ecaterina told him. "I don't want to look at you right now."

He nodded and left, a silent shadow.

She turned to Mathieu. "I trust you heard everything I said to him just now?"

"Yes." Mathieu looked nervous.

"And I trust you know that it applies just as much to you as it did to him?"

Mathieu's shoulders slumped. "Yes."

"Then you get out of my sight, too. I don't want to see you either."

She watched them both practically run away, and bit her lip in the sudden silence.

"I hope I didn't make a mistake," she admitted.

"Cheer up," Nathan said, with a shrug.

"Hmm?"

"If you were wrong you can always kill them later, right? But you couldn't undo killing them." He came to loop an arm around her shoulders. "Let's get these wolves set to rights and then go home and have a nice meal. I'm famished."

Ecaterina smiled at him. "Yes, let's."

NATALIE GREY & MICHAEL ANDERLE

She walked to the first cage and unlocked the door, holding out her hand to one of the wolves inside. "You're safe now," she told it. "We're going to get you food and fix that nasty cut on your side, and you're going to get to live out your days in the forest. You're safe now."

QBBS *Meredith Reynolds*

Marcus stared at the thermometer fixedly. It was climbing toward the temperature it should simmer at, and he adjusted the heat downward to slow its rise.

His head was aching fiercely, but he was determined not to lose focus for a moment.

He wasn't using the myrcene oil, and that meant he had to do everything else perfectly.

A timer went off and he poured the perfectly-leveled—and twice-measured—scoop of hops carefully into the wort after double-checking that they were the correct ones to add at this step.

"You're doing well," Barnabas said approvingly from the side of the room. He strolled closer to Marcus. "But this is, so far, just a trial for you. Instead of a trial, instead of a test, think of it as a devotion."

"What?" Marcus looked over at the former monk and hoped he didn't look as clueless as he felt.

Barnabas smiled. "You were never in one of the religious orders—I understand this—but you enjoy drinking a fine beer, do you not? You enjoy seeing the looks on others' faces as they relax in the bar and speak with their friends. You take pride in doing everything you do very well and to the best of your ability. Is this not so?"

Marcus hesitated, then nodded.

"Excellent. Well, for a monk such things would serve a larger purpose—all of them would reflect the greater glory of God. While I hope for such a thought in you, even if it is not in your heart, at least excellence and joy can still be your reasons for making this beer perfectly." He paused. "Think of what you wish to achieve," he said finally, "not of what might go wrong."

He glided away with an enigmatic smile on his face, and Marcus stared after him in bemusement.

He turned back to the wort with a new purpose. His headache seemed to be clearing up, and as he inhaled he tried to imagine the beer finished to perfection. It would be wonderful if he could manage it.

"I'm telling you, I went over the video three times. Marcus never used it—it was just Bobcat." William looked at Pete. "So do we add it or not?"

Pete looked at the measurements and the bubbling wort, then stared at the video and back at the myrcene oil.

"You said Bobcat was the one to beat," he said finally. "If he knows something we don't, we gotta think there's a reason. Plus, it's been how many hundreds of years since Barnabas brewed beer? There's new technology now. Let's add the oil."

William nodded. "Good call." He eyeballed the bottle. "It's just a little more than we need, so should we add all of it?"

"Yeah, might as well." Pete grinned.

Out in the hallway, Barnabas lifted his ear away from the door and shook his head as he glided off down the hall.

"Sloppy," he murmured to himself.

But he was smiling.

And Tabitha, watching from the opposite side of the bay, crossed her arms and narrowed her eyes. She was beginning to have a suspicion about this competition.

"ADAM?" She considered. "Would you help me look something up?"

Romania

Andrei turned sideways to examine himself in the mirror. The bruises had flared from a deep purple into a riot of greens and yellows, and they were now fading away.

His cracked ribs were, according to his doctor, healing well. He might always limp and it was likely that his nose would never be quite straight again, but he was alive.

And he had a new purpose. On the kitchen table were spread dozens of documents regarding a new venture he was researching. If it worked, he would have started his climb back to evening the slate.

The phone started to ring and he hurried into the main room to answer it before Mihai woke up.

"Hello?"

"Hello, Andrei." The voice was female. It was smooth and elegant … and it somehow made Andrei break out in a cold sweat. "My name is Bethany Anne."

"Do I… Do I know you?"

"No, you've never met me." Her tone was really quite

pleasant, he reflected, but he was utterly terrified all of a sudden.

"Ah, can I help you?"

"This call isn't really about whether you can help *me*, Andrei. It's about whether you can help *you*." He got the sense that this Bethany Anne person was smiling. "You see, I know what you did. I know how you earned a reprieve, but if you ever step so much as one toe out of line again... If you ever hurt any defenseless person, no matter how little you hurt them, I will find you and there will be no mercy. Do you understand me?"

Andrei had to brace himself on the table so as not to have his knees give out. His voice didn't seem to work when he tried to speak, and he had to clear his throat several times.

"Yes. I understand you perfectly."

"Good." The line went dead.

EPILOGUE

6 Months Later...

Ecaterina carefully placed the tiny vial of seeds in the holding container and made a check mark next to its entry in her log.

She waited for the microchip embedded in the lid to sync against the database and smiled. Now when anyone scanned this set of seeds, they would see what the plant looked like, what other plants its natural ecosystem involved, how best to tend it, and its uses both on its own and as an aid to the cultivation of other plants.

Meanwhile, searches that returned any of those same results would allow people to select this seed as a good candidate for whatever program they were running.

She was just reaching for the next vial when a crash and a shriek from the next room made her look around.

"Tabby?"

Tabitha popped her head around the door. Her hair had just this morning, been dyed a brilliant shade of blue, and she'd switched out one of her eyebrow piercings to match. "How did you know?"

"Given the crash it was a good guess," Ecaterina answered dryly. "What can I help you with?"

"They're going to start the brewing competition!" Tabitha danced back and forth. "Come on, let's go taste everything!"

"All right." Ecaterina put the vial back in the box, made sure she hadn't checked anything off that she shouldn't have, and joined Tabitha.

They walked quickly through the halls of the *Meredith Reynolds* to the bar, where a large crowd had assembled. People were drinking other beers made by Marcus and Bobcat and William, and they would periodically look up to the judging table to see if the competition had started yet.

The three kegs were being wheeled out, with the brewers guarding them as worriedly as mother hens.

At the table, Lance Reynolds sat back with a smile. He had been looking forward to this competition. It had been a very long time since he had proposed it, and he had been getting—to put things charitably—a bit impatient.

"Now remember," his daughter told him with a grin, "you have to be *entirely* impartial."

"The beer will be my guide," Lance told her, and smiled. "I would never lie about something so important as the quality of beer."

Bethany Anne grinned and took a seat beside him. She beckoned Jennifer, Stephen, and Nathan up to the table as well. "All right, the three of you are backup judges. In the event that my dad can't make a decision, your votes will break the tie."

"You are not judging?" Stephen asked curiously.

"No, just tasting." Bethany Anne grinned. "Queen Bitch's right, wouldn't you say?"

"Most assuredly," Nathan agreed.

Little bowls of coffee beans were set out along with beverages designed to clear the palate between tastes, and the beers were brought to each judge in a different order, marked so as to be anonymous to all but John—who had offered to oversee the rigors of the testing process.

In return for beer, of course.

Everyone watched as the judges sipped their beers and made notes. Sometimes they returned to one beer, other times they continued to the next. Each judge tried each beer multiple times with multiple cleanses of the palate, then John whisked away their notes and tallied the scores.

It was ten minutes before he emerged from the side room.

"Ladies and gentlemen, the winner of the beer competition is…"

Children shrieked and chased one another across their makeshift playground.

Over the past months Ioan's one-time hideout had become overgrown with weeds, but then it had been cleaned up using an infusion of cash that had arrived mysteriously at the mayor's office.

The grant had been very specific: the money was to be used to clean up the mansion and make it fit for families to live in, the surrounding land was to be kept as a nature preserve, and there was to be a new college established to teach people all sorts of skills for starting and running their own businesses.

In short, the town was to take care of those who needed it, and give them the tools to make their way in the world —and no one was to interfere with the nearby forest. Meanwhile, the fenced-in area of the grounds had become the village children's favorite place to play.

Andrei smiled as one child caught another in a game of tag. He was walking in the trees very slowly to allow for his grandfather's pace.

"You're not going to tell me where you got all that money, are you?" Mihai complained.

Andrei smiled. "As I have explained many times, grand-father, that money was not mine. I have no idea where it came from."

The first part was true, although the second was a lie. It had taken many careful phone calls and transactions, but he had managed to empty Ioan's illegal accounts and wind down the man's operations, ending up with a very large sum of money.

He still fielded the occasional call from a client, and explained that Ioan's business was simply too dangerous in the current climate. It hadn't survived.

He didn't mention that by "it" he meant Ioan, and by "dangerous" he meant 'prone to being ripped apart by wolves.'

Andrei, meanwhile, was making a good living working in one of the new shops in town. A few had come and gone since the money appeared, but most were staying.

Mihai smiled. He knew from experience that his grandson was lying to him, but for once he didn't mind. He also knew the tell-tale signs of guilt, and for the first time in years Andrei seemed to have none.

He was grateful for that, and grateful to see the town being built up by the younger generation. He and Alexi often sat over tea or a beer and discussed the young people who were coming home, or who had decided to stay after school.

It was beginning to look like their home was valued by others as much as they valued it themselves.

He looked up at the sky. *Whoever you were who came here and no matter why you did it, I'm grateful to you.*

John let the silence hang until someone yelled, "Just tell us already!"

He laughed. "The winner, by a very large margin in both our chief judge's vote and our secondary judges' votes, is Marcus."

The bar exploded into whistles and stomps.

Bobcat and William exchanged an incredulous glance and looked over to where Marcus was staring just as incredulously at the judges' table.

It was Bethany Anne who noticed the faintly smug smile on Barnabas' face, and she made her way through the crowd to his side. "Would you like to explain what you did to tip the scales?"

"I," Barnabas said confidently, "did *nothing* to tip the scales."

There was a snort from beside them and Tabitha tucked a strand of bright blue hair behind her ear. "As usual, Barnabas is being sneaky."

"As I have said many times—"

"It was sneaky, you were sneaky, the whole thing was sneaky." Tabitha raised her eyebrow at him.

Barnabas gave her a long-suffering look. "A matter of opinion."

"All right," Bethany Anne tried to keep her mouth from twitching, "*what* was sneaky, Tabby?"

"Barnabas laid a nice little trap for Bobcat and William," Tabitha said. She crossed her arms and gave Barnabas a look. "Which Marcus almost fell into, I'll have you know."

"I do know," Barnabas said. "I know you helped him almost fall into, and I know he *didn't* fall into it. I know that he spent a great deal of time on his process instead, and thus ensured a far better, more balanced beer than the others were able to make. They, on the other hand, felt that because they had a way to cheat, they could be sloppy."

"You sabotaged their beers?" Bethany Anne asked. "Barnabas—"

"I did no such thing." Barnabas held up a hand. "The ingredient they used was specifically formulated to do no harm to the beer, but neither did it help. A consummate beer brewer—and a worthy competitor—would either not have used the oil, having had no chance to test it before, or they might have used it but would have taken care on the rest of the beer. William and Bobcat did not do so. Marcus did."

Bethany Anne laughed and let her head fall back. "Oh, man, you have got to be kidding me. So you set up a way to trick them into thinking they'd have better beers?"

"Their choice to brew with sloppy technique was just that," Barnabas said. "*Their* choice. They didn't have to use the oil, and they didn't have to brew sloppily."

Bethany Anne exchanged a look with Tabitha. "Are you thinking what I'm thinking?"

"Never get in a fight with Barnabas?" Tabitha asked her. "Yup."

Barnabas smiled, then coughed discreetly. "There is... one more matter regarding this ingredient."

"Yes?" Bethany Anne asked with deep misgiving.

"I seem to have created somewhat of a...thriving business." Barnabas stared at the ceiling with a determinedly blank expression. "You see, in my attempts to establish myrcene oil as a valid substance to use, it was discovered by many other home brewers. It is now the subject of lively debate, and we find ourselves consistently sold out of it."

"*We?*"

"Well, I had to lease time in a factory to have the first orders made." Barnabas cleared his throat. "I understand they've hired many additional workers and are expanding the factory."

Bethany Anne dropped her face into her hands. Her shoulders were shaking with laughter, and she took a moment to enjoy it before wiping her eyes and giving a little groan.

"Oh, wow. Oh, Barnabas, you're a treasure." She leaned

over to kiss him on the cheek and grinned when he stiffened awkwardly. "A somewhat prudish treasure. I trust you'll manage the business well. Meanwhile, *I'm* going to go get more of Marcus' beer."

FINIS

When Michael and I talked about Seed Vault, back when it was still a nebulous concept, he knew he wanted to show the team unwinding and having fun. Of course, this is Bethany Anne & company, and trouble has a way of finding them - but what, exactly, do they all do on their days off?

Turns out, most of them are huge nerds in their own ways. Also, there's Tabitha.

I don't see how anyone could read the Kurtherian Gambit series and not love Tabitha. What has always struck me about her is her intense vulnerability. Though she kicks ass unapologetically, believes in herself, doesn't back down, and has plenty of snark, she also has a big heart, and she doesn't close it off from getting hurt. In many ways, that's one of the ways in which she's bravest - and this is a woman who does things like throw herself off roofs with surprising regularity.

In this way, Gabrielle is really her opposite: refined, elegant, and not very open with her emotions a lot of the time. But if anyone thinks Gabrielle's understated displays of emotion means she doesn't care for her friends … well, they have another thing coming (and they'll deserve it).

As always, the beta readers and behind-the-scenes team have been amazing. The energy of the KGU readers has a way of making my day, and I am so grateful to all of you.

I hope you enjoyed this peek into the world! For other works, including the Shadows of Magic books and a new standalone SciFi series, as well as a series centering on Barnabas (!!!), you can sign up for the mailing list here (no spam, I promise!):

https://landing.mailerlite.com/webforms/landing/w0k9j4

Happy reading,
Nat

AUTHOR NOTES - MICHAEL ANDERLE
JANUARY 24, 2018

Here we go!

Thank you for not only reading these stories, but ALSO reading through to the author notes, as well!

It is with a "WHEW" that we get this book (a little out of order) to you. Natalie had penned some books, but they got into a shuffle, (there was a baby, which if you haven't read what she and her husband call the little person, it's adorable), and a shitake-ton of challenges to get these stories out.

However, I'm to blame.

I am hoping (and crossing my fingers) that when you read these stories, you may forgive me for being so late!

We are tracking down Trials & Tribulations #3 which has more of the beer stuff in it now.

So, slightly funny story and it goes like this.

I'm JUST about finished with my 21st book in The Kurtherian Gambit and I am at the Aria (I had been writing there) on a conference call with one of my contacts (3D Artist) working to see if we can create a way for him to move full time into building covers for authors. As it would really help him and his family.

And you and I would get access to kick ass shit.

I get off that call, to check Slack (where all of the company communications happen) to see that Operations Guru and Zen Master Walking™ Stephen Campbell has informed me that for our release tomorrow (11 hours since he is in Florida), of this book you just read, he is missing:

1. 1.Title
2. 2.Blurb
3. 3.Author Notes
4. 4.Cover

OH SHIT!

Now, Title? Ok – not too hard.

Blurb? Grrr...

Author Notes... Well, ok...

Then, I see "Cover" and FREAK THE HELL OUT!

It's 3:30 PM in Las Vegas. My "guy" (Andrew Dobell) is in England for these things and I want to beat my head in frustration that I'd forgotten this little but *really* important part of the project.

So, I walk back home from the Aria and finish some family business before I have another CC with a collaborator, and start working down Zen Master Walking™'s list.

Takes me about five minutes to realize that both of these stories are a CHALLENGE. Great! So, Challenges becomes the title.

Blurb? Dammit! That takes me a while to dream up but I get it done. Then, Murphy bites me on the ass like a snapping turtle and won't let go! For whatever reason, the usual tools to help me make a viable blurb (with bold, italics etc for Amazon) just FUBAR's the HTML code and it takes me a good 45 minutes to finagle that and fix it.

SIGH...

Now, I have to deal with the cover.

I bring up the last Frank Kurns cover I worked on (December 2016) and after taking a couple of minutes to FIND said cover project, I pull it up in Pixelmator (MAC).

I jump on Slack and send a message to Andrew to see If I happen to be lucky enough and he is working super late...

Yeah, I got nothing. Family men who have to be up early tend to go to sleep on time.

(I tend to go to sleep *earlyish* too, but that's because I'm an old man who gets up with the stupid sun a lot of the time and peters out too early. *Nothing exciting to see here, move along...move along.*)

I start thinking about what I need for the cover, and how I would build it. Then, it HITS ME!

HUCKING FELL, Andrew and I did this cover DAYS ago! I was the one who failed to put on the typography.

I go back to our channel in Slack, scroll up, SCORE! There is the image and NOW I've got this sweet assed cover.

Crises averted as well as much embarrassment if I had failed to remember this. Although, I'm getting good at blaming age. This age defense is fucking brilliant, that's all I'm saying.

Now, all I needed to do was consider what I was going to share in my author notes.

... And then realize at that moment that I forgot to ask

Natalie for HER author notes on our stories call earlier this morning.

FML.

LOL

Ad Aeternitatem,
Michael

Shadows of Magic

Bound Sorcery

Blood Sorcery

Bright Sorcery

Set in the Kurtherian Gambit Universe

Bellatrix

Challenges

Risk Be Damned

Damned to Hell

Vigilante

Sentinel

Warden

Paladin

Justiciar

Defender

Protector

Metamorphosis Online

You Need A Bigger Sword

The New Queen Rises

Reign With Axe And Shield

Writing as Moira Katson

Shadowborn

Shadowforged

Shadow's End

Daughter of Ashes

Mahalia

CONNECT WITH THE AUTHORS

Natalie Grey Social

Email List

https://landing.mailerlite.com/webforms/landing/w0k9j4

Follow Natalie on Amazon

https://www.amazon.com/Natalie-Grey/e/B01MYG7K8P/

Facebook

https://www.facebook.com/Natalie-Grey-393234677682987/

Michael Anderle Social

Website: http://lmbpn.com

Email List: http://lmbpn.com/email/

Facebook:
www.facebook.com/TheKurtherianGambitBooks